a DUET *with the* SIREN DUKE

a MARRIED TO MAGIC *novel*

ELISE KOVA

Silver Wing Press

a DUET
with the
SIREN DUKE

a MARRIED TO MAGIC *novel*

ELISE KOVA

Published by Silver Wing Press
Copyright © 2023 by Elise Kova

Cover Artwork by Erion Makuo
Developmental Editing by Rebecca Faith Editorial
Line Editing by Melissa Frain
Proofreading by Kate Anderson

ISBN (paperback): 978-1-949694-57-4
ISBN (hardcover): 978-1-949694-58-1
eISBN: 978-1-949694-41-3

Also by Elise Kova

Married to Magic

A Deal with the Elf King
A Dance with the Fae Prince
A Duel with the Vampire Lord
A Duet with the Siren Duke
A Dawn with the Wolf Knight

Air Awakens Universe

AIR AWAKENS SERIES
Air Awakens
Fire Falling
Earth's End
Water's Wrath
Crystal Crowned

GOLDEN GUARD TRILOGY
The Crown's Dog
The Prince's Rogue
The Farmer's War

VORTEX CHRONICLES
Vortex Visions
Chosen Champion
Failed Future
Sovereign Sacrifice
Crystal Caged

A TRIAL OF SORCERERS
A Trial of Sorcerers
A Hunt of Shadows
A Tournament of Crowns
An Heir of Frost
More to Come

Loom Saga

The Alchemists of Loom
The Dragons of Nova
The Rebels of Gold

See all books and learn more at:
http://www.EliseKova.com

*for everyone who gave up on their
happily ever after... only to find it
when they least expected*

Table of Contents

Author's Note

Dear reader,

As an author, I know all too well that not every book I write will be for everyone. Sometimes, it is a matter of personal preference. Sometimes, books contain ideas, themes, or scenes that might hit some readers harder than others.

For this reason, I wanted to give a short note that to forewarn you that this book tells the story of a young woman finding herself and her second chance at love following a failed, runaway marriage. There are discussions and recollections of events that touch on thorny and complex topics like emotional trauma, memory loss, and the harm that can be inflicted by those whose faults we are blind to. While there is nothing overly explicit regarding these subjects on the page, in an effort to be truthful to Victoria's story they are not ignored, either.

While I hope that you are able to enjoy this story, it is also important to preserve your peace. But above all, I hope, dear reader, that you are safe and happy.

Your author,

Elise Kova

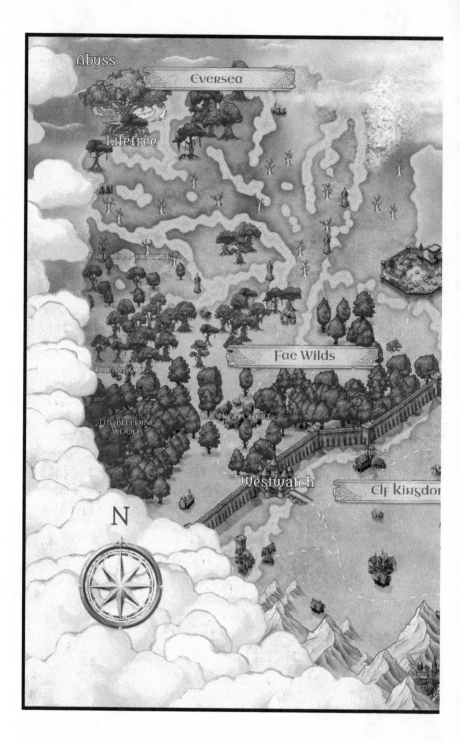

Vampir Mountains

Tempost

CASTLE TEMPOST
& GATE

Midscape

Quinnar

prologue

THE SEA WILL DEVOUR ME, IF GIVEN THE CHANCE. If not the waves and currents, or sharp-toothed animals, then the ghosts and monsters that haunt its depths. And if not those, if I am truly unlucky, the most fearsome creatures of all will be my demise: the sirens. They will sing a sweet requiem as they pull me deep below the waves.

My skin is gooseflesh the instant I step into the cold, dusky evening. The moon is rising from an inky sea. Fog and salt spray obscure the glowing orb, turning detail into hazy, curling strands of light.

Angry waves batter the rocks of the little island that I once thought of as my home. I've come to realize it has always been my prison. The ocean swells and churns, lapping at the land with its frothing tongues. Waiting for the moment it can consume all life that boldly stands against the tides.

I move quickly and confidently over the rocks. I've foraged in every tide pool for years. I've walked this path many, many times as I paced my cage. But, this time, as I head toward the back of the lighthouse, the rowboat is waiting for me.

Tonight, I am the one to leave.

The small vessel is old but sturdy. It's our only lifeline to the shore so Charles keeps it well maintained. I have only ever been in it once—when he brought me here two years ago.

Reaching out with one hand, I lightly touch the wood with quivering fingertips. Instantly, I look behind me. As if he'd somehow *know* I've broken his rules and will materialize out of nowhere. But the beach is empty and my gaze drifts up the dreary lighthouse. A few tiny, dark windows speckle its sides. I'm drawn to the one that is—*was* our bedroom.

After our argument at dinner, Charles will know where I've gone. But he won't be able to chase me. He'd have to signal another boat. Which is rare this close to the Gray Passage, but he will, eventually. He'll survive and I'll be long gone, past the horizon and far from his reach. I'll keep moving. Sort out affairs. I'll find a way forward without him. I know I can.

I have to.

I grip the basket I'm holding with white knuckles. The provisions in it clank together softly. Meager morsels I've managed to squirrel away as I've been secretly planning my escape—just enough to last for the three weeks it'll take me to get to my parents and sister, if I'm mindful in my consumption. The thought of confronting my family freezes me. What will I tell them? What will they think of me after what I've done—am doing? Should I even go to them?

I have to keep moving if I'm to make my escape tonight. But I'm stuck, staring up at the lighthouse and its slowly revolving beacon. Imagining what I might say to my family becomes replaying conversations with him.

I would've thrown myself into the sea by now, if I didn't have you, Lizzie. You are my lighthouse point. My comfort in the night, knowing you are always here to stand against the sirens. You were made for this responsibility. I could never let you leave. I hear Charles's words despite my cotton-packed ears. They rattle around my chest until my bones ache. Until I draw a shuddering breath and steel my resolve.

I can't back down now. I've made my choice. I gave him two years. I tried, I begged, I wept, I talked until my hands were exhausted from forming the words, and, above all, I hoped that our relationship would get better on its own. But he kept leaving the island…going off on the adventures he promised me and leaving me here. Alone. Yet I persevered.

But then…

Then two months ago happened.

The dust of his study was so thick it coated my fingers as I worked. Sweat on my neck, not from exertion, but fear. *Never go into my study,*

Lizzie. Charles had always made the rules clear. But he'd been so displeased by the dinner I'd made the night before he'd left. A little tidy couldn't hurt…or so I'd thought.

The stash of letters was in the lockbox by his chair. He'd left the key in the slot. I'd never known the itch of such curiosity before. One turn, and the whole world fell out from underneath me as I retrieved them one by one, traveling through time as I read dates and records of events that I should have known about years ago from a family that he swore had abandoned me. Every last one was addressed to me, and me alone. Rather than burning the evidence of his treachery, he kept it like some sick trophy.

I don't care if I'm an oath breaker. A contract ripper. A woman of loose morals. Or whatever else might be said about me. If the cost of my happiness is the world's judgment, then it is a price I'll pay.

It's amazing how easily the knots holding the boat untie. The way Charles spoke made it sound like my "delicate little fingers" couldn't possibly undo them. It's like finding out that I held the key to my cage all along.

I settle the basket in the bow of the vessel and push. The boat refuses to budge. Digging in my heels, I try again. The sand slips and piles under the balls of my feet.

Move. Move! I silently beg. Charles is not a heavy sleeper and it has been almost thirty minutes since I last crept from the bed.

As if sensing my fears, a candle flickers to life in the bedroom window.

Frantic energy brought on by panic fuels me and I heave with all my might. My meager muscles strain to what feels like the breaking point. *Move!* If I don't escape now, I will be trapped here forever. He will keep me like a doll in his house. Forcing me to play pretend that what I felt for him had truly been love and not naive infatuation.

There's so much more ahead of me. There must be. *This* can't be all there is. Tears are threatening to spill over my lids, but I keep pushing. The massive bell beneath the lighthouse tolls so loudly the island trembles. This is my chance, before Charles gets to me and while the siren's songs are disrupted. *Shove, Lizzie!*

For the first time in my life, the sea might be on my side.

The tide is coming in and meets the grinding hull of the small vessel. The resistance lessens before vanishing as the boat is freed of the shore.

A new fear grips me by the throat as I stare at the dark water rising to my ankles. I'll have to go in up to my knees to get in the rowboat. How deep is deep enough for sirens and their monsters or ghosts to claim me? How quickly can they recover after the bell? I should know this. You'd think as a lighthouse keeper's wife I would know this by now.

But Charles's study was always forbidden…

I glance back up over my shoulder. Charles is hanging out the window. Eyes wide and brows knitted with rage.

"What do you think you're doing? Get back here! Now!" he furiously says with his hands rather than his mouth. All those who live near the sea know hand signs so their ears can stay stuffed with cotton.

I gather whatever is left of the brave young woman I once was and race into the water, leaping into the rowboat. Charles has vanished from the window. He's coming for me.

The sea that was briefly my friend has returned to being my enemy. I'm straining against the tide that attempts to push me back to the man racing around the lighthouse. I pull the oars, the wood ripping the skin from my palms. Two years here has made me soft. Gone are the calluses from working with my father around the house. The muscles from hoisting Mother's crates and packages have left me. I've never felt so weak and…if I manage to escape him…I will *never* let myself feel weak ever again.

"Lizzie!" he mouths the pet name he gave me. He might actually be shouting. He's rounded the lighthouse and is racing to the beach, but I'm already gone. "Get back here!" He points to me, and then draws his hands to his chest, sliding them down his torso to point at the ground. He gesticulates, ending by drawing his fingers across his neck. "You maddening woman, you're going to get yourself killed!"

This is the closest he's looked to caring in years. He only ever wanted me when I was someone he had to save—a young woman on the outskirts of a small town who looked at him like he was a god. He doesn't love *me*. He never did. He loves feeling needed. Important. What he loves is knowing that at any time of day, I am there to be whatever *he* wants. That I am here on this rock every time he leaves and am waiting every time he returns.

"I'm leaving. You can't stop me," I let go of the oars to say, drawing my hands away from my chest and waggling my fingers hastily, and then I begin rowing again. The rowboat is moving more easily now. I'm freeing myself from the current pulling me toward him.

"And where will you go? Who would have you? You won't survive a day without me!" He gestures wildly. "You need me."

I need him? *I need him?* "I never *needed* you." He made me feel special. Feel...important. Desirable. All the things a young woman who never saw enough value in herself wanted. But none of it was a "need." I was fine without him. Father taught me how to hunt, cook, and keep the home. Mother was teaching me how to trade—how to be clever with numbers and negotiations. Charles, on the other hand... He taught me nothing but silence and subservience. "You were the one who needed me!"

"Why would a man of means like me need a woman like you? You lived in a back-roads hovel before me." He thrusts his fingers at me. "You were *nothing*. I pulled you from the dirt and gave you comfort and well-being. You should be groveling before me every morning and night. But you continue to try my patience with your insolence."

"You lied to me!" I scream with my mouth and my hands. The pain cracks through my voice, I feel it more than hear it. My throat burns from years of unuse. "You told me that my family didn't love me. That they didn't want me anymore."

But my family always did. Even when the dozens of letters I asked Charles to send were kept in a lockbox. They kept writing...and that is how I know that they will still love me, even as an oath breaker.

"Because it was true." Charles's face turns a scarlet that matches the last vestiges of sunset in the horizon as he continues speaking. His hands fly like wasps, trying to sting me with his words. My eyes burn as their meaning washes over me. "You are a sad, lonely, pathetic child. It is a relief every time I leave this island and can be free of you. Of course your family doesn't love you. How could they? Who on this wide earth could *love* you?"

The words batter my face and prick my eyes. He's told me them enough times that I can repeat them before his fingers move. They're barbs underneath my flesh. Constricting me. Holding me in place so tightly that I can't escape without giving my blood as payment. Without letting a piece of myself die here, tonight.

I keep trying to row, but my hands slowly release the oars. His words are a tether that tries to yank me back. Charles pulls on one side of me; the land and all the freedom to roam it calls from the mainland.

I'm caught between what I know I want, and every thought he has filled my head with.

What if...he's right? the barely eighteen-year-old version of myself that married him whispers from the depths of my mind.

Then, I see the letters as clearly as if I were still holding them.

Meeting Charles's eyes, I release the oars and stand. I am not the girl he knew. I want him to see me as powerful as the rolling sea beneath me that he fears so much. I want him to finally acknowledge the woman I've become. I don't care if it's all an act and I feel like a fractured pane of glass, only held together by tension. All that matters is he believes me.

"I am leaving you like you left me all those times; but I am never coming back. I'm going to the people who actually care about me," I sign slowly.

"And who would that be?"

"My family."

"You really think they care about you? They were relieved you were gone! I was the one who was here for you."

"They wrote to me!"

"You…" He stills, eyes as wide as the slowly rising moon. Charles's features twist into an ugliness that competes with his soul. "You would dare to defy my order and go into my study? Do not forget: I own you!"

I shake my head. "No." My teeth are almost chattering with my anxiousness. Instinct tells me to cower. It takes all my strength to stand.

"Your soul is *mine*. You swore it to me on the day we wed. You signed a contract. I will not let you break it, worthless wench! You will spend the rest of your life tending to this lighthouse, honoring me and doing as I say."

Before I can respond, a swell of the sea rocks the boat without warning. I sway, trying to get low to no avail. I'm loose. The sky rolls above me and I am plunged into the waves.

The water is ice. I barely get my head above the surface in time to inhale sharply. Another wave crashes over me, ripping away my earmuffs and cotton.

"Charles!" I scream, using my mouth rather than hands as the latter are too busy fighting to keep me above water. The scarves and coats I wore to fight the chill are waterlogged, trying to smother me. "Charles!" I reach for him back at the shore.

He stares in horror. He stumbles backward. Charles watched his family be sucked out to sea. I wonder if their ghosts are now in the water with me.

"Don't leave me! *Please!*"

He takes another step, shaking his head slowly. He no longer sees me as one of the living. I am in the sea and without protection for my ears.

I am dead to him.

Realizing it's no use, I turn away from him, thoughts frantic. I must choose between the boat and the shore. The boat is capsized, but the tide is still rushing in. I think the shore's a better bet. I begin to try to swim with the currents, trying to get back before the sirens or their monsters can claim me.

But it's too late. It's been too long since the bell tolled. There's already whispering on the wind.

A haunted hymn, barely audible at first, grows. It swells in me with a force greater than high tide. My eyes flutter closed against my will and my muscles relax. I exhale softly in harmonious relief. The sound soothes away my aches, physical ones and the frustrating pangs that never leave my heart.

The singer is masculine, a rich bass finer than any I've ever heard. He holds low notes, full of mourning and longing. As if he sings to the whole expanse of the sea…to every cold, lost soul condemned to its depths.

A smile cracks my wind-battered lips. He sounds so sad. So broken. So much like me.

The notes shift, pulsing. *Calling.*

It draws closer. Throbbing behind my eyes. The notes are almost a snarl and I am suddenly aware of movements in the waters around me. Darting shadows.

At that moment, the water hardens around my ankles with invisible hands. The current pulls my feet down. I don't let out a shout or a cry, but a gasp—before my head slips underneath the waves.

Rushing water fills my ears, roaring to the tune of the song. I fight for the surface once more, lungs aching. In a whorl of textile and color, I rip off the scarves and clothing I'd bundled myself in so I can swim better. I can't die like this. This can't be all there is for me. Not when I had just found the courage to feel real again—to live, really, truly, unabashedly *live*, no matter the cost.

I fight against the currents that pull at me with ghostly hands. My body is shuddering from the icy cold. My lungs are already stinging.

But it's not the currents that have taken me. The shadows have come alive in the form of a monster—half man, half fish, with hollow eyes. Milky and unseeing. His mouth is slightly ajar. In place of ears are fins, the cartilage pushing through the skin of his cheeks.

For a moment, I am stuck in shock.

The song begins to pulse, faster and faster. The singer is louder now. I can't tell if it's the siren before me, or the other one that emerges. Or another. All void of color and life. Somewhere between living and dead.

Panic sets in. I kick and push against them as they reach for me. I try to free myself, but I'm like a fish in a net and somehow only end up ensnaring myself further. Their hands are on me, grabbing. I shudder in the horror of what's to come. They will drag me down to their lair and allow their monsters to feast on me.

Lungs burning, I reach toward the pale moon high above. Umbra wraps around it.

I let out a silent scream.

The cold water burns as it crashes into me. Knives rip through the muscles in my chest, carving out my lungs, nicking my ribs. My throat spasms. Heart squeezes and seizes.

At once, the immense pain vanishes, and everything begins to go still. Numb. The night grows thicker around me. *It's over…that's it…all I got in life…* The cruelty of it all is astonishing.

There's a flash of light. *Lightning?* Movement in my fading vision. The song is at its loudest now. And then, all at once…silence. *Did the bell ring already?*

Two arms wrap around my midsection. *Charles has come for me.*

I can't believe he did. I never thought he would go into the ocean willingly for me…or swim this deep. *Maybe he does care…*

I'm wrong.

The moon vanishes completely, consumed by an ocean of night as I'm dragged farther down, consciousness slipping from me and mingling with the melody still buzzing in my ears. The other sirens seem to have vanished. One has claimed me for his own. For a second, there's nothing more than an endless void of water. But then, specks of light like fireflies dance on the currents—pulsing to the beat of his melody. The cold ebbs from my bones and heat flows in. Thoughts return to me. I blink awake.

I'm twisted, manhandled by the hands around my waist, and I meet the eyes of my savior. *No*, my enemy.

This man's face is different from that of his kin. Illuminated by the spheres of light that are floating along the currents, bright green and shades of cerulean highlight high cheeks perched over an angled jaw and sharp chin that is almost human in shape. These are not the hollow, skeletal angles of the previous sirens. But something fuller, more…real. As real as the curl of his tail underneath me.

Tracts of pale cartilage gently rise from his cheeks by where human ears would be, branching into fans of turquoise membrane reminiscent of a fish's fins. His brows furrow together. They're two platinum arches, the same shade as the hair that drifts around his face. More specks of light illuminate his cheeks and shine underneath intense, dark brown eyes. Not milky. Not void and dead. But the bright, intelligent gaze of a man in his prime.

His skin is fair and his right arm is almost completely tattooed with line and color—black, navy, white—that spread up his neck and chest, unfurling like ribbons. His left forearm bears similar markings. A wooden spear is strapped to his back. And while he looks not much older than me, he has an aura of timelessness around him.

He is unnatural. Uncomfortable. Forbidden.

He is terrifying.

And yet…I am keenly aware of his strong body pressed against mine as he holds me under my ribs with one arm. Our noses almost touching as he brushes his fingertips over my temple, pushing hair from floating into my face. My flesh is suddenly aflame, ignited by the barest

of touches. He beholds me in the manner one would a god, as if the
world starts and ends with me, here in this singular moment.

"A human..." His voice echoes between my ears, arms both arms
circling me again. He defies the laws of nature to speak without moving
his lips or hands. "You're dying."

I know this. It's a wonder that I'm still conscious. I felt the eternal
sleep settling upon me. But here I am...despite all odds.

"My song only stalls the inevitable. But, I could save you."

What? The thought ripples across my mind. Soft. Unbidden.

A smirk slips across his lips and the shadows around his face shift,
clinging to every ominous, almost sinister edge of his expression. He
leans in. Closer. My back arches, flesh aching, as if it is all suddenly
too tight. Hips and torso pressing into him as we tilt in the water and he
devours me with his eyes.

Somehow, even as he speaks, his song continues to buzz in the back
of my mind, smoothing over my worries and fears. Inviting me to sink
into it—into him. I fight the urge. Blink furiously to try and keep my
focus. I will *not* give in.

"Easy, easy," he soothes. "One way or another, this will all be over
soon. Either I save you. Or, I let you go and leave you to the sea."

No... There has to be more. *This can't be the end.*

"Very well. I will save you. But it will be at a great cost to me and
my magic, so it will bear a steep price. In five years' time, I will come
to claim what is mine."

Five years.

In five years I will be twenty-five, almost twenty-six. It seems like
an eternity away. Five years to see the world with nothing holding me
back. Five years of freedom. Or death.

"Do you accept?" Muscles ripple under the painted markings of his
flesh as his arms tense around me. His fingers splay over the small of
my back. Hot through the thin fabric of my dress.

Everything is a transaction, a barter. My life. My freedom. But this
I've known for a long time. As impossible as this all seems...I see no
other way. If I'm either dead now or in five years by the hand of the
siren, it doesn't make much of a difference.

I manage a nod.

"I knew you would," he purrs across the back of my mind then begins to sing once more. The siren encases me in his song. It flows over me. Into me.

I'm flush against his strong body. The water no longer passes between us, but the current still does. Energy, essence…no, it must be raw magic that ebbs and flows between us, pulsing, continuing to keep me alive. It swells and rises. I gasp soundlessly, my head tilting back slightly, eyes fluttering closed, as if I am to join him in the song. The endless repetition of words that keep pace with my fluttering heart.

The ocean is salty on my tongue; my body tingles as though a thousand hands run over it—holding life to me. The siren leans forward, his tail curling around my legs. I am slipping further and further into the song-spell he has me under. My thoughts are fleeting. Soon my mind will be as empty but endless as the void of the ocean around us.

His right hand slides down my left arm, fingers burning in their wake. His left hand rises between my shoulder blades, cupping the back of my head. My eyes meet his and the last of the tension Charles wrought into my meager frame leaves me. I grab onto the siren's strong, sculpted shoulders. I hold on for dear life and release everything else.

Bubbles rise around us. Air flows back into my nose. The sensation causes a giggle to burst in the back of my throat. It's like I'm in a glass of sparkling wine. Rising higher, and higher, and higher, until—

My head breaks the surface of waves. I inhale sharply but only for a second before a wave crashes and I tumble back underneath. I roll, clothes twisting, knotting, his arms still around me. The ecstasy of his caress transforms into a searing pain that shoots down my left arm, like a hot brand wrapping around bare flesh. I hiss. My shoulder nearly pops from its socket. I catch one last glimpse of him—a halo of nearly white hair in the moonlight, floating amongst a dark sea. In a blink, he's gone. The pressure around my wrist slides down my fingers and releases. The crunch of shell and sand heralds dry land.

I'm ashore.

Immediately my body revolts. I cough up seawater and the meager contents of my stomach. I heave until my throat is dry and throbbing. Abdomen spasming. I throw up until there is nothing left and I double over, collapsing back on the sand, waves lapping against my hand.

The moon is still overhead, watching. Waiting. Slowly, I recover enough to sit and stare out over the waves. Was the siren real? Or was it all a near-death dream? Kelp is knotted around me in place of his arms. I pause as I go to remove it.

Around my left forearm are swirls of magenta and gold. The former is nearly the shade of my dress and contrasts starkly with the hue of my skin; the latter nearly blends in. They are the same tattooed outlines that were on his right arm. A mirror.

I rub my flesh. The markings stay in place. Immune to my nails and seawater. It's then I realize that my wedding band is gone, ripped from my finger. Horror combines with relief. The emotions are muted by the sounds that fill my mind, manifesting as words in the back of my mind, as I stare at those strange swirls:

"An offering,
Of life so fine,
Unto the old
And ancient divine.

Er'y corner of the land,
Er'y depth of the sea,
Shall open unto thee.

No plant nor man,
Bird nor beast,
Shall hold you back
when you desire release."

The echo of a melody comes afar, as if singing with my thoughts, cut short by the low, loud resonance of a bell. How has it already been thirty minutes?

The lighthouse is now in the distance. I washed up on one of the distant shores that surrounded me for years.

After ten minutes of sitting and breathing glorious air and massaging my forearm—that I am pleased feels very much normal despite the new markings—I stand and put my back to the lighthouse, leaving it all behind me.

If I'm fast, I'll be gone by dawn. Charles no doubt thinks me dead, which means he won't report me as abandoning my marriage contract to the council. As long as no one knows I'm alive...I am finally free.

Five years of freedom on a siren's boon. Five years for the adventure I've always wanted.

Practically an eternity...

one

Four years and six months later...

THE FOUR CORNERS OF ONE SHEET OF PAPER HOLD MY FATE. The letter quivers in my fingers and the sound nearly takes me back to an afternoon a lifetime ago in a dusty, cluttered study. It started with a crumple of parchment. It'll end with one.

I begin reading.

NOTICE OF FINAL JUDGMENT

Regarding the Matter of:
Elizabeth Victoria Datch v. Charles Jol Vakstone

I suck in and hold a breath. *Final judgment.* This is it. For five years I've been working toward this moment.

Though, for all I want to read on, my eyes keep snagging on that second line. It's odd now to see my first name written out. That name died in the cold sea that long-ago night. There's only one person in the world now who uses that name...and it's purely out of spite.

I shake off that slimy, cloying feeling and continue reading:

The Council of Tenvrath has reached a judgment regarding the Forced Dissolution of Marriage requested by Elizabeth Victoria Datch.

Upon reviewing the supplementing documents provided by both Datch and Vakstone, as well as the full circumstances of the matter, the council has come to the following conclusion:

Severing of Marriage Contract: GRANTED

Ending of Reparation Payments: GRANTED

A noise somewhere between a muffled sob and a shout of triumph escapes on a hiss of air. **GRANTED.** One word has never meant so much to me.

I'm free. My person, my purse, my very soul is *finally* free of him...

"Victoria?" Emily shifts closer to me, no doubt worried about my expressions swinging like a pendulum. She still clutches the envelope I ripped the letter from to her chest. We're hunched around a booth against the back wall of the Tilted Table. Our usual spot in our family's tavern.

But I don't respond, I keep reading. There's still more. If there's one thing I know, it's that Charles is a small, petty man who won't remove his claws from anything he deems as his. He's been terrorizing me at every turn. From his demands of reparation payments to supplement his "hardship" at the lighthouse without me, to allegations of me being involved with the sirens, to doing everything he can to smear my name to anyone who will listen. There is no act that's beneath him when it comes to something that would hurt me.

The letter continues:

With the following terms applicable in consideration with Vakstone's suffering and Tenvrath's investment in Datch as a lighthouse keeper, as well as changing circumstances for Datch, Elizabeth Victoria Datch will owe:

10,000 crons to the Council of Tenvrath
5,000 crons repayment for each year the council funded Datch's room and board as a lighthouse attendant, inclusive of initial establishment costs.

10,000 crons to Charles Vakstone
200 crons annual reparation payment for desertion of marriage calculated across 50 years.

Payment will be due in exactly two years following delivery of this notice.

Should these payments fail to be made, the council will award Vakstone with an adequate replacement of lighthouse assistant from Datch's next of kin. Should there be no one willing or able, all those bearing the Datch name from the immediate family will be sent to a debtors' prison to pay back any remaining debts at a rate of one year per thousand crons.

There's more at the bottom but it's all the official seals and signatures of the Council of Tenvrath, followed by a long list of files and documents that Charles and I have submitted over the years. There's his initial notice of abandonment at the top, followed by his movement for reparations. My first request for the severing of marriage all the way to the third request—that Charles still refused—which led to the council being forced to finally step in and render a judgment that we clearly were never going to reach on our own.

It's easier to cut your own arm off than sever a contract in Tenvrath.

I make sure nothing is missed. No opportunity I lost to fight my way out of this corner I've been backed into. But every document I submitted is listed. Every appearance before the council. Every formal attack Charles has ever made against me filed in triplicate. The grim undercurrent of my adult life is cataloged with legal document and statement after statement.

They gave me one year to pay them more than what I make in several. It's a cruel sentence cast down by a council of old men who were always far more sympathetic to Charles than to me. The cruelty is made worse by what they don't know: I only have six months. My five years are almost up. And if I disappear before I pay this debt then my family will bear the cost.

Guilt turns my stomach sour. How could I inflict this upon them? I must find a way to fix this mess I've made once and for all.

"Well?" Emily whispers eagerly, interrupting my thoughts. "What did the council say this time? John wouldn't tell me *anything*. He didn't even want to let me bring the ruling to you tonight. I had to insist; even then, he only agreed because I told him how quickly you usually set sail."

There's a whole page of words in front of me and yet I can't find any to say. I've been staring at the letter for ten long minutes. Reading it again and again.

It's over…it's finally, at long last, over… Despite Charles and all his attempts to cling to me—to fault me for his every misfortune—I am finally free of him. Our marriage contract has been severed.

But my struggles are only just beginning. This moment should have been my triumph and, yet again, Charles manages to be the thief of my joy.

"Victoria, you're starting to worry me." Emily bites on her nails.

"No need for that." I rest my fingertips lightly on my younger sister's knuckles. "It's all right, Em." Or, it will be, once I come up with the money.

"Then..." She slowly lowers her hand, eyes widening. "Vic... you're finally free?"

I smile and nod. My sister practically vaults across the table and throws her arms around my shoulders. I barely have a chance to get the paper out from between us, shoving it into my pocket before she can see the terms. She squeezes the air from me. Every time I hug her I wonder where the little girl that was always on my heels went. She was thirteen and then, in a blink, a woman.

Though, it didn't help that I didn't see her for almost four years. There were the two I was on the lighthouse island, and then almost two after that when I was in hiding. Trying to find my feet and make a life for myself—on my own—before Charles reared his ugly head from that gray rock of his. Before I found out via getting back in touch with Em that he had declared me as abandoning my duty as soon as he was able—not dead, since my body could not be found—and went after my family for money as a result.

That was the beginning of our final battle. A war waged through papers submitted to the council, the rumor mill of Dennow, and an endless river of payments made from my purse directly to him for *his* pain.

"I knew the council would finally come around." Emily leans away and looks back toward the bar where Father is serving tonight's lone customer. "We have to tell Pa."

"Now isn't—" I don't get a chance to tell her the rest. She's bounding from the seat, racing over to the bar, slamming into it with raw enthusiasm.

"Pa, Vic is finally free!" Emily bursts with the news.

My father stills, eyes drifting over to me. A soft sigh turns into a slight smile. His shoulders relax, as if a weight has been lifted, which only causes mine to go more rigid. He looks relieved. Happy, at a glance, but it doesn't quite reach his eyes.

My parents' love story is one for the ages. A house filled with fondness, ripened, not soured, by distance and time as Father looked after us and Mother traveled. They've always supported me and Emily, without question…but I can't stop myself from wondering if part of them has grown ashamed of the path I've walked. Of the scandal and heartache I've brought upon our name.

Which is why I've worked to be the best captain Tenvrath has ever known. To bring pride. As if, somehow, that could outweigh the shame.

"The council nullified—"

"That is most excellent news," Father cuts off Emily with a glance to the customer.

The man at the bar slowly shifts to face me. His eyes widen slightly as if seeing me for the first time. I resist the urge to cover the tattoo on my forearm. The strange marking is as known throughout Dennow as my name.

I don't hide. Instead, a coy smile slides across my lips and I sink my chin into my palm. Somewhere between smug and sultry. My confidence makes them all the angrier.

The stranger scoffs at me, eyes shadowed with disapproval. I blow him a kiss. Without another word, he leaves. At least this customer dropped some coins on the bar first.

I am the best captain that there ever was…with the worst reputation. I'd be more loved in Tenvrath if I were a murderer than as an oath breaker.

Yet, when my eyes return to Father's, he's smiling. There isn't a trace of resentment. Of anger. My family's unflinching compassion only deepens the guilt I try so hard to hide.

"I think this calls for a round on the house." Father turns back to the tapped kegs, filling a flagon to the brim. "Vic, mind closing up?"

"Isn't it a bit early for that?" I ask as I somehow manage to stand despite the weight of the judgment in my pocket nearly gluing me to the seat.

"Hardly." Father puts a flagon on the bar and motions to the empty tavern before he begins filling the next one. "It's not as if we have many customers tonight."

Not tonight…or any night. If not for my crew, my father's dream of owning his own business would've long since died. Perhaps my disappearance will be a boon to them. When I'm dead, I can't tarnish their reputation any longer.

"I'll get it, then." I run my fingers over my inked forearm as I head for the front.

I spent years searching for information. For any word or clue as to what siren magic was used on me that night so that I could better harness it. If it has helped me so much throughout the years passively, what could I do with this power if I wielded it? I could be a sorceress of the seas. I could show Charles a sliver of the fear he instilled in me and my family. I would curse his name as he's cursed mine. Worse.

I became a sailor thinking that I might meet the siren again. To learn how to use the power or, perhaps, barter better for my life.

But all the rumors of the sirens are of monsters. Every whisper and bit of lore is of beasts that ravage the seas. And, in all my years on the ocean, I never saw another siren. That, too, is part of the magic, I've decided. To be immune to the calls of his people. This mysterious power and protection he gave me is immense in its abilities.

And yet I still could never harness it well enough to free me from Charles. I ball my hands into fists. If I were only stronger…

Before I step outside, I pack my ears with cotton. I learned long ago that it isn't necessary for me, but I do it anyway for appearances. The only siren songs that have any effect on me are the ones sung in *his* voice. Whispering in the back of my mind almost every night. Tingling across my skin whenever I run my fingers over the marking he left on me like a calling card.

Goosebumps dot the flesh of my forearm, rising around the tattoo, at the thought of him. I ignore it and pry open the heavy door of the tavern, stepping outside onto the Dennow docks. The familiar, worn sandwich board in all its peeling paint is only a few steps from the door. It reads:

TILTED TABLE TAVERN.
BEST ALE IN DENNOW.

Father's brewing skills are truly a force to be reckoned with and once I'm gone all of Dennow will finally realize it. Mother's trading has increased tenfold since I became a captain—I can only imagine what will happen when my reputation no longer is a reason for some to hold back. The job I managed to get Em with the Tenvrath Council is stable and steady and I'm sure they'll love her even more when they no longer have to deal with me.

They should have been fine after I was gone. But now I owe twenty thousand crons. More than I've ever seen in my life. More than the total mortgage of the Tilted Table. More than all the vessels in the entire fleet for the Applegate Trading Company.

I won't let my family bear that burden.

A woman walks by, muffs covering her cotton-packed ears. She brings her thumb to her mouth and bites on it in an offensive gesture. I lock eyes with her and relax my expression into one of cold, aloof elitism. *I'm better than you*, I try to say with a look alone. *You think me less than dirt, but I'm superior to you...so what does that make you?*

The look has the intended effect and she hustles faster. Disappearing. I keep the expression on my face, hiding how deeply the nasty words and gazes hurt. Even as I try to smile them away, Charles's voice echoes, persistent after all this time: *Who could love you?*

I return inside.

I've hardly had a chance to sit and take my drink when Emily claps her hands and exclaims, "So, when will there be a new lucky someone?"

I snort into my flagon, coughing up ale. "Em, the ink on the judgment hasn't even dried!" *Now is hardly the time for this.*

"You were married only on paper—to an ass, I might add—"

"Emily Datch," Father scolds.

She ignores it. "—but not in spirit for years. Your heart wasn't with him."

It was, once. At least I thought it was. Charles told me he loved me and in less than two years...

"Being married on paper was enough." I give her a firm look. She knows the lines I wouldn't cross. Even if Charles was possessive, cold, and cruel, I had made an oath to him. One I was trying to break but... until it was broken, I wouldn't cross that line. They all saw me as a scoundrel, a liar, an oath breaker. The only way I could keep my head high was to be a little bit better than they thought. I had to believe my word still meant something, even when everyone was trying to tell me it didn't. I might have broken if I gave that up.

"I've had my love story." *As pathetic as it was.* "It didn't work out.

That's fine. There are more stories to write than just love. I've more important things to focus on."

"You've always been 'focusing on what's important.'" She imitates me with her eyes halfway rolled back. It's rather unflattering but I can't stop a chuckle.

"Yes, and being focused is how I've become the best captain in all of Tenvrath and beyond."

"A heart forever on the road can never settle with one person," Father says gently. It's an echo of Mother's mantra—what always calls her home.

"Not you too, Pa." I groan. "Listen, my heart couldn't be fuller. You three mean *everything* to me. There's no room for anyone or anything else."

"You know what is important to us? You know what also needs to be important to you?" Emily points, leaning over to prod my chest. "*You.* Your happiness."

"Your sister is right," Father adds.

I sigh. This was not how I intended for any of this to go. But it's better than them asking for details I don't want to give. "I am happy when you are all happy."

Emily puffs out her cheeks and scowls at me. Her square chin makes her face look as round as a melon when her cheeks are full like that. She looks so much like our father, inheriting his hazel eyes and strong jaw.

Whereas I'm all our mother.

My eyes are like the tempest sea, stormy grays and churned blues, as restless as my spirit. That's what Charles told me when we first met. He was a child of the sea, too, so he could recognize it in me. He'd seen the majesty and the violence of the waves. How noble he'd sounded as he told me how he'd lost his family to it and dedicated his life to protecting others from suffering the same fate.

He told me stories of his life, full of excitement and danger. He could give me that life, too, if I wanted. That's what he'd said. What he'd *promised*…

I take another long sip of ale and try to banish the thoughts of him. It's a futile endeavor. I could love him, hate him, resent him, be frustrated with him. But the one thing I can't seem to do is *not care* about him. Everything is a reminder of him. Of the fleeting good times we once shared, so long ago they feel like a dream now. Of every reason I have to hate him.

"You know what I'm trying to say!" Emily continues, oblivious to my struggle.

"I do."

"Then why are you being so impossible about it?"

"Because I am your older sister and 'being impossible' is what I am made for." I grin slightly and push on her puffy cheeks, causing her to exhale with a *whoosh* of air and bat my hands away.

"Look, Vic, if you don't want to be with anyone ever again because it doesn't make you happy, then *fine*. But don't do it because you're 'too focused on taking care of us.' That's not what we want. Trust us that we'll be all right. You've been through enough; you deserve your happily ever after."

I smile faintly, swirling my ale in the flagon, entranced by the foamy amber. I believed those words once, that I "deserved" a happily ever after. That everyone did, whatever it looked like for each person. But now I see it for what it was: a child's daydreams. The real world is harsh, and cruel. Things don't always work out, no matter how hard you try, or beg.

"I'm going to go and get dinner started." Father sets down his flagon. "A celebratory feast won't cook itself."

"Father, you don't have to—"

He makes a *pish-posh* sound at me and waves my objection away as he heads for the side door that connects to the small kitchen. My stomach threatens to ruin the meal, souring at the thought that this might be the last time I ever eat his cooking. I'm going to have to get to work if I'm going to scrap together a lifetime of crons in six months.

"So, when are you going to tell me what's wrong?" Emily asks, nudging me with her shoulder.

"Nothing's wrong."

"Something *definitely* is."

"Why do you think that?" I hate how well Em knows me.

"You should be happier."

"I *am* happy." As happy as a dead woman can be. But ending my failed marriage has been the only real thing I've wanted to do before

I die. Not just because Charles went after my family before he'd even known I'd survived. But for myself.

I own you... Your soul is mine. I've carried those words with me for almost five years. Trying to prove them wrong at every turn. To show him that I am my own woman through word and deed...but it was never enough. There was always that last, whispering tether, holding me to him. A line now snapped.

"Victoria Datch." Even when she scolds, she doesn't use my full name.

"I'm sorry, what?"

"Talk to me, please." Emily lowers her voice and levels her eyes with mine. She takes both my hands in hers. "It's rare to see you so knotted like this." A frown crosses her lips. She works for the council and knows their methods. She's finally putting it together. "What else did they say?"

"The council has levied a fee on me as a cost of breaking the contract."

"What?" Emily balks.

"I have to pay back what I owe them for my care and pay while I was a lighthouse caretaker's wife." The words almost get stuck in my throat and I'm grateful for the heavy flagon once more as I peel my hand away to swallow a mouthful of ale. "I also must finish paying for his 'suffering.'"

"His suffering?" My sister looks as if she is about to flip the bar in her rage on my behalf. "What more could you possibly owe? You've been paying him two hundred crons a year—more than most could dream of." Just hearing her say "two hundred crons a year" emphasizes once more the impossibility of the amount my freedom has cost. I can't even die without being a burden on the ones I love.

"They want me to pay him ten thousand," I tell her so she doesn't have to risk her position with the council to find out—as I know she absolutely would've had I kept it a secret.

"Excuse me?" Emily pales, going still.

"And then another ten thousand to the council to pay back the investment they put in me while I was wife to a lighthouse keeper."

"You didn't see a single cron from him!" Emily has slowly learned the rough outlines of my circumstances over the years. I owed them all some explanation when I showed up, back from the dead, having—to their knowledge—ignored all their letters before the sea claimed me. But I've spared her the grimmest details. Still, my sister is a woman grown, and a clever one. She's figured out the worst of it.

"Keep your voice down, Em. Please," I hiss. "I don't want Father knowing."

"What are you going to do?"

"I have an idea." I stare into my flagon.

"It's not what I think it is…is it?" Em narrows her eyes at me. "Vic? Tell me you're not going to sail the north route."

I shrug and take a long, long drink.

"I thought Lord Applegate gave up on that route after the last close call?"

"He might have changed his mind." Rumor has it the Applegate Company is struggling, at present. The silver mines aren't producing at the rate they once were and the land route has been met with endless, costly setbacks as they've tried to tunnel through the mountains. Very little silver has been flowing to market, from what Mother says.

"No. I don't care. I forbid it."

I chuckle lightly. "You can't forbid me."

"I'm certainly going to try! It's not just the sea monsters anymore. I hear the sirens are worse in that area this time of year and it's too rocky for the council to erect a lighthouse closer than—" *The one you were at,* she stops herself from saying.

"Than Charles's," I say anyway.

She touches my hand. "Vic, a ship *just* went down."

"A lesser captain on a lesser ship." I squeeze her hand.

At that moment, none other than my employer enters the bar. I know he's here to check in on my last delivery, but opportunity never fails to present itself whenever I need it most. There's a little bit of siren magic opening the path I need before me, just as it always has. I rub my tattooed wrist in gratitude as I stand.

"If you'll excuse me a moment."

Emily catches my hand. "Please, don't do that run again. We can find the money a different way. It's not worth it."

"It's the last time," I assure her confidently.

"You said that last time." Emily sighs. "Vic, I'm serious."

I lean forward and tuck a strand of hair behind her ear, the same shade of honey gold as mine, as our mother's. She's the best of all of us, inside and out. "Me too—serious about looking after you and Ma and Pa."

She doesn't need to know about the council's ultimatum. She'll find out eventually, or just figure it out. There are only a few punishments for debtors in Tenvrath, and none of them good. But I won't allow the way she finds out to be when the collectors come to drag her and my parents off to a debtors' prison. Or…somehow worse…Charles demanding Em to go live with him in the lighthouse in my stead. I'll make a thousand bargains with a thousand sirens, and die a thousand deaths, before I let that happen.

"You can look after us better when you're not monster food."

"I've never seen a single monster in all my years. They're just excuses for bad captains or explanations for unexpected storms." While it's true *I* haven't…I'm also alive because of a siren. So I know better than to think there aren't any out there.

"We can help come up with the amounts."

"This is the only way."

She tugs on my wrist as I try to walk away. Lord Covolt Kevhan Applegate—simply Kevhan, among friends—is halfway across the small bar, pulling the cotton from his ears. "Please, you're going to get yourself killed."

I smile and kiss her forehead. "I'll be fine. I have been every other time."

"And each one was a close call. Vic—"

"Don't worry."

Em sighs and lets me go. What she doesn't know is that I have siren magic to keep me safe. And…I'm already a dead woman walking.

"Lord Kevhan," I say, keeping my voice low so Em doesn't hear *all* the details of our conversation.

"Captain Victoria, a pleasure as always." He smiles and the crow's feet at the corners of his eyes crinkle. He has the same beard as my father. One of their many similarities. This man has been as good as family to me when everyone else would cast me out. He was the first to take me in. The first to believe in me after years of Charles telling me all the ways I was a failure. He's been so much more than my employer.

"Everything looked good with your latest shipment. I wanted to make sure there weren't any issues I should know about?"

"None in the slightest," I report. But he can't be here just for that... My curiosity piques.

"You are a wonder." He pats me on the shoulder. I notice his clothes are a little dingier than I'm used to seeing. There are stray strings at his elbow that hint at a seam coming undone. Little imperfections that are unlike him. As much as my heart aches for the idea of misfortune falling on my benevolent employer, it also emboldens me. Perhaps the rumors are true and, right now, he needs me as much as I need him.

"I wanted to discuss something with you," I say.

"Funny enough, I had a matter I wished to discuss with you as well."

I hold up my hand. "You first."

He sighs heavily. "I know I had said you would not be sailing the north run again, however, I might require it of you and your crew. One *final* time." He emphasizes the last three words.

I smile grimly and nod. He's right. It will be the last time. One way or another. Without hesitation I say, "I accept."

two

MY CREW ARE ALL ON DECK. Some stand at attention, some sit. A few are perched on the railing. But all eyes are on me.

I lean against the mast, arms folded. No one has signed a word for a good five minutes. This is one of my tactics. I call these pre-sailing meetings every night before we shove off. No matter how long we've been in port, there are always stories to swap and catching up to happen on whatever shenanigans the crew got up to while in Dennow. This is the last wharf in Tenvrath, so it's one of the rare times we can dock and all disembark. I wait, letting them talk until the conversations have exhausted themselves. Until all eyes are on me.

"I'm going to get right to the point." I bring my hand to my chest, smooth it over the palm of the other, and then press the fingertips into the palm. Even in Dennow, protected by its three lighthouses and far from the Gray Passage, we keep cotton in our ears outside of thick-walled buildings with heavy doors and people to watch over us. Cotton is *mandatory* on ships north of the narrow river that cuts through the dark forests to the south and connects to the seas beyond. Even those who can't hear without the cotton still pack their ears tightly with it. Paranoia runs deep with sailors and some have claimed that siren song is the one thing that deaf ears can hear. I believe it, since, even with cotton-packed ears, I hear singing in the back of my mind. "Lord Kevhan has asked us to do a north run."

There are worried looks, some frantic hands asking me "Why?" and "Please elaborate."

I happily oblige. "As I'm sure you've all heard, the land route Tenvrath is trying to build through the middle mountains isn't panning out, at least not as quickly as desired. There's a massive backlog of silver waiting to be delivered." I hope it's a large enough backlog that my payout percentage from the cargo will be breathtaking. "We're departing at dawn. Three weeks up, three weeks back." It should give me enough time left over to settle everything before the siren comes to collect me. "It's an aggressive run under normal circumstances and we will be pushing hard to fight against the tides this time of year. And I know, I said last time was the last time. But I promise you this will be it. I *swear*, this is the final time I'll ever do the north run and risk your lives in the passage."

There are some private discussions. People turn their backs to me to exchange words unseen and then turn back around. Arms cross. Feet shift. Discomfort and unease become palpable in the air.

I take a breath, bracing myself before continuing. "While our crew has never had incidents before, a ship recently went down. Going *is* a risk to your lives, one you all know better than any other sailors. A risk you don't have to take. I'll give you the same choice I give every time before this run: you can stay ashore. I'll talk with Lord Applegate and find you work within the trading company until we return. And, *when* we do return, you'll still have a place on this ship if you still want it."

When I finish, it's complete stillness. There are a few worried glances. A nod or two reassure me. This lot is tough as nails.

All my crew has escaped some kind of hardship and misfortune. There are women and men who fled from their own partners—situations much worse than I was in with Charles. There are daughters and sons who escaped from homes filled with hate and depravity. Some I freed from debtors' prisons like the ones I'm trying to spare my family from.

The siren gave me an opportunity to live on past when my story should have ended. I was given a second chance. As deserving, or not, as I might have been. So I've made it my mission to try and share my fortune with others in need of the same.

Jivre, my reliable first mate, steps forward. I knew she would. Like me, she speaks with her hands. "You wouldn't ask this lightly. There's another reason for the north run, isn't there?"

I hesitate. They're all waiting on me. These men and women who have put their life in my hands, given me their faith, their livelihoods. I owe them the complete truth after all we've been through. Plus…most of them know the rumors. It's only out of respect for me that nothing from the streets of Dennow is repeated on my ship.

"As you all probably know…I've been working on…" My hands still. I struggle for words. "Resolving a matter in my past," I say finally. I shake my head. *Stop being a coward, Victoria.* I know the rumors and names they call me are just petty words and I should ignore them. Yet they stick to me. I continue to project bravery I don't entirely feel. I don't have the luxury of slowly processing, of wallowing in the news—I never have. I keep moving forward. "As most of you know—Who am I kidding? *All* of you know, I was married. It was a decision I made and it ran its course. It's been done for a long time in spirit and, as of today, it's done legally as well."

Smiles all around. Some cheers and clapping. I try to give them an encouraging smile in return. This crew really does want the best for me. Most of them have their own marks against them in the eyes of society. If anyone would know what I'm going through, it's them.

I really don't deserve this lot.

"However, for breaking the terms and expectations of the marriage contract, the council has demanded I pay back the investment Tenvrath made in me as a lighthouse attendant's wife, as well as a final sum to Charles for his suffering."

"Final sum of what?" Maree, my crow's nest spotter, asks.

"Twenty thousand crons."

"Twenty thousand…" Jivre repeats.

"Twenty thousand?" Maree balks. The rest of the crew joins her in her shock. Hands move almost too fast for eyes to keep up.

"Enough, enough." Jivre calms them and looks back to me. "How are you going to come up with the money?" It's a marvelous question, one I've been thinking of the answer to for hours.

"The north run is a few thousand to the captain, usually."

Jivre scoffs. "There's no way. Not after what we're paid."

I finally admit my long-standing secret. "I…usually cut my pay into a third."

"What?" Lynn, a deckhand, signs slowly.

"I wanted you all to reap the benefits of your labors. I always felt my pay was far too much. But this time I might—I will keep it all," I admit with some guilt. It's what I must do…but I hate not to give them all I can. "Beyond that, I have some things in my cabin that I can sell. There's a little bit squirreled away—"

"We know you don't have anything of real value squirreled away." Jivre shakes her head. "Especially not now knowing how you pay us, what you give to your family, *and* the payments you've been forced to make to that man for years. It's a wonder you have anything at all."

"I do have *something*," I say in defense. A hundred crons is technically "something."

"Take my share."

"Jivre—"

"Mine too." Maree steps forward.

"And mine."

"Please, don't." I will them to stop, but they don't listen.

"And mine," another says with his hands.

One by one, my crew offers me their portions of the profits from our most dangerous run. All of them. My vision is blurry and eyes stinging as the last one's hands settle. My gut feels as if it's been hollowed out to make room for all the guilt I feel.

"If the whole crew pitches in our shares for this run, that should get you close, shouldn't it?" Jivre asks me.

"It would be immensely helpful." I am grateful for my hands when I know my words would fail me if they had to be spoken. If I kept all of my share, and theirs, it'd get me almost two thirds of the way. Maybe three fourths, depending on how much silver there actually is. Still, woefully short. But suddenly the impossible amount seems attainable. "But what about all of you? I can't take what you need."

"We'll be fine."

The crew nods in agreement with Jivre.

"We owe this to you. You made sure Jork had the medicine for his girl. You got Honey out of that awful prison."

"And let's not forget how many times you've had your father clear our bar tab," Sorrea says with graceful movements of her hands.

If anyone owes anyone anything here…I'm the one who owes them.

"Let us do this for you." Jivre turns her eyes back to me. "Rely on us for once. And when we've returned, we'll all figure out how to get the rest. Together. Who knows, maybe we'll raise enough that there'll be some left over for you to go on a holiday with Emily."

I tip my head back and blink up at the sky. I can't cry, I'm their strong and stoic captain. But it has been a long, long day. And I am worn down.

A holiday with Emily...if only. There's so much I should have done for her when I had the chance. Done *with* her. Done for all of them. If I was going to owe Charles an ungodly sum, I should have just been late on payments so Emily could have new dresses. I should have taken my mother on more sailings and Father out to more dinners so he could sample more dishes and get new ideas for his own recipes. I should have stayed out later with my crew and learned more of their stories.

Now I'm out of time. But there's still one more run ahead of me. One last thing I must do before I am consigned to oblivion.

"Thank you all," I say, emphasizing each motion in the hope that they can feel my sincerity.

The crew disperses and I watch them go about their business. My shoulders sag with the weight of their lives. I've tried to take care of them as best I could—like they were my own family. Was it enough?

Shaking my head, I return to my cabin. It is a small thing, by most captains' standards. But I don't make money off of my living space. I make it off of my crew and cargo, so I made sure the ship I would be sailing on reflected that. My crew has as many amenities as I can afford them.

Still, as cramped as it might be, it is and has always been mine. Blissfully, entirely mine.

Just over three years of living here has cluttered it with dozens of tokens and baubles I've collected in my journeys. There's a box of incense on the shelf from the craftsmen in Lanton. A jar of herbs for sea sickness—almost empty—procured from a young but particularly talented herbalist who had just finished her schooling and opened her shop in Capton when I sailed through. There are candies from Harsham, the closest city to the strange walled town to the south that always orders more silver than the mines can produce. And a rare, framed stained glass from the plains regions near the dark forests of the fae, given to me as a gift from my boss during one of his famous parties.

"Every corner of land and sea shall open to you," I murmur,

paraphrasing the words I heard that night. They're as etched on my memory as the markings on my skin. I've never had any trouble going anywhere. I've never encountered a burden, a wall, or a gate I couldn't overcome.

Except for *one*.

There's one tie, one tether that holds me back. That continues calling to me with shouts and screams and ominous silence. One that has alarm bells chiming violently in my mind, louder than the lighthouse bell that tolls across the waters of Dennow.

But that tie has finally been undone. It's over. *You can let him go, Victoria.*

No, not yet... I still must pay the price of my freedom before I'm gone.

None of them know I'm going to leave soon. I never could bring myself to tell anyone, not even Emily. If so much as a whisper made it out, my family would be at risk. I already dealt with Charles's rumors of my being in league with sirens once. The last thing I can risk is a second time. I've already caused them too much risk and heartache.

Am I loathsome for keeping it from them? Does it make me a bad daughter? Sister? Friend?

The questions weigh heavy on my mind. Heavier than they ever have before. The hammock sags underneath me, swaying with the rocking of the ship.

Was I a fool for ending things with Charles? No, I had to. If not for me, then to protect my family... But what would've been if I'd never started things with him in the first place? That might be the greatest question of my life...what little remains of it.

Would I have begun my adventures earlier? Would I have unlocked the great secrets of the world, untethered and free? Would I have found my one true love like Emily's stories?

I chuckle bitterly. "Don't get ahead of yourself, Vic."

There's no one out there that would love me, not as I am. No person who would set my soul aflame with a touch. A person who would love me—all of me, the good and bad and all the ugly bits, no matter what. And, even if there was, it would be cruel to pursue anything with them. I'm a magnet for bad luck. I am marked for death.

I sigh softly as I wait, running my fingertips over the colors swirled on my forearm. Even from the watery abyss where my siren resides, I can hear him singing to me almost every night. Calling.

But tonight, my mind is silent. And the only sounds in my mind are my own torturous thoughts.

three

THE MINES ARE IN THE DISTANCE BEHIND US AND MORE SILVER THAN I HAVE EVER LAID EYES ON IS IN MY SHIP'S HOLD. The wind is in our favor today, as it has been this entire trip. Everything is going my way. I just need the magic to hold until I return.

I stand at the bow of the vessel and stare at a distant, gray speck on the horizon. This might be the last time I set sail. I wonder how the siren will come to me… Will he crawl up from the sea? Or will the song in the back of my mind become so loud that I am summoned to his lair, walking into the foam, never to be heard from again?

Will death hurt? Phantom pains burn my lungs, tasting of cold seawater.

Seeking a distraction, I return my attention to the decks below. Everyone is getting in their positions, doing what must be done before we start into the Gray Passage. What will come of everything I've built these past four years? The sense that I'm letting Kevhan down, after all this man has done for me, is as heavy as the silver belowdecks.

"Captain," Kevhan signs as he comes to a stop next to me. His ears are stuffed with cotton. Muffs over them. Those who were with the Applegate Trading Company years ago say that it was once rare to see him aboard. But, as long as I've been here, he's been insistent on almost always getting on a ship in his fleet and going somewhere. The sea must be as much his home as it is mine.

"Everything looks good, sir," I dutifully report. "Winds

are in our favor. We should make it to the Gray Passage within the next hour."

"Let's hope it's as easy on the way back as it was on the way here."

I huff but keep my hands still and thoughts to myself. Even with a captain guarded and guided by siren magic, the passage is never "easy." I merely repeat his movements. "Let's hope."

"There's something I wished to discuss with you—well—two somethings."

I motion for him to continue.

"The first is the matter of your compensation." Those words have my heart seizing. My mind is already racing. I knew the rumors that he had fallen on hard times with the land route being delayed, but if he needs to dock my compensation for the run...where could I make up the difference? "There was more silver in that mine than even our best estimates. My wife will be happy."

The Lady Applegate is a shrewd businesswoman. All of the sense of Kevhan with twice the cunning and half the heart—if that much, even. She's the one who inherited the mines from her former, late husband, making her union with Applegate a notable one in the Tenvrath region. The means of production joined with the means of transport.

"For that reason, there is enough for me to double your regular payment for this run."

"Excuse me?" I can barely move my hands to form the words due to my trembling fingers.

Kevhan turns to me with a knowing smile. I glance back at my ship—my crew—from the corner of my eye. *Someone told him.* I'm caught between panic and shame.

"Consider it a bonus."

"Sir, I couldn't... Your family..."

"My family will be fine," he reassures me. Yet, I know the tired expression he wears. It's the face of someone who's trying desperately, at all costs, to hold everything together. "This shipment will usher in a new era for the Applegate Trading Company. It's the least I can do for you helping me get to this point. I couldn't have done it without you."

"I—"

"You are like a fourth daughter to me, Victoria," he says warmly. How can something so tender strike me like a dagger between my ribs?

"And I feel like I've taken advantage of your skill for years by not paying you enough. I'd like to do this. Please let me."

How can I say no to that? Even if it makes me mildly uncomfortable, I raise my hand to my face and lower it in an arc to say, "Thank you."

"No, thank you. We've been through a lot, you and I." He chuckles. "You've come a long way from the slip of a girl I met nearly five years ago."

The first thing I did after washing up on that beach was walk to Dennow, the heart of Tenvrath. I knew that I could find some kind of work in the city...I never would've guessed that I might luck upon a lord expanding his business and in desperate need of captains who were foolish enough to sail the north route.

That was my first luck of the siren's song.

I didn't know the slightest thing about helming a ship. Lying about it had been as reckless as running from Charles. But it wasn't as if he had a lot of ship captains willing to sail through the Gray Passage, known for its sea monsters and ghosts. I was one of his only options and he was mine. I put in the work, had the magic, and it all panned out. My first lies to Kevhan were the best lies I ever told.

Lord Kevhan Applegate was generous to me, more so after I proved myself and quickly rose to become his most dependable and skilled captain. I worked hard and bided my time, going by Victoria instead of Elizabeth and even lying about my age to prevent Charles—anyone, really—from knowing I was alive. I wanted to protect my family; I believed that if Charles had known I was alive he would've gone after them. Little did I know Charles already had.

When I finally reached out to my family, as discreetly as possible, the truth came out. The council got involved. The orderly new life I had been trying to build for myself became messy quickly.

Fortunately, by then, I was in a position to pay Charles the cost of my freedom every year and have enough left over to help my family relocate to the city. We all worked. And struggled. And made something for ourselves.

Five years...*so much time*, I had thought on that cold night... over in a blink.

"We should begin preparing for the passage. Now, please, sir, get belowdecks," I say.

"Are you sure you won't reconsider me being on deck this time?" he asks. I give him a tired look that prompts chuckles. "All right, all right. I won't risk distracting you even though I'd been hoping to see a monster or siren." He steps away with an encouraging smile. I bite my tongue to stop myself from pointing out that he really doesn't actually want to see one of those horrific creatures. "Good luck, Victoria."

I hope his wish of luck works. No matter how many times I do this, how many times I charge into the tempest seas of the sirens' lair, my heart pounds.

The Gray Passage is a perilous channel weaving through a strip of fang-like rocks that jut out from a rocky coast and break the worst of the waves coming off the perpetually violent seas of the vast unknown—farther than any sailor has ever been able to sail before and live to tell the tale. Even I, with all my siren magic, never dared it.

There were always abnormal storms here, and rumors of ghosts. But after the sirens began attacking about fifty years ago, an already dangerous passage became downright lethal to all. I was the first captain to manage the pass in decades thanks to my immunity to the song.

But that doesn't mean it's easy.

"Dog hatches! Tie town! Ready sails!" I command the crew with large, sweeping movements so they all see.

They do as they're told, readying themselves and the vessel in the last hour of calm seas we will have.

As the rigging groans under the force of the winds, I head toward the bow with Jivre. The rest of the crew tie themselves to their places. There are four tubes strapped to the railing at the very front, two on my left and two on my right. Each holds a furled flag, not much larger than my hand. With flag movements, I can communicate to the crew behind me without having to turn or sign complex gestures.

Jork finishes fastening himself to the railing next to me. I nod to him and he nods back. He holds a chain in one hand and a stick in the other, each reflecting one of his duties in the passage. The stick is to get my attention—he's the watcher for if my crew needs to speak to me. The chain is connected to a large bell deep in the hull of the ship—a miniature version of what I would ring in the lighthouse to disrupt the siren songs. The bell on my ship is too small to make any lasting difference, but large enough to be better than nothing.

We pass a large, pointed rock that I know as the start of the Gray Passage.

The storm descends on us in a breath. Lightning cracks, closer to the ship than I'd like. We're moving at a good clip, tacking well into the changing winds.

I free my compass from my trousers and slot it into a spot in the railing I've carved just for this. It's part utility so I can confirm my instinct, and part good luck charm. As long as I've been out on my own, the compass has guided me. It was the first thing I bought for myself with money *I* earned.

As we pass the second landmark rock, the howling winds turn into screaming. The sirens are loud today. Hungry. Deadly.

I thrust out a finger and hear the first chime of the bell. It rings, loud and dissonant to the sirens' song. Confusing them, breaking their spells. I might be immune to the sirens' calls, but I've never trusted them to avoid my crew.

The muscles around my ears strain for when the song will inevitably pick up again. Rain begins to hammer the deck. Another strike of lightning illuminates the dark horizon, showing swirling shadows just underneath the waves. Monsters or ghosts, waiting to feed off our living flesh.

Even though we entered the Gray Passage in the early morning, it now looks almost like night. The clouds are so thick overhead that they almost completely blot out the sun. I take a blue flag from its canister, holding it overhead and waving it in a circle.

Sails lower, the movement says.

Then I take a red flag and hold it left. I can hear the rudder groaning against the waves as the ship veers. I listen for any abnormal sounds that might be a sign of my ship cracking under the strain. This old vessel is an extension of my own body. I know every creak and crack that's normal, and which ones are not.

The carcasses of other ships line the passage. Adding threats just below the water that could tear up our hull. The depth of the passage varies, from shallow enough to see the details of shipwrecks, to unfathomably deep as we pass through its middle section.

The singing is returning. The sirens are howling for blood in a tone

I've never heard before. It's so sharp that it's almost animalistic. I thrust out my right hand. The bell rings again.

I use the sounds of the song to help me navigate. They always come from the east, so far as I've ever been able to tell. That helps me keep heading despite the storm. The landmarks of ships and rocks give me time and place.

The song returns faster. I thrust out my hand again and raise a flag. We pick up speed. I can hear the crew scrambling on the deck behind me, as far as their ties allow, grunting and groaning. But I don't look back. I trust them to do as they know they need to—as they always have. I wipe the rain from my eyes and squint ahead, keeping my focus.

Everyone is a part of our success. Together, we'll make it through.

The ship is in a volley of waves. Every one is worse than the last, tipping us dangerously left and right. I grip the railing with one hand at all times, always keeping my other free to communicate with those behind me. We're in the thick of it now. Halfway through the passage. It only takes me half a day to navigate this violent sea but I swear I'm a week older every time I get to the other side.

The siren song picks up again, but this time it's shifted.

A low, lonely note almost shouts above the rest. Yet, even at that volume, it maintains its song. The flesh on my arm burns, as though the markings upon it have turned into razor wire, digging into my muscle as I grip the railing tighter. But I hardly feel it. The wind and sea, shouts of my crew, ominous creaking of my ship, it all fades away.

Come to me. It's a whisper, in a language I feel more than I know. The words shiver across me. Sink into me. Relaxing every knotted cord of muscle in my form. I breathe, as if inhaling the sound. His song comes to me like an old friend. Uninvited. But holding a key to the door anyway, letting himself in.

No. I blink, shaking the hold. For the first time…I had fallen prey to a siren's song.

The song stops and the world rushes back into my senses. The rain suddenly feels like icy daggers driving into my too-hot skin. My forearm burns to the point that, were I not gripping the railing, I'd be tearing at my flesh with my nails.

The song picks up once more without *his* voice. Pulsing. Thrumming. Frantic.

Calling for me.

No! I want to scream. But my throat is too dry to make even the faintest of sounds. *I have six more months. Not yet.*

The hymn of the passage has morphed into the song that's haunted me every day. The song even the calmest winds whispered. The song that nearly drove me mad the first year of hearing it every night before sleep, or every time my mind was still.

His song.

The siren is coming for me. My debts have piled. The payment for my life's choices is coming due.

But it's too soon. *Too soon!* I have six months left.

I raise two flags at once, thrusting them forward. Full sails ahead. I return the flags and point, twice. The bell rings twice. It hardly shakes the song. I point again. *Again!* The song continues. Relentless.

Not now. Not now.

There are other voices joining in. Others are calling for me with their wispy, ghostly harmonies. The siren has brought friends to collect my debt. Land and sea, there's nowhere safe for me, nowhere my dues are paid.

I turn, staring at the men and women who entrusted their lives to me. Jivre's hands go slack on the wheel a moment. Her eyes widen. I've broken my cardinal rule of the passage. My crew has seen my fear. I press my mouth into a hard line. I am not about to let these monsters take me without a fight. And I swear to every forgotten old god that I am *not* letting them have my crew.

We're just over halfway. *We will do this.* Grabbing a flag, I point. The ship veers. Left. Then right. Left again. One more turn…

It's a straight shot from here. Jivre knows the way as well as I do. She can do it.

There are shadows in the water, churning just beneath the foam. The song is so loud that it's become hard to formulate thoughts. There's no more time.

He's here to collect me. I feel it in the way each note scrapes against the inside of my skull. Maybe I can buy them time. They shouldn't pay for my choices.

My first mate's fear turns to panic and confusion when I step away from the bow and face her.

"Look after Emily for me," I say with my hands, mouthing the words for emphasis. "Please, pay my debt for me. Don't let her go to a debtors' prison. Don't let my parents. *Please*." I don't know how she could prevent all that. It's too much to ask or hope for, but I do so anyway. I'm out of choices.

Jivre goes to release the wheel to reply, but the second she does it begins to spin frantically. She grips it again, getting the vessel under control. All she can do is shake her head. Her eyes are shining, horror illuminated by strikes of lighting. She knows what's going to happen, because she knows me.

"Straight from here. Don't let them pull you away." I tap my compass, still nestled in the railing, and point ahead. "Thank you. Thank all of them, for me." I should have told my crew more, sooner. I should have found a way to ensure they knew my gratitude.

"Victoria!" she shouts my name, not knowing I can hear her frantic cry. Not knowing my muffs never did anything at all.

I go to the side of the vessel where the sirens' song is at its loudest. The noise causes me to wince. Underneath the dark, frothy waters, shadows whorl closer and closer to the surface. Bracing myself, I put both trembling hands on the railing.

Jump. *Jump, Victoria.* It's so simple. Yet terror holds me as I stare down at the churning seas.

The waves are getting worse. They're rising in the distance. The shadows are condensing into long tendrils.

The song reaches a crescendo. A hundred voices rise at once. No longer singing. They are howling. Screaming. I brace on the railing, readying to throw myself overboard.

Then, silence. I still with horror.

Those shadows aren't sirens!

"Hard left!" I scream with all my might, moving my hands as dramatically as I can.

Jivre doesn't have time to react.

Tentacles three times the size of the council building in Dennow erupt from the ocean. They stretch high above us, as if to rip the clouds from the sky. The ship tips. We're trapped in the grasp of a monster. Little more than a child's toy to this beast.

I barely have time to gasp before the tentacles come crashing down.

With a painfully brief crunch and an explosion of splinters and screams, the ship I built my life on and the crew who entrusted me with theirs is pulled below the waves and into the maw of the beast.

four

FLASHES OF LIGHTNING ABOVE GIVE GLIMPSES OF THE UNDERWATER HORROR THAT I'M PLUNGED INTO. Pieces of my ship are sucked down in a current that tastes like death. The faces of my crew are hardly recognizable to me, even though I have seen each of them for years. Even if I know them as well as my own. I have never seen expressions like this wrought across their features. Their mouths are twisted and tortured. They claw at their throats as they swallow water instead of air. Some have gone completely still, eyes wide open in silent, still, nauseating horror.

Others look almost peaceful, drifting in the small pools of crimson that seep from the places pieces of ship have skewered them.

Pain rips through me as though their wounds are my own. Every flash of lightning makes the cost of my bargain with the siren clearer. My life should have been the only one at risk. Not theirs. They never asked for this. They trusted me to keep them safe as I always had.

Even though the waters swirl around me and the storm rages, I am stilled by my horror. Time slows under the weight of my guilt; I'm unable to bear it as I always have. We'd made this run too many times. Pushed our luck too far. I'd made it seem safe enough that none of them harbored any real fear. They had faith in me when they shouldn't have, despite all my warnings.

Every member of my crew went because of me. *They are dead because of me.*

The monster that attacked us moves in the darkness. It's squid-like, with a body five times the size of our ship with countless rows of teeth and seemingly never-ending tentacles that rise up from the depths. It is a nightmare come to life. Survival instincts finally overtake me. I begin kicking, fighting as the monstrosity tries to suck us all into its maw. I reach, pulling water frantically as it tries to rip me down. My lungs are burning. I've been here before. I know what it feels like just before my body gives in.

Not like this. I refuse to die like this! Six months. I should have—

A massive tentacle moves behind me. I don't see it until the last second before it slams against me.

I spin out, hitting people and debris. The last of my air is knocked from me. My thoughts rattle, bouncing from one thing to the next as quickly as I am thrown. Emily's face flashes before my eyes, beaming. *Look, Vic, I got the job!* There's my parents, dancing in the tavern we all scraped together to buy. Charles above me as I convince myself that I am happy. That my apprehensive feelings are normal for a new bride.

Oh gods, this is it. I am going to die. Even as the sea pulls me down, I look up. I try to swim away.

A painted hand closes over mine. I look back and meet two wells of the richest brown I have ever seen in my life. Eyes that have haunted my dreams.

Warmth floods me. The world is still. There's no rushing of water. No hammering of the rain or waves. No silent screams of agony that somehow pierce my ears. Only a single note. Almost like a soft, *Hello. At last.*

The siren who claimed my soul is here. He is just as otherworldly as when I last saw him, though time has sharpened the edges of his jaw and worn shadows into his cheeks. Lines cast his brow in a nearly perpetual furrow; the shadows contrast with the halo of platinum hair that drifts around his face. He is as ethereal as a seraph, as timeless as a daemon, and far deadlier than both combined.

"Come. It is time." His voice resonates through my mind. Just like the first time, he speaks without using his mouth. He pulls me to him, his free hand slipping around my waist. A familiar song fills my ears and begs my muscles to relax. *Give in.* The water around us begins to shimmer like it did that night five years ago.

The lights begin to obscure the carnage and the abomination drawing my crew into the depths. The song nearly distracts me from them entirely, as if pulling me from my body. Consuming my mind. I battle to keep a grasp on my senses.

Let me go. I can't speak underneath the waves. I move my hands instead, awkward as he continues to hold me. "Let me go!"

"Even if I were to let you go to them, they are beyond saving. At least it is an honorable end." Despite his talk of honor, the words are bitter. I can tell he doesn't believe the sentiment by his tone, making the attempt at placating me even more grating. If he thinks he can convince me to abandon my crew with song or platitudes then he has another thing coming.

"Let. Me. Go!" I push at him, dig in my nails and kick. I fight with all my might to get back to my crew.

Maree is nearly to the surface. I can see Lynn's fiery hair in the night. Jork I know by his shape alone…though that familiar silhouette is still for far too long. Still, there are others fighting. But they won't last much longer. If I could help them, maybe they'd get a breath. There's a spire of rock not far from here…if they could get to it, they could have a chance. *I* could have a chance.

"We made a deal." His voice is a growl in the back of my mind.

I glare at him with ferocity usually reserved for Charles. "Yes, a deal that was just for me, not them. Moreover—"

"This is beyond us now. Lord Krokan has demanded their lives as payment to the churning seas. Now, we must go, it's too dangerous here."

"No, not—"

The light sharpens around us. With mighty pumps of the siren's tail, we cut through the water and move away from the horror at a speed unmatched by even the smallest, fastest ship with the strongest winds in its sails. We are a shooting star through the ocean. The rocks and currents that have always been a barrier between my world and the domain of the sirens are a blur—quickly left behind.

He holds me tightly as he takes us farther beneath the waves. I am helpless to fight him, but that doesn't stop me from trying. As pathetic as my attempts are when seawater is flattening my face and pressing down my arms. It's in my nose, ears, and eyes. It's in my lungs. It is as though he is trying to flay me with the force of the water alone.

The siren sings and bodily sensations slip away. My eyes flutter closed, lids heavy. I fight to keep them open. Fight for the sake of fighting.

Emily... Mother... Father... They're still depending on me. I still have so much I need to do for them. *My crew...*

I don't recognize the words of his song. They're low and fill my mind in the same way one too many strong drinks would, glazing over other thoughts. I'm vaguely aware of him releasing me with one arm. I try to use the opportunity to make an escape, but there's no time. He frees the spear from his back, pointing it ahead. The notes dip and rise.

With an explosion of stardust, we crash through a swirl of silver. In a blink, I find us adrift in a turquoise ocean. Bodily sensation slowly returns to me as the siren continues to drag me through the water. Every beat of his strong tail sends tingling ripples across my flesh.

We're somewhere else.

The sea floor is barren. Wrinkles of sand contrast against the streaks of light cast from a surface almost close enough for me to reach up and touch. In the distance is a strange, reddish haze.

Without warning, the sea shelf drops off precipitously. I squint and blink with force. It...it's not a shipwreck. My mind struggles to comprehend what is so clearly before me.

There, beneath the waves, is a city of light and song.

As we approach, details become clearer. I can see the archways that support arcades, which frame in courtyards. Terraced houses stretch up as organically as coral. Balconies are used as front doors that sirens swim to and from. In the distance, at the far end of a narrow cliff that stretches like a half-finished bridge across an abyss so vast that it consumes the horizon, is the faded outline of a castle. A wall of the red water is behind it, looming ominously like a cloud, barely held back by a bubble of silvery light. Faintly, I see the shapes of tentacles as more nightmarish beasts circle in the murk.

I shudder. Even though the landscape I behold is as stunning as a painting, I would much prefer if this were only real in brushstrokes. In life, *this* is the home of the monsters of the depths. The senses that were slowly returning to me numb once more.

All the stories about sirens that I could ever find stop at, "When they take you, they kill you." I never encountered anything about deals made with them or how to break them. And certainly no mention of a city beneath the waves…

As we get closer, the outlines in the red haze that I thought were tentacles sharpen some. I realize that it is not the swirling of many beasts, but a single, stationary structure. No, it's more organic than that. A *tree*? Squinting up, I try to make out the shape. But the water is too choppy and we're moving too fast away from whatever it is that looms above the surface.

We bypass the main city, swimming along the edge and out over kelp fields that stretch taller than the main mast of a barque. Most of the kelp is shriveled, a rusty muck covering their surface that releases tiny particles into the water when we churn the currents as we pass. There are a few other smaller houses along the way. The men and women stop swimming to look at us in what I read as confusion.

Most of the sirens are like the man who has yet to loosen his grip on me, not the milky-eyed, bloodthirsty creatures that first tried to take me. They are as diverse as humans. There are all shades of hair—even in colors I have never seen grow from a head or chin before. Their skin ranges from as pale as the siren who took me to deep browns. They are large and small, young and old. Some tails are narrow and others are wide. Some have fins along the sides of their tails, dotted with scales, and others are smooth, looking more like the lower half of dolphins than fish.

It's impossible to categorize them all. But one thing they all bear in common is painted markings upon their flesh. Some have only a few lines, wrapping around their torsos and biceps. Others are painted from nose to fin with artwork that is similar in style to what is on my forearm.

We crest a hill and a manor house comes into view. Behind it is a wall of rock and dead coral that the sea floor drops off behind. Somehow, illogically, the meager wall seems to keep out the swirling, reddish hue. The murk just stops, as if the barrier extends beyond the surface of the water invisibly.

The structures vaguely remind me of Lord Applegate's estate. My chest tightens. I had sent him belowdecks again for the passage. There was no way he wasn't the first to die. Was he one of the men I saw skewered on the wreckage?

I press my eyes closed, wincing. My mind torments me with visions of meeting his daughters years ago. All those girls have now is their mother, the wretched woman...and it's because of me. And Kevhan is just one man... I've taken all my crew from their families.

Kevhan Applegate. Jivre. Maree, Lynn, Jork, Honey, Sorrea, more, all, my whole crew. *Dead.*

Because of me.

I thought I had learned through coming to terms with my own demise that I must make peace with the world as it is, not as I wish it to be. But I suppose it's a lesson I never really took to heart. If I had, I wouldn't be slowly collapsing inward with the costs of my choices. With the guilt that just my proximity brought such misfortune.

I'm sick to my stomach as we slow and come to a stop on a wide veranda. Unlike Applegate's manor, there's no long drive leading up to the building. Just sand and skeletal coral stretching out in all directions. I suppose sirens have no need of roads, or carriages, or front doors when they can swim up to any balcony and through any window.

The siren's arms slowly unravel, releasing me from his viselike grip. But he keeps a hand on my person, preventing me from immediately swimming away, as he faces four others who have lined up, waiting.

There's a grizzled man with a gray shark's tail dotted with scars. Every pale line is outlined in red detailing that looks almost like lace covering his tail. His hair is a deep shade of purple. It must have been striking against his fair skin when he was younger, but now it's thinning on top and graying near the fins by his cheeks. Despite his potential age, he is more muscular than the man holding me.

Next to him is a young woman with broad shoulders and skin as pale as the siren next to me. Her light brown hair is pulled back into a single braid, decorated with pearls that contrast like tiny stars. She has distinctly familiar brown eyes, nearly identical to the man at my side, accented by the deep navy lines that swirl upon her cheeks and up her forehead.

At her side is a woman who looks to be my age, perhaps slightly older. Her similarly brown-tinted hair is somewhere between my captor's platinum and the younger woman's—a golden blonde, lighter than mine, and accented with brown. It's pulled into a bun, skewered with spiny shells, bone, and gems. As she approaches I can see her entire torso is painted with stark white lines that blended in from far away.

"Welcome back, Duke Ilryth." The woman bows her head. Her mouth doesn't move as she speaks. I hear her voice in my mind. "We are here to begin the anointing process."

"Thank you, Sheel, Lucia, Fenny, but I shall do it myself," the duke insists, nodding to each of them in turn. I can't stop myself from narrowing my eyes slightly up at him, which somehow only makes his eyes shine with amusement. "Our offering is as easy to hold onto as an enraged eel. The sooner we get her in her cage, the better."

Excuse me? I lean away from him enough to sign, "In my cage?"

"Speaking with your hands isn't necessary," Ilryth continues in my mind. "You are linked with me"—he touches his forearm—"so you can communicate with your thoughts as we siren do."

"Okay, great." Yet more unfamiliar magics. I focus on *thinking* the words, which is surprisingly difficult when all I want to think about is how I'm underwater and not...dead. "That doesn't answer my question."

"You gave your life to me." The duke tilts his head slightly to the side, as if challenging me to contradict him. We both know it's true, but...

"To...kill me?" I guess?

He smirks. "Aren't you happy that I'm *not* killing you?"

Sure, every minute they don't kill me is welcome, but it's confusing. "You wasted no time killing my crew and they weren't even a part of this. Unless you're sparing me so I get to live with the guilt?"

"You think me so depraved?" He scowls, offended. "Even after I saved your life? *Twice?*" Ilryth leans in, narrowing his eyes at me. Not speaking with his mouth gives it the freedom to twist in disgust as he says, "I told you, your crew's lives were not mine to claim. Nor did I want them. The will of the ancients intervened."

Sounds like an excuse to me.

His scowl deepens. "Now, follow me." He shifts his grip, taking my wrist. I notice that there are more markings on his skin than I remember. Every detail of that night is etched into my memory.

I don't budge. The water is different here. A little…thicker, perhaps? More resistance to it, allowing us to hover in place without treading. Just a small push and I tug away as he moves forward. His head whips back around.

"If you're not going to kill me, then take me back." It's difficult to make demands when I feel as if I might float away at any second. Respect is hard to muster when I imagine myself more like a jellyfish than an authoritative captain.

The other sirens are watching our exchange with a mix of emotions. The man radiates disapproval, bordering on anger. The older woman is equally bemused. But the younger, she seems to be fighting a little grin.

"Excuse me?" Ilryth's face relaxes with surprise. As if he's shocked I'd have the audacity to even ask.

"I will give you my life, as was promised—*when* it was promised." The only vow I will break is the one I made to Charles. No others. "I had six more months. You came early."

Though my ship is gone, Applegate is dead, and I've no idea how I'll make the twenty thousand crons now even if the siren did take me back. I still must return and do *something*. Helplessness tries to choke me but I force it down with a swallow. I won't let the dark thoughts have me. My family needs me to keep fighting.

"You selfish woman." With a mighty flap of his tail he is back before me, nearly slamming into me, but stopping at the last second. A rush of water follows him. "I found you practically dead. I saved you from sirens that were possessed by wraiths. I gave you my personal blessing during five more years' time than you would have had otherwise. Yet you *still* ask for more?"

"I ask for what I'm owed," I insist, leaning away slightly to gain some space and wishing the movement wasn't so overwrought. I want to rise with all the authority of the mighty sea captain Victoria. But I can't seem to muster the ability when I'm little more than human-shaped driftwood.

"Mighty sea captain." A scoff reverberates through my thoughts. My eyes widen with shock. *How dare he.* He leans forward, narrowing his eyes. "Yes, you might want to be more careful with what and how you think while you're here."

I try to force every errant thought from my mind. Gates upon gates lock shut on my musings. I might not know how this communication works, but I know how to guard myself and conceal my emotions.

"Please," I say simply. If one tactic doesn't work, try another. I soften my gaze and furrow my brow. It's an expression that usually worked on Charles. "I *need* six more months."

"This cannot be undone. You have entered the Eversea." He reaches for my hand and I'm too startled to stop him. Ilryth lightly runs his calloused fingers over the markings he put on my forearm, eyes distant and filled with a touch of sorrow I am not made to understand. "Lord Krokan knows the sacrifice marked for him is here. We cannot delay further." He leans away, a frown tugging on his lips. "I'm sorry." The apology almost seems genuine. But I don't believe it for a second.

The siren goes to leave again and I'm left staring at the curves and dips of his back where they condense into a narrow waist. The scales of his tail reach up his spine in a triangle shape, splashing bright turquoise against the pallor of his skin. This time he doesn't reach for me. He just assumes I'll follow.

He assumes wrong.

"Sacrifice?" The thought is as monstrous as the beast itself. The barbarousness of it overtakes me, breaking through my composure. "Your *Lord*," I sneer, giving the title no respect, "didn't get enough sacrifices for himself in my crew?"

Fenny winces at my side.

Duke Ilryth halts once more. But this time he refrains from bringing his attention back to me. I can almost feel a sense of sorrow, of worry, flooding the currents. He mocks me with feigned empathy.

"No," he says simply. "They were not anointed. So they couldn't ever be enough. But hopefully you will be, for their sakes—for all our sakes."

five

THE JOKE IS ON HIM. I've never been enough for anyone. Not to save a marriage, or my family, or my crew. It seems he picked the worst possible person for this sacrifice.

"Now. *Come.*"

I can tell by the word alone that I've pushed his patience as far as he'll allow. There's little point in resisting further, for now. I'm wildly outnumbered, and the shark-finned man looks as though he's about ready to manhandle me himself. With a push of my arms, I propel myself awkwardly forward. I'm at a disadvantage until I can get more information and a better sense of my circumstances. I need to play along, for now.

The archway into the manor reveals itself as a massive tube of coral. Tiny fish race overhead, glimmering like fireflies. Multicolored kelp is knotted and strung up as garland. Unlike the kelp I saw before, this is still vibrant and green.

Fenny swims ahead to the duke's side. I swim behind. The other two siren—Sheel and Lucia—take up the rear. I'm grateful that in the past four and some years I was able to get some additional experience swimming in the waters to the south—the seas without sirens. But I am nowhere near as graceful as them.

Ilryth and Fenny glance at each other, giving small nods and shakes of their heads, but I hear nothing. Their hands don't move, either.

Perhaps there is some way to communicate privately?

"That's exactly what it is," the grizzled man behind me says. Horror rips through me at the realization that he just heard my errant thought. "Once you master telepathy—if you're able to master it at all—you'll be able to speak with only the people you want. Though, if you master anything first, I'd suggest it's learning how to keep the majority of your thoughts to yourself." He has a slight smile, not unkind. A bit knowing, perhaps, as though what I am experiencing is a common issue. For a siren, perhaps, but not for a human.

Unless I'm not the first sacrificed to this Lord Krokan. Everyone assumes sirens kill humans *promptly*, given how none who are taken into the sea by them ever return. I never could find any mentions of sirens bartering with anyone else. Never, in all my travels, did I see any other markings like the one on my forearm.

But if we're all sacrifices for them, then that would also explain why there's little information. All these thoughts of sacrifices fill the back of my throat with a metallic taste. But I try and keep my face calm. If I could remain levelheaded every time I went before the council to defend myself against Charles's cruel claims, I can do it now.

"How do I master it?" The alternative is to live with people possibly reading my mind, and that's not acceptable. But there's also a curious streak in me. Magic is *real*. And, at long last, maybe I have the chance to use it, too? "I can't say I have a lot of practice with *thinking* my words to speak them above water."

"I wouldn't imagine you would. Given that humans are not inherently magical creatures, despite your origins here in Midscape as children of Lady Lellia."

Midscape?

"Yes, where you are now," he answers the question I hadn't consciously intended to broadcast. I curse inwardly and he laughs. He heard that, too, apparently. I'm struggling to tell which thoughts they hear and which I keep to myself. Perhaps it's the ones that are clear questions or strong wonderings? "Humans were originally from this land, back when it was one with the Natural World, before the Fade."

"And this place is called Midscape?" I intentionally try to broadcast my thought, trying to focus on how it feels when it's purposeful and I want other people to hear.

"Technically, you are presently in the Eversea, which is not *quite*

Midscape, if you ask me and many of the other sirens whose home this is." He adjusts the vest he wears, smoothing over the tiny mother-of-pearl disks that shine like the opalescent scales of Ilryth's tail. "Wedged between the Veil and the Fade, sustained by Lady Lellia of the Lifetree and guarded by Lord Krokan of the Abyss, we are not like the others of Midscape. Our magic is older than even the vampir. Though I'm sure they would argue otherwise. It is a hobby of many of the peoples of Midscape to debate whose magic is oldest and most powerful."

"The others are not descended directly from the first gods, as we are," the young woman, Lucia, says with a note of pride.

Others? Vampir? I have traveled the world far and wide, scoured every map and heard every tale, but I have never heard a whisper of Midscape, nor vampir. At most, rumors of fae… Though, if sirens exist then why couldn't there be more? Why wouldn't the old stories of the fae have some grounding in fact?

I am in uncharted territory. The first to explore a world of magic. *Think of the possibilities…*

I suck in my lower lip and bite on it, slowly releasing at the point of pain. The action focuses me. I can't get wrapped up in things that don't actually matter. Magic. Strange new worlds. As fascinating as it all is, none of it is my priority. I must stay focused on what's important: Getting back to and saving my family.

Siren buildings are nothing like the construction of human ones. There is little concern for protection from the elements. There are no stairs, and no doors. The structures are built from walls of compressed shells, coral, and rock. Balls of light hang in nets of kelp, or from rope. Some are stored in coral sconces on the walls. It all makes an unnatural-feeling and yet oddly organic world.

Other tubes branch away from the main atrium. Through two more, and we're in a birdcage of whale bones and coral.

"Sit." Ilryth points to the center of the room, where a lone pedestal stands.

I fold my arms and don't move. "Say please."

"Excuse me?"

"Aren't you a noble duke? Where are your manners?"

"The rest of you, leave," Ilryth snaps.

"Your Grace, she's not—if she tries to run—" Sheel begins to say.

"If she tries to run, I'm hunting her down myself." There's a deadly promise underneath Ilryth's words. But I don't shy away from it.

I keep my gaze locked with his as if to say, *challenge accepted.* Maybe he even hears the words. Let him. Let all of them.

Lucia drifts forward with tiny movements of her tail. "We could help, brot—"

"I said leave."

The other three hear the warning in his voice clearly. They all cast me wary glances, then look back to Ilryth with equal uncertainty. But, in the end, the three of them leave, dispersing through the whale bones and out into the open water that surrounds us. None looking back.

Even if a part of me yearns to let my gaze roam the boundless sea, taking in the sights around me, I bind my attention to the last remaining siren as he approaches me, his muscles rippling in the shifting light cast from the surface of the sea. I am acutely aware of just how alone I am with this man—the man who took me from my world and claimed my life as his own. Who wants to make me into a *sacrifice.* I face him as I would the Gray Passage, I am serenity before the chaos.

I never gave Charles the satisfaction. I sure as shit won't give it to Ilryth, either. My glare is matched by his up until the moment he looms over me, taller, thanks to his tail.

Yet, without warning, his expression softens. "This will happen, one way or another. So, please, don't fight me."

It's the nearly serene tone of his voice that almost pushes me to the breaking point. I force every word to be placid. "I won't, if you let me leave."

He tilts his head and cocks a brow. A slight sardonic expression slides across his lips, as if he can feel every bit of quivering displeasure I am actively working to suppress. He looks at me much like how I would look at an oncoming storm. A challenge. A test. An opportunity to pit my own might against a force of nature and win.

He lifts both arms, motioning around him. They address him as Duke, but his physique is more befitting of a laborer. Of a man who has been cut and carved by the sea. He would be able to best me in a fight without much effort.

"Where would you go? You are only alive right now because of magic I have given you. Because of my protections allowing you to be beneath our waves. Protections that, if I do not reinforce them, will end. And what do you think would happen then?"

The question seems rhetorical, so I do not answer.

"Is that not motivation enough for you? Then, perhaps I should tell you of the wraiths… Or the monsters that prowl just beyond our fragile barriers."

"Bring me back," I request as calmly as I'm able, focused on my sole mission. "Give me my remaining six months and I will be as peaceful and compliant as you want. You won't get so much as the idea of struggle from me."

"And this is an idea you have now?" His tone is impossible to read. But I can assume he is not pleased by the notion.

"I've played nicely so far." I allow the words to hold a note of caution. "You don't want me to start putting up a fight."

"You always seemed like a person who respected their word." The sentiment has an air of superiority.

"I do. More than you will *ever* know." The calm, dangerous quiet to the statement has him pausing. His smug expression vanishes, becoming blank and impossible to read. I've negotiated with more insufferable and insulting men than this siren. "I know the bargain I made and all I want is what is owed. We uphold our deals and pay our debts in Tenvrath. The question is, siren, do you respect your deals here?"

"How dare—" he growls.

"Because if you did, you would let me go have the six months you promised."

Ilryth folds his arms and stares at me. I'm not sure what his assessment will render. But he's looking for something. I make it a point to be as much of a blank slate as possible. Judging from the slight quirk of his lips downward, the blank slate I can transform my face into frustrates him.

Good.

Now an outright frown. I wonder if he heard that thought. I hope so.

"The timing was never meant to be exact, given the anointing…" His words crush me, but I don't let it show. "Since Lord Krokan intervened, it was a sign that it was time to begin. And if not for me, you would've been lost, and with you the hope of the sirens."

Hope of the sirens? How could I possibly be that? If he hears the thoughts, he doesn't answer.

"Even if I wanted to return you to the Natural World, I couldn't. Your mere presence here has triggered the start of the anointing." Ilryth's gaze falls to my forearm. I touch the drawings that have stained my flesh. No…they've marked my very soul. "You will become more magic than flesh. And if you were to leave the Eversea—depart from underneath the waters of the Lifetree—you would fade away. I'm sorry, but you cannot be brought back to the Natural World now. Not ever."

"You bastard." The thought races through my mind before I can stop it, but I don't regret it either.

"I see you've picked up a foul mouth since we last spoke." He seems more amused than bemused.

"I'm a sailor—a captain. The very best in all the seas. I've salt on my tongue."

"Yes, yes, I know of your exploits, Victoria." He sounds so bloody *dismissive*. But that's not what I focus on.

"How do you know my name?" I can't remember ever telling it to him.

"I know much about you." Ilryth sinks lower and I am forced to lean back, otherwise his chest would be pressed into mine. It's as if he is trying to devour me with his eyes. When he reaches for me, I know there has to be magic that has taken hold, because I do not pull away. "I know you have sailed the vast seas. That you have fought with every hour you were given."

He's not wrong. *But how…* His hand closes around my wrist, above the markings he made. A thousand whispers hum across my skin, sinking deep into long untouched parts of me. I fight to keep my focus. *This connection…*

"Yes," he answers the unfinished question that only briefly flitted through my thoughts. "And we shall deepen our bond with the anointing. You will learn the Duet of Sendoff. And you will be presented before Lord Krokan before it is too late for us all."

I am about to object, but he silences me with one demand.

"Now, take off your shirt."

six

"*EXCUSE ME?*" I lean back and he releases me. A wise choice.

"I will need to anoint all of you. I cannot do that if you are wearing clothing."

I fold my arms, as if to press my shirt onto me. "Do you often ask ladies you hardly know for them to remove their clothes?"

"I don't 'hardly know' you." Before I can object, he continues, more impatient, "Now, your shirt."

We have a staring contest. A silent battle of wits. Frankly, I couldn't care less about removing my shirt. My notions of modesty are a bit different than most because of my line of work. My crew saw me in all manner of dress and undress as the need arose. But…something about a man seeing me when we're very much alone… It stirs other thoughts, belonging to a reality that I have not even allowed myself to entertain for years.

I grab the hem of my loosely fitting shirt with purpose. If he wants to turn this into a duel of comfort and discomfort then, fine, I won't allow him to have the upper hand. I peel it off.

My corset underneath is a well-structured, over-bust style, and stays in place with the aid of two straps. It took three fittings to get the garment absolutely perfect, but what I ended up with was a highly functional and comfortable piece of clothing. After sailing once with my chest coming loose from its binding and flopping about, I was converted. I was not graced with a smaller bosom and it is impractical and uncomfortable to have my breasts flopping with every jump and dash across the deck.

The moment I let go of the shirt, its color drains. The garment fades slightly, turning from solid to little more than an outline. A shift in the currents wipes it away, as if it never existed at all.

"What the—"

"It was no longer a part of you. Therefore, the magic of the old ones didn't extend to it any longer," Ilryth explains. "So, it could not sustain here in the Eversea and faded."

I make connections to everything else he's said so far. "I'm alive because of this magic." I hold up my marked forearm. "It connects with these old gods—the same ones you want to *sacrifice me to.*" The words have enough bite that a hard look passes over his features. Good. "But the second I'd leave the sea, or break that connection, I'd fade away like the shirt?"

"That's an accurate summary," he says after a moment of consideration. As if there's more he wants to explain—finer points— that he omits.

I'm in desperate need of a chair. Or, better, a hammock. I want to curl up and close my eyes and have a nice, long sleep. *Everything is clearer in the morning*, Mother would say. But I doubt anything will be clearer then. Or any morning to come.

The inking on my forearm takes on new meaning. I might have freed myself from Charles, but there are still shackles around me. I exist only because of a magic tether that I will never be able to escape from, not even in death. I dig my fingernails into my palms and swallow past the lump in my throat.

Keep moving, Victoria. Don't stop. Don't look back. Forward.

"I hope this will be fine for whatever this anointing entails." I motion to the corset I'm still wearing. I'm not going to help my family if I disappear so allowing this anointing to proceed is the only option I have.

"It is acceptable, for now." Ilryth approaches. I willfully ignore the "for now."

His fingers hover above my neck. The siren's eyes shine in the fading light. Small, glowing motes ignite in the water around us—luminescent jellyfish, like fireflies, swim effortlessly on the currents. Everything is cast in a starry, twilight hue.

There's something unique about this siren, distinct from any other soul who has come close to me, ever. My crew is my crew. They are friends—family in their own way. I don't see them as men or women. They just are immutable forces in my life.

But this creature...this *man,* who's practically a sculptor's study in perfection of the male form, from his strong jaw to his delicate lips that could beckon so dangerously with a smile—with a song. He is something else altogether. The curve of his eyes and swell of his powerful arms carved from years of swimming. I allow my gaze to explore his physique, down the swirls painted across half of his broad chest, to the muscles of his abdomen, rippling like waves to the V of where the scales of his tail meet his hips. It's such a strange, unnatural sight. To see a human melt away into fish. But I don't find it as unnerving as I might have otherwise imagined. Perhaps it's because under the waves he looks natural, *right,* as much an expected feature of this aquatic realm as kelp or coral.

He must feel the weight of my attention, because his eyes are waiting for mine as I return my gaze to his face.

"Are you all right?" His words are a low rumble in the back of my mind. Like summer thunder. Hot. Ominous.

I manage a nod.

"What is it?"

It's been so long since I was touched by a man and his hand hovers just beyond my flesh. Long enough that the mere thought of it has me fighting shivers. I ache all over and hate myself for it. I've been strong for years, fighting the pull of a warm set of arms. The appeal of carnal urges. For the first time, I don't *have to.* I am as free on paper as I have been in spirit for years.

But, really? Here? Now? Moved by something as simple as a bare chest?

I hate that the mere idea of a touch from a man has me fumbling over myself—like the girl I was when I fell for Charles. *That* thought sobers me. I am not *her* any longer. I have struggled, and wept, and bled to not be her. I have fought these urges every day and I will continue fighting them until the last.

"It's nothing." I glance askance. Avoiding those piercing eyes allows me a moment to compose myself and hide my inward anger.

"I don't want…" He trails off.

"Don't want what?" I demand when he doesn't pick up the thought.

"I don't want to force this upon you." He lowers his hand slightly.

That brings my attention back to him. Every muscle in his face pulls with tension. He almost looks in pain.

"Then don't," I say, matter-of-fact. "You never had to. You are very much in control of this situation."

He leans forward, hand hovering still between us. "You think I'm in control?" There's accusation in his tone, woven with anger that doesn't feel entirely directed at me.

"You're the one who brought me here. Who holds my life in his hands. Who could let me go if he wanted."

"You honestly believe I had enough power on my own to save you that night without marking you—and you alone—as the anointed, the offering? That I could stave off death itself without marking you for it?" The closest thing I might know to hatred flashes across his expression. A note of bitter laughter tickles across the back of my mind. "Oh, Victoria, how I *wish* I had that much power. If I did, my people wouldn't be starving, rotting away, or falling prey to wraiths. If I were truly powerful, would I be resorting to sacrificing a human in the hopes that it might abate our hardships?"

I don't have an answer, so I say nothing. Part of me wants to think he's lying. But to what benefit would that be? He already has matters in hand. He doesn't need me to sympathize with him. But…I do. I know the kind of desperation that comes from trying to wrench back control from a situation turned sideways.

"If I was in control then I would've—my mother would've—" He keeps stopping himself short. Then, he continues after a moment of gathering his composure, "None of us are in control so long as Lord Krokan rages, threatening to kill us all. The Eversea is the last barrier between his wrath and rot permeating all of Midscape, perhaps all the mortal world. I must do everything I can to protect my people and stop that from happening."

The sentiment stills me. That, too, I can understand. It's a want I know all too well: protect the people that you love most.

Perhaps he can be reasoned with. If there's a way I can use his needs to serve mine…

"Then, do what you must do." I take his hand in mine and slowly bring it to my body. Being the one to cross that line offers me some sense of control. A sense both of us so clearly, desperately need. His fingers splay across my chest above my corset. My heart is a tiny bird trying to escape its cage and I hope he doesn't feel it.

"I am not supposed to touch you," he murmurs.

"Why?"

"No one is. The offering must sever all ties to this world." Yet, even as he says those words, his focus is solely on his flesh against mine.

I release him, feeling a little silly in my assumption of what his outstretched hand was intended for. "Do what you must, then."

"Very well." He hums as his fingers pull away from my skin. The small orbs of light that had appeared before collect on his fingertips like dew on leaves. He moves them over me, the light creating lines of color that land on my skin with the warmth of sunlight.

The song that guides his hand is rich with sorrow. I heard it that first night, all those years ago, too, and I see it now. As he sings the markings upon me, the emotion fills him to the brim, threatening to overflow into me. His fingers sweep three arcs on either side of my neck—markings reminiscent of the gills of a fish. They trail down both my forearms, circling my palms. With one index finger, he draws a line down the bone of the center of my chest. Every marking comes to life, pulsing and undulating with his song, taking shapes of lines and swirls I don't understand.

I never realized how *almost* being touched could drive someone almost as mad as the actual thing.

Finally, he stops, and the light fades, but the colorful new markings on my flesh do not. "That's enough for the first day."

"What are they?"

"Words of the ancients—their songs and stories as music given shape. It is a language nearly impossible for mortal minds to comprehend," he answers. I half expected him to say that it's not my business to know.

"If you can't comprehend it, then how can you mark it?"

"All life came from the hands of Lady Lellia, Goddess of Life. Her mark is still upon our souls and hearts. Even if our minds cannot comprehend the ways of the old ones, the eternal parts of us remember," he answers. "Lucia can explain more if you would like to know. She studied at the Duchy of Faith."

A moment passes where neither of us say anything. His statement sounded like a dismissal of any further inquiry and a conclusion to our conversation. But he doesn't leave. Instead, he continues to stare at me. As if…he's waiting for something?

"I shall return later for further anointing," Ilryth says quickly and swims through the whale bones that make the birdcage. With a few flaps of his tail, he's gone, disappearing among the buildings of the manor that spread out beneath me. Almost like he's running away.

That's…it? The question hovers in the water around me. Begging an answer I don't get.

I wait to see if he'll come back. I expect them to. Foolish of me or not. I can't believe they're actually going to leave me unsupervised and without any further explanation. I swim over to one of the openings between the whale bones, taking stock of my position.

It's hard to tell exactly what direction the sun is moving. The surface isn't that far—close enough that I could swim for it on one breath, if I'd taken one. But at this time of day it's almost directly overhead, and the light through the waves is playing tricks with my eyes. So far as I can guess, east is still east here in this other land of Midscape.

I reach for my compass to check. My hand hits the empty pocket on my thigh that's usually reserved for it.

It's gone. It sank with my ship. My compass was the first thing I ever truly bought for myself. It helped me find my way for almost five years… Now, I must find my own direction.

There aren't many sirens swimming over the estate. I could start heading west. If I go west long enough, I should make it home, right? But his warnings about fading away… I saw what happened with my shirt.

Maybe running isn't the best idea yet, but I can get a better sense of this place, at least. I push off the shell-crusted floor and expect to glide past the whale bones. But I am stopped short.

Two invisible hands clutch my torso, shoulders, and face from behind, pulling me back. I choke on instant panic that rises up in my throat. Hands on me, forcing me to stay. Forcing me down.

I'm suddenly aware of the lack of air. I want to breathe. *Breathe!* Feel air moving through my lungs and bringing with it life-sustaining calm.

The ocean around me suddenly feels so vast, so immense. On its surface, I could move as freely as the wind. I had the power to go anywhere and do anything. But the siren whose magic freed me now traps me. The water is almost too heavy. Alive. It is pushing me down. Pulling me back. The measured calm I've worked to maintain is fracturing. *Calm under pressure, just like on the ship.* But the thought only feeds into my guilt.

My ship is gone, crew dead, my family is at risk, and I am trapped. For the first time in nearly five years I cannot escape. I will be kept here forever. The feeling of Charles's hands wrapping around my torso. Even here in the siren's domain, he exists within me, clutching me so tightly that I can't breathe... That's why there's no air. Why—

Calm, Victoria, he's gone. He can't reach you now.

I close my eyes and still myself. My mind is a vortex, a relentless spiral that whorls further and further down. No matter how far I go. Or how fast I get there. A part of him continues to come with me—to haunt me.

I ball my hands into fists and willfully banish the thoughts. Charles found out what happens when someone tries to tie me down. This siren has no idea what's coming for him.

My skin is raw. At first, I rubbed and scratched to try and see if the markings would come off. I didn't suspect they would, as they never have, but it never hurts to check. Then, I kept rubbing and scratching because of a new, strange phenomena—whenever my skin is broken, it magically knits before even a drop of blood can be spilled.

More magic than flesh.

I try every archway of whale bones. I try to scratch away the lacy markings carved into them, thinking that's what is keeping me here. There's little I can do, but I try it all—dozens of times, in dozens of ways. But each time I'm yanked back by the invisible leash that's been placed upon me.

Dusk has been inked across the top of the waves. Filtered through the ocean blue, it's become beams of honey fading into ambient light that coats everything in a misty orange hue. The sky is as angry as I feel.

It's been a long time since I spent so many hours pacing, lost in my thoughts. Well, not quite pacing...treading water in circles? Any awkwardness I felt about being completely submerged has vanished. Twelve hours of nothing to do other than swim, float, and drift has made it all seem completely normal.

I wait up for Ilryth to return as promised. I've gone days without solid rest before. Sleeping regularly isn't a luxury a ship captain always has. So, I'm trained for it. I'll be fine and manage to be sharp when I need to be. At least for a few nights.

But, usually, when I don't sleep on my ship it's because my crew needs me. It's because the ship is being thrown by waves almost as large as the vessel itself—because nature is challenging me, testing the magic I possessed and seeing if it could thwart my will. And if it is my mind that is in a torrent on a calm sea then there's always something I can do to occupy my hands.

Being wide awake but lacking anything to do other than *wait* makes every second feel like an entire minute. Hours creep like days. All my thoughts catch up to me.

My crew is dead...because of me.

Their faces haunt me, over and over. I know if Jivre were here, she would flash me her lopsided grin and tell me not to feel guilty. She'd say, "Victoria, we are all men and women grown, we made the choice to sail with you of sound mind and body. We knew the risks and reaped the benefits time and again. You cannot accept responsibility for the choices we made."

But Jivre is not here, and those hypothetical words are faint in the back of my mind. Easily countered by my racing thoughts. By the hot and cold that washes over me like sickness.

I shouldn't have made the north run. But if I hadn't, I would've doomed my family. I shouldn't have tried to end my marriage to Charles. But, if I didn't, he would've continued going after my family. Even if I can't be certain what would've come to pass, I know his relentless cruelty.

Just as I know one thing for sure, I should have never married him. If I hadn't, who knows what my life might have looked like. I probably wouldn't be here now.

There's no possible way of knowing what could've been. I will drive myself mad, walking—swimming—in circles as I turn my thoughts over and over. As if I could look at all these concerns and problems from a new direction and think, *Aha, that's the answer, that's the right course. That's what I should have done.*

But I'll never know if what I did was right or wrong, and that's the hardest part of it all. That's what my mind can't seem to let go of. *What if?* Those two words have haunted me my whole life, and all I can do is run; when I'm still they're able to catch up.

I try to think forward—of what will come next. I've been on the move for five years, always pushing ahead. Always striving. I can't stop now. I can't fix the problems of the past; I can't make different choices. I can only think of what I'll do next. Keep moving. Forward. Next thing. *Next thing…*

When Ilryth comes back, I'll ask for more information on this magic. No, freedom first. Then maybe I can bargain with him, once I have knowledge of what powers I hold.

The sound of faint singing disturbs my thoughts. It sounds like a thousand voices rising all at once. Shrill. Circling over a single word.

I turn in the direction of the ominous noise. A pack of dolphins armored with carved, wooden helmets are a blur in the distance. There are sirens holding on to their dorsal fins with one hand and wielding spears made of sharpened wood in the other. The weapons seem to glow faintly, cutting through the dark sea like shooting stars. A handful of the sirens are adorned with armor made of the same pale wood—a strange choice for protection.

Especially when I see what they are racing toward.

In the distance, barely visible through the night and haze of the rusty murk that clouds these seas is a silhouette of a massive beast. It drifts up from beyond the distant barrier of coral, wood, and shells, as if it is crawling through the thick murk that hovers beyond that barrier, pulling itself through, one tentacle after another. Trying to break into our world. My stomach churns with nausea brought on by panic. It is the same beast that came for my ship…

Coming for me once more.

I look back to the sirens. At the front is a familiar turquoise tail. Ilryth leads the charge, glowing spear in hand.

The song reaches its crescendo as they fan out, releasing their dolphins and launching an attack. The animals and sirens swim down and around the writhing tentacles. They take blows, spiraling through the water. I swim to the edge of my tether, leaning against the whale bones.

What he told me was true…he really didn't send the beast after my crew. They're as much his enemy as mine.

The voices continue to rise in volume. I don't hear the sounds with my ears, but in my soul. The staffs the warriors carry glow brighter, as though they are banishing an evil spirit.

I find myself cheering for them, even though my throat is too tight for me to swallow. I want to help. I don't care if these are the sirens who took me. All I see is a fight against the monstrosity that killed my crew. I want vengeance. I want something to *do* other than sit on the sidelines, trapped. I'm not made for stillness. For confinement.

The sirens pitch downward, chasing the monster and disappearing into the reddish haze on the other side of the drop-off.

The song fades and the sea grows still. I continue to stare, waiting for them to return. Scanning the estate, I search for more warriors. Other sirens who could help them. But none emerge.

I wait for the warriors to return. But they don't. The minutes pass by, the moon's progression telling me that time has crept into hours.

They're still not back.

If Ilryth dies, am I free? Can I leave this place? Or will I disappear? I stare at the markings on my forearms. They're still as sharp as ever. Even the old lines Ilryth gave me years ago…he must be all right. I don't know why, but I feel like I would know if he died.

Finally, a silhouette crests the hazy horizon, now turned a deep red in the dawn filtering through the water. I don't know if it's from the same reddish haze, worse than it has been since my arrival, or from blood.

I squint and it doesn't take long for me to realize the figure is Ilryth. Every beat of his tail seems weaker than the last. His shoulders slump. He does little more than drift.

Leaning farther past the whale bones, I strain against my invisible tethers as all his movements cease. Ilryth's arms are limp, head hung. Waiting is agony to see if he'll move again.

"Lord Ilryth?" I think, imagining my voice resonating in his head alone.

He still doesn't move. My heart begins to race. He's been too still for too long. Something's seriously wrong. How could it not be? I saw the monstrosity…

"Lord Ilryth?" I think, louder. I don't care who might hear. In fact, let them all hear. Maybe it'll wake someone else and I won't have to feel like his life has suddenly become my responsibility.

Why is no one else awake? Why weren't they all helping him?

Still no movement. No change. He's as still as death.

"Someone help him!" I shout with my mind. "Duke Ilryth needs help!"

There's no movement, from the estate or from the duke, as a cold dawn breaks across the sea.

seven

THERE'S AN INSTINCT THAT WAS AWOKEN IN ME FROM THE FIRST TIME I STEPPED ON A BOAT AS CAPTAIN: NO MAN OR WOMAN WOULD EVER BE LEFT BEHIND.

Not on my watch.

None would be forsaken, abandoned, spurned, dismissed, or disregarded. Every soul is worth diving into the choppiest of seas to save. No matter how grim a situation is on the surface, if there's even a glimmer of hope, if there's breath in me, I'll be the hand that reaches out.

That instinct is stronger than any animosity I feel toward this siren. Compounded further by the feelings of uselessness that I steeped in all night, watching. Uselessness amplifying in me.

Without consideration for the magic tether holding me, I launch myself from the whale bone. The tether snaps taut, attempting to hold me back. Those invisible hands claw at me, pulling my skin. *No.* I grit my teeth, muscles straining, legs kicking. *I will not be held back a second longer*.

There's a *pop* between my shoulder blades. I glide effortlessly out into the open water that had mocked me just a few hours ago. I look back at the cage for a second, betrayed. *How dare you*, I want to say. I had been trying all night to escape and now the magic snaps. *Rude.*

Pumping my arms and legs, I swim as fast as I can without having the aid of a tail, keeping a close eye on the distant wall the warriors had disappeared behind. I scan for any signs of the monstrosity they were fighting. Before I know it, I'm at the duke's side.

His head continues to hang, lips slightly parted. He doesn't stir at my sudden presence. There's no twitching of the fins on either side of his face. Circular bruises ring his midsection and arms, plus a few other minor scrapes, but he seems otherwise all right... But looks can be deceiving. I reach out and press my palm against his chest.

Lightning cracks through me. Light flashes behind my eyes, as bright as staring into the sun, momentarily blinding me as scorching pain runs up the new and old drawings inked into my flesh. I hiss but refuse to withdraw. Instead, I hold it more firmly against his chest.

His heart is beating, but faintly.

"*Fine*, you're alive, come on then." I can't decide if I'm grateful or not that I feel his fluttering heart. It's not as if I am particularly fond of this man. But...that doesn't mean I want him to die, either.

I grab his arm and sling it around my shoulders. The pain is subsiding, but in the back of my mind I begin to hear murmuring. *Coward...how dare...do it...* As unnerving as the whispers are, I work to ignore them. Right now, the only thing that matters is getting help. I try to swim but it's awkward with his mountain of muscle, and I've no idea where to take him.

"Fenny! Lucia! Sheel! Someone!" I imagine my thoughts echoing across the manor. I think of each of their faces as I say their names, hoping that it will connect with them.

Maybe I'm a quick study with magic, because it works.

"Your Holiness?" Lucia's soft voice laps as gently against my thoughts as a small wave would on the hull of a ship. It's an odd sensation when I can't see the speaker. Though, not as unnerving as it otherwise might have been had I not had a song humming in the back of my mind for years.

"Holiness?" The word rips across my mind in confusion.

"Yes, you are the offering, the holy extension of our Lord—"

"Duke Ilryth is hurt!" I blurt, sensing the explanation was going to drag on far longer than necessary. *Marked with the old gods, seen as holy, got it.*

"What?" So much confusion in that one word.

Oh bloody... Did she hear my other thoughts? So much for being a quick study. I focus on two words, "Come here!" The young woman rises from one of the coral towers of Ilryth's grand estate. "Over here!"

She turns and finally sees us; we've just about crossed the small gap between the wall and the estate. Her lips part. With mouth wide open, she sings a sharp note. I know an alarm when I hear one.

Sheel is the second to arrive, a wooden spear in his hand as he emerges from a balcony. Fenny also swims up above the rooftops, wielding a short sword made of sharpened bone and looking surprisingly fearsome for a woman who had seemed only uptight and matronly so far. Lucia is already halfway to us and Sheel is quickly catching up.

"What are you doing out of your anointing chamber? And the offering should not be making contact with others, lest you disrupt your disconnection from this world!" he growls at me, baring his teeth. I notice he has six canines—four on top, two on bottom—rather than just two as humans have. As if his mouth is part shark. "What misfortune have you brought upon us for your blasphemy?"

"The next time your duke needs saving, I'll gladly let him die if that's your preference," I snarl back, baring my own teeth, even though they're not nearly as fearsome as his. Sheel seems taken aback by my tone, straightening away.

"Die?" There's genuine confusion in the question. It gives way to horror as he really looks at Ilryth for the first time. "Don't tell me he went with the warriors into the trench." The words feel like they slipped out, unintended. A thought Sheel had meant for himself.

"I certainly didn't give him these wounds." I shift my grip on Ilryth. It's awkward trying to swim with the mountain of muscle this man is. He is still completely limp. "They seem serious."

"They are," Lucia says as she takes the opposite arm from me. Her eyes are wide with worry. A panic deeper than even Sheel's. The familial resemblance between her and the duke was apparent from the first moment I laid eyes on them both. Even though Lucia's soft features are nothing like Emily's strong jaw and intense eyes, I see my sister in her worry. "But his physical wounds are not nearly as worrisome as the ones we can't see."

Isn't that always the truth? I think. Lucia gives me a weary smile. She must've heard. I pretend she didn't.

"You need to stop touching him, Your Holiness. Let me help." Sheel takes the arm I'm holding on to as Fenny arrives.

"What happened to him?" Fenny's words are filled with worry, but her brow is furrowed with disapproval.

I don't miss how Fenny also looks in my direction with accusation. I give her a small glare as well. Why is it that they all think I have the ability to bring misfortune upon them when I'm the one who's been sitting in a cage; the one who they plan to *literally sacrifice*?

Fenny glances away. I'm not sure if she heard my agitation or not.

"The worst, I suspect," Lucia says gravely. "But we'll look after him. Go and lead a hymn with the people of the duchy—one of protection and safety."

Fenny nods and speeds off in the opposite direction of where Lucia and Sheel are headed. I glance between them and ultimately decide to go with Ilryth. The only reason I have a chance to catch up is because they are burdened by Ilryth's weight.

I get a better sense of the estate swimming over it than I had on the initial approach. Like a reef, many structures have been built upon each other, dotted around the rocky and sandy ocean floor in a seemingly haphazard, almost organic way. Many are connected by coral tunnels and archways, but not all. Towers stretch up, spiraling with gnarled branches.

We head for a cluster of buildings toward the center that are mostly disconnected from the rest of the estate. Rising from among them is a large structure with a domed roof of brain coral. We descend to a balcony attached to a room connected to the structure, parallel to the wall that serves as a barrier against monsters and the ominous red haze. It's a bedroom, I quickly realize. Even though it looks unlike any bedroom I've ever seen.

There are carvings on each of the columns that line the small balcony we enter through, their lines and shapes like the markings on our bodies and the whale bones of my former cage. On the far wall, opposite the opening to the sea, is a tunnel. Mosslike seaweed grows up from a stone platform opposite me, snaking along the wall, and across the ceiling, trailing into the tunnel. Small, glowing flowers are nestled within the kelp, illuminating the room.

Sheel and Lucia bring Ilryth to the platform before taking places on either side of Ilryth. They begin humming, swaying back and forth. Other, unseen singers meld with the melody and the resulting harmonies resonate deep into the core of my being. The silvery glow of the flowers budded in the mossy kelp brightens, encompassing all three people before me. Ripples distort the luminescent haze, changing in frequency with every high and low shift of note. Tiny bubbles form across Ilryth's skin and loosen into ribbons of airy pearls.

After a few minutes, their swaying stops and the two share a brief exchange I cannot hear. Sheel drifts away and Lucia adjusts to float over Ilryth's head, resting both her hands on his temples. Her tail is straight up, arcing lightly against the mossy seaweed of the ceiling. Her face is close to his and she continues to sing softly in harmony with the music that still rides on the currents around the estate.

"What happened to him?" I dare to ask Sheel when it looks like he's no longer joining in the song. The sharklike man looks positively incensed. His large, scarred arms are folded over his chest. A scowl is etched across his face.

"He went when he was not supposed to—after swearing he wouldn't. The rest of us hunkered down and I thought he was too. It was going to be fine without him." Sheel shakes his head. "I told him it's too dangerous down there for him these days, especially since Dawnpoint is occupied. But he's been insistent it's the 'Duke of Spears's duty to be on the front line of defense.'"

The sheer quantity of names and places and people would be dizzying if I weren't already accustomed to quickly learning such things for my work. "Went 'down there?' Over the ridge?"

Sheel glances my way, anger in his eyes. But it fades quickly, as if he remembers that I have no idea how things work underneath the waves. "Yes. To the Gray Trench."

"And that's where the monsters live?"

"Monsters and wraiths." He pauses. "You saw one, then?" I nod. Sheel's scowl deepens. "No wonder he felt obligated. Lord Krokan's emissaries are venturing closer…"

The aside makes me feel far less safe. Wraiths. Monsters. All on our doorstep.

"He went with warriors."

"Yes, if they go, he goes."

I can respect a man who doesn't order others to do something he wouldn't do himself.

"But he was the only one who returned," I add softly. My attention drifts back to the still unconscious duke. I know how horrible that feels... to be the sole survivor. The unyielding guilt is relentlessly chasing me, threatening to catch up every time I'm still. "You said he felt it was his responsibility as the Duke of Spears?" Repeating the names of people and places helps me remember...and pushes other thoughts away.

"Yes. Every duchy has their own primary responsibility to the Eversea. There's the Duchy of Faith, of Hunt, of Scholarship, of Craftsmen, and of Spears. Of course, each duchy is expected to be self-sustaining. But they specialize in unique areas to cover the gaps of the other duchies. They are led by a chorus composed of all five dukes or duchesses, the eldest of the bunch serving as our king or queen when a single head of state is needed," Sheel explains. He offers an extensive explanation while saying nothing of the other men not returning. I pick up on his intention, subconscious or not, and allow the conversation to move on.

The notion of the duchies makes sense to me. It's not so different from a specific region of Tenvrath having the densest collection of farms because the land is more fertile. Merchants tend to specialize based on their proximity to specific goods. Even crew members know one post on the ship better than others because it is what they are inclined toward, despite also being required to be able to fill in for anyone else.

Sheel remains focused on Ilryth, concern evident in his eyes. "As the duchy closest to the Gray Trench, our duke is responsible for the protection of the Eversea from wraiths."

Ilryth had mentioned something about wraiths possessing the sirens who had tried to take me years ago.

"Are wraiths the same as ghosts?" I ask, taking advantage of the fact that he seems to be forthcoming when trying to distract himself from other matters.

"Not quite. Ghosts will still have their wits about them—they're a more intact soul, still. Wraiths are ghosts that lost themselves and now only carry hate and violence. They cause turmoil within the living and, once they've weakened a soul, can destroy it to possess the body." Sheel finally averts his eyes, motioning to the wooden spear he carried.

"The armor our warriors wear, the weapons we use, and the defenses we create against these monsters are cut from the trunk and roots of the Lifetree. Only a spear of wood from the tree can destroy a wraith."

I assume the Lifetree to be that massive tree I suspected I saw near the castle when we first arrived.

"Why didn't the duke have armor?"

"He didn't?" Sheel is shocked.

I shake my head. "A few of the warriors did, but not him."

Curses I don't know crash across my mind. Sheel rubs his temples and they vanish. "Apologies you had to hear that."

"I'm a sailor, I don't mind foul language. Though I am impressed you have words I didn't recognize."

"Old tongue of the siren. It's what we still sing many of our songs in."

"Ah, you'll have to teach me some sometime. I'd love to bring back some new, deliciously foul language to my—" My thoughts halt. *My crew.*

A brief frown cuts into Sheel's formerly harsh expression. Yet, he refrains from apologies or condolences, and for that I'm grateful. I don't think I could bear the apology of a siren, not when there are still instances when I resent their kind for my current predicament. Still, I recognize the hand I played; the choices I made that brought me here, save for the six months of which Ilryth robbed me.

"You will learn our old tongues, just like you'll learn our ways." Perhaps his forthcomingness wasn't merely a distraction. "You must before you are sacrificed to Lord Krokan."

My turn to divert the conversation. "Why wasn't the duke wearing any armor?"

Sheel presses his mouth into a hard line. "There's not enough to go around."

"He forfeits his armor to his men so that they might be more protected," I realize.

"Yes." Sheel regards me thoughtfully. His anger has given way to something that almost resembles curiosity. "How did you know?"

I stare at Ilryth's unmoving form. He's a duke. A leader in his own right. There are merchant lords in Tenvrath, and from among them the council is elected—a system not unlike what this siren chorus sounds like. I am familiar with the responsibilities of leadership from my land, as well as from my ships.

"I am a captain." The words are still projected thoughts, but it doesn't feel like they come from my mind. They come from my heart. I *am* a captain, even without a ship. It is woven into my very essence. "I know what it's like to be willing to sacrifice *everything* for the people you're responsible for. Those you love…"

The guilt has caught me. Can I even call myself a captain when it's because of me that my sailors are dead? I, *the great Captain Victoria*, who never so much as lost one crew member, lost them all in one night.

What if… The question returns, haunting me relentlessly. In my darkest nights, when my only company is my own worst enemy, I cannot help but wonder if those around me would've been better off if they never met me. The doubts poison my blood, fueling my muscle and the relentlessness of my work. Perhaps, with enough sweat and toil, maybe, one day, I will be worthy of their loyalty and admiration.

"Your Holiness." Lucia lifts her head, locking eyes with mine and jarring me from my thoughts. "I might need your help."

It's still odd to be called holy. But now is hardly the time to try to convince her to stop. "Help how?"

"Float over him."

"Excuse me?" Even in my mind, the words have a bit of a stammered shock to them.

Lucia shifts, her hands still hovering on either side of Ilryth's face. The light seems to flicker as she interrupts her song to speak. "Horizontal—nose to nose, feet to tail."

"Why?"

"You are anointed with the songs of the old ones, by his hand…" She pauses to sing a verse, joining what sounds like Fenny in the distance. "You are like a bridge to their power, and to him. And I—" She pauses again, brow furrowing, mouth twisting into a frown. "I'm not strong enough alone to save him."

"Will it hurt?" I ask, but I'm already moving. I push lightly off the stony floor and drift midway between the ceiling and his bed. I've come this far to save him. I'm not stopping now. Plus, the best chance I have of getting what I want is by helping to keep him alive. He's going to owe me for this.

"No, it shouldn't."

"All right, then." With small twists of my wrists and kicks of my feet, I move over top of him, drifting to a stop. I'm acutely aware of our positioning. It's been half a decade since I've been over a man and the radiant heat of his body serves as a vivid reminder. The coiling need is all too happy to ignore the blatant fact that now is very much not the time or place. I swallow it down, well trained in not letting emotions or urges get the better of me.

"Closer, please. I need your hands on his temples, under mine."

"I thought I wasn't supposed to touch him?"

"This will be fine." Her words are filled with desperation. I'm not sure if it's "fine" or not. But I don't think Lucia cares right now. Not that I blame her. If it were Em, I'd break every rule—old gods or no—to save her.

With a few somewhat awkward movements, I've lowered myself enough that I can reach his temples. Lucia's hands make room for mine to slide underneath hers. I rest my fingertips on the duke's skin.

Tingling shoots through my body akin to the last time I touched him. I am an eel, electrified from head to toe. For a brief second the world falls to a hushed thrall, music pulsing in the distance.

My lips part slightly. The glow encompassing the duke is changing colors from a soft silver to warm gold. The bubbles are not just coming off his skin, but mine. They grow in quantity, as if they are trying to carry me away in their effervescence. But I can't move my hands from him. It's as if we've been glued together.

Emotions war within me—attraction and repulsion lock horns. The pull toward him intensifies; my urge to wrench myself free grows in equal measure. Curiosity begs to see what's next. Duty to save him— *no man left behind*—fuels my resolve. Yet, at the same time, hushed whispers in the back of my mind are present to remind me that this man took me and has possibly damned my family. Every story, every sailor's instinct, tells me that my sworn enemy is below me—to shift my hands and wrap them around his throat.

No. I refuse to meet cruelty in kind. I made my choices, willingly got myself into this—I'm going to see it through.

A pause. As if the whole world has sucked in a breath. No movement. No sound.

Then, the stillness gives way to a different melody. This is not the one the sirens were singing to heal him, but something new. A song in dissonance with the one Ilryth imprinted on my soul that night long ago, the two clashing against a third singer that is borderline howling underneath it all.

The cacophony grows in tandem with the light. I no longer feel the bubbles on my skin, or the currents around me.

All at once, I am blinded by unfiltered sunlight.

eight

I AM STANDING ON A BEACH AS WHITE AS BONE. The sand is so fine that it almost seems to shimmer with prismatic iridescence. Waves are broken on roots as large as ship hulls that wrap around this sandy place in a way reminiscent of a bird's nest. They connect upward to a massive tree that looks as if it is a thousand smaller trees wrapped into one. It towers so tall that its uppermost branches pierce the heavens and tangle with the clouds.

The beach itself is skewered with pieces of wood. Some have the same golden-brown hue as the tree wrapping around it. Others have been sitting out in the sun for so long that the woodgrain has been bleached to a pale ash.

This must be the Lifetree and its beach that Sheel was just describing. But why…*how* am I here? The questions intrigue and excite me. My better sense says I should be afraid. But I have spent the best years of my life stepping into the unknown—going places that no one else would dare to even dream of venturing.

As I whip my head around, I notice that the world has a faint haze to it. Blurry at its edges. I don't feel the heat of the sand or hear the whisper of wind. Everything seems distant, faint.

It's then I notice that on the far side of the beach, closest to the trunk of the tree, is an older woman and a young man. They look like humans at a glance, but on closer inspection have the faint cartilage tracts that run up their cheeks and split into the fin-like ears of the siren. On their fair skin are the siren's markings. However, there is one noticeable difference between them and the siren I know.

They walk awkwardly on two legs, slowly making their way to the main trunk. I fixate on them, trying to reason through what I'm seeing. Is this a different being than the siren? Or perhaps a transformation? The latter seems more likely.

In the water they are powerful, unstoppable rulers of the seas…but on land they're akin to baby deer.

I take one more look around myself, and then begin to walk over to them. It takes no time to catch up with their slow pace, and I notice when I'm about halfway to them that the young man has a narrow trail of scales along his spine, disappearing underneath a wrap around his waist, in an all too familiar shade of turquoise.

"It's not much farther now." The woman still speaks without moving her mouth. I wonder if they would be able to speak above land, or not. I wonder how they're able to walk on two legs at all.

"Mother, I feel as though I will shrivel and crisp up here." The young man looks like he couldn't be older than fifteen. Even that might be generous.

"You can do this. It's not much longer. I wouldn't give you a burden you couldn't shoulder." The woman gives her son a warm smile. The familial resemblance is unmistakable. Though her hair is long and loose, flowing down to her waist, and the young man's is cropped close to the scalp, they have a similar cut to their jaw and the same sharpness in their eyes that betrays a clever and warm-spirited nature. "Soon we will be back in the water."

He carries on, leading the charge with every determined step. But he's too ambitious. Off-balance, he falters and falls. The woman is at his side instantly, helping him up. She has much more control over her two-legged body.

"I can do it. I can do it," he insists with all the headstrong pride of youth.

She gives him space to struggle to his feet.

"Hello?" I speak, but they don't turn. I suspected such would be the case when I approached and they didn't so much as glance my way. There's not another soul on this beach, so there's no way they couldn't see me…*if* they could see me.

They finally arrive at the foot of the tree. Here, a doorway is set against the trunk itself. Branches and vines have grown over it like thick bars. It's barricaded against the world. The only signs of attempted entry are five woody vines that have had pieces cut and pried away. The wounds still weep a dark red sap.

"Now, just as we practiced," the woman instructs.

The boy—young man—a young Ilryth, from what I can tell—drops to his knees and places both palms on the doorway. He tilts his head skyward and parts his lips to unleash a soaring song that weaves between the falling silver leaves. His voice has yet to completely deepen and he can hit notes of near-piercing intensity.

My forearm tingles at the sound. It's the first real sensation I've had since arriving here and it draws my attention to the markings on my skin. They seem the same as always.

When the song is finished, they wait, staring at the door.

Ilryth's shoulders sag. "I could not hear her song."

"I did not either," the woman says in a tone that contrasts warm support with tired dejection. "Her voice has been silent for centuries now. Even the oldest among us have not heard her words. There is no shame to it."

"But I thought Lady Lellia might tell us another way." The young man continues to hunch with his back to her. His next words are so small that, were they spoken normally, I doubt I could've heard them. "That I might be able to help…"

"My child, the best way for you to help is to assume the mantle you were born for." She kneels beside him.

"If I do that then you—you will—" His voice cracks.

"I will do what I must to protect the people I love." She sits and pulls him to her, clutching him tightly. The woman places a kiss on his temple. "Now, you must do what you must to protect our home, those we love, your sisters and father."

"I'm not ready." He buries his face in his hands. "I can barely sing the song to walk on her holy ground."

"You will be ready when the time comes," the mother reassures her son. But she doesn't look at him when she speaks. She stares over his shoulder with a relaxed and distant gaze that reaches well past the horizon.

"Could there not be another way?"

"Ilryth…" She draws her attention back to her son and then to the tree high above. Ilryth's mother's mouth is set in a hard line of determination. But her eyes nearly overflow with sorrow. "Duke Renfal says that Lord Krokan wants women who are rich with life and who have held Lady Lellia's grace in their hands sacrificed to him every five years. That was the knowledge he gave his life for. The other sacrifices haven't worked; our seas grow more and more dangerous."

"Yes, but why does it have to be *you*?" He looks up at his mother.

She smooths hair away from his brow. In the arms of a mother, every man becomes a boy. "Because who is richer with life than the Duchess of Spears? Who holds a stronger grace in their hands than I, with Dawnpoint? Who better than a singer of the chorus?" She smiles but it doesn't quite reach her eyes. "My duty is to protect our seas and our people at all costs—as is yours. You must take your oath so that my anointing might begin."

"I don't think I can…" He glances away in shame.

"Of course you can."

"Do it." A new voice enters the mix. A familiar one. I look over my shoulder. Behind me, farther back on the beach, is the Ilryth I know. A man grown.

He doesn't have two legs and instead hovers, tail and all, as if suspended in water. He moves like he would in the sea, though here he soars through the air.

"Ilryth?"

Somehow, he doesn't hear me. Perhaps he can't see me, either, because he rushes past me to the young man.

"Ilryth, what is this place? What's happening?" I try to call out to him.

Ilryth looms over his younger self, oozing disdain and hate as the young man pushes away his mother's arms and assumes his position before the tree door once more. But he doesn't lift his palms to the wood. Ilryth tries to push his younger self forward. The adult's muscles ripple in the sunlight, bulging with effort. His brow is lined with rage. But the child might as well be sculpted from lead, he is oblivious to the straining of his adult self.

"Ilryth!" I shout.

"Do it!" he yells at his younger self. "Don't delay! Don't be the one that holds her back!"

"Now, swear your fealty to the old gods and to the Eversea that you are sworn to protect," his mother instructs gently. "Take your oaths so that you may wield Dawnpoint."

"Mother, I…" The young Ilryth hasn't moved, oblivious to his older self.

The woman opens her mouth to speak again, but closes it with a sigh. Resignation softens her brow. Her head tilts just slightly.

"Very well," she relents and kneels at his side once more. "It was too much to ask of you so young. No other duke or duchess has ever been asked to assume their role this early. If you are not ready to pledge your life to the Eversea and take up Dawnpoint as the Duke of Spears, then you don't have to."

"Loathsome, wretched, weak, coward," Ilryth seethes. He grips his younger self's hand, trying to press it directly against the tree. Still, he cannot influence anything in this world.

"Ilryth, is this your memory?" I dare to ask, thinking of no other explanation. He still does not hear me.

The younger Ilryth looks to his mother. Fear wells in the young man's eyes. Vulnerability. He's terrified, but also relieved. "Mother, are you certain?"

"Yes. This is a duty one must be ready for when they accept. It is an honor, not a bane." The woman gives him a warm smile.

"But the anointing—" the young man starts.

"Does not take *that* long." She wraps her arm around her son's shoulders and helps him to his feet. "When I must begin in earnest, you will be nineteen. You will be ready to take Dawnpoint then, I'm sure of it."

Despite his obvious efforts to contain his emotions, the young Ilryth's eyes shine. His lip quivers slightly. "Are you ashamed of me?"

Somehow, even on land, even awkward and clumsy, the woman moves faster than I thought possible. She grabs her son behind the head and around his shoulders. In the same movement, she presses her lips to his forehead.

"No. Never, my boy."

"Yes!" The older Ilryth continues to try to pry his younger self away. To force him to the tree to take up the mantle of duke. But his efforts are waning. His strength is leaving him. Instead his shoulders are slumping. "Yes," he rasps, somewhere between rage and tears. "She will always be ashamed of you, you pathetic coward. It's because of *you* that her death meant nothing…that she couldn't sever her mortal ties sufficiently to quell the rage."

"Ilryth, that's enough." I take a step forward. Still no reaction to my presence.

"You are my son, the light for the tree of my life. I could never be ashamed of you." She strokes her son's head once and then releases him with an encouraging smile. "Now, let us return to the sea. We'll come back in a few years."

The two begin to leave, but the older Ilryth doesn't move. He sinks down to the sand where his younger self was, tail bent under him. He hides his face in his hands.

"Come back and fulfill your duty…coward…" He heaves over, digging his hands into the sand and unleashing a scream that causes the world around us to splinter. "How many times must I be reminded of my failures? How many times must I watch you die?" Ilryth leans back, arm outstretched, as he reaches toward his mother, well beyond his grasp.

I cross over to him with deliberate, purposeful steps. His every word resonates palpable pain within me, as if this agony were my own. It rumbles through the foundations of this illusory world, causing lightning-shaped cracks of darkness. At once, it shatters, like a mirror crashing into stone. Between the edges of the fractured images, ghostly hands reach out, grasping at the boundaries of this reality, clawing.

"Ilryth, I think we should go." I place a hand on his shoulder, but my focus is on the monstrosities trying to tear apart this dream turned nightmare. There are faces moving behind the separating picture of this memory. Entities that have the tiny hairs on the back of my neck rising are trying to break through.

The duke is as still as a statue. His unseeing gaze is transfixed on a spot of sand right before the door. His skin has turned cold. The luster is fading from him. All color drains from his body.

I kneel at his side, tilting my head, looking up into his face. He still has yet to even register my presence.

"This isn't real," I say purposefully. Though it feels quite real to me now. Every rumbling of the earth. Every roar of the monster that has haunted my own dreams is tangible. I *hope* this is not real. "We must leave whatever this place is. Now. It's over, Ilryth, time has moved on and so must you. There's no point in losing yourself in what you can't change. You have to move forward."

Ilryth doesn't move.

I shift, trying to place myself directly in front of him. There's no way he can't see me now. "You have to get us out of here. I don't know what's happening, but Lucia sent me here to tell you that, I think. You must come back to the real world, with me."

"Worthless. Coward," Ilryth whispers with raw loathing. "If I had just…let her go. But I couldn't. Like I couldn't hear Lellia's words. *I* held her back. She was too good to die. It should have been me offered that day, not her."

The words are a dagger between my ribs. I inhale sharply. My hands fly to his and I clutch them tightly.

"I know…" I whisper. "I know what it's like to feel like you're a burden to all those around you. That, no matter how hard you try, it's never good enough. You can't love them enough, sacrifice enough for them…"

He still doesn't react. Still looks through me. The world around us continues to tremble. The shadows are consuming the edges, eating away at the details.

"Ilryth." My voice has gone firm. "You're the only one who can save us from this crumbling reality. You are not that boy any longer. You're responsible for people, *they* need you, still. I—" The words stick to the inside of my throat. I swallow, trying to dislodge them. They make me sick, churning my stomach. But they're the truth and right now I can't be proud. I can't allow my own fears of being dependent on another to hold me back. "*I* need you, Ilryth."

He blinks and there's a moment of clarity on his face. "Victoria?" he whispers across our minds. There's something unexpectedly intimate about the way he says it, made more intense by our hands being interlocked.

"Ilryth, we—" I can't speak fast enough.

A loud roar interrupts me and a blustering wind rips over the beach.

The roots of the tree groan and crack, falling into a pale sea. In the distance, the fog condenses into a face that is locked in an eternal, angry scream. The visage of hate itself.

Ilryth hunches once more, his eyes going blank as they drop to the sand. He's reverted to his numb, statue self. "What was the point of it? Of any of it? Have the gods truly abandoned their stewards?"

Mention of the gods draws my eyes to my forearm. It's words—song given shape upon my flesh. Lucia wanted *me* to do this because I had their magic. I look between it and the distant face that is sharpening as it grows nearer.

I don't know what I'm doing but... "I'm a bloody wretched singer, Ilryth. You see what you're driving me to?" No reaction to my bitter words. Damn. "*Fine*. Here goes nothing..."

I open my mouth and begin to sing. Not with my mind, but in my throat. It's a few wobbling notes. Terrible, really. I never was a good singer. But I sing words as they come to me on instinct, whatever feels right,

"Come to me.
I call to you.
Come, come—"

Clarity dawns on him. Ilryth's eyes widen slightly. I stop singing immediately. He grabs for my painted forearm.

"You sang."

"Told you it was bad."

Yet he stares at me in wonder, as if I were finer than the most skilled prima donna. But the moment is short-lived as Ilryth looks around, finally seeing the degrading world. Yet, he's not surprised by it. He sighs softly and it betrays an exhaustion deeper than the lowest point of the ocean. His eyes land on the face in the distance, rushing toward us, as if to consume this whole island in a single bite.

"We need to go," I urge.

"You should never have been here." His eyes shift to me and, for a moment, all the sorrow a person was ever capable of is mine. He gives it all to me. Sympathy. Empathy. Longing. "This is a nightmare no others should endure."

Ilryth rises, suspended in the air as though it were water. He extends a hand to me and I regard it warily. My palm slides against his and, for a heartbeat, he does nothing but grip my fingers. I meet his intent stare and a thousand unspoken words pass between us. Nothing is said. But an understanding that transcends words sinks into me like the warmth of his fingers. In that fleeting breath, the barriers between us aren't as strong as either of us would like. We gain a rare glimpse into the other's soul.

There is a part of me that wants to withdraw. To hide my face and my heart. But a lonely corner belonging to a woman who cried one too many nights alone, craving the comfort of an embrace, wants nothing more than to linger here. For this moment to drag on long enough that my pain becomes a shared burden. Even if the idea of someone else truly seeing my raw and tired heart is as terrifying as carving out a piece of it and handing it over.

"Let's get you out of here," he whispers as the howling begins to pick up, breaking the trance.

I nod, unable to say anything more.

With a flap of his tail, he swims upward through the air. I am pulled along with him, weightless. The air rushes across my skin and it's the first thing I feel.

No…not air.

Tiny bubbles.

I blink ahead as we rise toward the sun and away from the roaring underneath us. The world continues to fracture, spiderweb cracks chasing us upward. Ilryth glances down, continuing to soar with strong strokes of his tail.

"Hold on."

I squeeze his hand tighter.

The bubbles rush over me. We crash into the branches of the tree and are met with blinding light. I let out a gasp and flinch on instinct, waiting for pain. But there is none.

I blink as the light fades—no longer blinded by it. I am still hovering above Ilryth in his bed. Lucia's fingertips are still over mine, resting on his temples. But now, his eyes are open.

The duke stares up at me, as if he is trying to crawl back into my mind. Then, as reality crashes around us both, his brow furrows with anger. His gaze shifts to Lucia, who lets out a surprised chirp and pulls her hands away.

"How dare you involve *her*."

nine

"Your Grace, I—I—" Lucia quickly swims away.

"This is not the business of a human. She should not even be here," Ilryth seethes.

I take that as my cue to swim away as well. The sound of a man's rage has a cloying, grasping feeling working its way up my spine, gripping the back of my neck. *Get away*, every instinct demands. The water is cooler with distance between us. Easier to move through. There's a riptide to Ilryth's proximity that's almost inescapable. I stare at my yet-tingling fingertips, half expecting them to still glow and bubble.

"Ilryth," Sheel says firmly. I've never heard one of them say his name plainly, without any kind of honorific attached. I'm surprised the first I hear do it is Sheel, rather than one of the women whom I presume are his sisters. Now that I've seen their mother, the familial resemblance between him, Fenny, and Lucia cannot be denied. Sheel's act does the trick and Ilryth stills. "You were in a bad way. Not even responsive this time around. Lucia needed to resort to drastic measures to pull you back before the wraiths consumed your soul and took over your body."

Ilryth looks back to the young woman with a hateful glint to his eyes. I can't stop myself from crossing to her. I rest a hand on Lucia's shoulder. He doesn't mean his anger, he can't. Goodness knows there are times I wanted to throttle Em and all it took was a reminder of how in the wrong I was in the moment to quench my rage completely.

"She did everything she could to help you. You should be *thanking* her, not scolding her," I say firmly.

"You don't even know of what you speak." He seems like he's barely able to hold himself back from redirecting all that rage at me. But he *is* able…which makes him better than many I've known.

"I might not know the details of your magic—since all of you have yet to properly tell me," I add with a slight bitter note. "But I know what a man misplacing his anger and hurt on a young woman who doesn't deserve it looks like." The words echo in my mind, chafing, a little too raw. They're words I wish I'd had the grace, or opportunity, to say to Charles. Instead, he always seemed to get the better of me. The young woman I was back then cowered time and again to the point that I'm surprised her spine didn't break.

But I'm not her anymore. I'm better. If I can fight Charles to the bitter end, through all his threats and jabs, I can stare down a siren duke.

Ilryth points at me, eyes narrowing. A noise of disgust ripples across my thoughts and he shakes his head, turning away. With his back toward Lucia, he murmurs, "Thank you for your assistance, Lucia."

"Always, Your Grace." Lucia bows her head. She glances in my direction. "Thank you, but that wasn't necessary."

I get the sense the words were only to me and try to reciprocate, focusing on her and her alone. "I don't care if he's a duke or a pauper. I'm not going to stand by and let someone treat you that way."

"It really is fine. I know my brother," she says with a note of sorrow. Almost of pity. And confirms my suspicions about the familial resemblance. "The trench is hard on any…especially those with many burdens to bear. The wounds of the wraiths are deep and difficult; they're meant to destroy the soul."

"We all endure deep and difficult wounds. They're not an excuse for handling oneself in a boorish manner." I squeeze her shoulder before releasing. "Never compromise your worth, not for anyone, not even for family." The words come naturally—I said variants of them enough to my own sister.

"I'll keep that in mind." Lucia shares a smile with me.

"Everyone but Victoria is dismissed."

"Your Grace?" Lucia's smile falls as she looks back to him.

"I'll be all right. I can handle men like him," I reassure her.

"I heard that," Ilryth says dryly. I shoot him a challenging look with a shrug to convey how little I care that he did. His lips are slightly pursed, but the frustration doesn't quite reach his eyes. He pierces me with his stare as Lucia and Sheel leave without objection, swimming out over his balcony.

I keep my stance relaxed, but don't back down as I wait for him to say something. The sensation of unsaid words clouds the waters between us once more. They hum against me, even after the singing that reverberated across the manor stops.

Somehow, I feel like I win the unspoken debate when he relaxes, body slackening in the water. The tension evaporates when he averts his eyes. Yet, my guards don't drop. Retreat can be its own war tactic.

"I'm sorry," Ilryth murmurs.

"What?" The word is blurted with shock.

"Really?" He chuckles and shakes his head, still not looking at me. "You're the kind of woman who's going to make me say it again?"

"It's not that, I—"

"I'm sorry, Victoria." Ilryth returns his gaze to me. There's the same fierceness of determination to him as before but, this time, it doesn't feel combative. I don't know how to react to a man apologizing so quickly. In my moment of surprise, he continues. "You were absolutely right, I shouldn't have lashed out like that. It wasn't your fault and Lucia was merely doing what she thought was best."

I fold my arms. I'm not going to let him use forgiveness to catch me off guard. "You should apologize to Lucia as well."

"I will." He glances away again. "And I'm sorry as well that you had to witness...*that*."

"I don't know what you're talking about." I shrug. Ilryth looks at me from the corner of his eye, skeptically. "All I remember is a bunch of bright light. Maybe some bubbles? Nothing else."

He knows I'm lying. I don't really care that he knows. I'm too busy asking myself *why* I'm lying. I helped him to try and use it to my advantage. I'm not even making an effort to imply I want something in exchange for my kindness.

"Why?" he asks, the same question I'm asking myself.

A bitter chuckle rips through my mind, and I can't stop the tired grin from splitting my lips as I shake my head. It's my turn to avert my eyes. *Because no one should have their darkest secrets held against them.* Yet, I can't bring myself to say that. It'd admit too much. If he hears anyway, he makes no indication. So, instead, I say, "Don't ask or I might reconsider."

"It's not as if I've been particularly kind to you," he's quick to point out.

"No, you haven't."

"I'm going to sacrifice you to a god."

"The reminder really isn't necessary." I glare at him.

"Why?"

"Are you always so insistent?" I snap.

"You're not really one to talk."

"Good Gods, man, and here I was trying to be kind to you." I throw my arms up and drift back awkwardly.

"I didn't ask for your kindness." He has the audacity to glare at me.

"Oh, *forgive me* for giving it to you then. Would you rather me tell you that I only did what I did because I was hoping to somehow use it to barter with you to get you to bring me back to my world?" And, yet, when I was in that strange place in his memories, the notion of doing that had completely vanished. All I see is that sad boy and tortured man.

"I suppose it'd make it easier to comprehend." Even though I told him what he wanted, he doesn't sound delighted at being right and now we're both sulking. "But I already told you, I *can't* bring you back. If you were to leave the Eversea, you would begin fading, immediately. You'd have minutes, *maybe* an hour. It's too great a risk."

The words feel like someone is physically ripping out the last places hope had attached to my bones. *I can't go back...* Even if I could, I couldn't do anything. My back curls and I am aware of just how weightless I am. The want to breathe chokes me again. But there's no air. My chest rises and falls, but I don't feel water. I don't feel air. I'm not the woman I was. *More magic than flesh...* I'll never be her again.

I drift, turning away from him, catching myself on a pillar as if I could catch my breath. The shimmering dawn through the surface mocks me. Close enough to draw golden lines across my face. Far enough that I'll never be able to reach it again.

"You should have killed me." I wish he had.

"You have a greater purpose."

"*I had a purpose!*" Rage and hurt bubbles over. "I was a captain, responsible for my crew—the crew that you killed."

"I didn't—"

I won't hear his excuses. I don't care. "I was a daughter, a sister, responsible for my family. And you...you took me from them. Six months. I had *six* months... And now, they..." I trail off and shake my head. This was foolish. There's no world in which this siren would care. Why would I ever expect him to?

"They what?" he presses.

Twisting, I face him once more. Ilryth's eyes in the sunlight remind me of the sun between the leaves of fall. Cozy. Warm. They're eyes that beg you to trust. Which is more dangerous than any cruel glare.

I'm not sure why I tell him. Perhaps it's because it feels fair. I found out something about him—something he clearly never wanted anyone to know—and now I feel obligated to tell him something of me. Perhaps it's because part of me desperately wants to believe that maybe, *maybe* he'll find a way to help if he knows the truth.

"I owe a good deal of money to the council that oversees my home. If I don't pay it, and am not present when it comes due, it's my family who will pay the price." It's an oversimplification of my circumstances. But I default to assuming he wouldn't be interested in any additional information.

I'm wrong.

"They will be killed for money you owe?"

"No, the council won't kill them...but they might wish for death, if that fate comes to pass." I think of them, toiling in a debtors' prison. "Do you have debtors' prisons here, Duke Ilryth?"

"No, I cannot say I am familiar." He sounds genuinely intrigued.

"They are cold, brutal places where a person's freedoms are stripped from them. People are treated as less than animals and made to labor on whatever tasks the council requires hands for—constructing roads, buildings, whatever else. They work tirelessly, and without pay. In exchange, their debts are forgiven...but only after years of compliant service."

"We do not use our freedom as currency, here in the Eversea." His mouth has pulled into a frown, brows furrowed. "It sounds like a monstrous practice."

"Monstrous?" I scoff. "Says the man who intends to sacrifice me to the god who claimed my whole crew." I can't keep in the remark. The sea between us is electrified again the moment I throw the verbal jab.

It feels as though we've squared off with each other. Opposed. Equally horrible, if I think about it, his old gods…our prisons.

At least a debtors' prison doesn't take your life, I want to think. But it does. Either literally, as a result of the squalid conditions. Or practically, from the years of work and opportunity that it steals from the people thrown in.

I've always hated the debtors' prisons. I can't in good faith defend them. But they're a staple of the world I knew. Of the sun rising or the pull of the tides. The idea that there could be another way is as foreign to me as Sheel's siren curses.

"Everything in Tenvrath comes down to contracts and crons." I deflate from my conflict. "Even if that's taken to a debilitating extreme… We all understand that payment comes due and there's nothing worse than not having it in hand at the time. Once I am declared dead, the man I owe the money to will immediately move to collect. It will be claimed that I abandoned my oath—the contractual amount I was obligated to pay."

I touch my chest. Tingles shoot out along the lines he marked upon me, causing my heart to flutter briefly. Perhaps it is simply my desperation. "Please, I'm trying to keep my word. Surely you understand that? I would rather die a thousand cold, lonely deaths than break this obligation and allow misfortune to befall them."

Ilryth hardly moves. His stare is intense, as if he is trying to not just hear my thoughts but peer into my skull. To root out if what I'm saying is true or not. His silence is the breeding ground of my desperation.

One last chance, Victoria.

"Ilryth, I knew you would come. I didn't plan to fight you when you did. I worked so hard to get everything settled"—*everything neglected to settle for me with your magic*—"and this is all that's left. My family is all I have left. If they are taken care of, then I will do whatever it is you wish without concern or objection. We had a deal for time, and since you didn't—or couldn't, allow me the full amount of time owed, then please help me settle this matter. I give you my word once this is done, I will put my full effort and every skill into being whatever it is you need me to be as your sacrifice."

Once more, I'm bartering myself away. My heart. My mind. My time and my coin. It all slips between my fingers. Given away. But at least this time will be for my family. I can find comfort in that.

Finally, after what feels like ages, he says, "Very well then, come with me."

"What?"

Ilryth turns, starting down the tunnel connected to the wall opposite by the balcony, to the left of his bed.

"Where are you going?"

He glances over his shoulder. "To get your family the money they need."

ten

NO...IT COULDN'T...HE CAN'T POSSIBLY MEAN...

"I do mean it."

The words slip out and I curse inwardly. Ilryth chuckles and starts swimming again. I pulse my feet as fast as I can, trying to catch up.

"Why are you helping me?"

A heavy sigh sinks into my mind. "You asked me to help and now that I've agreed you're trying to convince me to stop?"

"No," I say hastily. "But if I can't understand why, I'll have a hard time trusting you."

He halts, pushing the water forward to cease his momentum, tail curling under him and twisting for him to face me once more. I am not as graceful and nearly slam into him. I would have, were it not for Ilryth reaching out to catch me by the shoulders. He quickly releases me, a moment of shock passing over his face. At first I think it's because of my directness, but given all he's said, I took him as a person who'd understand my feelings. Then, I realize, *He's not supposed to touch me.*

"Part of your anointing is letting go of your connection with this world so that you are a blank slate for the words of the old gods. That way when you are presented to Lord Krokan, you will be nothing but prayers and the Duet of Sendoff. If you are to go before him—the old god of death— with ties to this world, longing for the living, then he will reject you as a proper offering and his rage will continue,"

Ilryth explains, matter-of-fact, as if trying to ignore the contact. "It will be easier for you to succeed in your goal if you are *willing* to let go of this world. Which, you've made clear, involves knowing that your family is taken care of."

I object to his general notion that it is *my* goal to have anything to do with being sacrificed. But I work to keep those thoughts relegated to the back of my mind. If my family is taken care of, I can work to be at peace with everything else...

"Good, I'm glad we have an understanding." I feel better knowing that he is getting something out of this. It is easier for me to think of relationships in simple transactions, rather than pure kindness.

"Indeed." Ilryth doesn't move. His brow softens slightly, lips parting with words unsaid. Thoughts unshared. Is he...guilty?

I intentionally try not to pick apart the meaning of that stare. His guilt doesn't matter to me in the slightest. In fact, he should feel it. If his magic had been stronger and able to break the bond between Charles and me, I wouldn't be in this mess. Even when I know there is blame to fall at my own feet, placing it at his is such a guilty pleasure.

Without another word, Ilryth turns and continues deeper into the tunnel.

I would think that being semi-magical, I'd be able to somehow propel myself through the water at a faster speed than kicking and moving my arms. But alas, that isn't the case. At least I don't seem to tire. That's the only thing keeping me from being completely left behind in his wake.

We swim through a narrow stretch, illuminated still by the faintly glowing flowers that grow from the kelp along the ceiling. The tunnel opens into a domed room—I recognize it as the brain coral I saw earlier. That's easy enough to figure. But what I can't seem to make sense of is exactly what it is I'm looking at.

The main source of light is the oculus in the ceiling, so the room is illuminated exclusively by a hazy, filtered twilight that feels almost... magical. And yet, given the contents, eerie.

All manner of bauble and oddity are trapped within nets and strung from them, suspended from the ceiling. Twine has been tied around the hollow centers of crons, like garland, and they dangle like wind chimes. Hundreds of crons...pinned up like paper party decorations.

Hooks of all sizes, from the largest fishing boats to the smallest, connect the nets to each other, and to the walls. Sailcloths of ships I recognize have been hung like tapestries—ships I mourned on the docks after word arrived that they never made it through the Gray Passage.

There's an anchor. A part of a mast leans against a wall, framing a figurehead of a half-naked man in the corner. Ship rigging holds together the various nets. There's astronomical navigation tools, sundials, and countless chests lining the floor—their heavy locks torn off.

I slow to a stop as I reach the center. The sand is equally cluttered. Scattered around are pots and pans, tinderboxes rendered useless, bottles of rum still corked and sealed with wax.

"What is this place?" I take a turn about the room. Piles of odds and ends are stacked as far as I can see. Flagons. Boots. All of it hoarded reminds me—more than sirens, living underwater, and confronting wraiths in a man's memories ever could—that I am very far from home, in a place very different from anything I've ever known.

"My treasure room," he says, only after I look back to him following a long silence.

"Treasure?" I balk. The thought was so quick I couldn't adjust my tone to be more polite. There are a few things of value here, certainly. The crons tied up, for one. Some of the navigation tools are worth some pretty silver to the right buyer, those that aren't ruined by the seawater. But most of it…is random waste.

"Yes, *treasure*." As expected, he bristles slightly at my tone. "I have spent years filling this place with precious items."

"A shoe is 'precious' to you?" I gesture with an open palm to a worn-out boot.

"I did not bring you here for your judgment." He glances away, clearly uncomfortable. His posture communicates he is trying to maintain his dignity.

"Then what did you bring me here for?"

Without another word, Ilryth swims off into a different coral tunnel than the one we entered from. I'm not sure if he still intends for me to follow, so I wait. He confirms my suspicions by not calling after me and I'm left to my devices.

Ilryth's treasures… I take one more slow lap around the room, the words repeating in my mind as I look over all the various items. A flagon catches my eye, perched on a shelf. I take it gingerly, treating it with far more reverence than I ever did at the Tilted Table. I've drunk from these clay mugs how many times without thought? Now, it's like a relic from a world that is unbearably far, impossible to get back to.

Will the men and women of the wharf look after my family? I briefly imagine all the people I worked with in Dennow chipping in, banding together to help them avoid the debtors' prison. Every bit of goodwill the four of us worked to scrape together coming due. The ones who knew me beyond the rumors stepping forward. Or maybe the ones who whispered about me behind my back will do it out of pity that my family would have to endure the consequences of an oath breaker.

Even in the best iteration of either scenario…there's not enough generosity in all of Dennow to bring together twenty thousand spare crons. I always hoped the few friends I'd made would help my family with small things. Getting through their grief after my being lost to the sea. Making sure my parents paid their taxes on time. *Father always gave away too much ale to my crew in his kind enthusiasm…*

I return the flagon to the shelf where I found it. As I do, I notice a small chip in its bottom and remember a night, a year, maybe two, ago.

We were stumbling back to my vessel, Emily supporting me. A bitter, sad smile passes briefly over my face. She had been relentless that night.

"He was quite handsome." *I don't know who you're talking about.* "Yes you do, that other captain for the Crosswind Traders. He was clearly interested." *I'm married, Em.* "Only on paper." *It's not the time…,* I'd said. But what I'd meant was, *No one would be interested in me, not romantically, at least. People have made it plenty clear what they think of oath breakers.* "When you're free of that wretched man, you will find love again, right? You deserve it, Victoria." *We'll see.*

I never did have a good answer for her. Mostly because I knew if I were ever free of Charles, I'd be dead soon after. Eventually, she just stopped asking.

What good is my heart, anyway? It's been chewed up and spit out. Rotted away from neglect. It stopped beating in a cold sea. Even when it was young and wild and full of hope, I couldn't trust it…how could I now?

That night, I should have told Em that I already had all the love

I needed. I had her and Ma and Pa. I had my crew and Lord Kevhan Applegate. Even if, at times, I felt like I had somehow used the edge of the magic to fool them all into loving me. I didn't need anything more.

Love like what Em was talking about stopped mattering to me long ago.

That night, right before I could get on my ship, my flagon had slipped from my grasp, despite my promising Father I'd return it to the Tilted Table the next day. It had fallen into the water, hopeless to be recovered from the deep dredges of Dennow's wharf.

Was Ilryth there?

It couldn't possibly be the same flagon. My homesickness is getting the better of me. I shake my head and move along.

There are more oddities, like a silver cane. But what catches my eye next is a stained glass of two people dancing. I run my fingers over the lead between the shards of colored glass.

"That's one of my favorites."

I hadn't heard him return. But he's back with a chest in his hands. This duke becomes stranger and stranger by the minute. I can't make sense of what might be going through his mind at any moment. Or what his motivations are. "I was just thinking it'd come from very far, to make it to your waters."

"Is that so?" He seems genuinely curious, so I indulge him.

"This type of glass was made to the south-southwest of Dennow— *very* far southwest of where you collected me from. It's an older art form and most of the expertise has been lost. Only a few craftsmen still engage in the practice." I tap the glass lightly. "I had a piece in my cabin, on my ship." The ship that is now nestled at the bottom of the Gray Passage.

"The fae are the ones who perfected the art of glass pictures, originally. Makes sense, given their glass crown," he says as if it is a well-known fact. "From what I know of your lands, it sounds like that area would be adjacent to the fae wilds."

It's true that I sailed the passage through the mysterious woods that were said to be occupied by the fae.

"Sheel said that there were once humans here in…"

"Midscape," he finishes. "Humans were made by the dryads—Lady Lellia's favorite of all her children and the ones to most closely bear her likeness. She oversaw their work personally, guiding the dryads. Despite humans' magical lineage, humans lacked their own abilities. Perhaps because they were made by mortal hands, rather than immortal, as the rest of the peoples of Midscape were."

"Lady Lellia made all the other species of Midscape?"

"You sound surprised. She is the Goddess of Life, after all." His mouth quirks into a small grin. "If the stories are to be believed, the fae tried to teach your ancestors their ritumancy, and some humans went west, to see if the vampir could help them harness powers from their blood. But nothing ever came of it, I believe. If any progress had been made, the Fade was erected shortly after and severed all chance at humans mastering magic."

"Why was the Fade made?"

"It was created by an Elf King—a direct descendant of the first Elf King, who erected the Veil between our world and the Beyond—to protect the humans from those who would seek to take advantage of their lack of powers. It was a time of much upheaval in our world."

"The power to sever worlds sounds mighty. Did you ever think of asking this Elf King for help with Lord Krokan?"

Ilryth shakes his head. "When the seas began to rot, we flooded the land bridge that connected the Eversea to the rest of Midscape to contain the blight. We began closely watching our traveler's pools— limiting their use—and kept our people to our seas. No one may go in or out."

"You came out to collect me," I point out.

Ilryth purses his lips. "That was different."

Rather than fighting him on that, I focus on what might be most useful to me here and now. "You wouldn't even try to see if these other powerful kings and queens could help you?"

"No Elf King or Human Queen has come to pay homage to Lord Krokan or Lady Lellia in nearly a thousand years. I suspect that they have turned their eyes from the oaths of their forefathers." It's hard to tell how he feels about the idea. If the notion wounds or offends him. Or if it is merely accepted as fact. Probably both. I know all too well how easily pain can numb into bitter acceptance.

"I see."

"I imagined a human would reject the truths of their world more." Ilryth wedges the chest in the sand at the center of the room.

"I fell into the ocean, was attacked by what I now know to be wraith-possessed sirens, saved by a siren duke, had a strange marking put on my arm that gave me some kind of magic I could never quite figure out the extent of but now know it has something to do with being a human sacrifice"—I count on my fingers—"was shipwrecked by a sea monster, lived after death, saw *another* sea monster, walked through another man's memories, and am currently still existing underneath the waves…consider me primed to believe the impossible." There are not enough fingers on both my hands for all the oddities.

"Laid out like that, it seems all the more improbable for you to believe me."

I shake my head. "Not for me. I spent my whole life looking for adventure. Granted, I went searching in all the wrong places…" I quickly recover before I can go too far down that line of thought. "But I've spent years learning all I could, pushing the borders of maps. What greater adventure is there than old gods and sirens?"

He holds my gaze. It's unlike any other time he's looked at me. This is steady. Almost warm. Perhaps a glimmer of understanding and appreciation. Just when it's at the point of awkward, he looks away and motions to the chest.

"Well then, now that all that's out of the way, what should we put in here?"

"Excuse me?"

"To pay your family's debt. I told you I would help you. Take what you need."

I'm slow to move, a bit uneasy about picking through his "treasures." Unfortunately, there's not much for me to select. I resist pointing out all the relative garbage in this room. I don't want to insult him when he's doing something to help me and my family and, more so, because he seems to have a genuine interest in humans. Why else would he collect all this and call it treasure? Insulting someone for not knowing when they have an earnest curiosity and will to learn is the lowest of low.

"Let's see…" The items I put into the chest need to be things I would realistically have, something that people won't question my family for possessing. The last thing I want is for people to accuse them of stealing.

The items will also need to be things that my family will be able to extract immediate value from. Pieces of art, navigational tools, and other relics might have immense value, but Mother would have to search far and wide for the right buyer. That kind of wasted time isn't something I should risk.

They might have a year in theory, but for all I know Charles is going to go to the council right after word reaches him that my ship went down. He could appeal for an immediate payment. I wouldn't be there to fight him. Emily could file on my family's behalf. She knows the system but… I fight a wince. This shouldn't be my sister's battle or responsibility.

A glint of gold catches my eye, jarring me from my spiral of self-deprecating thoughts. It's such a small thing that it's a wonder I saw it at all. Perhaps because this item is set to the side. It's on a shelf alone, resting in a half-opened clamshell.

I swim over, hovering before it. This room is like a cemetery of memories. Things I tried to keep buried, all rising to the surface.

My fingers close around my wedding band. It's undeniably mine. I know every last scuff. Down to initials I no longer use etched on the inside that marks it to me.

"Are you all right?" Ilryth swims over. I can only imagine what expression I must've been wearing from the first moment I saw it.

"I'm fine." I shake my head and return the band to the clamshell. The ring doesn't matter. Unimportant. *Forget about it, Victoria.*

"But I can see you're not."

"I said I'm fine."

"It's clearly something," he insists. "It slipped off that night and—"

"There's no need to discuss it," I interrupt him curtly.

"Are you always like this?" He scowls slightly.

"Are you?" I thrust my chin out at him, matching the expression.

Ilryth won't relent. He's encroaching on my space. "If you'd like it back, all you have to do is ask."

My face twists with disgust. "I most certainly would not."

"Ah, then it's not what I thought it was." He chuckles. He almost sounds relieved.

"What did you think it was?" I should let the topic drop. Damn my curiosity and slippery thoughts.

"Why don't you tell me why just seeing it seemed to upset you so?" he asks, rather than answering my question.

"You aren't owed any insight into the workings of my heart," I fire back. If he isn't answering then neither am I.

"Ah, so it *is* a matter of the heart." He folds his arms and leans back slightly, as though he's looking down on me. That expression reminds me of every cruel jeer, every side-eye and whisper of "oath breaker" I endured in Dennow. Instinct renders my face passive. "I should have known a man was likely involved."

"Excuse me?" I arch my brows, intentionally making my expression muted. *Don't show that you care. Don't let them know their words hurt.*

"You said you owed a debt to protect your family and I assumed it was your parents, or siblings, perhaps."

"That is exactly what I—" I can hardly get a word in.

"But now I see clearly that you have a lover you wish to get back to. It makes sense, such a lovely ring and all." Fascinating that the idea of an ex-lover doesn't seem to cross his mind at all.

I twist slightly. I'm not sure how I don't sink to the ocean floor with how heavy my entire body feels. I am pulled down, weighted. And yet I still am suspended—in the same stasis I've been for years. I want to put Ilryth in his place. To tell him how this is all his fault because there was one bond his magic did not undo.

But doing so would require me to explain myself to him. To explain Charles and those raw complexities I don't think I could handle baring before him. So I resort to the same cool indifference I worked to maintain around my family and crew; that way they never had to see how deep my hurt was. How long the scars run.

I smirk slightly, almost mischievously. Ilryth's eyes narrow slightly, as if he can't see so clearly anymore. "So what if there is a lover? What does it matter to you?"

"It would just be another tether to this world to unravel. The less you have holding you back, the better," he says curtly. "Love just makes things unnecessarily complicated."

"I couldn't agree more," I say, my sincerity surprising even me.

"Then, you don't have a lover?"

"Not even a man I'm remotely interested in," I say with all the confidence in the world. For good measure, I gesture to the ring, "This is nothing more to me than a worthless trinket." Then, I decide to turn the question back on him. "And you?"

Ilryth bristles. "That's hardly your business."

"It's not fun when someone puts their nose where it doesn't belong, is it?" Hopefully this puts an end to discussions on matters of the heart.

He purses his lips, knowing I'm right. Yet, he makes an excuse anyway. "You are the offering. I must know about the ties that bind you."

"Well, now you know, and you should leave it at that." My tone is laced with wariness. I level my eyes with his, holding his gaze with determination. Allowing my expression to caution that this is not a topic for him to pry further into.

Ilryth's expression shifts; apparently he's seeing me in a new light. "Good." There's a hint of resignation in his tone that feels like victory in my mind. "Well then…take what you need and let's be done with it."

"That's the problem." I ignore how thick the water has become with the discomfort of Ilryth's presence and thoughts of Charles. I'm so close to securing my family's safety. I won't let anything stop me now. "There is nothing in here even *close* to covering what I owe."

"But—"

"I know these are your treasures," I say gently. "But I owe…a *lot* of crons. Even if we took down every one of your strands, it wouldn't even make a dent."

"What would we need? What do your people value so much that could pay the debt?"

I sigh and run a hand through my hair. It miraculously doesn't knot under the waves. "There are only a few things that are worth as much as twenty thousand crons…diamonds, rare and precious metals—" I stop short.

"You have an idea."

"I do…but I don't think either of us are going to like it very much." I slowly turn to face him. He's waiting. Well, let's see just how far I can push this siren's good will. "I know where a whole ship worth of silver is—one of the most precious commodities we have—and it's all just waiting for the taking. Easily triple the amount I owe."

"Where?" He's piecing it together as he asks. A frown crosses his lips.

"The bottom of the Gray Passage."

eleven

"IF THIS IS SOME PLOY TO ESCAPE—" HE STARTS.

"Firstly, didn't you say I *couldn't* escape since I was already anointed with the words of the old ones, in the Eversea, and all that?" I interrupt, moving my hands through the water to encompass all the warnings he's previously given me.

"Yes, which is what I was about to remind you of," he backtracks slightly.

"Secondly," I continue as if he said nothing, "you know what I need to 'sever my ties' and this is the only way to get it. *One* of the silver bars we were carrying is worth a thousand crons. All twenty—and then some—could fit in there." I gesture to the chest with a palm. "This is the best plan we have."

"You would go back to the wreckage of your own ship?" His expression is torn between horrified and impressed. Accurate.

"If there was another way, I'd suggest it." I keep my emotions guarded, along with all the thoughts I want to keep private. "Sometimes, the only path is into the storm."

Ilryth curses softly in the back of his mind and puts his hands on his hips. "This is foolish. It's too risky for us to go into the Gray Trench, cross the Fade, and linger in the Gray Passage. I should never have agreed to indulge this."

"But you did, and now you have to see it through."

"Do I?" He arches his brows, whirling in the water to face me again. To loom over me. I sigh dramatically enough for him to notice that his posturing has no effect and tilt my head slightly, conveying that I'm not backing down.

"You gave me your word that—" I start.

"And you gave me your word that in five years you would be mine."

"Well, who came early?" I arch my brows. "All of this could've been avoided if you'd let me get through the Gray Passage."

"I went because if I didn't, you would be turned into chum by one of Lord Krokan's emissaries and then all of the Eversea would be damned for it," he growls, leaning in. I still don't back away. Our noses are almost touching. "Moreover, I never specified it'd be five years to the day."

"You also never specified otherwise," I counter.

He opens his mouth to say something. Abandons it. And then starts again. "Have you ever had a day in your life where you haven't been unrelenting?"

"No." At least not since I began life anew as Victoria. And I'm proud of it.

A low rumble crosses my mind as he eases away. I didn't realize just how tight my chest was with him being so close. The tension between my shoulder blades eases some.

He swims over to the opposite corner of the room, rummaging around. I can almost hear him muttering to himself, and I close the gap he put between us. As if that'd somehow enable me to hear him better. Of course, it doesn't, since the words are entirely in our heads.

"Yes. Here—" He lifts a large slab of wood that looks almost like a cutting board until he sets it on a barrel. A map I instantly recognize from sailing its waters countless times has been carved onto its warped and waterlogged surface. "This is your Gray Passage." He points to a rocky stretch along an arc of land by northern mountains. "About here is the Fade." He gestures on the edge of the map with the side of his palm. It's the sea to the east of the Gray Passage, where none could sail and return from.

"Which means, this is Midscape?" I reach over and point on the other side of his hand.

He nods. "And right about where you're pointing is what we call the Gray Trench. It is a deep ravine that leads from Lord Krokan's Abyss."

"I was wondering if it was connected, given the names…"

"We were once one world, after all." Ilryth shifts his hands, pointing now on the other side of my palm representing the Gray Trench. "And here is where we are, right now."

"The Gray Trench is what's on the other side of the reef." My growing suspicions are finally confirmed. Ilryth nods again. "And where the wraiths, monsters, and rot come from."

"Exactly. It stretches all the way…" He drags a finger over mine, pointing at nothing but water far to the northeast. "To Lord Krokan's Abyss."

The perpetual storms. The ghost stories. The ships going down. It all has an explanation. "The Gray Passage is connected right to your old god of death."

"Yes." Ilryth relaxes his hand and I can't help but notice how it brushes mine again when he does. "The Gray Passage is on the other side of the Fade, where siren magic is weaker, so it's too risky for my warriors to patrol. Beside, most wraiths who cross the Fade don't last more than a day or two in the Natural World, at least not without possessing a host."

"Like the ones that attacked me," I say. Charles's lighthouse is at the end of the Gray Passage that's closest to Dennow.

"Yes." He doesn't meet my eyes. His expression is soft. Haunted. "They were my men. I'd led them on a reckless mission; it was my fault that happened to them. I was chasing after them to give them a clean death."

"If the wraiths move from the Abyss up through the passage, then it is likely we'll be attacked on our journey," I reason. He nods. "Why not avoid the passage altogether, then? Use the same magic you used to bring me back quickly when Krokan's monster attacked?"

"That was something special, I can't do it again. And, traveler's pools? I told you, they're restricted to prevent the spread of the rot. I might be able to use them once, undetected. But it's better to save that for bringing the silver to your family."

"Fighting it is then." I raise my hand to my mouth, biting on the cuticles. "There's a way through the Fade at the end of the passage?"

He nods. "It was how I followed my men on the night we met. I saw how the wraiths made it through."

"Good. Then you can do it again."

"I did it *one time*. When I was younger and far more foolish." There's a bitter note to his voice. It has the same tone as the self-loathing he admonished himself with in the memory. I can't stop the slight ache between my ribs. I know that endless cycle of self-deprecation. When every little thing somehow serves to remind you of your failures and shortcomings, yet also inspires you in equal measure to fight to prove that terrible inner voice wrong.

"Well, thank you for being so foolish," I say softly. Reluctantly. "Otherwise I would've died that night." Have I ever thanked him for what he's done for me? I can't recall. Even if it didn't work out how I might have hoped…I had five years of life that I wouldn't have, without him.

Maybe I haven't. Because, at my gratitude, his face turns in my direction. His lips are parted with the slightest bit of surprise. It feels like there's so much there that he's not saying. For the first time, I wish he was as clumsy with his thoughts as me. That I could have a glimpse within his mind.

Keeping his eyes locked with mine, Ilryth shifts, gliding through the water to perch on the edge of the map. He leans over. I still, and the world seems to hold its breath a moment. "The only way for us to get to the Gray Passage and to where your ship is will be to go through the Gray Trench here in Midscape. It's perilous, risky, and—I can't believe I'm even saying this—if we're going to do this then I need to be more confident you will be protected."

"I'm useful in a scrap. I've ended more than my fair share of bar fights, even fended off pirates."

"Above water and against mortal men, I've little doubt you can hold your own." His confidence in my abilities surprises me. "But how do you fare beneath the waves against wayward spirits?" He arches his brows. I give a small shrug, pride not allowing me to outright admit he's probably right. "We will teach you, though."

"Teach me, how?"

"You'll learn more of siren magic, and the words of the old ones."

Learning these words sounds a lot like he's getting what he wants… "This isn't some trick where you're going to back out of helping me once I know the words, is it?"

His fingers settle under my chin and the scowl my face was working into relaxes away. He's as ethereal as always, a fitting acolyte for the god of death. So gorgeous it hurts. Seductive enough with a glance to have a woman throwing herself overboard for his arms. *Don't trust a pretty face, Victoria, you know how that ends.* "I shouldn't have to trick you. You already agreed."

I nod, his fingertips continuing to press into my chin. I fight a shiver when I say, "All right. Let's begin, then. The sooner the better."

"Follow me." He pushes off the map and swims into one of the four tunnels connected to the treasure room. I do as he says.

The tunnel pitches downward. Coral becomes carved stone. Intricate lines are etched into the rock, similar to the whale bone cage I was previously kept in.

We emerge into a landscape of deep blue, richer than the purest indigo dyes Mother could ever procure. Sunlight dances through beams of wood that crisscross the opening above, more carvings upon them, and across the surface of steps carved down in a semi-circle to a half-moon platform at the bottom. It's an amphitheater, I realize.

"We'll practice here," he announces, heading to the lowest point. I continue to follow. "Now, let's begin—"

I hold up a hand, halting him. "Wait, I have questions."

"*More?*" His tone is exasperated, but a slight smirk curls just the very corner of his lips. As if he's fighting amusement.

"I am trying to grasp a whole world beyond my own. A magical one at that." I sink down onto the lowest step. "While I've gathered bits and pieces, I feel like I'm still missing the whole picture, which it would be nice to have. Plus I think it would help me understand the magic better."

"You seem fairly sharp; I'd be surprised if you didn't have the sense of it all." He folds his arms. The smirk spreads wider.

"Flattery will get you nowhere."

"And here I was hoping to soften up your crusty exterior."

"Sorry, 'Crusty' is my middle name."

He snorts. "Victoria Crusty…"

"Datch," I finish. "My family name is Datch."

"Victoria Crusty Datch."

There's something about hearing my name—even with the "crusty" and not Charles's—that brings a slight smile across my lips. "Now, indulge me. Start from the beginning and explain everything to me like I know nothing."

"If you wish." His expression turns serious. "Roughly fifty years ago, Lord Krokan began to revolt. Our seas became dangerous. From an increase in storms and deadly currents, blight in our crops and lands, his leviathan emissaries turning hostile, an increase in wraiths indicating souls are not able to cross the Veil as they once were, to the rot…every year was harder than the last."

This aligns with the history I know from my world. In all my research, the earliest stories of siren attacks were from about fifty years ago. And if those attacks were caused more by wraiths than the sirens themselves, it all lines up.

"We tried many things to appease Lord Krokan and, when we could not, we began to carve pieces of the Lifetree to protect ourselves. Using Lady Lellia's magic was the only way that we knew to shield the living from the plague of the dead. But it wasn't enough.

"Our previous Duke of Faith, Duke Renfal, spent many years in quiet meditation on the hymns of the old ones. His studies bore fruit, and he was finally able to commune with Lord Krokan."

I recognize the duke's name from Ilryth's memories. But I refrain from pointing it out. "And what did Duke Renfal learn?" I ask, though I suspect it has something to do with the sacrifices.

"The duke received a message from Lord Krokan. The old god wanted women who had a zeal for life to be sacrificed to him and his Abyss on the summer solstice roughly every five years." His words are void of emotion, as though he has practiced many times over saying them without betraying his thoughts. But, in so doing, he strikes me as deeply uncomfortable. Even with his trained presentation, his eyes lose some of their focus and he peers right through me. The small muscles of his jaw tense.

His mother in the memory ties to all this, somehow. From what I've gathered, the wraiths draw out the worst in individuals—their most horrific memories—to feed on their souls. Out of all the memories that Ilryth might have suffered from, it was *that* one.

There's more to the story… I have my suspicions, but I don't probe. There are questions about my own past that I don't want him to ask. We don't need to know too much about each other to work together. This can be as professional as the rest of my business dealings.

"But the sacrifices clearly haven't been working," I say.

"No."

"Why?"

Ilryth shakes his head. "No one knows."

"Nothing more from Duke Renfal?"

"The only other thing we learned from him was that the anointing must take place before any could be sacrificed to Lord Krokan. Merely communing with the old god destroyed his mind and then took his life. No sacrifice would survive the Abyss long enough to even stand before Lord Krokan. The anointing clears the mind and purifies the soul, creating a worthy offering that can exist before an old god."

When I'm not thinking about it relative to myself being the sacrifice, it's fascinating. Horrifying. But also fascinating.

I shift, leaning back slightly on my hand. "And then, you wanted me because none of these other sacrifices were working?"

"Yes. Though it could've been any human. *You* were purely by chance."

"You really know how to make a lady feel special," I say dryly.

He chuckles. But his tone turns serious once more. "When I became the Duke of Spears, I gained access to the songs of Duke Renfal. There was a line of the song he'd sung recounting his time communing with Lord Krokan about 'hands of Lellia.' Most sirens took it to mean that Lord Krokan wanted those touched by life—still living sacrifices. Others assumed that it was that he wanted blank vessels to mirror his wife."

"His…wife?"

"Lady Lellia, Goddess of Life, is wedded to Lord Krokan, God of Death. Together, they complete the circle and maintain the balance."

"The giant sea monster is the husband of a…tree?" I blink as if somehow that could help it all make sense. It does not.

"They are literal old gods, Victoria." He grins slightly, as if the question and all its unspoken implications and wonderings had crossed his mind before, too. "Besides, Lady Lellia is *inside* the tree. Not the tree itself."

"Right…" Something he said earlier strikes me—about how humans were crafted by the dryads but guided by Lady Lellia. "You think what Lord Krokan wanted was a human, and not a siren. That's what the 'hands' bit meant. That's why the other sacrifices didn't work."

His expression is almost proud that I've pieced together his logic from everything he's told me. "When I saw you in the water that night right after... Well, it was too good of an opportunity to pass up."

Right after the last sacrifice, I realize, if one is owed every five years. Meaning, the last one was a failure, too. His mother? Likely. But I don't pry and instead focus on keeping the thoughts from escaping.

"That's why you gave me five years," I reason aloud. He nods. It wasn't kindness, it was pragmatism. He had no use for me until now. He probably couldn't even anoint me with the magic needed to keep me under the waves of the Eversea without me dying. "There I was, in a position to agree to anything since death was my only other option. You had a willing participant. Someone who agreed to sever their connection from the world and be sacrificed."

Another nod and then Ilryth levels his eyes with mine. "Five years ago, I swore to myself and to my people that I would find an end to the blight of our seas, brought on by Lord Krokan's wrath. That no siren would ever have to sacrifice themselves ever again."

To my human mind, it sounds callous and cruel. He would sacrifice humans to spare his people. But can I blame him? It's no different than what the Council of Tenvrath would do if the roles were reversed.

Moreover, that's not really what he's saying...

"No *person* will ever have to sacrifice themselves again." I push off the step, floating up. Hovering just before him. Even though Ilryth is much taller than me from top of head to tip of tail, one of the magical things about being underwater is being able to look him in the eyes. "If I do this, if I can be a 'worthy' sacrifice and quell Krokan's rage, then no human or siren would ever have to be killed again?"

"Yes, if you're able."

If I'm able... Have any words been more of an invitation than that? There is nothing like a challenge that will prompt me to action.

"I've overcome more fearsome challenges than an angry old god." Charles is at the forefront of my mind.

"I hope your confidence isn't misplaced."

"It won't be." Perhaps there is one last thing for me to do while I walk this earth. One last good I can do in a life that's been full of punishments for good intentions. "Now, teach me how to use this power."

twelve

"Sirens wield magic through our songs, for song is the language of the soul. There are common anthems—ones which we all know. Personal ones sung in the tongue unique to our bones." He reaches forward, as if about to touch me, but refrains. His fingers ghost over my skin. The sensation of the water moving between us is like a caress and I am momentarily captivated. "Then there are the hymns of the old ones, passed down in our people for thousands of years. They are words of great power, but whose meaning has long been lost to time, not meant for mortal comprehension."

Ilryth's other hand lifts, and his fingers trail over the newer markings he made. An urge to inhale, to stretch my chest and push my skin into that touch, nearly overtakes me.

"We'll start with one of my songs. That will be easier for you to get a feel for how to draw out power through song before we focus on the hymns of the old ones."

Magic. I'm going to learn magic. The idea is twice as thrilling as it is improbable. This feels like the grand adventure I was waiting all my life for. Searching for across the seas. How many humans have the opportunity to wield power like this? Probably none. As macabre as it is, what is a more epic beginning to an adventure than dying?

"For now, merely repeat after me." The water around Ilryth begins to pulse as he emits a low note. It fills up the space, resonating off every surface. The water shivers at the sweet sound.

His voice was my lullaby for years. How he haunted me with the constant reminder of my impending demise. I never properly enjoyed it as a result.

Never once did I fall asleep in awe of how lovely his voice was. Never once did I think of how wonderfully he drew the notes from the depths of his chest. How they complemented the high falsetto he sang from the top of his throat. For nearly five years, a siren sang me to sleep almost every night, and I have only just now appreciated the sound that would make sailors leap to their deaths for want of merely hearing it a bit better.

His voice—his song—it feels as if my very soul aches for it. Simple notes fill me to the brim, leaving no room for thoughts, for pain or doubt. As if...all the secrets of the world were hidden within those sounds, waiting for me to uncover them. Inviting me to stay in its melodic embrace.

Without warning, he stops. I don't remember closing my eyes, but I did. Ilryth stares at me expectantly.

It's my turn.

Taking a deep breath, I try to match his previous tone and volume, but there's something about *singing* with my thoughts that's harder than speaking them. Song is a more mechanical thing. Felt, rather than thought. It was easier in the dreamscape of his memory where I perceived myself on land. Here, I can't even make a note.

"Relax, Victoria. *Feel* it. Don't think it."

"Don't I have to think to make sound?" I counter, a bit playfully. He huffs and rolls his eyes.

The coy smile slips from my face as I close my eyes once more. I try and retreat to that place he just created for me with his music, to force the muscles in my body to relax. The notes are somewhere within me, I know it, waiting to be freed. If I can just force them from me... But I remain frustratingly silent. I can hear the song in the back of my mind louder than ever, as if it's screaming to break free. But it can't—won't escape.

A soft caress down my forearms has me jolting. My eyes snap open. His fingertips trail down the markings he has painted upon me to my hands, this time actually touching me, hooking my fingers.

Ilryth begins to sway, like the ebb and flow of the tides, and I find myself instinctively moving along with him. We move in perfect synchronicity to the music that only we can hear. A hazy sensation akin to drunkenness settles on me. Yet, though my senses are dulled, my awareness is heightened.

The melody in the back of my mind changes. No longer is it just one singer. There are soaring harmonies of joy, two voices tangling together. Whispers of passion and forbidden secrets. Low, aching pain. A lifetime untold. Unshared.

The song of *my* soul. Every corner of my body vibrates. It's a delicious tingling, one that feels like invisible fingers racing up my thighs. I can't stop myself from savoring it. Something so wholly different than anything I've ever felt before. Something that feels unnatural—that I should fear. And yet…almost decadent.

My fingers close around his. I should stop this, but I don't want to. It feels like the dozens of hands of men who stared at me with lustful eyes over the past few years—men I refused out of obligation to my oaths—coming back to touch with wet, warm fingers now that those vows are severed. It is every forbidden urge being set free. The satisfaction of every lewd act I could've ever fantasized over rippling through my body, alighting pleasure without the stigma of shame.

I shudder. I'm losing control—losing the one thing I've tried so desperately to have. These primal instincts beg surrender. Yet, I hold myself back. *Don't give in*, a scared voice whispers in the back of my mind. The last time I gave in to such urges, I ended up on an island alone.

The song reaches a sudden stop.

"Don't fight it," Ilryth says quickly, twisting me without warning. He yanks me to him, my back to his front. His bare skin against my shoulders and upper back has a yelp racing up my throat. It has no escape into the water and I gulp soundlessly. The action reminds me that we are deep beneath the waves, in a world of magic—that *I* am magic.

"Ilryth," I murmur, at war with myself. Numbed and yet so alive by the song that has consumed me.

"Sing for me, Victoria." His nose brushes my temple, as though he is actually whispering in my ear.

My lips part. But it is not a gasp, or a sigh, that escapes, but a clumsy and sharp note. Brief and fleeting. A pathetic attempt compared to his song and what I was feeling within me.

A low chuckle rumbles across the back of my mind. His grip slackens. The failure breaks whatever trance we were under.

"What do you think you're doing?" I ask, but don't pull away. My chest heaves, breathless. As if I just sailed the Gray Passage. My body is more sensitive than it has ever been in my life.

"I am getting you out of your head." He continues running his fingertips up and down my forearms. I bite my lip and try to force my mind to be blank. I shudder to think of what he might hear if I lose control of my thoughts.

"I thought you weren't supposed to touch the offering?" Yet I'm not pushing him away. I'm not telling him to stop.

"The most important thing is that you learn the songs. We'll focus on severing your connection after." His tone is nonchalant. Typical noble thinking the rules don't apply to him. "Besides, there's no one here to know—to report my transgressions. Unless you will?"

I swallow thickly and shake my head.

"Good." One word vibrates in my very core. "Now, sing. *Feel* the song. Don't think it. Don't force or command it. Let it flow as an extension of you."

"How? I don't really know what to sing."

"You sang in my dream without knowing what to sing," he points out.

"That was different," I counter.

"How?"

"I had a mission, at the least. I need direction. A headwind." The destination I'm pushing toward. The goal.

"Song isn't about the end point. It isn't about having sung. It's about the act itself."

"But one must prepare and plan for what they will sing." Even I must admit, it's a new level of stubborn to argue with a siren over singing.

"If you're so worried about what will be, you'll lose what you already have in a moment." His hands settle on my abdomen, over my corset. "Has there ever been a time in your life where you just…let go? Where you lost yourself?"

My eyes flutter closed once more. The sensation of his body is distant as my mind retreats to my past. There were times I let go...of everything. Of my future. Of myself...

I can still smell the water on Charles's skin as we swam naked in the creek in the woods not far from my house. He had only been in town for a week...stopping in because the wheel on his cart had broken.

I can taste how sweet his words were on my tongue on our wedding night. All his promises of love and respect. Of partnership.

The whirlwind I was swept into when I let myself go—just acted on instinct. It blew me off course, farther than I could ever recover.

What my life might have been if I'd just stayed on the path. Yet, my heart could never resist the call of adventure. My soul is divided between everything I want and everything I know I should pursue.

"The times I lost myself, I was just that, *lost*. Those times are not exactly memories I savor. It's not a place I want to go back to. Physically or mentally." I can't stand the shame lurking behind my eyelids for a second longer. But I'm not sure I said anything until he shifts. The water is cold on my back where he just was.

Ilryth releases me. His brow is furrowed with what looks like genuine concern. I don't know if I can trust it—trust *him*.

"What?" I say when I can no longer take his assessment.

"You're shaking."

"I—" I stop short. I am. "I don't know why," I say softly.

He frowns and almost reaches out to touch my face, but abandons the motion halfway, for some reason. He's already touched me more than I would've ever expected.

"There is something more I should tell you about anointing..."

"Something *more*?" I give him an incredulous look, trying for playful.

His expression grows even more serious in response. "I was holding it back because I thought it might frighten you."

"Frighten me more than being sacrificed to a god? You have an odd scale of terror."

It's Ilryth's turn to look away, to get lost in memories far deeper and more tumultuous than the one I saw on the beach. But because I saw that memory...I can suspect what might be haunting him as we discuss this process.

"The anointing has two elements, both to a singular end. The first is to mark you with the hymns of the old ones—so that you are granted passage to the Abyss and Krokan knows you are for him."

I still hate the idea of being "marked" for any man or creature. But I just say, "All right."

"The other is to sever your ties with this world. Leveraging the magic of the old ones—what little we still remember from our ancestors—takes a toll on the mind and body. Duke Renfal is the perfect example. You will not be able to stand before Lord Krokan with a mortal mind as you have now."

"Yes, I understand this in principle. But I'm guessing there's something more that you have yet to share?"

"I will see that the hymns are written across your body." He motions to the markings on my skin, a single finger dragging against my collarbone. "But placing them on your soul is something only you can do through singing them yourself. And every word you sing will come at a cost. You will have to make space for this new power. And when you—"

"Enough. Say it plainly," I demand. Firm. But not harsh. I know when a man is stalling.

"Every word of the hymns of the old ones that you learn will eat away at your mind—at your memories. And you must let it happen. Otherwise you will go mad from trying to keep too much mortality in your mind alongside the power of the gods."

Plainly is still complicated, it'd seem. But he said it straightforwardly enough at least. I take a moment and allow this information to sink in. "Do you do this when you sing? Do all sirens?"

"Our personal songs require no such cost. We're drawing from our own magic, not trying to connect with an old god to summon theirs."

"I see…" I hold out my forearms, lightly trailing my fingers over the markings. I always wondered how the siren's magic works, and now I know. Small spells come from innate magic within them. But greater acts come with a price. "And this is what I must master for us to go to the Gray Passage?"

"The stronger you are with the blessings of the old ones, the more confident I will be that the wraiths and Lord Krokan's emissaries will allow you passage. Or, should they put up a fight, that you will be able to defend yourself," he says. I notice there's no comment about his own safety.

"Then let's focus on the words of the old ones instead." I meet his eyes again so he can see my resolve. "No more of the other songs." *And no more touching*... Yet, I can't bring myself to say it.

"We can continue trying to learn the simpler songs until—"

"My family has no time," I object. "Will I get to choose the memories I lose, at least?"

He dips his chin slightly. "I have been led to believe so."

"Exceptional, then. Let's not waste time with the simpler things. I'm more an all or nothing kind of woman, anyway." I know he can hear my conviction, but Ilryth doesn't make any motion. It seems it's his turn to take a moment.

His face finally dissolves into a disbelieving smile. Though I can't tell what it's toward when he shakes his head and looks away. "I thought you might say as much."

"Care to share your private amusement?"

"Just that you too are someone who has things you'd prefer to forget." He glances at me from the corners of his eyes.

I shrug, trying to seem more casual than I feel. Had he heard my thoughts of Charles? If he did, he's a good enough man not to say anything about them. "Who doesn't? Now. Let's try again. For real, this time."

"I won't be able to say complete words for you, otherwise I risk my own mind. However, I can say pieces until you can learn how to read the markings on your own." Ilryth takes my hand, holding my arm between us. He points at the markings on my forearm. "*Kul*."

"*Kul*," I repeat.

His finger moves up another line, stopping on a dot, as he says, "*Ta'ra*."

"*Kulta'ra*." The word is hard to say. As if I'm holding a dozen marbles in my mouth. I try to shape it, but fight to.

"Remember, Victoria, don't fight. Give in," he says gently. All my life I've fought. I've struggled. I've pushed forward. But perhaps to move ahead I must release it all. "I will sing underneath you, to prevent the hymns of the ancients from sinking into my mind. You may sing with me, or above me."

"All right." I nod.

He closes his eyes and begins to hum.

"*Kulta'ra*," I whisper. "*Kulta'ra.*" Again. This time there's a shiver working its way up my spine. I can feel the tingling. But there's no release. No tremble to rush across my skin and alleviate the tension. It just hangs there between every vertebra.

"*Kulta'ra.*" I pull my hand from his as I say it again. Ilryth releases me, but I hardly realize he's there anymore. The fingers of my right hand brush over the markings. "*Kulta'ra...*"

The more I say the word, the more melodic it becomes. Easier on the mouth but, just as he warned, it's harder on the mind. Pain is budding at the base of my skull.

"*Kulta'ra.*" That time was almost like singing. I tilt my head back and sigh, "*Kulta'ra.*" The notes start low, then high, then low again. I repeat it, changing the intonation. High, then low. All low. Again, and again.

As I sing, images flash before my mind. My life is like a violent thunderstorm across a night sea. The visions spin before me and I pick one as if I could reach out and pluck it from the rest.

It's that memory of the creek. The first time Charles told me I was beautiful. The first time he kissed me.

"*Kulta'ra.*" With a word like a sigh, that singular moment in my history slips through my fingers, gone forever.

I open my eyes, blinking down at the markings on my forearm. The markings Ilryth had pointed to have shifted. Gold now lines the magenta in new shapes.

"Well done," he appraises, his own song ending.

"Let's do another," I say.

"I think that's enough for one day."

"There is no time," I remind him forcefully. "Another."

Ilryth merely stares, long enough that I worry I've somehow offended him. Finally, he says, "You are a truly fearsome but impressive creature."

I throw him a look that's somewhere between forced smugness, and all my hard-won confidence. "I know."

We begin to sing again.

Hours later, he brings me to my new room. A lovely place of carved coral walls, perched higher up on the far back of the manor, with a balcony that overlooks the distant trench. Ilryth leaves me, his expression as guarded as I have ever seen it. But I am too exhausted to try to parse out what it is that's bothering him this time.

So far as I can tell, I was *exceptional*.

I mastered three words. Which means…I gave up three memories?

As I lay atop a bed of sea foam, I wonder what memories I gave up. I slowly replay my life, from the earliest details I can recall—or, I think I can recall—in order to this moment. My thoughts snag around eighteen years.

There's a blank void shortly after the first time I met Charles in the market, but before him asking for my hand. What was there? Something…surely. Something to do with *him*.

A wicked smile crosses my lips. He thought he had marked my soul. But I unraveled his hold on me legally. And now, I will eradicate all memory of him.

My life's only regret might be Charles not knowing just how easily I could expunge him.

thirteen

THE NEXT MORNING, LUCIA COMES TO ME AT DAWN. She sings, moving her hands over my body, unlike Ilryth, she's diligent to never quite touch my flesh. Markings appear with her songs in deep red strokes. Though, my body doesn't flush in quite the same way as when Ilryth last marked me.

The thought of him has me searching for a topic to distract myself.

"Do the colors mean anything?" I ask as I hover, waiting for the next series of markings.

Lucia is behind me; based on the tiny currents, her fingers are somewhere between my right shoulder and spine. As the song-turned-color seeps into my flesh and begins to writhe, it almost feels like she's lightly scratching with her nails.

"They do. Red is for strength. Blue for luck. Black for truth. Green for vitality. Magenta for promise. Yellow for prosperity…"

She lists off other colors, most of which I've yet to have upon my flesh.

"It sounds like I will be quite the masterpiece when I'm done."

Lucia laughs lightly. A melodic and easy sound. "Yes, indeed."

"And the gold?" I point to the area that changed with my song yesterday.

"That means the anointing has imprinted on your soul. You are truly becoming one with the old ones so that you might stand before them without giving in to madness." She pulls her hand away. Today was a shorter anointing than previous. Not that I'm complaining.

Fenny appears at my balcony. "Come. Lord Ilryth has asked for you in the amphitheater."

"Of course."

"Take care, Your Holiness." Lucia bows her head.

"Just Victoria is fine," I remind her. Lucia merely smiles. I don't know if I'm going to have her giving up on the honorifics any time soon.

I follow behind Fenny. At first, I think it is the dawn that is clouding the seas. But then I realize it's that faint, reddish haze I've seen since I first arrived. *It must be the rot.*

"That, in the distance?" Fenny asks.

I bite back a sigh that the thought slipped out. "Yes."

"It is. Duke Ilryth helps keep it out of our lands with the grace of Dawnpoint. But some rot will inevitably seep in, especially on days like today, when it seems that the currents are slow and it is not moving through the trench."

"Could it make it through the trench and up into my world?" If the wraiths and monsters have a way to slip through the Fade, why not the rot?

She pauses, but only for a second before she catches herself and continues swimming. "I do not know—matters of the old gods are more Lucia's domain—but perhaps it could. Should Lord Krokan's rage and the duchies of the Eversea fall, then I see no reason to believe it couldn't escape. We already fear the blight escaping to all of Midscape."

"And quelling Krokan's rage falls to me..."

"Should we be so blessed."

"You don't sound confident," I point out.

"A human has never been the offering. You are an unknown."

Little does she know that telling me I can't do something makes me want to do it even more. "You know...you should have said all this to begin with."

"How so?" Fenny glances over her shoulder as we swim through the ceiling and into Ilryth's treasure room.

"Because protecting my family is something I would gladly sacrifice anything for, even my life." It's the least I can do for them after all they've done for me and all they've stood by me through.

"Then I'm glad you know now." She swims for the tunnel, but I pause once more in the room, taking in all the strange baubles and reminders of home.

"Fenny."

"Yes?" She stops the second she sees I have. Her tone betrays mild impatience.

"How did Duke Ilryth acquire all this?"

"Humans are very good at cluttering their seas," she answers simply. "So I hear, at least. Since the Eversea closed, only the dukes are permitted to leave with permission, and I did not venture beyond much before."

"Ilryth scavenged all of this, then?"

"Yes."

"It must have taken him years."

"Indeed." There's a lot of weight to that one word that I don't quite understand.

"Why?" It's still difficult to imagine a duke swimming around and collecting trash. Perhaps it's resentment for us littering his seas with garbage? But if so, why would he save it all? And why would he call it his "treasure?"

"That is his fascination to explain to you. It's not my place to comment on." Fenny clasps her hands before her. I study the woman. She glances away.

"You don't understand it either, do you?"

"My focus has always been here, in the Eversea. If there is a matter His Grace can't handle, for one reason or another, I take care of it. If there is something he cannot do, I will do it. I am solely focused on and dedicated to our family and our people," she says, somewhat curt.

I don't have to, or want to, understand, is what I read between the lines. There's something more, too. *Dedicated*. Does she see him as not being fully committed to his role? Everything I've seen of Ilryth so far makes him seem far more dedicated than most leaders I've ever known. Certainly more than half of the lords of Tenvrath, sitting in their salons with cups full and ambitions thin.

"You think little of your brother, don't you?"

Fenny goes still, clearly taken aback. "You are too bold."

"Perhaps," I admit. Her offense is fair. I was pushing the boundaries with that remark. Testing the limits. Despite my prickling her, she rewards me with information anyway, just as I expected she would. Pushing someone past the point of offense usually prompts them to correct with a truth they might not have otherwise proffered.

"I think the world of my brother. He carries the weight of the duchy on his shoulders." Her eyes sweep across the room. "There are choices he makes that are different from mine. But my confusion doesn't mean I think less of him. Judgment is not my place so long as he acts with our best intentions."

A soft chuckle escapes me.

"What is amusing now?"

She must've heard. "I wonder if my little sister would've said much the same of me." *Oh, Em*...always so optimistic. Hopeful. Pushing the boundaries without overextending herself. She was the better one of us two.

Fenny continues to inspect me, then says softly, "I imagine she probably would. I imagine most siblings do. Now, we shouldn't keep His Grace waiting."

"Wait, Fenny, there's one more thing." I swim to the half-open clamshell with the wedding band upon it. Such a small thing to haunt me the way it did throughout the night. But, perhaps Ilryth is right; there are some tethers holding me to this world that will be a fight to let go of. Lifting the band from the shell, I glance at the initials I no longer bear one final time and hold it out to her. "Get rid of this, please."

"You have no right to—"

"It was mine," I admit. "I have every right to decide its fate and I want it gone."

"Why not get rid of it yourself?" The question is laced with skepticism.

An excellent question. *Why not?* Because just holding it causes my hand to tremble? Because the mere thought of it has Charles's voice relentlessly reprimanding me in the back of my mind for even thinking of getting rid of it? Haunting me. Berating me.

"I hardly have the time. My focus is on the anointing." I shrug, trying to hide my unease. "And I suspect that your brother would struggle to rid himself of it, as I doubt he readily removes anything from this room."

Fenny swims over and assesses the ring. With a glance between me and it, she plucks it from my fingers, turning it over in her hands. "What is it?"

"Something that now belongs to a dead woman, nothing more or less. So, can you get rid of it for me? Somewhere Ilryth would never look?" I would keep it on me, but I don't want to risk it. Moreover... the mere idea of holding on to that wedding band for longer than I want threatens the stability of my stomach.

"Very well." Fenny pockets it in the wrap around her breasts. "Now, if you'll come with me." She starts down the tunnel and I follow. Swimming is a little bit easier knowing that I will never have to lay eyes on that ring ever again.

Fenny leaves me at the entrance to the amphitheater. I swim the rest of the way down to the stage at the bottom, where Duke Ilryth is already waiting. He lounges on the lowest step, straightening away as I near.

"I've realized something," I say.

"And what is that?"

"You lied to me." My toes land on the edge of the step above him. I seem to be in an antagonistic mood today. Or perhaps I've caught my footing enough in this strange world to be my usual, challenging self.

"Excuse me?" He arches his brows.

"You led me to believe that it was hard to cross the Fade. That you didn't cross regularly, and that when you came to claim me was one of the rare times you had done it." I fold my arms, perfectly poised. I've already grown quite accustomed to the sensations of moving in the water. "But that can't be true, can it? If it were, you wouldn't have a whole treasure trove of human items that could only be collected by moving between worlds."

His lips quirk slightly into a frown but he still says nothing. I push off the step, my body moving of its own accord, unable to take his nonchalance for a second longer. His eyes follow my movements and the water between us grows heavy.

"You know what I can't stand about men like you?"

"No. But I suspect you're about to tell me." He's goading me. But

I let him. I'll allow him to have the sense of power only because I was going to tell him anyway.

I slow to a stop before him, halting myself by prodding him in the chest with my finger. "Men like you—the ones so used to being in control—will lie without hesitation. And even when you're caught, you don't feel the slightest bit of remorse. If anything, you'll make the other person think that they were the one who misunderstood."

He grabs my hand, holding it so tightly my knuckles *almost* hurt from the compression. "Do not insult my integrity."

"No?" I tilt my head and fight a scowl. As disgusted as I feel, I won't permit him the satisfaction of causing me to lose my composure. "You mean to tell me you don't see the whole world as a collection of fools?"

"Most of the world might be fools." It's as if he's trying to burrow into my mind with his stare. To expose every weakness or insecurity I've ever had. "But there are a good few who are not. Those close to me. I didn't take you for one, for example."

Was that a compliment? "What did I tell you about flattery?"

"It's not flattery if it's true."

"You hardly know me."

"Don't I though?" His grip relaxes some.

"Then tell me the truth, now."

"I didn't lie to you. It is difficult and dangerous to cross through the Gray Trench. But I also admitted we have other methods of moving— the traveler's pools." He's still holding me in place.

"You said they were closed due to the rot." The reminder eases the edges of my anger, bringing back details of our previous conversation.

"Only recently." He frowns. "And before you look for places to make accusations where there aren't any, I brought you back using a rare boon given from the Duchy of Faith—an elixir of crushed leaves of the Lifetree, ground with the sand on the beach and mixed waters from its roots to create portable transport that returns one to the heart of the Eversea with a song. That was the only one I had and there's no way for me to get another. I'm hiding nothing from you, Victoria, and I have not lied."

I relent with a sigh, glancing away.

"Has my explanation satisfied you?" He finally releases my hand. I'd forgotten he was holding onto it yet am painfully aware of its absence.

Why does it feel so natural for him to touch me when it is proclaimed to be forbidden?

"For now."

"You're too kind." Ilryth moves for the center of the amphitheater stage, holding out his hands. I go to him with little hesitation. The sooner we do this, the sooner I will be able to save my family. Our fingers curl around each other's once more. He draws me close. The feeling of the smooth scales of his tail against my legs as we bump together sends a jolt through me. "Now, let's begin," he declares, his voice low and commanding.

I stand at the top of the lighthouse. The flame is hot at my back, beacon forever churning slowly thanks to a paddle wheel on one side of the island that's regularly bombarded with waves. The spotlight flashes across the rocks of the distant shore. It reaches out toward the impenetrable Gray Passage and promptly halts against the wall of storms that churn in the distance.

It's a dark wish to hope that a storm might break free of the passage and reach the lighthouse...but it would be something to break the monotony.

Every five minutes, the beacon illuminates the distant supply house on the far shore and the little rowboat tied up there. It's been there for three weeks now. Unmoving. As tied to its location as I am here.

Charles had said it'd be only a few days. Something important must've kept him...

I force myself awake. It's a dream I know too well. A dream that's haunted me many, many times—enough that I can recognize it even in sleep and reject it.

It's hard to tell whether it's very early or very late. The moon has gone from full when I first arrived to now being nothing more than a sliver. I push away from my bed, drifting to my balcony to see if the faint light is from the moon or a distant dawn. Is it worth it to try and go back to sleep, or should I wait to meet the sun?

Right when I cross out from underneath the coral shelf that hangs above me, a low, ominous note trembles across the earth. It's followed by a high-pitched sound. To call it singing would be generous. More like shrieking. The noise immediately puts me on guard.

Other voices join in to form a similar chorus to my first night here. How long has it been? Two weeks, based on the moon? Time has gone painfully slow and yet fast at the same time given how my every day has been filled with learning their words and songs.

I look to the trench, but see no sign of tentacles. I squint, trying to make out any shifting shadows in the inky night. Still nothing.

There are no warriors moving. No chatter of dolphins. Yet, the song continues. It rolls like a wave. Hasty and frantic before suddenly collapsing into silence. The voices seem to come from across the manor. All distant, and yet close, given how they resound in my mind.

The water is still. There isn't the slightest bit of movement to it. When the next doldrum of silence overtakes the song, it feels as if the sea itself is holding its breath.

Something is wrong.

A flash of light has my attention jerking in one direction. It's gone in a blink. Like a firefly vanishing into the dusk.

Without warning, there's movement at my side. I see it out of the corners of my eyes. A chill sweeps down my spine and my breath catches in my throat as two invisible hands encircle it from behind. I choke on nothing.

For the first time, it feels as if I can't breathe. The water is weighted in my lungs. Heavy. Pulling me down, and down, and down...

Charles is back.

I wait on the shore for him, patiently, as he ties up the boat. It's been four weeks now—a full month. The longest he has ever been gone. I'm practically bouncing with barely contained excitement at finally seeing my husband again—at seeing another person.

"My darling." I rush over to him the second he steps away from the boat, throwing my arms around his shoulders. "I've missed you so much!"

"Enough with the hysterics, wife. I've only just arrived; allow me a moment to catch my breath." He places both hands on my sides and

sets me down. Away. As if I am a toy placed back on the shelf when it is no longer amusing.

"Hysterics? I—"

"Can a man not unload his things without being assaulted?"

"I'm sorry," I say quickly. "It was a long time here...alone. And I—"

"Are you saying that you cannot even handle a month by yourself?" He pulls his satchel from the boat. "I took you for a stronger woman."

"No. I mean yes." I take the satchel that's thrusted toward me, slinging it over my shoulder. "Of course I can. I missed you is all."

"Update me on the lighthouse," he demands briskly.

Not on me. The lighthouse. But that's his priority; it's understandable...it's what keeps Tenvrath safe. Of course it'd be the focus. He'll ask about me next, I'm sure of it.

"Everything is running smoothly. No issues. The bell has been rung every thirty minutes. All the timing mechanisms have been greased and updated, checked throughout the night as you like. I even cleaned from top to bottom."

He stills. Like a viper, his hand shoots out, grabbing my face by the chin and cheeks, forcing my lips to pucker slightly with his hold. "Did you go into my study?"

"No," I say awkwardly.

His hand relaxes and a smile slips across his face. Charles leans in, kissing me lightly. "That's a good wife. Now, I hope dinner is ready."

"Yes, it's started—I mean, it'll be ready soon."

"Good. A man needs a home-cooked meal and a loving wife when he returns." Charles starts around the lighthouse.

"How was your trip?" I ask, following.

"All the questions, must you be such a nag? I am tired." He sighs, muttering under his breath.

I pretend I don't hear the words. But—

There's a flash of light.

A distant scream. Not my own. Or maybe it is? I'm left gasping, doubled over.

The water is as cold as ice. As black as pitch. I blink, thinking I've somehow been blinded. But, slowly, colors and lights fade back into existence. My ears hear a song again. It's slower, more purposeful. Led by a familiar voice that's…

Right behind me.

Ilryth's powerful form hovers, radiating otherworldly strength. In his hands, he wields a staff of pale wood that pulses a faint, silvery light. Tendrils of shadow fade in the currents around him; the water moves once more. I gaze up at him, my heart still pounding with fear and stomach churning with disgust at the images that are behind my lids every time I blink. Something in my expression causes him to ease away slightly. Slowly, as if trying not to spook me, he rests the spear against one of the pillars lining the balcony.

"What did you do?" I finally find words. But they're raspy and thin. Weak. Harrowed.

"A wraith broke through our defenses and made it into the manor," he says. An apologetic tone breaks through the severity of the statement. His intimidating presence lessens as he sinks to meet me on the floor, tail curling beneath him. Every movement is filled with a gentleness that slows my racing heart. "It sought you out and was trying to rot out your soul and steal your body."

"A…a wraith was here?" I am dazed.

"I banished it." He motions to the spear, still with slow, purposeful movements. "I was fast enough to you that there shouldn't be lasting damage on your mind, or the anointing. But not fast enough to spare you…" Ilryth balls his hand into a fist. It's the only thing that betrays his anger. "It should never have been able to lay a hand on you. Forgive me."

I dig my nails into the coral beneath me. The sensation of touch, the pressure of the water on me, grounds me in the here and now.

"Thank you for getting it when you could," I murmur. "I suppose our lessons haven't been enough. You were right…I'm not ready for the trench."

A moment of heavy silence passes between us. His lack of denial cuts deeper than I expected. I'm right, we both know it. Even after two weeks of work I'm still weak in this world. Still struggling. I press my eyes closed as if I can physically hide from the shame.

"Victoria…" My name is a whisper. With it, he gently beckons my eyes to him, holding my gaze with an intense stare. "You remember the state I was in when I returned from the trench, don't you? How hard it was to pull me back?" I nod. "This was blessedly easy. Resisting whatever torture it tried to inflict upon you is a sign of your strength. Even the wraith being drawn to you is good, in a way; it shows the magic of the gods is taking hold in you."

Ilryth moves to rest a hand on my cheek. I flinch at the sight of a man's hand reaching for my face, the memory of Charles as sharp as shattered glass. He pulls away instantly.

"Sorry," I murmur.

"You've nothing to apologize for," he says softly. "I know what it's like. To have your deepest horrors, your most closely held regrets, be drawn out with the grace of a disemboweling."

Gutted is a fitting metaphor for how I feel.

"Believe it or not, Victoria, you're making progress," he emphasizes.

"I don't feel it."

"I see it," Ilryth says firmly, enough so that I glance over at him despite still being hunched. My hair slowly drifts around my face, obscuring him now and again. Pulling him in and out of focus. "If you can't believe in yourself, believe in me."

My lips part, an objection ready on my tongue. *How dare you say I don't believe in myself.* But there's a flicker of knowing in his eyes. He has felt just as exposed as I am now. I have seen him in that state.

Perhaps that's why, when he says, "Now, I'll leave you be," my hand shoots out, grasping his before he can swim away.

"Wait!" I blurt out, desperately. "Wait," I repeat, softer. "Please...I-I don't want to be alone. Will you stay a while?" I hate feeling weak. Feeling needy. But there are a million more memories the wraith pulled to the surface that I now need to push back into obscurity, far from all conscious thought. If I'm left alone, my mind will wander to them, I know it.

Ilryth sinks back next to me, our sides flush, as if drawn together by an instinctive force. Slowly, he collects my hands in his. Our fingers intertwine and I've never been more fascinated by how my fingers move. It is surprisingly intimate.

"You're all right," he says softly. "I will not let any harm come to you."

"Until I'm sacrificed," I say with bitter laughter. Who would've thought sacrifice could be used to lighten the mood? I was expecting him to chuckle along with me. Not for his brow to furrow and his eyes to flood with conflict I've never seen from him.

"Your Holiness! Are you—" Lucia stops short, swimming up over the edge of the balcony. Her eyes fall to our locked hands. There's confusion, concern, and accusation in her look. "Your Grace, I came to attend Her Holiness and make sure none of the markings were disrupted."

"I was just finishing doing so," Ilryth lies with ease. He releases me, swimming away a little faster than normal, as if he needs to get distance between us as quickly as possible.

But Lucia stops him by swimming in his path. "You should not touch her." She could've said it only to him, but she clearly intends for me to hear. Does she think *I* was the initiator? "She needs to sever her ties to this world, not deepen them."

"She needs to keep a clear head about her," Ilryth counters. "And the wraiths can distort one's mind. I was ensuring she was all right."

"She needs to lose *all* thoughts. Those of harm *and* comfort."

"What good to us is she if she loses all the latter and is nothing but the former? She'd be rendered a wraith the moment we send her to the Abyss."

Ilryth is on my side, and that has me sitting a bit straighter. How is it that the man who intends to sacrifice me is also protecting me? And, more importantly, why does that fill me with such ease?

"She will be nothing more than an empty vessel when she is sent to the Abyss. So that she can stand before Lord Krokan as a fitting offering." Lucia moves toward me. Her expression is that of cool indifference. But there's also a touch of sorrow to her eyes. She's better at fighting the guilt than Ilryth, however. "Now, Your Holiness, if I may check your anointments?"

I push myself off the balcony, drifting up.

Ilryth leaves without another word. Without so much as glancing back at me. I stay still as Lucia moves around me. She motions for me to lift my hands, looking on both sides of my arms. Swims behind me. Prompts me to stand.

"Lucia," I say softly, when I can no longer bear the silence. At least I've enough distractions to keep my mind focused.

"Yes?"

"I will do this. I swear it to you. I know what's at stake." For my family *and* for the Eversea. The thought of sacrificing myself still sends a chill down my spine, but there's no other option. This is the path that my actions have led me down and I must follow it to its bitter end. Perhaps my resolve is a pathetic attempt to make this one, final act seem like my choice. To reclaim some power in a situation where I have precious little. But it feels like more than that. Like a calling I can't ignore.

I have a role to play in this fight. A duty. I made a promise to Ilryth that at five years, I would be his, and I swore I would only ever break one oath.

Sometimes, the simplest choices are the most powerful.

Lucia pauses, tilting her head slightly, as if seeing me from a new angle. "Oddly enough, I believe you."

fourteen

FOR ALMOST FIVE WEEKS, I SPEND EVERY DAY IN THE AMPHITHEATER. After the wraith attack, I have all the motivation I need to fully dedicate myself to Ilryth's song training.

My day begins at dawn with Lucia or Fenny arriving to escort me. It ends at dusk with Ilryth bringing me back. While I was never specifically forbidden from leaving my chambers at night, I never have. I'm either too exhausted or the sensation of the wraith wrapping its spectral hands around my throat is too sharp.

There have been a few other nights that are filled with song. But nothing so ominous or dread-filled as the two attacks I've endured. At first, the music meant nothing, but the longer I work with Ilryth, the more of an innate understanding I have.

The occasional nighttime hymns are songs of protection, I think. *Stay away*, the sirens sing with a dozen voices, each saying a different word on a different note, yet in somehow perfect harmony. *Stay away…*

Every night, I fall to sleep listening for Ilryth's voice among them. I can always find it, like a lighthouse beacon striking a distant shore. I cling to the sound, allowing it to ease over the gaps in my memories, left behind by my work. It fills and soothes the wounds that I try to keep hidden.

His voice is achingly beautiful. Toe-curling. It fills my chest and soothes the beast of my pain that paces its cage. I can't deny the pull of his voice, even when I know I should. His words, though sweet and melodic, roar within me like a storm that I am powerless to stop—that can only be chased. It is every lost moment of savoring his songs condensed into what I know will be the final days of my existence.

One morning is not like the rest.

It is not Lucia, or Fenny, that has come to collect me. But rather both. They hover over my balcony at dawn. I'm up. Usually early to wake. So I saw them from the moment they crested the far edge.

"You won't be meeting with Lord Ilryth today in the amphitheater," Fenny announces.

"No?" I arch my brows. I've made good headway on turning lines throughout my markings golden and chunks of memories into voids. Much of my skin is inked. But more still is blank—there's still much work to be done.

"No. Your attendance is requested for a small gathering of nobles in the duchy." Fenny's tone makes it clear there's to be no argument. I object anyway.

"Is that the best way to be spending my time?" I push off from the bed. "I should be learning more words and gaining more markings for my anointing."

Lucia's eyes flick toward Fenny. There's a spark of agreement in them. She's an unlikely ally. But she doesn't speak up.

"You still have nearly five months until the summer solstice, when you will be offered to Lord Krokan. But there are only a few weeks before we must surrender you to the Duchy of Faith for final preparations before the solstice. It would be improper if we didn't allow our nobles to meet you first. Moreover, as a human, you will already be scrutinized enough. It is better for you to gain some allies here first. Where people are more inclined to be on your side."

I find it interesting that Ilryth has mentioned nothing about introductions, nobles, or formalities. "I was under the impression that people didn't have a choice in me being the offering or not."

"They do not."

"Good," I say hastily, before she can get another word in. "Then I think I would much prefer to focus on my actual task instead of being paraded about."

"Do not insult our customs," Fenny says curtly. "Just because you are designated for death doesn't mean the rest of us are. Don't be so selfish as to think that your actions don't impact the rest of us."

"*Selfish*?" The word strikes at my core, ringing with anger.

"Fenny," Lucia scolds, but not nearly firmly enough. So much for an ally.

"You are marked for death and—"

"Take me to Ilryth, now," I demand, interrupting Fenny.

Fenny folds her arms and doesn't budge. Lucia looks between us, a bystander to the wordless battle of wills. I narrow my eyes.

"I did something for you, as a personal favor," Fenny says coolly. Lucia's expression turns to confusion. "Now I'm asking for you to do this for me."

Damn her. She's using the ring against me. But at least it's confirmation she did get rid of that stupid band once and for all.

"Fine," I relent. "But only this, and then we're even."

"And you will hold yourself well before our nobles." Fenny smooths a few strands of hair into the wrap that's fastened by the spiny shell. "Ilryth tells us you are quite capable, when motivated."

"I have all the motivation I need. I might even surprise you," I inform her. I might not particularly enjoy stuffy affairs, and will always take a warm ale at the Tilted Table with exceptional company over the finest wine in a crystal chalice when everyone around me is scheming and plotting. But… "I've been to my share of fancy parties with the nobility of where I come from."

"Good. But I do not think human sensibilities translate to the sirens."

"Try me," I challenge.

Over the next hour, I am given a very different, and very condensed, education on the sirens than I have received so far. Fenny teaches me of siren compliments and taboos. Of etiquette and the dance of politics and nobility. My mind swirls with new information that I am determined to remember. I will not make a fool of myself. And I will surpass Fenny's expectations of me. Anger and frustration are strong motivators.

The most surprising thing I learn is that the sirens have very different definitions of "appropriate attire" for a formal event than humans do. I imagine most people would be utterly scandalized by the options that are floated by me. At least, as a sailor, I am familiar with men and women who work in all manner of dress…and undress. The job is hard enough, might as well be comfortable while doing it.

My one insistence was that I still wear my strapped corset—much to Lucia and Fenny's mutual dismay. At first they wanted my bosom to be free, covered by some layers of chiffon that would hide nothing. Then they wanted to apply shells over the peaks of my breasts held together with strands of pearls and silver beads. A bold statement that I didn't inherently dislike. But I might as well be naked in that instance, as it wouldn't stay on for more than a second.

While I might not be too particular about modesty, I also don't want to give up my ability to be clothed, as the second I release my corset it will disappear like my shirt. I *like* my corset. It's the one perfect piece of clothing I ever had tailored and was the hardest to make. I'm not ready to part with it just yet. Especially not when I have the trench ahead of me.

Our compromise was that I would wear a necklace of their choosing, which ended up being a similar style to Lucia's, with cascading arcs of pearls and beads wrapping my shoulders, arms, and torso down to my waist.

My undershorts they also left, mostly because they didn't quite know what to do instead of them as they didn't have any other options for two human legs. Over top the shorts, from my waist to my thighs, they repurposed the fabric formerly intended for my breasts to cover my lower half and make it somewhat more "presentable" than my shorts alone.

"Here, I have one last thing for you." Fenny swims over, fishing a necklace from the satchel around her hip. It's a simple thing, corded with leather rather than glass, stone, or pearl. There's only one shell at the base of the necklace—a small conch etched with symbols that mirror the ones inked upon my skin. They've been filled with silver, giving the piece an almost mysterious glow in the shifting light under the sea. "It's something given to children when they're first learning their words and speech. It helps them focus so that only the thoughts they wish to be said escape them. I should have given it to you sooner, but it took me a bit to hunt down."

I stand, a bit stunned, as Fenny ties it around my neck above the other loops of pearls. The woman always seemed a bit brisk toward me.

I didn't expect a display of affection, however minor. But she clearly went out of her way to get this for me.

"This way you won't embarrass yourself or the duke."

Maybe I gave too much credit. Still, I say, "Thank you. I appreciate it."

"Don't let us down." Fenny drifts away, giving me one final look. "I think she's sufficient."

"Ooh, *sufficient*," I say with mock excitement. Fenny ignores the sarcastic remark.

"Do you think they will find her presentable?" Lucia asks uncertainly.

"I do." But Fenny doesn't sound entirely convinced. "Now, follow me, if you please."

I make every effort to, but they've bound my legs so tightly together that it's awkward to move. My options are bending and kicking from the knees down, or moving my whole body in a wormlike motion similar to the sirens. They, however, have no problem achieving both speed and grace swimming in this manner. Meanwhile I look and feel like a fumbling buffoon. This is going to go exceptionally; I can already tell.

Lucia slows and wraps a length of fabric previously pooled over her hips around her arm before linking it with mine. "I can help you." I suspect the words are for me alone, as Fenny doesn't glance back.

"Thank you." I focus my reply.

"You're welcome." She smiles and we swim together. It's awkward, but a little easier than trying to do it on my own.

I keep my focus on Lucia as my thoughts wander back to the night of the wraith's attack. "How is it that this touch is all right?"

She seems startled by the question and then purses her lips in thought. Shifts her grip. "There's the fabric for one. And for two, it's…"

"What?" I press.

"Different."

"How so?"

Lucia gives me a look that almost seems to say, *you should know*. But the thought doesn't entirely manifest. Instead, she forces a smile. "It's much more practical. Necessary. It's not a touch that could bind you here to this realm. And the lack of skin-to-skin contact is important."

Comforting me after I had just had nightmares forcefully played at the forefront of my mind wasn't "necessary?" I think bitterly. It's a forceful thought and I glance over at Lucia. No reaction. Then at Fenny. She doesn't slow or even glance back.

The shell works.

I heave a silent sigh of relief. I hadn't realized the mental toll it'd been, constantly trying to shield my thoughts. Worrying what might escape. For the first time in weeks, it feels as if my mind is mine and mine alone.

"Thank you for the explanation," I say. Lucia nods. I wonder if she really believes I found it sufficient or not. Luckily, there's no chance for her to ask.

"We're here," Fenny announces. Lucia quickly unwraps her arm from mine before her sister looks back.

A pavilion stands amid a coral grove. Schools of fish swim in a lazy circle, encircling the central structure like walls. We swim over them and down through the hole in the center of the pavilion's ceiling.

Large clamshells padded with sea sponges are positioned in a somewhat free-form oval. In the middle of one side is an especially adorned shell, decorated with silver gilding and sea fans that extend from the back like massive wings. I can assume who will sit there.

The shell directly across from what I am assuming is Ilryth's is the second most opulent. Instead of sea fans, bright coral grows from the beds that surround the pavilion to frame it with almost crown-like points. It is empty, as is the shell directly to its right.

I would assume this is the space for the lady of the manor, Ilryth's spouse or second-in-command. What kind of a person would that be? I assume one does not exist, given that I've yet to hear or see anything suggesting otherwise.

The rest of the shells are full. Five women stop all movement from the moment I arrive. They are all shapes and sizes, some fair-skinned, some dark, some with short hair, and others with long, flowing tresses. All their skin is adorned with paint, the markings far more delicate and carefully drawn than my own, but each is of a different color and design. The only quality they all share is that they are all immensely beautiful.

"You will sit here." Fenny motions to the empty shell at the right hand of the second most adorned shell.

Poise and grace. Poise and grace, I repeat to myself as I propel myself through the water. I am a beautiful dolphin, elegant and sleek. I will not vault into this shell like a flopping seal. By some miracle, I think I manage it. The sponges cradle me.

To my surprise, Fenny sits in the large shell next to me. This further supports my working suspicion of their family—both of the three siblings' parents have passed. The mother, I think, was sacrificed. Father is an unknown. But I know for sure that Fenny is not Ilryth's wife. Nor is she his mother. Which means she's sitting in the shell for the lady of the house because she would be the individual with the next most authority and claim to the duchy after him.

"Go and see to the meal, please," Fenny says to Lucia, taking on an air of superiority.

I shift in my seat. There's not really an uncomfortable position to be in. It is made of the same sponge my bed is. So soft it cradles me, and yet, supportive at the same time. I wonder why no one ever thought to make beds back home out of the stuff. I've certainly never heard of divers pulling up sea sponges large enough to lie on. But perhaps they exist only in too deep waters.

Home… A pang of longing shoots through me. I knew I would be taken, but I never imagined I'd live long enough after to miss it. I imagined Ilryth consuming me and picking his teeth with the smallest finger bones. Not keeping me in his manor, teaching me, being obsessed with ships and humans or anything close to kind.

It's been over a month now. Dennow will have realized our ship didn't arrive on schedule. They'd probably give a grace period with the backup at the mines and the Gray Pass being what it is. But Charles would've been watching from his lighthouse. He would've seen my ship go by and not come back. Even if the council gave me the benefit of the doubt as the great Captain Victoria…it will only last so long.

Which means, my family should know by now. Or they will very soon.

They have mourned me once before and I imagine that will make this time worse because they might hold out hope that someday—a week, a year, several—I will emerge from the sea foam and return to them. I will defy all logic and reason and turn up alive, because I did before.

My hands ball into fists. Their pain is a wound on my soul. But, at least, thanks to Ilryth, they will be taken care of. *If he keeps his promise.*

We'll have to move quickly. The amount of time that's passed is hitting me all at once. As soon as Charles finds out I'm dead, he'll begin trying to claim I deserted my responsibility again. He'll fight until he's destroyed everything I ever loved.

"So you are Duke Ilryth's sacrifice?" A woman with bright yellow eyes jars me from my thoughts. The rest of them stare at me expectantly. I didn't realize until now that I am the center of attention.

I nod. "I am."

"That much is obvious, Serene, by her markings," another, with brown hair braided thickly, says dryly.

"Even without her markings, how many humans do you see in the Eversea?" Another laughs.

"You honor us with your presence today, Your Holiness," a woman across and to my right says.

"Just Victoria is fine," I try to offer politely.

"Oh, even as a human, we could never disgrace you as such." Serene waves a hand. I resist glancing at Fenny to see if I upset her with my attempt at being casual. "You have the markings of Lord Krokan upon you. We must show you the utmost deference."

"Is it true that Duke Ilryth himself has anointed you with his own song and hand?" the woman seated at what I assume will be Ilryth's right asks.

"Yes…" Now I'm fighting not to think of his hands running over my body again. Coaxing me with an index finger dragging up my throat to hit the highest of notes.

"How lucky! What an honor." Her eyes flutter closed as if the idea is akin to the sweetest dream.

"Victoria?" Ilryth's voice echoes through my mind. Before I can reply, he arrives, swimming through the circular opening of the ceiling.

The rest of the women rise off their shells, bowing their heads respectfully to him. He freezes in place, the muscles in his jaw and neck going taut. I see a flash of anger and confusion in his eyes that lands on Fenny.

"Just what is happening here?" he demands to know.

"We discussed this…that it would be good for our court to see their

duke, and to meet the woman you've chosen as the next offering."
Fenny's tone is hard to discern but I get the immediate impression that
this was certainly not discussed.

The other ladies must as well, because the woman with the brown
braid says, "The invitation bore your personal seal."

Ilryth purses his lips. I can almost see him physically holding himself
back from looking at Fenny. "Right, now I remember, of course."

"Lord Ilryth, it is an honor to dine with you this day," Serene interjects
with some force and a tense smile. The others speak agreement.

But Ilryth seems to pointedly ignore them all. He drifts to a stop
before me, inspecting me from head to toe. I sit a little taller, rolling
my shoulders back and keeping my neck long. My hands are folded in
my lap, face relaxed. I don't have a full grasp of what's happening yet,
so the best I can do is stay poised and polite. Fenny seems to have the
upper hand at the moment; making her happy is probably the wisest
course.

Without warning, Ilryth leans forward, expression shifting from
frustration to intensity. I'm too stunned to say anything as his face
hovers so close to mine. We have been this close in the amphitheater,
but given Lucia's reaction to him holding my hands, I'd begun to think
that his way of teaching me the hymns of the old ones was somewhat
a secret.

The other women share looks. They are no doubt also exchanging
words in their minds. He's scandalously close to me. And without
warning, he reaches for my chest.

fifteen

I LEAN AWAY SLIGHTLY. I don't care how rude it might appear. Here? In front of all of them? Lucia might not be present but I'm sure the rest of them would scold us all the same—

Ilryth's hand closes around the shell necklace at my throat, his fingers careful not to brush against my bare skin. The absence of his touch has me fighting the urge to lean forward and force the contact. A flush of embarrassment, shame, and need threatens to rise to my cheeks.

"Where did you get this?" he asks thoughtfully.

"That would be from me," Fenny interjects. I can't tell if she heard the question or just assumed.

"Is it all right?" I ask Ilryth, keeping my focus only on him. "I can return it, if you would like me to."

"No, keep it." He releases the necklace. "I haven't used it since I was a boy."

The necklace was Ilryth's? His markings are already on my body. I'm not sure how I feel about wearing something of his around my throat. He seems oblivious to my uncertainty and thankfully the shell keeps it that way, reminding me of just how practical it is. Symbol or not, it has an essential use to me.

"You clean up well." A smile curves across his lips. It looks almost prideful. He has yet to acknowledge any of the other women and there are a few wounded looks. "I admit I am surprised."

"You thought 'salt-crusted and dingy sailor' was my only state of being?"

"Don't forget crass," he quips.

I smirk.

"But you look beautiful," he adds. "Dressed like this, and when you're 'salt-crusted and dingy.'" The words catch me off guard. When was the last time someone called me beautiful without shouting it half-drunk across the street?

"Your Grace, I would hate for you to not properly spend time entertaining the other guests *you* invited," Fenny says, slightly terse.

"Yes, of course." Ilryth gives his sister a sharp look. It's a quick flick of the eyes. There and gone. I only catch it because I'm looking straight at him.

But he's saved from having to engage further when sirens swim through the opening above, interrupting the discussion. They carry shells piled with slabs of fish meat and balls of kelp, which they place in the water surrounding Ilryth and the women. None are placed before me. Which I would find stranger, if I were hungry.

In fact, this is the first time I've even *thought* of food since my arrival, despite it now having been weeks.

"I haven't eaten... Why don't I need to eat?" I keep my thoughts only for Ilryth. To my delight, thanks to the shell and my practice with magic, it works.

"As your body becomes more woven magic than physical mechanics, you won't require sustenance in the same way as you once did," he says matter-of-factly.

I stare at everyone as they begin to unwrap the kelp balls placed before them. They reveal seemingly solid bubbles—almost like gelatin—with sea vegetables contained within. It looks nothing like any food I've ever eaten, but now that I've realized it's been literal weeks, all I want is food. Even though he's right and I'm not actually hungry.

"May I kindly request some?" I ask no one in particular.

Ilryth and Fenny both look over in surprise. The other ladies stop eating, exchanging glances. I would've assumed my taking an interest to be a good thing. But now I'm not so sure.

"You would like some?" Ilryth seems uncertain.

"I would be honored to try the cuisine of my hosts," I say, trying to emphasize that I am sincere and well-meaning in my request.

Ilryth stills. I suspect he's mentally requesting another order. My suspicions are confirmed when a siren rushes in and a small kelp bubble is presented to me. I slowly unwrap it. It's about half the portion everyone else was given, but that's fine. A little sampler is more than I need to satiate my curiosity...and my desire to feel human.

Humans need to breathe air. Live on land. Need to see unfiltered sunlight... I've already lost so many of those things that connected me to my humanity—my mortality. I need something left to remind me that I'm not just magic. That I'm still Victoria.

"I apologize; I believe humans would eat with a...*furnk*? So you must find this quite barbaric." Ilryth reaches inside his bubble, and plucks raw vegetables with ease, eating with his fingers.

I snort amusement and can't fight a smile. "I've lived my years on a ship, where I'm lucky if we saw anything fresh for days on end. There's usually not much room for 'etiquette' in my world."

I make a point of reaching into the bubble while he's looking to show him that I truly am not bothered by the practice. All eyes are on me as I take my first bite. It's a bit like a too soft pickle. Briny. Sharp in flavor. The texture is slightly off-putting and that makes it something I might not otherwise gravitate toward. But for the purposes of feeling a bit human, it satisfies. I have the act of chewing and swallowing, as awkward as that is under the waves.

"You hold yourself well," Ilryth appraises.

"I've had to be adaptable in my life. I worked for Lord Kevhan Applegate as his fleet captain. My reputation demanded I attend formal gatherings not unlike this." I pause. "Well, much less water."

Ilryth chuckles. "I'm glad for it. Seeing you be so adaptable is a relief," he admits. The words are gentle across my mind. A soft caress of the barest of thoughts. My skin prickles to gooseflesh at the compliment. Knowing I've managed a job well done will never stop being a rush.

"Lord Ilryth, we would most enjoy getting to know Her Holiness as well. If you don't mind..." Serene is clearly getting annoyed and Ilryth doesn't seem to care in the slightest about her—or any of the other women's—presence.

"Yes, Your Grace," Fenny chimes in, "I was about to say much the same. You have such *lovely* guests here all eager to chat with you."

"Apologies," Ilryth says to the group. "I find I have been most occupied with my obligation to prepare the offering for Lord Krokan. I might have been neglectful of attending to my court."

"Worry not," Brown Braid says, peering at Ilryth through fluttering lashes. "We would wait an age for you, Your Grace."

"It is my honor for my brother to be surrounded by so many who love him," Fenny says warmly.

"I will love His Grace faithfully for all his rule."

"As will I," another chimes in.

Serene is not to be outdone. "Me as well."

The women eagerly speak up, one by one. They all profess how much they love—or will love—Ilryth. Yet, he doesn't look delighted by this. If anything, with every declaration he looks more and more uncomfortable.

I'm getting a sense of what this gathering is really about. It probably had nothing to do with me being "presented" at all. Fenny wanted to get Ilryth here and he was going to come looking when I didn't show up in the amphitheater. I wonder if he was waiting for me. Should I tell him what happened this morning? Maybe later… I don't want to risk someone else hearing, even with the shell.

"Tell me, what enjoyments do you fill your hours with?" Fenny asks them, fueling the conversations in the wake of Ilryth's continued silence.

The ladies list off the things they enjoy. The world of the siren is fascinating, filled with dolphin riding and kelp weaving. I try to listen to the first three attentively in an effort to be respectful. But then I notice Ilryth has hardly touched his food. While he listens to the ladies, it is with listless eyes. Obviously obligatory. In a way, he looks beyond each of the speakers—staring through them at the coral and dancing fish beyond the pavilion—as though they don't even exist at all. As if he's a world away. I'm sure I wore that look many times at Kevhan's parties.

"Lord Ilryth," I blurt. All eyes are on me, including one particularly annoyed lady who must have been speaking. "Apologies for the interruption when you looked so attentive. But I feel I need to return to my chamber…this is a great amount of contact with the world of the living and I am becoming disoriented, given the words of the old ones upon my flesh. I need some time to detach myself and focus on my anointing." I hope my manipulation of all the lore and history I've been told up until now sounds convincing.

"Yes, of course." He eagerly straightens off his shell. "If everyone will please excuse us."

"First, Your Grace," Fenny bites out, stopping us both with the remark, "I had brought Her Holiness here today in the hopes that she could show us her skill with singing our songs."

Wrenching, panicked tension grips my chest. I'm not ready for a demonstration of any sort. Moreover, we've been focusing on—at my request—the words of the old ones. Not other siren songs.

That's it.

"While I would *love to*, my focus has been on learning the hymns of the old ones. I would not want to risk your mental wellbeing by singing those words," I say boldly. From the corner of my eye, I can see Ilryth staring at me with what seems to be an impressed, pleased expression.

"Surely, Ilryth, you have taught her some of our most important songs and not just all hymns of the old gods?" Fenny presses.

Ilryth moves to my side. His hand hovers behind me, right at the small of my back. Not quite touching but so, *so* very close. "The offering is not your personal performer," he says firmly and escorts me from the room, out through the roof. Careful not to touch me the entire time their eyes are on us. I work to swim with all the grace I can manage, still awkward with the wrap around my legs.

I can feel him still silently fuming. I don't say anything. Mostly because it's not my place, but also because I can relate to him in a strange and unforeseen way.

"Thank you for trying to get us out of there," he says finally, the words soft in my mind.

"Of course. That was hardly fun for me, either." We slow. My hand moves of its own accord; my fingers closing around his is surprisingly easy after the past few weeks. Ilryth looks between the contact and my face. I think he's about to pull away. But he doesn't. Instead, he gently probes with a stare alone. Thousands of unspoken questions wrapped up in a single look. "I didn't know that was going to happen. I wouldn't have done it if I'd known the truth. I thought you were the one who organized it."

Even if I find Fenny's machinations to be a bit underhanded, she's still his sister. I'm not going to berate her in front of him.

"Fenny means well." Ilryth shakes his head and mutters, "At least that's what I tell myself."

"Sisters, right?" I tilt my head to the side with a slight shrug.

He shares in my knowing smile. "Unbearable, truly."

"But we love them anyway."

"That we do," he agrees. Ilryth's attention drops back to our hands. He unlaces his fingers, shifts his grip, and hooks them once more against mine. The smallest gesture has my heart skipping beats. It's been a painfully long time since someone beyond my family touched me in a way that was gentle and reassuring.

The sirens are right. Touch is dangerous—*his* touch. It alights a part of me I've long thought shriveled and gone. Dead from neglect. Maybe, a part that should stay dead…

"You did wonderfully," he praises warmly.

"Thank you, I was trying." I smile slightly. "But I appreciate not having to sing in front of them. I know that I'm not very good at it, still."

"Don't say that. I didn't get you out of there because I didn't think you could—"

"It's all right if you had," I say with a tired smile.

"Victoria…" Ilryth searches my expression, as if in disbelief that's what I truly think. "You are—"

"Ilryth," Fenny calls after him, swimming over. Ilryth quickly releases my hand. I don't think she noticed our linked fingers. "You *may not* leave like that."

"I am the duke of this manor; I may come and go as I please."

"And as the duke of this manor you make a fool of your sister?"

"My sister made a fool of herself when she forgot her place and acted without my approval," Ilryth says curtly. "Victoria is not your pawn and neither am I."

Fenny halts all movement. But her scowl only deepens. "I was trying to show your court that you actually came through on your promise of acquiring the sacrifice. You wouldn't know it because you spend so much time tucked away, holed up doing who knows what, but people were beginning to whisper in disbelief that you'd procured an offering at all. I took it upon myself to try and accomplish a few goals at once. *Someone* must hold this place together."

"Watch your tongue," Ilryth growls. "I have done many things for our duchy."

"Have you? Name one, other than the offering."

"Sister, you cross a line."

"Give a man enough time and he can fulfill any duty." Fenny shakes her head. "The anointing has been only the past few weeks. Mother died nearly five years ago."

"Enough—"

"And I know that you never wanted to be the duke, but you had the honor of being born first." *And Fenny can't stand it*, I realize. She would've wanted the responsibility to fall to her. Clearly there's precedent for women leaders in the Eversea, as Ilryth's mother was a duchess. "If you want to be the duke then act like it, always, not just when it suits you. If you want to be respected then respect your responsibilities."

"I do," Ilryth snaps.

"Do you?" Those two words are sharper than a blade edge. I lean back, easing away slightly, as if I could vanish from this conversation that I really don't feel like I'm meant to hear. But, if she didn't want me to, she could conceal her words to be for Ilryth only. The fact that she's not makes them that much harsher. "Because what you just did in there is hardly indicative of 'knowing your responsibilities.'"

"That is enough." Ilryth's tone is so sharp that it's Fenny's turn to lean away, looking wounded.

"I just want you to take these matters seriously," Fenny says, calm but direct.

"I assure you I do," he says with a note of exhaustion. "But I must focus on the anointing right now. Not your games."

"You are trying to use one responsibility to avoid another." Fenny still doesn't look at him. "You are twenty-five now—"

I didn't realize that he was only a year older than me. Ilryth always seemed so much more mature and put together. Timeless in appearance.

"—and you are *still* without an heir or wife to give you one. I know you have always been a late bloomer. I know you have always come into responsibility in your own time." Ilryth winces. She doesn't see it because Fenny turns her gaze back to him after the fact. "But you must act sooner rather than later. The Eversea is not the safe place it was in our parents' time. Krokan's rage worsens with every passing month. The rot threatens the well-being of all, children included. We all need strong leaders with capable heirs *now*."

"I know." Ilryth sighs heavily. "Listen, let me take Victoria back to her room and then I'll return to the ladies you have brought for me to consider. I will make amends, and I will be the epitome of charming."

"Good." She smiles proudly. How quickly Fenny's tone shifts when she gets what she wants—what she clearly thinks is right. "I know you will find your songmate soon and she will make you as happy as Mother made Father."

Ilryth barely hides a flinch. "My happiness will be found when everyone else is happy." The words echo mine from weeks ago. A deep sadness stirs in me. Is he covering up the same complex emotions I was? "Now go and entertain the ladies until I return."

She nods and swims away, leaving just the two of us. Ilryth rolls his neck, as if trying to release the remnants of tension that conversation left in him. Judging by his shoulders being nearly up by his chin still, I don't think it works.

"I'm sorry you had to see that," he says finally.

"It's all right," I say softly. "I...I can understand better than you think."

He looks at me with obvious confusion. "You know what it's like to be obligated to marry for the good of your people?"

I laugh lightly. "All right, no. I don't know *that*... But I do know how frustrating it is for people to try and tell you to fall in love, set you up, tell you to do this or that, what you *should be* focusing on... when you clearly have everything under control. When you know what your headway is in life but no one else seems to accept it because they always suggest you should have or be something more. Like, you could do everything right and yet—"

"It would never be good enough," Ilryth finishes, staring at me for a long moment, blinking, as if seeing me for the first time. "I didn't expect to find camaraderie with you in this way."

"Neither did I."

"You had expectations to marry?" He swims over and takes the lead once more. I follow at his side, undoing the wrapping from around my legs to swim in just my shorts.

"I wouldn't call them *expectations…*" I release the silken fabric, allowing the current to pull it away. Someone will find it. "But I did have a good many people asking if I would find a suitor. It was hard for them to imagine a successful woman not being in want of a man to 'complete' that area of her life."

"I imagine many men were drawn to your success." It's amazing that he seems to really mean those words, believing they're true.

"Some were," I admit. "Many were intimidated. I was interested in neither. Like you, I had responsibilities. Unlike you, I had the convenience—if I look at it that way—of knowing that my days were numbered. I never had to worry about growing old and being alone."

"Sometimes being alone sounds like a luxury," he says dryly.

I laugh. I know I'm going to sound like my sister, but I can't help but ask, "You have no interest in a wife, or husband?"

"It is not a matter of interest. It is a matter of choice. Of which I have none. I have two main duties to the Eversea—beyond anointing you." He counts on his fingers as he lists them. As he moves his arms, his elbow brushes mine slightly. "Protect my people from the wraiths, demented emissaries of Lord Krokan, and whatever other horrors creep up from the Abyss. And procure an heir, so the Granspell line lives on to carry Dawnpoint and continue protecting these lands."

I stare out at the open water, thinking about his words. Trying to find my own. "I know it is not my place…" I stop and he stops with me.

"Why do I get the impression that you're going to say whatever it is anyway?" He doesn't seem genuinely annoyed. If anything, he sounds amused.

I smirk. "Because I am." Because I must. If I can stop just one other person from making the same mistake I did… "Marriage is an oath that should never be taken lightly, nor should it be taken without the proper thought, or if you feel like you are forced into it. It will only yield heartbreak. But I also understand responsibility… So if it is something you *must* do, make sure the woman you choose knows the design of your heart. Make sure you both go into it with open eyes. *Talk* to each other, treat each other well. Even if it is not love, at least ensure she is someone you respect and be her friend."

He studies me thoughtfully. I expect him to be offended by my sticking my nose where it doesn't belong. To tell me off. But instead, he nods.

"That is sage counsel, Victoria. Are you sure you're not married?" He grins slightly.

"Quite sure I'm not." It's a little strange to say so, but it feels *so good* at long last. It's a reminder of just how free I am.

"Then you are a wise individual by nature." He smiles, looking down at me over the swell of his cheeks. Yet again, the siren doesn't seem to consider I might have been married once. I suppose divorce isn't something that's done in the Eversea. "Savvy, strong, intelligent, capable, honest, and loyal... I lucked into quite the woman that night in the sea."

I find myself fighting a blush for a second time in one day. But, this time, there is no anger, only the warmth of his praise. His compliments fill me in a way that I haven't been filled in a long time. He has no reason to praise me, really, which means his affections are sincere. Not knowing how to handle myself in the face of such kindness, I glance away and shrug.

"I assure you I have my shortcomings."

"You will have to let me know when they rear their head, otherwise I might begin to think you are too perfect." He swims ahead again but I'm too stunned for a moment to follow. It's then I notice he's heading away from my room.

"Where are we going?"

"There's a task I need your help with."

"Didn't you tell Fenny that you were going to return me to my room and head back?"

Ilryth looks over his shoulder with a smirk. "Do I look like a man who can be told what to do?"

No. And, dangerously, I like him even more for it.

sixteen

"WHERE ARE WE HEADED?" I ask as we swim higher above the estate. I notice that Ilryth doesn't swim in front. Instead, he remains at my side.

"Sheel's house."

"Sheel's?" I repeat, surprised. I haven't seen the sharklike man in a solid week or two and haven't really interacted with him in longer. It seems our paths stopped crossing after Ilryth's injury. To neither of our complaint, I'm sure.

"Yes, there's something there that I think you'll be able to help with."

"Which is?" I swim a bit ahead of Ilryth to look back at him.

"You don't like surprises?" The corners of his mouth quirk slightly into a knowing smile. Mischief dances in his eyes like sunlight on the sea floor. Somehow the expression manages to be both coy and seductive. When he can wield expressions like that so effortlessly, it's no wonder the ladies at the breakfast were practically throwing themselves at him.

"Not regarding matters that seem important."

Ilryth slows and drifts to a stop. I do so as well, ending alongside him. He swims around me, tail arcing behind my back—slow to catch up with his torso—as his arm wraps around my shoulders, hovering just over my skin. Every almost-touch is more and more unbearable than the last. *Just touch me*, my skin screams, aching for the real thing despite my better judgment. It's made worse by the memories of his hands smoothing down my arms, over my stomach. Our contact is a forbidden secret, made potent whenever we're in public.

Ilryth points past the barren field of sand and shells to a small reef ahead—one I can see houses built into.

"See that? It's a small township of my duchy. That's where Sheel and many of my other vassals reside. At his home is someone that needs you desperately."

"Needs *me*?"

"Yes, you."

"How?"

"She is sick with the rot." His tone becomes serious. A shadow passes over Ilryth's face, making him look haunted and distant. "And I believe you can heal her."

"How?"

"The rot is a product of Lord Krokan's rage—a blight of death. Lady Lellia's magic keeps it at bay. You are working to learn their magics, so I believe you should be able to undo it," he says, full of hope and confidence.

Emotions I don't quite share. "We've never practiced anything like that."

"But we've worked for weeks. You're ready."

I can't go and fail. I can't let someone down. "Ilryth…"

"You want to go to the trench, right? You need to save your family."

"How dare you bring them into this." The words are cold.

He boldly grabs my hand and ducks his head, locking his eyes with mine. There's nothing but determination. As if he's trying to mentally pour the raw confidence from his mind to mine.

"Show me you're ready." He smirks and adds, "I didn't take you for someone to back down from a challenge."

"I got out of that room as fast as I could earlier." Rather than rising to the challenge of singing in front of others.

"True. But that didn't matter. It was petty, showy, noble nonsense. This matters. Someone's life is on the line and I know you, Victoria, you won't abandon someone in need."

I still and take a deep and bracing breath. "How do you know me so well?"

An uneasy sensation glides across my skin as I realize just how much I have exposed myself to him, leading me to question the boundaries I never intended to allow him to breach. Somehow, with every conversation, every wordless afternoon of song, he's managed to find the rough outlines of my hidden scars and unspoken secrets. When Ilryth looks at me, he sees me. He is as familiar as my crew, as comforting as my family. He is forbidden and yet is also liberation in every stolen moment and touch. Being here, working with him, learning magic…it makes me feel alive in a way I never have before.

"You've handled everything in your stride—with grace. All because you want to help the people around you and the people you love. It's admirable."

His words paint me as a paragon of selflessness and a bitter smile twitches my lips. The truth is far more complex, blurred with hues of genuine compassion, and the shades of an underlying, gnawing yearning to be worthy. For so long, I've existed in a muddy contradiction: stubborn yet wanting to bend to appease others, independent yet craving approval, needy and somehow not needy enough.

I've managed to convince myself that as long as I'm working, striving, helping and giving, then I can compensate for my flaws and be worthy of the love of those around me.

Perhaps I was wrong. If he thinks my motives so simple and altruistic then he doesn't know me at all.

"Now, grab on to my shoulders." Ilryth releases my hand and puts his back to me, ignorant to the emotional murk he's churned in my soul.

"Excuse me?"

"It'll be easier, faster, and it's no trouble to me."

"Wouldn't it be degrading as a duke to have someone ride on you like a dolphin?" My thought escapes me and not even the shell holds it back.

He glances over his shoulder, narrowing his eyes. "I hadn't thought of it that way, previously…but thank you for enlightening me on how you might perceive my kindness. Now, are you grabbing on or not?"

"Are you sure it's all right if people see us touching?" I glance back to the estate. There are a few sirens darting about. But none seem to be paying much attention.

"This is a practical touch. Harmless. Not enough to deepen your connection to this plane. No one would care." The way he says it makes me wonder if he's working to convince himself, as much as me.

"I can swim on my own."

"You are slow."

"There's no rush, is there?"

He turns to face me, folding his arms. "Do you always have this much trouble accepting help?"

"I'm trying to prevent us from getting in trouble." I roll my eyes. "Forgive me for caring."

"Don't hide behind your compassion to conceal the fact that you just don't want to feel indebted or vulnerable."

"Excuse you." I lean back and fold my own arms, as if I could protect the heart he's trying to poke at. Making a bit of a mockery of his stance is a fringe benefit. "We are not analyzing me." Even if he's absolutely right.

"Victoria, you don't have to hide." He rests his fingertips gently on my forearm. "I understand." The way he looks at me... "Leaders like us, those responsible for warriors or ship crews, can never *need* help. We're the ones supposed to be helping others, aren't we? Asking for help would mean imposing on the people we're meant to protect—showing vulnerability when there can be none. We are ready to give everything, even our flesh and blood, if that's what the cost is."

The words are tender, introspective even, and they feel as much a critique of himself as of me. My hands twitch, wanting to retort in the same manner I would when defending myself from Charles. But as exposed as I am...I don't feel defensive. Perhaps it's because he is lumping himself with me in his assessment. Somehow, in this moment, I feel less...alone.

"There are worse things than sacrificing yourself," I say softly.

"Of course there are," he agrees with ease. "But you don't have to."

"Don't I though?" I grin and give a small shrug. Ilryth opens his mouth, as if to object, but then closes it when he rightly thinks better of it.

"You really are something else." He chuckles and shakes his head, as if he can't believe it, either. "Fine. Around me, just you and I, you don't have to sacrifice everything. As you are is more than enough."

Ilryth gives me one last warm smile and then puts his back to me again. Waiting.

We hover over the edge of his estate. Beneath us, sirens go about their business. In the distance, a group arrives at the main pillars that seem to delineate his duchy. But he is as still as a statue. Poised.

I stare at his broad back—the markings that swirl and dip into the grooves cut by water into the muscles under his skin. Touching him now, taking his shoulders, feels like so much more than merely accepting some help in this moment. My fingertips on his skin are an unspoken promise. A forbidden connection beyond sacrifices and anointing.

What are you doing, Victoria? a tiny voice whispers from the far recesses of my mind.

My fingers press into his muscle and I whisper, "Thank you."

"You're welcome." He begins swimming.

Keeping my elbows bent and locked against my sides, I ride atop his back, acutely aware of the ripple of powerful muscle beneath me. His rear bumps against my groin now and again, sending a jolt straight into my body. While I cannot feel the water pressing against my face as sharply as I would've otherwise expected, I can certainly feel *that*.

Charles was my first. My only. Even when he thought me dead, I did not seek the arms of another. Not just because I didn't know if a man would want a woman who was running from her oaths and former love…but because I was still married. Even if I did not wear a ring, even if I didn't live under his roof. He was still marked upon my soul. Seeking out the arms of another didn't feel right at best, and, at worst, promised to be something that would knot my insides with turmoil I didn't have time for.

Maybe, if I'd had more time…

Bump. Bump. Bump.

I press my eyes closed and swallow thickly. Trying to focus on anything but the unexpected pressure of Ilryth against me is futile. The strength of his muscles presses into me. His body moves like music. The siren is as tempting in form as he is in song and power.

All of him, so much, so close, is overwhelming. For the first time in years, I feel like the girl who ran off with Charles. So hot between the legs. So eager to explore. Believing anything would be good just for an opportunity to have the tiniest of tastes. Luckily, I now have experience to help keep my wits about me.

We leave the edge of the estate. The buildings connected by archways and coral end. A barren land of sand and rock stretches toward a series of small homes in the distance.

The homes are modest versions of his estate—constructed of coral and shell. Ilryth tips downward, and as we pass, the people pause what they're doing to bow their heads before resuming their daily activities.

Sheel is perched outside of a home carved into a massive mound of brain coral, polishing a bone blade with a rock. But the second he sees Ilryth and me, he's at attention. "My Lord, Your Holiness, I thought you were hosting court; to what do I owe this unexpected honor?"

Ilryth ignores the mention of "hosting" and says, "I was thinking about what you were telling me the other night about Yenni's condition and it occurred to me that, perhaps, Victoria might be able to assist."

Sheel blubbers, opening and closing his mouth, looking between Ilryth and me. The shock and, dare I say, admiration on his face is such a different emotion than he showed me when he thought I was escaping my prison. "Your Holiness…I am not worthy."

"Just Victoria is fine." I allow a calm demeanor to hide my unease at his about-face in perception toward me. It's surprisingly easy, given that I know the type of man Sheel is. I've met his type across the years—the order-following general. He is happy so long as everyone has a place and occupies it. I can sympathize, and understand how I've been a disruption in his tidy order.

"Please, come in." Sheel ushers us through the curtain of braided rope, weighted by polished rocks, hanging from the top of the archway that leads into his home.

Inside is an odd dwelling—odd to me, at least, as a human. There is a glowing orange pool situated in a basin of rocks. More rope and kelp are draped from the ceiling, looped and braided like swings. At the center of the home, where I might have expected a hearth to be, is a small, ghostly twig, spiraling up around a pale shard of wood that's been stabbed into a crack in the stone floor.

The moment I lay eyes on it, I am drawn over, as if pulled by an invisible tether. The leaves of the ghost tree glisten like silver, emitting a faint, cool light. They sway as they're pushed by unfelt breezes. Or, perhaps, swaying to the music I hear whispering in the back of my mind.

"What is it?" I murmur.

"It's formally called an anamnesis—it is a memory of the Lifetree, stored in the cutting our spears are made from." Ilryth is at my side. "It offers protection, and the blessings of Lady Lellia, warding against the grip of death." He glances over at Sheel. "Has it been helping?"

"It has. Thank you for allowing us a shard of the Lifetree to bring Lady Lellia's blessing into this humble home."

"It is the least I can do." Ilryth sounds like he means it. The sentiment is riddled with guilt.

I resist the urge to touch him. Ilryth must've had the same need, because his little finger hooks mine. Briefly. So briefly that I almost wonder if it was just a curl of current rather than a conscious touch.

"This way." Ilryth leads me to the right of the two archways in the back of the room, Sheel right behind us.

We're in a coral tunnel. Kelp hangs from the ceiling between strands of silken thread that are adorned with crystal beads and opalescent shells. Carvings similar to the shapes drawn on me are etched into the coral walls—similar to what was etched into the whale bones.

"When the roots in the trench died off, Lady Lellia's blessings could no longer reach this distant domain," Ilryth says softly. I get the impression he is speaking for me alone. "We were at the mercy of the rot until I managed to use the sacred spear of my family, Dawnpoint, to make an anamnesis strong enough to hold off the tides that brought the rot into our homes. Since then, all the duchies followed. But it's a temporary stay on a worsening problem and the rot gets more and more of a foothold each year."

A spear... I think back to how Sheel mentioned Ilryth going into the trench without his spear. Was he sacrificing his own safety for that of his people in yet another way? Another tendril of admiration for this man worms its way into me. But I don't linger on it; I'm too distracted the moment we pass through another rope curtain and the full extent of the rot's consequences are instantly brought into clarity.

The farthest room in the house is dim, save for some pale lilac flowers that glow across the ceiling. But their light struggles against the reddish-brown rot that floats through the water in clumps.

The source of the rot isn't a current, or a distant trench, but a girl laid out on a bed of stone and kelp. Her breathing is labored, chest struggling to rise and fall with each shallow breath. She is covered in a thin layer of what looks almost like rust. It clings to her, irritating her skin, and if her raised purple veins are any indication, it is also poisoning her blood. At her side is a woman who, until the moment we entered, had been clutching the girl's hand despite the physical manifestations of her ailment, holding it to her forehead as she sang in prayer.

"Sheel?" The woman looks between us.

"Sanva, His Grace has brought Her Holiness—Victoria—to come and aid Yenni." Sheel crosses to the woman, giving her a brief kiss and then wrapping his arm around her shoulders. "As the offering, she has been learning the words of the old ones. She might be able to help."

The woman clasps both her hands before her, holding them out slightly. "Your Holiness, we are not worthy."

"I'll do what I can," I say, wishing I were more confident. I've no idea what I'm doing and the two of them are looking at me as if I am the only hope for their daughter.

With a pump of my arms, I drift to the other side of Yenni. She's the spitting image of Sheel, save for the pustules that cover her entire body. Some of the boils have ruptured and they don't ooze blood, but clumps of the red algae—no, rot. No wonder Sheel was so aggressive when he thought I was disrupting the anointing. He sees me as the cure to the rot itself.

Ilryth had said that the rot seeps from the Lifetree. If so, then it is no longer a tree of life, but rather one of death, and it is poisoning the people of this land. I've been working to comprehend the scale of what I am facing and thought I was doing well…up until this moment. This isn't an illness I know. It is one that stems from a force beyond my comprehension.

But I don't have to understand it to see when someone needs help. And if I can assist, I will. I'll do this so we can go to the trench. So Ilryth will lend his aide to me and my family and because…

Because I couldn't live with myself if I didn't help when I thought I could.

Charles might have taught me how to emotionally manipulate someone through the necessity of my own survival. But he also taught me how it felt to be manipulated. The wiry tethers that wrap so tightly around one's soul that they cut into your very being. That knowledge is what keeps me from being able to be the mercenary I wish I was.

I'm not doing this for me—to get something from Ilryth. I'm doing it because it's the right thing to do. Now, the question remains…can I do it at all?

"I would like some space," I announce, hoping I give an air of authority. Sheel and Sanva leave. Only Ilryth remains, lit ominously by the low light and red haze. I look to him, panic rising. But I keep it from taking over my head, remaining level. "What am I supposed to do?"

"Command the words of the old ones to banish the rot," he says calmly. So matter-of-fact.

"I've no idea how to do that." I shake my head. "Ilryth, this is serious. I—I don't know how to help her…"

He glides behind me. The moment his body presses against mine, all worries melt into the heat of his form. One hand settles on my abdomen. The other slips up my side, resting on my collarbones. The feeling of him behind me is more reassuring than I would've wanted. I hate how I want his stability. How I've come to associate his touch with this strange power.

"Victoria, you are incredible. You can do this." His nose brushes against my neck as his face settles by my shoulder. I try to suppress a shiver and fail. He feels it. He must. Because his fingers press into the stiff fabric of the corset that covers my stomach, as if he's trying to grip the need he's placed in me. "All you have to do is sing."

"What do I sing? What words?"

"You know them in here." His hand slides down my chest, resting just above the swell of my breasts. "You are more magical than you think. As a human, you are a distant descendant of the old gods—of a people who were handcrafted with the help of Lady Lellia. You have been marked with their power. Your soul is music for their songs. Search the voids in your mind where their words have taken residence and find the right ones."

I take a deep and unnecessary breath, my chest swelling against his hand. Ilryth clutches me even tighter. Our skin seems to merge. His nose brushes my neck as he tilts his head.

"Now, just like in the amphitheater," he whispers. "Sing for me, my Victoria."

My will…I intend to heal her. I will it so.

But my mind is silent. I'm keenly aware of how still everything is. I can imagine Sheel and Sanva in their main room, waiting anxiously for me to save their daughter. I've been singing for weeks now. But in the moment I need it most, the words don't come. I'm back at the beginning.

Ilryth was right to pull me from the breakfast with the ladies. I would've made a fool of myself. I can't do this.

What can you do, Elizabeth? Charles's voice sneers at me through the barriers I try to put up in my mind for him.

"Great things," Ilryth whispers in reply.

My eyes snap open and, like that, my mind is filled with music. The last of the hesitation leaves me. Just like in the amphitheater, I part my lips and begin with a note—not a word. I hold it, sustaining. I know what will come next. I heard it going to sleep countless times and it instantly has the muscles in my shoulders unknotting.

Ilryth begins to hum in harmony. As if that was what he was waiting for. His voice moves effortlessly around mine. The melody supports me while protecting his mind.

I find the first word. It's one on my forearm. "*Kulta'ra*…" Then the second. "*Sohov*…"

Images flash before my mind, just like during all our practice in the amphitheater. My life, the good, the bad, the ugly. It's all pulled to the forefront like strikes of lightning on a stormy sea.

I pick a memory to thrust into the void. I must make room for the magic. There's too much of me otherwise…I have to make space for the power to command it.

Behind my eyelids, memories of my wedding are blotted away. First the color of my dress…the expression on my mother's face…dancing with my father.

Ilryth's grip tightens on my corporeal form, as if he's trying to hold me in place.

The moment the memory is gone, there's nothing but a void for the words of the old gods to fill. The second they occupy that space, understanding follows. I can wrap my hands around them. The power is mine for the taking.

The song reaches its peak and I open my eyes to find a faint, silvery haze shining in the water around us—the same as what hovered around the anamnesis. It fades to reveal clear water, plants vibrant and healthy, shining a happy purple light down upon us. There is not even a trace of the rot. I am breathless as Ilryth's arms slowly unravel from me.

"I knew you could do it." There's a note of pride in his voice that makes my toes curl. "You're ready for the trench, I think."

Before I can respond, Yenni's eyes open. Sheel and Sanva must have heard something of my song, for they come rushing in. Stop. And stare.

With an outburst of tears, they both throw their arms around their daughter—scarred from the rot, but sharp-eyed and otherwise healthy.

seventeen

SANVA AND SHEEL TRY TO CONVINCE US TO STAY. They offer us an early dinner and Ilryth politely declines, saying that we are needed back in the estate. By the time we're leaving, I have a small bag of gelatin candies that Sanva thrust into my hands, refusing to let me leave without any gesture of gratitude. Sheel tried to get me to take two bags. Somehow, in an afternoon, I've warmed to him enough that I genuinely consider it.

"Are we actually needed back at the estate?" I ask when we're alone in front of their home.

"Not in the slightest." Ilryth twirls in the water. "I thought it would be nice for them to have some time alone, as a family."

"How long was she like that?"

He doesn't respond for long enough that I worry I've somehow upset him. Though I don't know how I could've. The question seemed harmless enough.

"She was the first to fall ill, and the worst. The only one Lucia couldn't manage to stave off the rot within before the barriers were established." His gaze sweeps across the landscape, landing on the trench. "Yenni became sick because of me."

"Ilryth…"

"It's true," he insists. "I sent Sheel into the trench on a deep mission with one of the new recruits. The rot was on him when he returned. We were careless and Yenni paid the price. I sent Sheel out again too soon. Sanva was assisting Lucia with attending the warriors… Neither of them were home when they should have been. No one knew Yenni was sick until the rot took hold."

I think of Ilryth swimming with the other warriors. Of Sheel's anger that Ilryth had personally gone on the defensive. "That's why you go yourself, now, isn't it? Even when Sheel doesn't want you to, you go anyway."

He nods.

"I'll heal any others, too," I offer without hesitation.

"They're managed, for now."

"But—"

"The best thing you can do is continue preparing yourself for the presentation to the court and the offering. If you can appease Lord Krokan and heal our seas, then the rot will end in our water and in the bodies of those afflicted. Our lands will be as fertile and as magical as they always were before his rage began," he says with desperate optimism. He's so determined, so hopeful.

But something doesn't sit quite right with me—and it's not because my life is the one on the line to bring about this new utopia… The more I learn about this place and its histories, the less everything seems to make sense.

"Shall we?" He interrupts my thoughts, presenting his back to me. I grab on to his shoulders and he launches off. I shift, settling on his back. But I can't find a grip that's comfortable.

I have no doubt that Ilryth believes every word of what he's told me. I can see it in his eyes. But, for some reason, the words don't ring true with me. I try and search my thoughts to find a reason why as I stare listlessly at our shadow blurring over the rooftops of the estate. In the end, I can find no explanation for my sense, so I say nothing.

We slow to a stop, hovering over the balcony to my room as the sun begins to set. I release him, but we don't drift very far apart. His fingers trail lightly down my forearm. I almost think it's by chance. But the touch lingers long enough that I doubt it is. I wonder if Lucia saw any of our traveling today. Or would it be the "practical touch" that is less of a concern for her? Whatever that means…

"I'll come to you tomorrow and we'll prepare for the trench in earnest," he says, soft but firm. "We should move quickly, for the Duchy of Faith will come asking for you soon to take over the anointing."

"What will they do to me?" I never relished the idea of being here. In fact, I outright resented it at first. But now the notion of leaving is as terrifying as it was when I first arrived. This is all I know of the Eversea and, more than that…Ilryth makes me feel safe here. With him around, I don't have to worry.

He is not the monstrous siren I first thought him. Nor is he a coldhearted ruler that relishes cruelty. I stare out over his estate. At the sandy and kelp-covered hills, spilling down along an underwater mountain range toward the castle I can barely see as a shadow in the distance, encased in a haze of silver light. How much of this is his duchy? How much is his responsibility? How many more names of people suffering from the rot has he imprinted on his mind? I can almost feel their weight tugging on his every move. It's what drove him to do something as grim as pulling a young woman from the ocean and telling her to sacrifice herself.

"They will anoint you as we have, but their castle is closer to the Eversea, so you will be able to commune directly with Lord Krokan, and be ready to do so. Things will move faster then and, when the summer solstice comes, you will be cast into the Abyss." The words are little more than a caress.

I'd ask him if it will hurt. But I doubt he knows. No one has ever returned from the Abyss. I want to ask if he thinks I will be good enough, despite all my flaws and all my doubts. But I know, no matter what, he'll say yes…because I'm the only option he has.

"Will you be there?" I don't know why, out of all the questions I run through in my mind, that's the one that escapes.

"Where?" He seems as surprised as I am.

"Will you come with me to the duchy? Will you stay with me to the end?"

Panic crosses his features. "Victoria, I—"

"Never mind," I say hastily with a shake of my head and a forced, bitter smile. "I shouldn't have asked." In the end, no one will be there for me. But that's all right. I've long since come to terms with that truth. Even Charles, the man who "bound his soul" to mine, left at the first chance he got.

"It's not that—"

"I don't want you to placate me. I'm fine," I say gently, reaching out to pat his bicep. He catches my hand, sandwiching it in both of his.

Ilryth stares at me with breathtaking intensity. I couldn't look away if I wanted to. "My mother, you see, she..."

"I know," I say softly. He doesn't need to say that she was the last sacrifice.

"You do?" His eyes widen. "Did Lucia or Fenny tell you?"

"No one needed to tell me. I put it together." I give him a gentle smile. "That's why I shouldn't have asked."

"You..."

"I'll be all right." I pull my hand from his as Lucia rounds the building. Ilryth isn't surprised, but he does have a brief expression of frustration. I suspect he summoned her before the conversation shifted.

Lucia glances between us with confusion on her face. But she doesn't question the tension in the air. If anything, she forces normality with a smile.

"Shall we begin tonight's anointing, Your Holiness?"

"Yes," Ilryth answers for me, drifting back. "We will ready ourselves in the morning." He swims off without another word. I almost call after him, but I've nothing else to say. No reason to call him back other than...

Other than...

I want him to be here? But why? And why did I ask him that question? I fight a scowl. The answers are something I know I'll have to search within for...though that's an exploration I am not looking forward to.

"Let's begin," Lucia says, and she moves to my left ankle.

I wake with a start. Chest heaving. Smoothing hair from my face as it floats around my eyes.

Charles's words are still in my ears. *Did you see how relieved they were to let you go? Your family not having to be burdened with you any longer is a relief.*

I'm not a burden.

But don't worry, I don't mind. I will gladly take you under my wing.

I'm not a burden, I insist to myself again, and again. I am strong. Capable. I am the best captain that there ever was in Tenvrath. I've sailed the seas. I've supported my family and my crew.

Because of me, the Eversea—and Tenvrath at that—will be saved. I will give my bones for it. A dream. It was just a dream. I try to calm myself. He is gone, nowhere to be found. I look around anyway. For him, or the wraith he might as well be manifested within.

It was a relief every time I left you, Lizzie.

I push myself off the bed, drifting through the water and out to my balcony. The night is quiet. There's no singing. And yet, my heart is thunderous, as if the wraiths are coming for me and me alone. My toes brush against the sandy, shell-filled stone and I push off again. I swim over the estate in a hasty rush.

Moonbeams strike the sea floor, dancing across my balcony and casting everything in shades of silver and deep blue. They shift and move with the currents above. My shadow casts a striking contrast against the sand below.

It's easy to spot Ilryth's treasure room. From there, I swim over the coral tunnel that connects with his room, coming to a stop just above his balcony. It strikes me that I am about to venture to a man's room at night.

What would Charles— No. I refuse to think it. He is not a part of my life any longer and never will be again. He no longer has a hold on me, my body, or my heart. I need to stop worrying about him…however hard that will be to learn.

In fact, I will swim down because I can. To spite him if nothing else. Charles might never know I've moved past him, but I hope that he can somehow feel it deep within his soul.

Ilryth's room is dimly lit by the small, glowing buds that dangle from his ceiling and the ambient moonlight. He lies on his bed, on his side, kelp piled around him like a nest. In slumber, he looks peaceful, almost innocent.

I breathe a sigh of relief at the sight of him. He's here, which means there's no attack. No cause for alarm. I turn, and start to swim back… until I notice a shadow looming over me. I startle, looking up. Every part of me is on high alert. My eyes meet a now all too familiar pair, the brown nearly black in the night.

"Is it common for you to be found sneaking into men's rooms at night?"

"Y-Your Grace," I stammer.

He frowns. "If you were thinking of killing me in my sleep, let me tell you all the reasons why—"

"What in my nature, after all this time, has led you to think I would cut a man's throat in his bed while he slept?" I say, flabbergasted and more than slightly offended.

"I see you've already meditated on the how." He folds his arms with a slight smile. My shock fades with a roll of my eyes. He's teasing me.

I hold out my hands, motioning to myself. I am in nothing more than my shorts and corset—the same ones he has seen me in practically this entire time and with a woeful lack of pockets. "With what weapon?"

"Strangle me, then."

"You flatter me by suggesting I could overpower you enough to choke the life from your body."

That elicits a dark chuckle of amusement from him. "Are you saying you think I'm strong, Victoria?"

"What? No. I... Not to suggest you're weak. But—"

A rumble of laughter stills me. I fight a flush on my cheeks. His grin is mildly infectious and I can't help but mirror it, though only for a moment.

"Besides, do sirens even...breathe?" I realize I don't know.

"Not in the way you think. Though I don't believe I'll tell you how, lest you try to use the information against me."

"Fine, I'll just ask Lucia in the morning. She will tell me because she is kind and good." I turn, beginning to swim away.

He balks. "Kind and good? Are we talking about the right sister?" I laugh. "And what? Unlike me?" He says my implied words.

I glance over my shoulder and shrug, still smirking.

"What have I done to make you think I am anything less than 'kind and good'?"

"You—" I stop short.

"Yes? You have me waiting on bated breath." Ilryth folds his arms.

I was jesting. But it has me thinking...What has he done? Taken me early? Yes. But, Krokan had basically killed me—my second death. An old god who no doubt disrupted Ilryth's magic. He imprisoned me when

I first arrived…but it was necessary so I could continue existing in this world. He's pushed me to learn his magic songs…so I can first go and get the silver my family desperately needs. Everything I thought might have been bad or wicked about him turned out to have an explanation that only made him shine all the brighter.

"You're all right, I suppose," I admit.

"Just 'all right?' And you 'suppose'?" He swims up to me. We hover in the open water, filled with small, luminescent, blob jellyfish that make the dark ocean around us feel like a sea of stars. "You really don't want to give me much credit, do you?"

"The last thing I would want is for you to get a big head."

"I assure you I am at no risk of that around you." The words are dry, but he wears a slight smile. "Why did you come to my chambers? Is everything all right?"

The genuine concern in his voice gives me pause. Even when I should know better. He seems like he cares…genuinely cares.

I confess, "I had a nightmare and I was afraid the wraiths were back. But it doesn't seem like it. Merely some dark memories I still have yet to sacrifice to the void of the words of the old ones. Really must keep practicing my magic…" I laugh softly. "Now that I say it aloud, it sounds silly."

What am I? A child scared of the dark? Running for their security blanket? And…what does it mean that Ilryth was the one I ran to?

"I don't think it's silly in the slightest." He tilts his head to meet my eyes. "What was the nightmare about, if you want to share?"

He stares at me with earnest intensity. I can't look away. My barriers fracture. My armor is peeled away. I have been working so hard, for so long…and what do any of those barriers matter now, anyway? Ilryth will never know my family or my friends. He will never tell them of my weakness. Of how burdensome I really can be.

"I dreamed you left." The words are a quivering whisper and leave so much unsaid. They're a lie. That's not what I dreamt of. But it's part of the truth of what made me come here—fear of being left behind. "I was afraid you went ahead without me—to the trench, to get my family's silver."

"Victoria…" He searches my face. I'm convinced he can see right through me and the idea terrifies me so much I can't move. "Why would I leave without you?"

"Because I would just slow you down?" I shrug, trying to hide how heavy the words are on my shoulders. "Because I am little more than a burden?"

Ilryth slowly takes both of my hands. There's no pretense about it. No tension. Nothing awkward or uncomfortable. The gesture is...one a close friend might give another.

"I wouldn't leave you behind, ever. You're too important for that."

There's so much more to this.

All my earlier thoughts. My hidden worries. The things I never explored with myself because I didn't want to.

My stomach twists itself into a small knot, one I instantly work to undo.

I know this feeling. That small bubble of affection that clings to my insides and breeds more until, before I know it, I'm practically floating with the effervescence of infatuation. I will not let myself be taken in by a handsome smile and kind eyes. I cannot let my guard down around him or any other.

I lasted three years after Charles without succumbing to a handsome gaze. At this point, I'll guard my heart until the day I die. I won't ever allow it to be held carelessly again. And since I am already, quite literally, marked for death, I don't think it will be hard to keep that vow.

"Because of my magic?" I say.

"Because...you're you." He quickly adds, "And I wouldn't want to take from you the opportunity to protect your family."

"Of course not." We can pretend that's all it is, that's all that's happening. I've yet to pull away, even knowing I should. This is not a "practical touch."

"We'll leave tomorrow, together; I gave you my word." Ilryth's fingers slowly glide against mine as he shifts his grip. I wonder if he knows what he's doing—the affection he's brewing. He can't possibly, because if he did I'm sure he would stop. "So rest easy tonight, Victoria."

"Thank you," I say softly as he releases me. The seawater is cold against my fingers.

"Now, I am going back to sleep. You exhaust me." The dry remark pops the little bubble of warmth that'd been floating up in me. My lips crack into a smile. How is he so effortlessly comforting, and also simultaneously baffling, with a dash of charming annoyance?

"I exhaust you?" I call after him as he swims away.

"Most definitely. You seem to require all my energy and attention these days; I can think of nothing else but you."

I stare as he retreats into his room, drifting to the bed and settling once more in the nest he made without looking back at me. His tail curls up and around him, much like a cat's. It's oddly…adorable. I shake my head and banish the thought as I begin swimming back to my own room.

When I try to go back to sleep, the words, *I can think of nothing else but you*, float through my mind. Not in Charles's harsh, demanding, or dark tones. But Ilryth's deep and warm notes…as soothing as his hands on mine.

eighteen

THE REST OF THE NIGHT IS PEACEFUL. No more nightmares haunt me.

I don't quite sleep, but I'm not quite conscious either. I've noticed that I need sleep less, much like how I don't eat any longer. The more I am marked by the old ones, the less I need to tend to my physical body. Still, my awareness slipped from me at some point in the night for long enough that when I stir and sense the presence of another hovering at my bedside, I'm so startled I spring from the spongy bed and shoot halfway across the room.

"You wound me with your reaction to my presence." Ilryth folds his arms.

"You startled me! You cannot just come into my bedroom without warning." I grab my chest. This man is going to be the cause of a third death pulling things like this.

"Why not? You didn't seem to have a problem with sneaking into my room last night. I thought this was merely how you preferred to be greeted—a human custom I do not understand." He's fighting a smirk and I can't tell if it is a result of my reaction or if he knows full well that this isn't a human custom.

"Humans do not enter other people's bedrooms without invitation," I huff, erring on the side of him genuinely not knowing.

"But you—"

"I know I did." I roll my eyes. "But you, sir, are an exception."

"Lucky me," he says playfully enough that I can't discern his true feelings on the matter. But his expression quickly sobers. "We should begin our preparations early. The wraiths are worse at night so we will want to leave while the sun is still high."

Today is the day, at long last. I'm going to get the silver and save my family. While relief surges through me, it's also tempered with a gut-wrenching horror about the unknowns that await me in this infamous Gray Trench. The glimpses I have seen of it are horrifying enough. What else lurks in those depths?

"I'm ready," I say with confidence. I've faced the unknown before. I can do it again.

"If you would rather—" He crosses to me.

I stop him with a gentle hand on his chest. When we're alone, touching him is easy—natural. "My mind is made up; I'm going, Ilryth. They're my family, my responsibility. I cannot abandon them."

His fingers close around mine and he gives a firm nod. "I understand."

"I know you do," I say softly. I truly believe he does. After all I've seen, all that weighs on him, there's no doubt in my mind. "Now, let's begin these preparations." I free my hand and busy it by smoothing it down my front, pressing out invisible wrinkles on my shorts, my attention snagging on the colorful and golden markings that shine on my arm.

It's very odd to not be regularly putting on fresh clothes. But in this form, I don't sweat; I don't seem to collect grime. My skin is as clean as it was when Ilryth first took me here. My hair remains untangled no matter how long it drifts through ocean currents unbound by braids. As uncomfortable as it might be to constantly have a nagging feeling that I am living in filth, it's also terribly convenient as my mornings and evenings are much more streamlined without worrying about maintaining a physical form. Becoming more magic than flesh and blood has its benefits.

"Are you all right?" he asks.

"Yes, just thinking about how much I've changed over these past few weeks."

Ilryth pauses. I turn my eyes to him. I half expect him to tell me that I haven't changed. It seems like the polite thing to say. The kind thing to say. But he doesn't. And somehow…well, it doesn't make me feel better, but there is comfort in it. In knowing he's realistic. Pragmatic. That he's going to tell me the truth and not just cozy platitudes. I admire that in a person.

"It's all right," I say, mostly for my own benefit. "I've gone through many journeys, many evolutions." I chuckle softly. "I even changed my name once."

"You did?"

"Well, I began going by my middle name." I avoid mentioning how the more official name change was dropping Charles's family name.

"Why?" He seems genuinely curious with how he leans in slightly, as if he's hanging on my words.

"Because the woman I was died in the ocean the night we met. I didn't want to be her anymore. Her name didn't fit me any longer." Maybe, in a way, forgetting the memories of Charles, and all else that I've lost, is stripping off the last of Elizabeth's old skin that still clings to my bones.

He opens his mouth, almost as if he's going to say something more. But he refrains. I don't press for whatever thought it might have been.

Instead, Ilryth says simply, "We should go."

"Right. Lead the way."

Ilryth swims over the balcony and I follow at his side. We head for a square building toward the center of the estate. This building is blockier than the majority of the constructions. There are no open archways or flowing kelp screens. It's a solid structure—cut into a hulking rock—with only one entry, which is curiously sealed by a door that looks like a porthole. Ropes are wrapped around it.

Lucia and Sheel wait on either side of the entry with worried expressions.

"Lucia. Sheel," Ilryth greets them each in turn.

"This is a terrible idea," Sheel grumbles. Lucia is silent but radiates agreement.

Ilryth ignores the remark and begins to unfasten the ties of silvery kelp that hold the large porthole shut. He hums softly as he does, and the ropes shimmer with a rainbow sheen as he loops them around a knob off to the side. Pulling open the porthole, Ilryth leads us all into a dimly lit room.

The room reminds me of the houses of worship to the old gods I saw in the countryside where Lord Applegate was from—the buildings with the tall towers and rare stained-glass windows. This has no such glass, but it is ornately carved inside. Giant roots of stone wrap around the sandy floor of the room, coalescing into the base of a sculpture of a tree that stretches to the ceiling. Its carefully rendered canopy supports the roof as rocky beams. Lifelike leaves glisten in the hazy light brought in through the porthole.

The carved roots and branches slowly tangle across the walls, changing with the skilled hand of a master sculptor into tentacles. The suction-cupped limbs collect and weave together. Like rolling waves crashing into each other. They circle around the sunken visage of a beast.

No...not a beast. A god.

Krokan is portrayed with an almost humanlike face. He has a flat, elongated chin and a jawline that stretches up to his temples, shrinking at the eyes before flaring out like the spiked mantle of an armored beetle. Four eyes are set in two diagonals, opposite each other. His beaked mouth grips the porthole we entered through. The rest of his body is impossible to discern. It is lost behind all the tentacles. Perhaps completely unknown.

I stare at the figure in awe. In horror. The markings on my skin become ropes upon me. My whole body feels tight in a constricting, wrenching way. I almost want to claw my skeleton out of my flesh. Carve my mind from the skull to escape the whispering song that's humming in my marrow.

Look away, Victoria, I command myself. But I can't. I'm stuck. Staring. I am going into the trench that connects to his Abyss. Where his emissaries lie in wait. Will Krokan feel me there? He knows I'm marked for him. He's calling me. *Calling...*

...Victoria...

"Victoria?" Ilryth jolts me from my thoughts. I whirl. The room spins until I lay eyes on him. Then everything comes into focus. "Are you all right?"

I glance around him, at Lucia and Sheel down below. They've all collected around a ghostly tree at the far back of the room, wrapped in a nest of sculpted roots.

"I am," I say just for Ilryth.

He nods and swims away. I glance back at the statue and the same creeping feeling is there...but I don't let it overtake me again. I cannot worry about the things beyond my control. The what ifs. The beast will have me when it is his time. I will relinquish myself for my family, my friends...even for the Eversea.

"Are you sure this is the right course of action?" Sheel asks as we swim over. At the center of the ghostly tree in the far back of the room is a spear. It's not different in shape or material than the dozen others skewered into the floor of this room, but the wood seems paler. It has an aura of importance.

"It won't be long enough for the magics holding back the rot to be disrupted," Ilryth reassures him.

"How can you be so confident?" Sheel is less than convinced.

"I will lead a group in the songs of protection here. Fenny in the amphitheater," Lucia says.

"And you will be at the ready with men. Take the spears you need from the armory. But I do not think you will have to use them." Ilryth motions to the sand around them. Then he reaches for the spear at the center of the ghostly tree.

Sheel grabs his wrist. Ilryth gives him a look that conveys offense at the boldness—at the challenge. Sheel slowly unfurls his fingers and drifts back.

Without another moment of hesitation, Ilryth lifts the spear from its spot on the floor. The shift in the waters happens immediately as the anamnesis fades. Everything stills. Shadows are longer. Colors duller. It's colder.

"If something happens to you, and subsequently Dawnpoint, the rot will claim the duchy. That is one of five great spears, there is no replacement." Sheel drifts forward slightly as his torso pitches. He's pleading.

"Do we need to take Dawnpoint?" I eye the spear. This must be the one his mother was carrying in the memory. The infamous weapon that Ilryth left behind the first time I saw him go into the trench because it was protecting the duchy.

"It will be safest, and fastest, this way."

"I don't want to leave the Duchy of Spears at risk because of me."

I'm supposed to be helping people, not hindering them. I *won't* hinder them. I can't prove Charles right and be a burden…though I suppose I already have by demanding this trip to begin with. My stomach knots. What is worth more, my family? Or the whole of the Eversea? I know what the answer was, for me, and what it should be. But what it is now, I'm no longer sure.

"Yes, Your Grace, please. Reconsider this risk," Sheel encourages.

"It'll be all right." Ilryth speaks mostly to me. "I'm taking Dawnpoint because it improves our chances for success. If I didn't, we'd risk more because we'd risk your life."

I go, and I risk dying to the wraiths or monstrous emissaries of Krokan or rot or whatever other horrors are down there. It would leave the Eversea in turmoil. They'd have no other sacrifice and only a few months left before the summer solstice. Given how much time they've already spent anointing me—and I'm not even halfway through the process—I doubt they could find someone else in time. And if I died… the Eversea, maybe the world, would be at risk.

I don't go, and my family will go to a debtors' prison. Charles will demand Em's hand. She will be his lighthouse attendant and suffer the fate I escaped.

I love my sister more than anything. I owe my parents everything. I can't let them down. I won't. But I also won't fail and leave the Eversea struggling. I can accomplish both.

"I won't let you all down," I say with conviction. Everyone's eyes are on me. But I'm focused solely on Ilryth. I match the intensity of his dark eyes, trying to show that I understand how serious this is. "We can keep each other safe. We will do what must be done, as we have until now."

"What do you think you can do?" Sheel asks plainly. It doesn't come off as intentionally rude, but the words still sting. He must realize it, because he backtracks slightly. "I am grateful for your help with Yenni, but cleansing rot and fighting a wraith are two very different things." He's not wrong.

"Ilryth has been teaching me how to use our duet and harness the magic within me. We've been preparing for this."

"For just how long?" Sheel side-eyes Ilryth, who ignores him, focusing on Lucia instead.

"She might actually be able to help a great deal," Lucia chimes in, as if on cue. I suspect Ilryth had been consulting her on our plans long before now. "As an anointed, she's been given unique immunities from the call of the Veil and the Beyond. It might offer her similar protections—better, even, since it's imprinted on her soul—as the armor from the Lifetree. In fact, it could be possible that she is like a tree spear just by the virtue of her existence."

"I did see her power against the rot," Sheel says thoughtfully. "But the wraith targeted her specifically."

"Weeks ago," Lucia says gently. I didn't expect her to turn to me, but she regards me with wary confidence. I try to reassure her with a look alone. "She is stronger now. Even if she does attract them, she can defend herself."

"There's only one question that matters." Ilryth swims up to me. His intense, dark eyes are like the space between the stars—infinite, cool, and dangerously inviting. "Are you ready?"

"I am." Once more, I will charge ahead into the vast unknown. Keep moving forward. Keep putting distance between myself and the past.

"Lord Ilryth, I should give one cautionary note, we've never tested all this before. It's impossible to know how her markings might be impacted by the trench, or going back to the Natural World," Lucia cautions. "Everything we've discussed has been my speculation."

That further confirms my suspicion that they've been in cahoots. My opinion of Lucia is increasing by the moment.

"Your Grace, as your general, I must still advise against this." Sheel's attention darts between Lucia and Ilryth, prompted to action once more by her hesitation. "We shouldn't take any unnecessary risks with the offering. Think of what the Duke of Faith would say if he caught word of this."

"We're doing it," Ilryth declares, as if emboldened by Sheel's continued refusals.

"If you must…but let's not be hasty, please." It's evident by Sheel's tone that he's struggling to come to terms with this. Part of him wants to follow orders. Part knows what Ilryth is risking. Part of me feels for the position he's in. "Lucia, could you perhaps consult with your scrolls from the Order of the Lifetree on this before we go rushing in needlessly?"

She bristles slightly. "There isn't anything in the records. I know them quite well and would remember anything regarding the offering." I take it that this isn't the first time Sheel has questioned her on matters of faith.

"There's no time for consulting scrolls," I interrupt. "I can do this. I must do this." All eyes are on me. "I give you all my word. I will keep both of us safe. What's the point of me learning the words of the old ones if I'm not going to use them?"

Ilryth studies me. I must measure up, because he holds out his hand to me. I hesitate a moment, trying to ascertain Sheel and Lucia's expressions from the corners of my eyes. But it's impossible. All that truly matters—exists, even—is Ilryth and me. It doesn't matter what they think or feel, what matters is what I do.

I take his hand before them. His palm is larger than mine, but his grip is equally firm and calloused. I took his physique for a laborer's originally, but now I see him for what he is—a warrior.

"Please, Your Grace," Sheel objects. "If you leave the Eversea you risk her disappearing—You're—"

Ilryth whirls in place, his lips part, and he lets out a low note—one of warning, of danger. He dips his chin, leveling his eyes with Sheel's. The general stills, swaying slightly. His gaze softens and jaw slackens.

Lucia raises a palm to her chest, bowing before her lord. A soft melody emits from her as well. One that pulses in harmony with Ilryth's.

The sounds would've once been unintelligible to me. It is as though every language of the world has been merged into one. There are the beginnings of words, given up and mashed together with other sounds before disappearing.

Yet, I can glean meaning from it. I hear Sheel's worry and pain. How he fears for my anointment and the very magic that makes up my form. I hear Lucia's understanding and support. All the sounds combine in my mind in wondrous harmony—a sound human ears have probably never heard before and certainly wouldn't have understood if they did.

Ilryth closes his mouth, and the song stops. Sheel is still in a dazed state. The duke looks to me. I nod before a thought is exchanged. No need for words. I'm ready for what awaits us.

His body compresses in on itself. Ilryth bends at the hips, drawing his tail in, elbows back. He explodes with power, jetting out into the open water and taking me with him.

I twist, reaching up to his right shoulder with my right hand. Ilryth understands my movements and reaches back to help me. I settle behind him, gripping both his shoulders. Our bodies move together effortlessly. The feeling is familiar enough and my thoughts are too far elsewhere for me to be too distracted by our proximity. I'm focused on the trench ahead.

We soar over the coral barrier and wooden walls that serve as the defensive line for the trench. Much like how the water changed when Ilryth removed Dawnpoint from its place, the water shifts instantly when we pass the barriers. There's a faint, bloody tint to the seas. The sand is paler. Gray. It looks like it would be cold to the touch.

Not far is a large chasm, greater and deeper than any I've ever imagined. We run parallel to it for some time. I regard the swirling depths of thick rot at my right warily, peering into the darkness for any sign of a wraith that might creep over the edge…or the curl of a massive tentacle.

Eventually an underwater mountain range begins to obstruct our path.

"Hold on tightly. It's difficult for light to penetrate the depths so you'll need to stay with me."

"I'm not going anywhere." I squeeze his shoulders.

"Good. I want you nowhere but my side." The words leave no room for doubt. I wonder if he knows all the ways I could read into them but choose not to.

We pitch over the vast trench. Night has pooled in its depths, like a sea within a sea. The water beneath us is somehow denser still and swirls with ominous curls of rot.

Ilryth descends. There is no time for hesitation. It is just like charging into a storm at sea.

Steel yourself, Captain, I tell myself.

The gloom and red swallows us whole. All light has vanished. Ilryth cuts through the darkness with the spear. It's begun to emit a faint, shining glow. He waves it from side to side now and then, swirling away the muck that begins to cling to his arms.

Frost creeps up my legs, biting into my marrow. I imagine that without the magic woven into me, I couldn't survive the pressure between my ears, or the rot that clots my nose…and certainly the cold would've killed me by now. This far below the waves there is no light, no warmth, no life.

This is a place only for death.

Yet, we are not alone. I can sense movement in the waters around us. Monsters? Wraiths? Large, or small? One or many? Impossible to tell. I can't see anything other than a night more intense than I have ever known.

The phantom sensations of Krokan's tentacles wrapping around me have me fighting a shudder. The monster of my imagining cradles me in one of its suckers before it crushes me, bringing me to its toothed beak for consumption as it did my crew. For a brief second, I feel as if I might never see the light of day again.

"Hold steady, Victoria," Ilryth says, cutting through the grim thoughts. "Don't let them take your mind."

"Them?"

"The dead. They're here." The words are as solemn as church bells tolling for a funeral. I feel that cold grip sliding around my neck once more, prompting me to glance over my shoulder. But there's nothing there. "Steady yourself and guard your mind. Don't let them drag out your thoughts."

"I know how to protect my thoughts from others." The Eversea helped—since I first arrived, I was having to be mindful of what I thought, and how. But well before that, I was practicing. *Bury it all, deep down. Don't let anyone—don't let him—see what brings you joy or it will be taken and destroyed.*

"Good. That skill and more will be needed soon."

"Soon?" The way he said it has me wondering. There was an ominous tone to the word.

"Now!" Ilryth twists, nearly throwing me. If not for my years clutching the deck railing of ships, I might have been. He thrusts out his spear and lets out a sharp sound, followed by a descending trill of notes.

The light flares, illuminating the unraveling, wispy, and tortured visage of a wraith.

nineteen

IT ISN'T UNTIL I'M STARING INTO THE EYES OF A WRAITH THAT I REALIZE I'VE YET TO SEE ONE IN PERSON. The first time I encountered wraiths, they had possessed the bodies of Ilryth's men. The next time, the wraith caught me from behind.

This is the first time I've ever laid eyes on one outright. And it's exactly how I would've imagined. The ghostly man is more condensed fog, or mist, than anything corporeal. He moves as if by dissipating and reappearing—parts never quite catching up and floating through the undersea currents as tiny tendrils outlining where details once were.

In life, the soul belonged to a man with long hair, tied at the neck, and a thinly bearded face. I'm almost reminded of my own father from the hair on his chin. But this man wears clothes that would've been considered in fashion almost thirty years ago. I've only ever seen my father tie a cravat in that tight-necked, stuffy style...

The thoughts evaporate. The memory of my father tying his cravat. Staring in the mirror. A barely eighteen-year-old me kisses him on his cheek, he smiles, and...*nothing*. Whatever he was dressing up so formally for, I can't recall.

The wraith retreats with a scream, summoning me back to the present. He shies away from the light of the spear, expression twisting with utter loathing. All the contempt in the world is on his face. As though it is our fault he is no longer among the living.

Rather than continuing to fight, Ilryth speeds away, deeper

still into the rot-filled chasm. He propels us mostly by his tail as his arms are occupied with tapping his spear into his opposite palm. With every beat, light pulses around us, scaring away the monsters that lurk in this sea of death. I'm reminded of the bells we use to keep away the sirens. A similar strumming to disturb the singing enough to allow us passage.

"Victoria, I need you to sing."

I don't hesitate or falter. This is like all the times in the amphitheater—like with Yenni. My mouth knows the words of the old ones now like my hands know the ropes of a ship. The best thing to do is not overthink.

My eyes flutter closed for a moment. My grip on him relaxes enough that it's less viselike and more steady. The first note escapes me, as low as a growl. Ilryth joins in. We find the harmony quickly and it sends a shiver down my spine with just how sweet our two voices sound entangled. Even our bodies are moving now in perfect synchronicity.

Consciousness fades into the rhythm. Into the harmonies. I slip into my memories that begin to flash the moment I look for a word of the old ones to sing. Something for protection, to guard and guide… That will do. I settle on a word and I can feel the pull of the power in the back of my mind. Rising from my toes. Swelling through my body to the point that my bones almost ache.

It demands I give something up to claim this power. A price I am all too happy to pay if it keeps us safe. I've begun working from the oldest memories of Charles and am going forward. I pick a memory of a cold night, one where I grew so exhausted from maintaining the bell while we were waiting on a part for the mechanism that I fell asleep on the stairs, unable to make it back to the bed. Charles had been gone, again. And when he returned to find the bell not ringing…

It's gone.

What was I thinking of?

This word. That's what I needed. "*Solo'ko…*" I sing the word of power and Ilryth's staff shines even brighter.

Singing grows easier as we continue our descent. My mouth opens and closes, miming the act of breathing in, as if I still can, as though there is air and not endless water surrounding me. As if I am singing with my lungs and not with magic etched onto my skin. I feel nothing moving through my body. In fact, I hardly feel my body at all.

As the words and the light of Ilryth's spear wash over me, they scare away more memories. More flashes of moments in my past that are paid as the cost of our safety—paid to part the seemingly impenetrable gloom. Waves of light from Dawnpoint strike against the darkness and clotted rot, making a hissing sound—like water dropping onto hot iron, instantly bubbling and searing away. It accompanies the sounds of distant screams.

Finally, we begin to slow. My eyes flutter open. I don't remember closing them. The wraiths seem to have left us, for now.

The light from Ilryth's spear strikes against something that isn't water and rot. There, far beneath the surface of the sea, is a ring of stone pillars. They tower around a paved circle, an empty bowl at its center. The sea floor around the structure is upended, appearing almost like waves carved into the sand and stone.

No...not waves. And not sand or stone, either. Roots. Giant, stony roots, coated in crimson rot that pours from cracks in them like festering wounds.

They are as massive as ships and puncture through the rocky cliffs that converge down toward the bottom of this deep valley. The roots wrap around the lone stone oasis in a way that could be cradling, or consuming.

They must be the roots of the Lifetree, I realize. Dead and rotting in this watery grave. Ilryth heads toward the circle of columns far below.

Rather than swimming into the arched grotto from above, Ilryth takes us down along the roots. A compelling urge to touch them nearly overtakes me, but I cling to Ilryth instead as he swims under one of the archways of the circle and right up to the stone basin in the center of this underground altar.

The basin is much larger up close—large enough for me to curl up within if I wanted. But I don't release him. Ilryth dips the tip of his spear into the large, chalice-like structure. As he does, I notice spots of rot that cling to his skin, as though he has been splattered with blood. Ghostly ribbons unfurl from the tip of his spear into tendrils that take the shape of leafy vines. They grow at an impossibly fast rate, spilling over the edges of the basin and flowering, winding against each other to weave into a small sapling at the center. As the glow radiates over

Ilryth, the red rot on his skin vanishes like dew evaporating in the morning light. My own skin remains clear.

"It's safe here now. You can relax." He eases away from the stone bowl, resting his spear against the pedestal upon which it sits.

The last note hangs as I slowly uncurl my fingers. With the slightest push, I drift away from him, looking up at the nothingness above us. The light from the ghost tree illuminates this small circle, but it does little to show much beyond it. Had I not seen the cliffs on either side of us, I wouldn't know we were at the bottom of a vast trench. I wouldn't know anything about this location at all.

I'm like a broken compass, spinning with no heading. Screams echo in the back of my mind. They're all around me. Vertigo claims me and I sway. It's hard to tell which way is up, suddenly. Underwater, there is no up or down, not really, not in the same way as on land.

I know the way we came, I try to remind myself. The earth itself is beneath me. And yet, my mind doubts itself. I've never been in a place so completely void of any markers. There's no light. No landmarks. Even in a calm sea and empty, blue sky, I have the sun. I have—

"Victoria?" Ilryth says, though his voice seems at a great distance. Are my senses beginning to leave me as well?

A part of me is in the dark bell room underneath the lighthouse. I'm in the tiny closet adjacent, embedded into the thick rock of the island, where it is safe for the cotton to be out of my ears. Where no sound can reach.

Safe to scream and weep without him hearing…

I press my palm against my thigh, where the pocket for my compass would be. But it's long gone. The thing that always guided me—that I could depend on to lead the way—is gone. I have nothing to lead me from the darkness. I—

"Victoria." A hand clasps my shoulder. I spin, startled, looking up at a pair of eyes as dark as the void that surrounds us.

Will I be trapped here forever? Will I become one of those things?

His eyes widen slightly. Ilryth heard me. Even through the shell he heard my fears.

"You're not trapped and you won't become one of them." Ilryth shakes his head. "As I said, it's normal to feel panic, sorrow, or anger in the presence of the wraiths. They feed off life in a vain attempt to steal it."

"But I don't see any wraiths."

"That doesn't mean they're not still there. Lurking. Waiting to see when we'll reemerge from this haven, or if they can convince us into doing so," he says gravely.

"This isn't from the wraiths," I murmur with a shake of my head, trying to calm myself.

"It's perfectly normal—"

"I know my emotions, don't question me on them," I interject firmly. When I first began captaining ships, there were a few sailors who would question if I was "too emotional" to helm a vessel. After proving them wrong, that I was quite capable of having emotions and leading a crew, I promptly showed them off my ship at the next port. "How to keep a firm hand on my emotions was something I learned very, *very* well."

"Which makes it all the more terrifying when they're out of control." He speaks like he knows the feeling, the terror of finding yourself trapped in a mind you can't recognize. A maze of nightmares of your own design. "Come. The closer you are to the basin, the better you will feel."

His arm slides around my shoulders to guide me over. I notice how the inked markings of his bicep press against the tattoos that swirl on my upper arm. As though we are one—meant to fit together.

Ilryth sits on one side of the square pedestal that holds the anamnesis; I sit on another next to him. Both our backs are against the stone. Our hands relax to the ground. Almost touching. With just one shift my pinky would brush against his… Instead, I draw my knees to my chest.

"What happened to this place?" I ask. "How did it get like this if the Lifetree once grew here?"

Ilryth stares out at the darkness, not looking at me as he speaks. Instead, he's focused on the roots around us, or something beyond. "Some called the Gray Trench the 'bridge between life and death.' It was the long march for souls to traverse down to Lord Krokan's Abyss. They would be guided by the anamnesis, and places like this were opportunities for my ancestors to pay last respects and sing songs of protection on the dead.

"But…we siren slowly forgot the words of the old ones. Lady

Lellia's songs were harder to remember than Lord Krokan's." He stares out at the nothingness with a sad expression. I remember in his memory when he lamented not hearing Lellia's words. "It was postulated that the roots died when we stopped paying homage to her. Then, with Krokan's rage allowing the forces of the dead to bleed into our world, the roots began to rot; it is now solely Lord Krokan's domain. The balance is off. This is Death's grave."

"Do you think Krokan was the one who killed the roots?"

"He would never. Lord Krokan is the old god of death, but he does not wield his power with malice. He bridges our world and the Great Beyond with his wife, Lady Lellia. The Lifetree is what roots her to this world. He would never intentionally attack it. The impacts on the Lifetree are the failure of the sirens and a casualty of his rage."

"He would never attack Lady Lellia, assuming he was still in his right mind," I say as gently as I can. "But I'm sure it would've been said that Krokan would've never attacked the Eversea, either, right?" Ilryth continues to stare. I know he heard me so I don't press for a response. "Do the sirens have any idea of why Krokan is raging the way he is?"

"If we did, it would've been long since mended." Ilryth sighs heavily. "The siren viewed the bond of Lord Krokan and Lady Lellia as the most sacred connection in our world, and the next. It is why we value our oaths to others so much. Why, when we marry, we do so for life."

It's my turn to look out into the Abyss. It's not the first time I've wondered what Ilryth might think if he knew the truth of my debt, but this is the first time I've dwelled on it. Oaths sound like they're even more important here than in Tenvrath, especially marriage. I suppose I have my answer for why he never considered me having previously been married.

A sad smile crosses my lips. I'm mildly surprised to find that I dislike the idea of being seen as less than favorable to Ilryth. It makes the bud of affection for him that had been growing within me, despite my wishes, stint. *Who could ever love you, Victoria?* I ask myself, in my own voice. Not Charles's. But he's the one who answers, *No one.*

Maybe I'll give up all my memories of Charles and our time together before Ilryth finds out. That way, if Ilryth ever does, I can look him in the eye and tell him I've no idea what he's speaking of. I will remove that shame from me by force. With every sung word I'll wring it from my bones.

"What is it?" he asks softly. "What are the wraiths making you think of?"

"What do you mean?"

"You look sad."

Ah, sweet man, I can make myself sad all on my own. No ghostly evils necessary.

"I was thinking we should start moving again," I lie. Then to ensure he won't probe, I add, "You said they are more active at night. We're racing the dusk."

Ilryth straightens and looks down at me. The light of the anamnesis casts half of his face in silver, the refraction of the rocks casting the other half in a deep blue. He looks like the image of the balance of life and death that he previously described. As effortlessly handsome as always. As untouchable as this whole world previously was to me.

Yet, Ilryth extends his hand. Like a bridge between two worlds that should have never been, I take it and Ilryth pulls me up. He isn't expecting me to push off as well, and I float right into him.

My body slides against his, too much, too quickly. The little shorts I wear bunch between my thighs, generating uncomfortable friction. Reminding me of just how little touching has happened in that particular location. I shift my legs, but that only makes it worse as they brush up against the scales of his tail, sending a shiver up my spine at the smooth, cool sensation.

We ease away slightly. I avoid his probing stare.

"It's not just for the wraiths." Ilryth seems to gather his thoughts as well before continuing as if nothing happened. "It's easier for souls and spirits to travel at night. Yes, that includes the wraiths, but also you."

"Unless I died without knowing...I'm not a spirit." I certainly hope I would know about that sort of change in status.

"You're not," he agrees. "But the magic holding your body together has been imprinted on your soul. Much like the souls of the wraiths being held together by the magic of death. When we cross the Fade, there is a chance of it unraveling with the dawn—just like a wraith or ghost would."

Sheel's worries return to me. Yenni. The whole of the Eversea...

They told me that I might not survive beyond the Eversea, and that was a risk I was willing to take for my family. But the cost could be all of them. The scope of my selfishness comes back into focus.

"We…we should return," I whisper.

Ilryth startles, then a serious expression overtakes his features, shadowing them. "You don't mean that."

"I can't…" *Am I really doing this? Am I really sacrificing my family for them?* "How can I go to my family at the cost of the Eversea?" It was so clear to me what was worth more when I first arrived. Now, I'm not so certain.

"These doubts are the wraiths speaking for you." Ilryth grabs my hands. He's as immovable as the giant roots around us. "We will save both. Your family and the Eversea. Together."

"How can you be so sure?"

"I…" It's his turn to trail off. To lose himself in his thoughts, words knotted. "I have no reason to be," he admits. "But when I'm near you, I find myself believing that anything and everything is possible."

I stare, stunned.

"So keep your strength a bit longer, for us all."

Somehow, I manage a nod.

"Good." He smiles and it is as if dawn itself has broken over this dark, forgotten corner of the world. Ilryth points through one of the archways. How he knows what direction is what escapes me. "Just beyond there is the Fade. On the other side of that is the Gray Trench, and your ship. We will go and get the silver you need and return before night falls."

"I'm ready."

Ilryth puts his back to me and I position myself on him. Without another word or thought of hesitation, we charge off once more into the vast and dangerous depths.

twenty

WE SPEED THROUGH THE DARKNESS, PAST THE SECOND CIRCLE OF STONE ARCHES WHERE HE SPROUTED ANOTHER ANAMNESIS AND WE CAUGHT OUR BREATH, BUT ONLY BRIEFLY.

The song I'm singing has now become second nature. The notes flow from me without thought. At first, I thought deeply about trying to ensure I continued to pronounce every word and sound correctly, but I've since let that go. Now they're muddled, running over each other.

Memories continue slipping through my fingers. My ties to this world weaken as I strengthen the power of those mysterious, old gods within me. What I sacrificed in the amphitheater before was nothing like this. Vaguely, behind all the words and song and magic, I wonder if I will forget everything… *Will there come a time where I don't even know my name?*

The idea is so horrifying it almost makes my mind gutter. My song stop. If that is the cost of my family's safety, here and now, but also protecting them from an old god's rage seeping into my world, then of course I'll pay it.

We reach a final ring of stones. This one is different from the others. It has a taller archway that faces a wall of living shadow. Carved into the stone are musical markings of the old gods. With their ancient language fresh in my mind, I hear whispers of mysterious melodies in the back of my mind—as if the shadow itself is the singer.

"What is this place?" I ask as Ilryth lights the basin with his spear, sprouting another anamnesis.

"It's the gate of souls. The one spot in the Fade that allows passage through. When the Elf King erected the Fade, this was left in accordance with the bargains made between the old gods and his forefather. This is the final push back to the Natural World, but it won't be an easy one." He glances over his shoulder, back at me. "Are you ready?"

"As I'll ever be."

We plunge into the living night that is the Fade.

It's oppressive, clouding my lungs, even though they can't breathe. It stings my eyes and burns like hot smoke. For a moment, it feels as if I am being ripped apart. But it passes quickly.

In the distance is a faint light, like a keyhole, that grows large enough for us to swim through. We emerge into a choppy, gray sea.

The sea floor is barren. No shipwrecks. No rocks. No coral. Just smooth sand and the occasional skeleton of some primordial beast whose frame I can't recognize.

Torrential currents try to rip me from Ilryth. I clutch tighter to his shoulders, hanging on to him with all my might.

Among the unbroken sand is another altar that was once used to sprout an anamnesis, not too far from the archway we emerged through. However, we do not stop. The pillar has been toppled, basin shattered. If I hadn't seen those small outposts not long ago, I wouldn't have even been able to tell what it had once been intended as. Magic has forgotten this place—my home.

Though, it doesn't feel like home. Even back in my world, this place is strange and terrifying.

I am in the depths of the Gray Passage.

It feels as oppressive and dangerous down here as it does atop the waves. Sharks and other ominous shadows swirl through the darkness. In the distance, I see a monster twice the length and girth of my ship. Lights dance on its side, three flashes. It writhes and an overwhelming sense of being watched overtakes me. I see its maw open—a silhouette on a deep blue-gray background. Sickles of sharp teeth are hidden within, sending a chill down my spine.

In a blink, it's gone.

"Ilryth, did you see that?" I whisper, keeping my focus on just him. I don't know what senses those beasts might have.

"I did," he says just as softly.

"Was it—"

"An emissary of Lord Krokan? Yes."

I fight a shudder. My training is overtaking me. Years of practicing to look calm and in control when terror wants to grip me by the throat.

"What other monsters are here?"

"Some that are no doubt worse than our imagining... It is a rare breed of creature indeed that will feed off the carcasses of the living and the souls of the dead." Ilryth slows, shifting. He reaches up, taking my hand, turning in the water. His fingers trail up my arm as he swims underneath me, continuing to pull me along. I'm briefly enamored with the grace of his movements. The elegance of how we change positioning is breathtaking...almost intimate, seeing him beneath me. Ilryth drags his fingers down the markings on my arm. "How are you feeling? You seem all right."

"I feel fine. Other than slightly unnerved." I'm grateful I don't have to speak my words, otherwise they might not have been as strong as I wanted.

"Yes, we should move quickly." He twirls back around, propelling himself back and into me. The heat of his body is even more apparent and I pull myself slightly closer to him. Ilryth is my only waypoint in this dangerous and unknown sea. He holds out his spear, using its light to guide us. "Now, keep singing."

It doesn't take long until we are weaving back through an underwater mountain range. Though, like everything else beneath the surface of the sea, these mountains are unlike any I've seen before. More like flat-topped columns and sinking valleys. As if the floor of the ocean has fallen out even farther beneath us. I dread to think what might be lurking in those depths, well beyond my realm of sight.

Then, we finally arrive at my ship.

Even shattered and broken, I know it in an instant, and everything grinds to a halt the moment I lay my eyes upon it. Ilryth still moves beneath me. I can still—albeit barely now—feel the water against my face. But everything within me freezes.

The vessel has been cleaved in two by the mighty tentacles of

Krokan's emissary. The stern has been reduced completely to pieces, most of it missing. The bow is hole-ridden and cracked, but at least resembles its former glory.

I want to weep. I want to howl, clutch my gut, and emit screams of my grief. No person should be made to look upon the innards of the tomb of their loved ones. It is as if I am staring into the eyes of Death himself and he is mocking me.

It is because of me that they're dead.

"No, it is because of a raging god," Ilryth says solemnly.

"Why is the shell no longer helping to conceal my thoughts?" I blurt, frustrated its protection seems to have vanished.

"Perhaps because we're in the Natural World. Or perhaps because…I am closer to you than before."

Horror seizes me. This can't be happening. Especially not here and now. "What do you mean?"

"We've sung together."

I keep in a sigh of relief. "Of course that's all it is."

Ilryth twists, holding me by the shoulders. He looks me in the eyes. "You know this wasn't your fault, don't you?"

"I… We need to keep going."

He stops me from swimming away. "Victoria, look at me."

I relent, but only to get us to move along.

"You know that, right?"

"I do."

"If only you said it like you meant it."

"Look at it!" My voice pitches, sharpening. "My ship is wrecked. My crew is dead. They followed me because they believed in me. They stood by my side for me. And what did they get for it? A cruel, painful, horrifying death."

"No. Their death was fate's hand. What they got from you was years of companionship." Ilryth's lips part slightly and he seems to be bracing himself. "A life at the side of a woman of your caliber would be a life well lived."

"We have to keep going," I say. His words are under my skin, hooking into me and flooding the freeze I've tried to put on my emotions with warmth.

"Not until you—"

"This isn't the time!"

Ilryth's face scrunches in an expression of frustration and disgust. He looks between me, the wreckage, and the deadly water surrounding us. "You're right. But whenever you are ready to—want to discuss what you've endured…I will be here for you."

He has no idea what I've been through. But that's all right. He doesn't have to.

People say they'll be there…but so few can be trusted when the time comes. People are happy to be there for you until things are tough and messy and hard. Especially when it's a mess they can walk away from.

Ilryth has been kind to me. But what he's offering is not what our relationship is. What it could ever be. I'm his sacrifice. And he is nothing more to me than a business partner. That was the only thing that brought us together and soon it will be over…which will be for the best, for both of us.

"I'm fine," I say warmly, even giving him an easy smile. The trick is making it not look too forced. And getting the tone just right.

So I'm all the more surprised when he turns out to be one of the select few who see through it. "You're not."

"Ilryth—"

"But I won't press further, here and now." Ilryth unhooks the bag that's been attached to his belt. "Get what you need and be quick about it. The sun is setting and we have a narrow window until the wraiths will be more active. I'll keep a patrol."

"Thank you." As I drift away from him, he begins to circle the remnants of the ship. The deep chasm beneath the vessel almost has me frozen in terror, waiting for a tentacle to reach up from the darkness to pull me below.

I make no noise. My face is absent of fear. I shove those emotions deep, deep within me, into the reinforced basement bell room of my soul. To what benefit would howling be? What would tears give me? It will not change my circumstances. It will not bring back my crew.

I must keep going. No matter the pain. No matter what I must endure…I have to keep moving forward.

Keep moving, Victoria, I remind myself.

I swim into the wreckage.

Even though no silver was kept there, the remnants of my cabin distract me. I can't stop myself from pausing briefly. Running my fingers over the stained glass that's shattered across the wall that's become the floor like a constellation that spells doom. All my oil-dipped map canisters are scattered; half are missing. Every precious token I'd collected, reduced to nothing…

I leave it behind. How many times in my life will I just ignore everything that I once had—once was—to become someone new? Is there any part of me that's actually…me? Or am I nothing more than a shape-shifter, becoming whatever I need to be to survive?

Survival is all that's important now. But not my own.

Farther down is the hold—where the silver was kept. I work to get there. But something else catches my eye. I drift, staring into the gloom of the half of the ship that's still mostly together. Barely visible is the torso of a man, crushed under the weight of the wreckage. All manner of monster and fish have fed upon him, but I still recognize a tuft of brown hair, a string out of place on the elbow of a waterlogged coat…

Now, please, sir, get belowdecks.

Those were my final words to Kevhan Applegate. Firm. Businesslike. Casual.

My trembling fingers cover my lips. Even though I can't scream, I'm trying to hold in the sound. My chest aches. My whole body aches. I've eaten nothing and yet I want to upturn my guts.

I never meant for this to happen to him—to any of them. *It was all my fault.* All my fault for fighting to be free. For not being strong enough to breathe despite feeling Charles's invisible grip upon me.

I grasp above my collarbone. I run my fingers over the markings that have given me power that would horrify Charles. In the end, I won.

But at what cost?

Would it have been better to have endured for eternity?

"Victoria."

Victoria, Charles sneers at me from a distant past.

"Victoria."

You are mine.

"No!" I rear back. Two strong hands are closed around my shoulders. Holding me in place. "Let me go!"

The grip relaxes instantly. It isn't the sound of his voice but how quickly Ilryth releases me that brings me back to the present. I push the hair from around my face, staring at him in silent shock.

"I—I'm sorry. You shouldn't have seen that." I'm not sure if I'm referring to me, or to the corpse.

His expression is nothing but thoughtful concern. "It's all right."

"No, it's not." I go to swim past him, but Ilryth is much faster and more nimble in the water.

"What do you need from me?" he asks.

"Nothing."

"Victoria—"

"Now isn't the time," I remind him coarsely.

"Please, let me help you."

Those five words almost have me at the point of breaking. "*Help me?* Help me like you took my life?"

"I gave you life. You would've drowned in that sea." He is calm and patient in the face of my emotions, even when he has every right to snap.

"Only because you needed me to be a sacrifice!" It's easier if he doesn't care at all. If I'm nothing more than a thing to him. It's more painless that way because it's something I can comprehend. "And even then…you mocked me."

"Mocked you?" He seems genuinely surprised and confused by the remark. It burns all the more when he asks, "How?"

"You told me I wouldn't be held back. But all I've had is the illusion of freedom as I've grasped at straws, fighting futility for just a glimmer of happiness—a moment to live on my own terms…for me. I've had to keep running, and running, and running, or else it would all catch up." My mask is crumbling. I can feel it on my face as my chin juts out slightly. My brow furrows. My cheeks tense and relax, unable to make up their minds. "And it was all an illusion, wasn't it? If not him, then you. If not you, then your god. Surely I'm more than a thing to be claimed. That can't be all there is for me…there must be more."

"Victoria…" Ilryth's eyes flutter closed. A pained expression crosses his features, as though he is mimicking mine.

I seethe. "You mock me."

His eyes open and in them is all the sadness in the world. Enough to drown the seas. "I hear you. *I feel you* as though you are near even when we are oceans apart." His hands run up my shoulders to cup my face. "So tell me, who is 'he'?"

Every muscle in my body goes rigid. I am tense from head to toe. I can't...

I won't...

A fresh wave of nausea sweeps over me. I should be able to say it without fear—*my ex-husband*. I should be able to hold my head high. I am still the great Captain Victoria. No matter what I've been through in life...it doesn't diminish what I have accomplished. I know that.

And yet...I can't. I don't understand why, even. And I hate myself all the more for it.

I'm still searching for a response when movement distracts me. There's a familiar shadow—a silhouette I've seen on many a dark night. Her blonde hair has turned ashen in this ghostly form. Her green eyes have lost their luster.

"Jivre," I whisper. Ilryth turns and makes a low noise of alarm. Of warning.

The shade of my former friend and first mate opens her mouth and lets out a dizzying howl.

twenty-one

"Jivre!" I shout, moving my hands in case she can't hear my thoughts like the sirens can. "It's me."

"That is not your friend, Victoria," Ilryth growls, pulling me close.

I know it's not her...not as I knew her. But this is a fragment of who she was. Of a woman who was so near and dear to my heart. How could I—

Jivre lunges.

Ilryth spins. She's nothing but mist, shadow, and the fading light of life. Ilryth stabs his spear forward, straight into her gut.

My first mate's fingers close around it. She howls again, gnashing teeth. The illumination at the tip of his spear grows as Ilryth sings.

"Please, Jivre, this isn't you. I'm sorry." My hands move as fast as my thoughts.

She's gone with a burst of light.

I blink away the blue haze of where she just was. The dancing lights aren't even gone from my eyes before I slam into Ilryth. "How dare you! She—"

"She was a wraith." Ilryth catches both my wrists. One grip is halfway and awkward as he still holds his spear. It digs into my skin and I feel it more keenly than the water or even his fingers around my other hand. "That wasn't the woman you knew. She would've tried to steal your soul from your body and replace it with her own if you'd given her the chance."

I manage the slightest of nods. Shock and horror are numbing my senses. I am reverting to what I came here to do. Nothing more. Nothing less.

"I need to get the silver. I had a whole crew; there will be more wraiths." If Jivre could be one of those things…any of them could be.

"I'll keep an eye out. Move quickly." Ilryth swims away, trusting me to do what must be done despite my earlier faltering.

I force myself to move. To swim down into the remnants of the hold. The slim, silver bars that had been so carefully stacked are strewn about, barely glinting in the darkness.

My family's safety. Freedom. Future.

Each one I hastily shove into the bag Ilryth gave me is a number in my mind. A rough tally. But more is more. I keep grabbing, the bag bulging but not ripping, until a sharp note distracts me.

There's a flash of light. A grunt. Movement in the darkness. I can feel the wraiths drawing near, clawing their way up from the depths. They cry and scream for us—for me—with a noise that sounds like the frantic singing of a funeral dirge.

It's as I feared. As I knew. They blame me for their deaths and now they want their revenge. But I can't give myself to them for it. There's still more I must do.

I'm sorry, my heart says, even though none of them will hear.

"Ilryth, I have it!" I swim back out, the bag heavy on my shoulder. My siren is over the remnants of the bow of the boat. Two more wraiths surround him.

"Start swimming back!" he shouts.

"Wha—Ilryth!"

He tips down beneath my field of vision. I try and swim over as fast as I can. But, weighted by the bag, he's already coming back up.

"Start swimming, Victoria!"

I do as I'm told. I've become so accustomed to being the one in control, the one calling the shots, that falling into the role of support is uncomfortable. It feels like stepping back into shoes I wore as a girl that no longer fit. But, because of my time as a captain, I also understand it's important to trust the person who has the expertise and knowledge in perilous situations. Sometimes, even the best leaders must follow.

A deep voice fills the seas. I look over my shoulder. Ilryth is death in the water. Wielding a shining spear, he impales wraiths as they descend upon him, exploding them into nothing but a shimmering current. Some of them I recognize. But the majority I do not. My eyes struggle to keep up with the chaos.

Ilryth is skilled in battle. Every movement is trained and graceful. His combat instincts are as honed as mine are to the wind and tides. But he's just one man.

A wraith reaches for him, grabbing his arm. Ilryth does not so much as let out a cry, but I can see pain flash across his face.

I move to call out to him. It draws a wraith's attention. The specter locks eyes with me. Charles's voice fills my ears: *Ring the bell, Lizzie.*

I open my mouth but there is no sound. There are no words, no song. I'm back in that dark bell room during those early weeks that I haven't thought of in years. I thought I gave up this memory…sacrificed it to the words of the old gods. How did the wraith find it within me?

Another wraith swipes for Ilryth, landing a hit on his chest. It hardly registers, even though I'm staring right at him.

Ring. The. Bell. Lizzie, Charles snarls from across time, trying to distract me from the present.

"Victoria!" My name in Ilryth's voice is what brings me from the wraith's trance. The wraiths are pressing into the glob of light around Ilryth. The strength of his spear is wavering.

I am not Lizzie. I am Victoria. And I am no longer in Charles's control. I have not been for years and I will not allow these wraiths to dredge up my horrors and use them against me.

My eyes dip closed. I think back to our practice and feel Ilryth's phantom grip as he holds me around my middle. As he sings into the crook of my neck and shoulder, teaching me down in his amphitheater.

The quiet stillness. The calm. The peace I somehow found in these mysterious songs.

Be gone, my heart demands, *be gone, shadows and shades of the past. I am no longer yours.* That is what my song says in words of my own, layered around the hymns of the old ones. I am louder than the hissing, growling, or screeching of the wraiths.

As my song reaches its peak, light bursts forth from Ilryth's staff. This is different from any power he's used so far. It's brighter, stronger, warmer. It expands out much farther than the previous bubble of protection he drew—so far that it crashes against the rocks and wreckage.

The noise of the wraiths is silenced as they burst into stardust that briefly collects in faint outlines of men and women, who almost immediately disappear with soft sighs. I feel every one of them on my heart. Their pain. Their pleasure. It is as though they each pass through me with palpable strikes on parts of me that should not even be able to be seen. Parts of my very soul.

Slowly, the light fades. The outlines of the undersea carnage of the Gray Passage are nothing more than hazy glows left behind whenever I blink my eyes. But the light is not entirely gone. It clings to me. It is within me...it is...them.

Thank you, I hear in the back of my mind. The words are little more than a butterfly's wings. Brief and fleeting. Gone the moment you feel it. But...it almost sounded like Jivre.

I stare at my hands and the faint, silvery aura that surrounds me as Ilryth swims over. He glows as well. Every marking across his strong body is shining and illuminated, as silver as mine. Even though I know the wraiths landed strikes on him, he doesn't show any signs of the battle. It's as though it never happened.

"What have I done?" *What have I become?*

"You wielded the words of the old ones with all the skill and might of a Duke of Faith. More than, even," he says solemnly, almost reverently.

"Your arm." I reach out, touching it lightly. The markings are warm under my fingertips. Liquid gold, like mine are. However, unlike mine, the magic lining his fades back into flat blue, white, and gold. "I didn't hurt you, did I?"

"No." Ilryth takes my hand in both of his. He holds me by my fingertips alone, but I feel like his arms are around my torso. That he's crushing my body against his. When I look into his eyes, I hear the echo of the song that I made—that we made. Something that was unique only to the two of us. Powerful. "You..." A flash of pain rips though his eyes. He quickly puts his back to me. Once more, I wish I could hear all his thoughts and not just the ones he allows. "We should go. Even though that removed the wraiths in the immediate vicinity, there are still dangers."

I grab his shoulders without another word. I'm too dazed to form cohesive thoughts. As we speed back, I wonder vaguely what memory I must have given up to save us at the wreckage. I wasn't paying attention to plucking one of Charles. I try to think, but there are too many gaps now in my personal record of my history to know for sure.

We pause on the other side of the Fade.

I slowly unravel my fingers from the death grip I had on his shoulders. Ilryth slows to a stop and we break apart. The anamnesis he lit earlier is little more than a flickering outline of what it once was. He crosses to it, reigniting the silvery foliage in the basin.

My own shimmering outline has slowly faded, completely vanishing as we crossed back into the realm of Midscape. I drift over to one of the pillars of this little altar that offers us a brief reprieve and press my forehead against the cool stone. My thoughts are jumbled. It feels as if someone stuck a fork into my mind and whipped my brain.

A familiar grip clasps my shoulder. "Are you all right?"

"My thoughts feel a bit scattered," I admit.

"Once we return, we'll give you a bit of a break from the anointing." He sounds genuinely concerned.

I shake my head and push away. "I'll be fine by then, I'm sure." I force a brave smile. Once more, he doesn't seem convinced. "What did I do to them? I know I wielded the hymns of the old ones, but what happened?"

"Once a soul has lost its way, and all the things that made it mortal are long gone, all that remains is a shell," he says delicately. "Wraiths are husks of what they once were. They left the Abyss and cannot find their way back. Either through fading, or by force, they must be destroyed."

Bubbles prick under the surface of my skin. Faint voices hum in the recesses of my mind. Voices I've never heard before, of people I've never known. They echo the sounds of the wraiths when I let out the burst of light. Jivre's gratitude haunts me—the last of her humanity, spent on me.

"I killed them." It's an odd thought, as they were dead to begin with. "That burst of light... I killed them all. Didn't I?" I look to Ilryth, hoping I have misunderstood. Hoping my analysis of his words is wrong. "Their souls are completely gone? Are you certain I didn't send them to whatever is next?"

"There is nothing 'next' for a wraith but finality," he says, gently but full of sorrow. Ilryth reaches out and places his hand on my cheek. My throat is thick. "You did them a kindness. An end, even a final one, is better than roaming the world as they were, torturing the living as they go. Bringing the rot with them as they spread Lord Krokan's realm of the dead…only to dissipate when all their hate has been exhausted. You gave them a clean death. A moment where they could know humanity once more thanks to Lady Lellia's magic within you, rather than dying as a monster. I know it's what I would want, should such a fate ever befall me."

I hang my head, shaking it slowly. "It's not fair."

"None of this is." His tone is nothing but agreement. "It's not fair that souls must suffer. That Lord Krokan has stopped honoring his bargain made with the first Elf King and escorting souls to the Beyond. That he rages and pillages our seas of life. That in his tortured state his realm bleeds into Lady Lellia, threatening to poison her as well. Nor is it fair that a sacrifice must be sent to him every five years on the summer solstice—an innocent woman who might give her life and have it mean nothing."

I think of his mother. Ilryth watched her go through what I am. Watched her be anointed. Watched her memories be offered up, one by one, before her body was. Did she even recognize him in the end? *Will I?*

The pain that courses through me on his behalf is almost too great to bear.

"It won't be for nothing," I say softly. He startles. Before he can speak, I continue. "If—*when* I go, I will do all I can to quell his rage. To be worthy." If I'm ever worthy for one thing in my life, please, let it be this. "But even if I fail, it won't mean nothing."

He leans back slightly, straightening, as if he's drawing a slow, deep breath. His brow turns in slightly at the center. My chest is tight in sympathy. I reach forward and grab both of his hands, trying to share in his pain—to prove to him that it's really all right.

"It will be worth it to me just to try. Now that I know my family will be safe." I pat the bag of silver that's at my hip. "Trying to keep them all—and the Eversea—safe for eternity will be a good way to go. I've watched people die for a lot less."

Ilryth's eyes, as deep as the mysterious wood, dip closed. He releases the tension that's built within us with a barely audible sigh, leans forward, and rests his forehead on mine. I can't resist raising my chin slightly, on instinct, pulled by a fragile, tenuous thread. Our noses almost touch and, for a minute, we float in a stasis of our own making. The cool waters of the Gray Trench give way to the warmth of our bodies. Our fingers stay interlocked, neither of us willing to break this moment of connection—of comfort.

"Why are you so willing to give everything up so gracefully for people who will never know?" he murmurs. Had he spoke the words, I would've been able to feel his breath graze across my lips. He is that achingly close. "How can you be willing to give everything without a second thought?"

"I think I've had many second thoughts," I quip. A low chuckle rumbles across the edges of my mind, drawing a smile across my lips. My tone turns serious once more. "Because, Ilryth, I've been a burden on so many people around me. Doing this—possibly, literally, saving our worlds—is the very least I can do." Honesty comes with surprising ease.

"You are not a burden. I doubt you ever have been."

"You clearly don't know me." I pull away slightly to meet his eyes as they flutter open, retreating from the almost inescapable pull of the moment before it got the better of me.

"I know you better than you think." His voice is deep and full. Stare intense.

It's too much for me to handle. This topic. The small flutter of my heartbeat. The undeniable want to kiss him in a way that would've consumed me whole.

"We should keep moving," I say.

"We can stay a bit longer, if you need to." His fingers tighten slightly, not yet ready to give up.

I shake my head. "I want to—need to keep moving." I need to see this one thing done. Because I'm afraid that if I stop moving now, I might never start again. Forbidden temptation might win, and I might seek refuge in the embrace of this enigmatic, intriguing, and unexpectedly gentle man who has begun to ensnare me, despite all my best efforts to protect my heart.

twenty-two

IT'S NOON BY THE TIME WE RETURN. Hard to believe that we were gone for only one night. We go to the armory first. The soft singing from within stops the moment we enter. Ilryth swims over a group of men and women—some of whom I recognize from Fenny's failed breakfast. Lucia was leading them in song and continues to do so once Dawnpoint has been returned to its place. The spear supports a rebloomed anamnesis and the Duchy of Spears is back under the protection of Lady Lellia's magic.

We then head to the treasure room. The chest Ilryth had brought me weeks ago is still in the center of the room.

"Go ahead and fill it with the silver," he instructs me as he lowers the satchel off his shoulder. Despite its weight, it hardly seemed to bother him as we swam back. "I'm going to check in with Fenny and Sheel, then I'll return."

I nod and set about my business as he swims off to attend to his.

The chest quickly fills with the silver we took from the wreckage—every bar is a bit of hope for my family's future. I neatly arrange them into lines. He's still not back by the time I do that, so I find a dagger and carve my name into the chest—that way, there's no questioning to whom it belonged and hopefully to whom it should go.

But my name alone still doesn't feel like enough, so I begin to roam the shelves. Poking about the various items. *The mug, perhaps? No…*

"What about the mug?" Ilryth jars me from my explorations. I didn't
see him enter. He hovers by the chest, assessing my work.

"Oh, I was thinking I would leave something else with the treasure.
I wrote my name on the chest, but I thought it couldn't hurt for my
family to have further proof that it belonged to me. Moreover…I want
to add a personal touch that might offer them some kind of peace."

He hesitates, his gaze turning soft. "It would be cruel to let them
know you still live."

"You don't think I know that?" I tilt my head and give him an
incredulous look. Ilryth's expression remains unchanged. Internally
sighing, I wrap my arms around myself. I am back on that beach he left
me on after I escaped Charles. There is a wet cold so deep it would set
into my bones, and my lungs, and make me think that the sea and sirens
gave me back only for the chill to kill me. But I would carry on. I would
survive. For myself—for them.

"I *don't* want them to think I'm alive. If anything, I need them to
know the opposite. I returned from the dead once already; they could
still harbor hope," I say softly. "After that night at the lighthouse, they
heard of my demise only to have me return a few years later, better than
they left me. Thanks to your magic, I made a name for myself as the
unsinkable captain. I pulled through, time and again, no matter how
impossible the situation seemed. My sister once told me that, no matter
how much she worried, she didn't really believe death would ever
be able to hold me. After all that, they might spend years expecting,
hoping, and living like I could return any day. It'd be cruel to put them
through that when there's no hope for me, this time."

"Ah." The sound is a soft hum across my mind, sinking into all the
dark places I previously thought only these grim musings could reach.
"You want to kill their hope early."

"Yes. I don't know how," I admit. "I'm not sure what I could leave
in this chest that would tell them I am gone—to not wait for me to
return. But I have to try something." I shake my head. "I know you will
not understand it. I know I have no right to ask anything more of you."

"Yet you do." The words are slightly amused. Ilryth isn't bothered
in the slightest by my demands. "Very well."

"Pardon?" I meet his eyes, startled.

Ilryth approaches, fumbling at a small pouch in the belt he wears at his hips. He comes to a stop before me, holding out a small, golden compass that fits in the palm of his hand.

Every crack and ding are exactly as I remember, every scuff in its place, plus a few new ones. I slowly reach out, my fingers gliding across the fractured surface of the compass.

"I put this in its spot at the bow of my ship when I went into the Gray Passage," I whisper. Then, I think of Ilryth swimming down by the bow. The wraiths surrounding him. "You…"

"When I was patrolling the wreckage while you were getting the silver, it caught my eye. I knew it was precious to you, so I grabbed it," he says as if it's no matter. I remember when he told me to swim. When he dipped down out of sight at the bow. This was what he was getting.

"How did you know it mattered so much to me?" While it wasn't a secret, it also isn't something I've told him. He shrugs. "Ilryth," I say with a probing tone, so he knows he's not getting out of this.

"There were a few times, when you were setting sail, that I caught glimpses of you."

"You visited me?" I whisper. "Why?"

"You fascinated me." He gestures to the room. A room of seafaring "treasures." Even though I had my suspicions, I also had my doubts; it couldn't all be because of me…could it? "Besides, I had to make sure my protections on you were still strong," he adds offhandedly.

"Was the compass going to become part of your room of treasures?" I'm uncomfortable with the idea of something so important to me being little more than an item on his shelf. One of dozens. Like my old wedding band had been.

He shakes his head and rubs the back of his neck, fingers catching in his hair. "I was thinking it could be a parting present before you went to the Abyss. Something to help you find your way in the world of the gods."

Gifting this to me at any point sounds a lot like holding on to a tether to this world. But I don't say as much. This gesture was profoundly kind. It was something he didn't have to do—something that benefited him in no way and, if anything, risked much. Yet he did it anyway. For me.

"Well, thank you." My fingers close around the familiar compass. It feels heavier than its metal, as heavy as my heart. This compass saw me through the worst of my days. It guided me through countless storms.

It was the first thing I bought for myself—a free woman, out on her own, finding her own way.

It was by this compass that I convinced Kevhan I was a ship captain—a pathetic façade, but it worked. Such a seemingly insignificant thing felt as if it held my freedom in its spinning pointer. It guided me into the unknown for five years…and now, its time is over. That freedom, however fleeting and limited it might have been, is gone.

I place it in the chest. If my compass returns to my family…they'll know I'm not coming back. My life ended with that shatter across the glass. I close the top of the chest. My fingers splay across the surface as I hesitate. It feels as if I just closed the lid of my own coffin.

Farewell, Captain Victoria.

"Now, how do we get this back to Dennow?" My words are level, fueled with purpose.

"We'll cross the Fade again." Ilryth has the decency not to press me on the emotions that I'm sure he knows are swirling within.

"And you're willing to risk taking me across once more?" I know how important my role is, not just to him but to the entirety of the Eversea and everyone beyond. This is the path I'm now choosing. The last course I'm charting in my life.

"I gave you my word. And, as I told you, our word holds weight here in the Eversea." He meets my eyes with brief intensity and then shrugs. "Besides, you'll need to tell me how best to leave this so your family finds it. It'd be pointless to go without you."

Reaching out, I take his hand in mine. The same hand that plucked my compass from the darkness and carried it back to me. "Thank you, Ilryth," I say with all the sincerity in the world.

His face relaxes into a smile, a tender and earnest one. "For you, Victoria, anything."

The words crash upon me like a wave, carrying me back to that moment just on the other side of the Fade. The moment where I realized, undeniably, that I would like to kiss him. As I stare into Ilryth's warm eyes, it dawns on me that these urges might not entirely be one-sided. But…acting upon them would be our undoing.

I force a smile, feign ambivalence, and say a simple, "Thank you."

This time, I don't think Ilryth told anyone we were leaving. I would've expected to hear another objection from Sheel had he known. Another song of protection echoing over the duchy.

We swim off as night falls. I hang on to Ilryth's shoulders again, riding on his back while he holds the chest. At least, this time, we didn't take Dawnpoint, so its barrier of protection still stretches the length of the Gray Trench at our right as we head in a westwardly direction.

I've no doubt that we've timed our departure perfectly to avoid any of Sheel's patrols. I regard the swirling depths of rot warily, peering into the darkness for any sign of a wraith that might creep over the edge…or the curl of a massive tentacle.

But everything is quiet.

After what feels like an hour of swimming, Ilryth banks and descends in a wide arc. Far beneath us is a landscape that resembles the tide pools of the lighthouse island I lived on with Charles. Rocks have been smoothed by time and currents, cradling ponds that look like slowly spinning mercury. The area is illuminated by glowing amber vents of steam and heat that rise from the molten earth below. Stone archways encircle the area, much like the anamnesis altars in the trench, separating it from the black sand of the sea floor that stretches around as far as the eye can see.

"What is this place?"

"These are the traveler's pools. Almost all water is connected, somehow. If not on the surface, then through underground channels and unseen rivers. There are few corners of this world where the magic of my people cannot reach," he explains. I vaguely remember the mention of this when I first asked about going to the trench. "We use these channels and connections to speed our ability to traverse long distances."

"This is what you were telling me about earlier—the stable pools akin to the magic you used to take me here."

"Yes, I used a vial containing a drop of this magic—the relic and song I mentioned earlier."

"I still find myself envious of this ability," I admit. "To easily transport oneself from one place to another would've completely changed my world. Though, I might have been out of a job if it were that simple."

"Then I suppose it's good you didn't have it."

"'Good' is relative. I'd rather be out of a job and still have my crew—and the crews of all the other vessels that sank trying to complete dangerous routes—alive." My tone seems to sober him, and rightfully so.

"It's not your fault they're gone," he reminds me, the words an echo of what he said in the trench.

"They followed me, thinking I would keep them safe."

"And I know how hard it is when someone who trusted you with their life ends up losing it." The words could be curt. But they're not. Instead, they're full of understanding and tenderness. "Sometimes, we make mistakes, and must live with those consequences. But sometimes fate simply deals a cruel hand and the blame rests at no one's feet."

He would know as well as I. The urge to wrap my arms around his middle so I can press my cheek against the dip between his shoulder blades is almost overwhelming. We can understand each other. In ways I never expected, I find myself sympathizing with a siren. We came from vastly different worlds. Different expectations and upbringings. And yet…there's so much about him that I understand on an innate, almost visceral level. So much that enables him to connect with me more than anyone else I've ever met.

"Are you sure it's all right to go?" I ask as he banks. He'd said they were monitored.

"We'll be fast." Ilryth dives deeper before I can express any further hesitation or doubt. "Hold tight; we'll be through in a moment."

I shift my grip, pressing my body closer to his. My forearms are nestled between his body and biceps, elbows just above his. *Sturdy*. The word fits him so well. Every solid muscle. Every mighty flap of his tail. The duke is a sturdy, solid man. Feeling so much power against me stirs a need in my core—one I haven't felt in ages.

Focus, Victoria, I caution myself. Carnal needs are only slightly less dangerous than the knot of affection my stomach has been attempting to twist into. While it is entirely possible for many to indulge in pleasure without affection taking root…as much as I would love to be able to divide the two, as much as I wish I could fall into bed with a strong and handsome man, I know I cannot. If I tangle my body with his, my heart will be equally ensnared.

Yes, Ilryth is a man with a body worth appreciating. But that is and will be all I shall think about him, ever. I can admit that much without too much danger to myself.

I try to hold my breath on instinct as we plunge into the pool. There's the same blink of darkness and the feeling of weight that I felt the first time we crossed over via magic. But this time there's less chaos, so I can focus more. Or perhaps it's easier to travel as I am now. Specks of light appear, coalescing into a single point in the distance.

In a blink, we're swimming back toward the surface. Vertigo spins my head at the sudden and dramatic shift in direction. The world has flipped and the sea has changed.

We swim up from a single mercury tide pool, barely visible in the dimming light. An archway has been carved into the stone cliff behind it, but that is it as far as adornment. The rock is the same dark stone I recognize from the cliffs that frame Dennow.

"We're here," I whisper.

twenty-three

"I TOLD YOU THIS EXCURSION WOULD NOT TAKE LONG."

"How did you know where to go?" I ask.

"You mentioned Dennow before. I am familiar with human maps, at least of the shorelines." That much I can believe, given all the navigational tools and maps I saw in his treasure room.

However, there's something I don't quite believe. "I don't think I mentioned Dennow before."

"I'm sure you did."

I shift, staring into the pale strands of hair that sway over the back of his neck. All the nights I spent listening to his song are in the forefront of my mind, along with everything else he's mentioned. All the other little asides that add up. "Ilryth, you said you came to check on the status of my blessings. On me. Did you ever come here, specifically?"

A long stretch of silence. Long enough that it removes all doubt in what he's going to say before he does. "Yes."

I'll give him credit for not denying it. "Why?"

"You were the offering I had chosen for Lord Krokan, the one the Eversea was waiting for. I wanted to ensure all was well, that the blessing I gave you remained strong so it would keep you safe." Practical. What I would expect. But then, he adds, "Over time, however, I grew fascinated with your world. With your adventures and the courses you charted. As if you were so determined to explore my domain without ever really sinking into it."

"I always thought the song was just in my head most nights...how often did you visit me?"

"As often as I could." He slows his pace as we near the surface. Refuse litters the plateaus of the upper levels of the cliffs near Dennow. Abandoned lines and nets capture nothing but water. There are lost children's toys bedded down in the sand.

I think of him, swimming through this odd collection of discarded effects most nights, seeing a part of my world I never gave thought to. Above us, the lights of the city are blotted out by large silhouettes of ships and boats, lined up in the wharf and smaller docks. I imagine him drawing as close to the surface as he dared, no one any the wiser of the siren being able to come so, so close to our homes. Or that the siren weren't the ones to fear at all.

"And you might have heard the song echoing across the Fade, from me to you, from time to time," he adds. "It wasn't always from me coming to sing you to sleep." Ilryth chuckles softly. "I wasn't sure if you'd hear me at all. Though I should have known better. After forging our connection, it only makes sense."

Part of me thinks I should be aghast at his presumption to come to me every night. But it wasn't as if he invaded my space. He never came aboard the ship. He never *demanded* my attention.

"Your treasure room..."

Our connection must be deep, because he knows what I'm about to say without my needing to say it. "Yes, *you* inspired me. Every trip, I'd take something back."

So it was the same mug as that night...

"I enjoyed trying to see where you'd end up next, even if my traveling pools wouldn't permit me to always follow, or your lighthouses wouldn't allow me to stay for very long." I can almost hear the smile in his words. "At least I could be there before you crossed the Gray Passage in your world, trying to ensure you had all the protection I could offer."

"You..."

He must not have heard me. The thought was weak to begin with.

"Though little good I could do the last time. I truly am sorry for that. I hope one day you can believe me that I never meant to go back on my word. I really, truly tried, Victoria, to protect you."

My ribs seem to collapse on themselves. My throat constricts. I rest my forehead between his shoulder blades, up by the nape of his neck. I'd thought so little of him. I'd spoken so harshly…when all he'd done was try to protect me.

"Victoria? What's wrong? Should we go back?"

"I'm fine." I hope the firmness and strength in my words gives him calm.

"What is it?"

"I just need a moment." My masks are breaking. It's been a long, exhausting day, and my strength is waning.

He slows to a stop, saying nothing more. Allowing me to cling to him. My body pressed against his sturdy frame. We hover in the ocean as I steep in my thoughts.

All those years I spent alone. All those years that I spent looking out for myself, feeling that if I didn't, no one would. I was strong because I wanted to be, but also because I had to be.

I couldn't depend on anyone to take care of me. I truly believed that. Part of me still does, I suppose… My crew was like family, but just like my actual family, they were my responsibility. I could trust them all to do as they needed. But it was my job to look after them, not the other way around.

But they were there for me. Just as Emily was looking after Mother and Father in my stead when I wasn't in port. Even Ilryth…even as I cursed him underneath my breath every day for not giving me power enough. He was there, too. It was him protecting me—not just his magic, but *him*. Even as I was trying to hunt for folklore or magic to undo the hold he had on me.

"I gave so little credit," I whisper. He doesn't say anything, so I continue, "Everyone… I thought I was alone for so long. That I was surrounded by people who needed me and the best thing I could do for them was provide. *That* was what they needed me for—everything I could offer—and I was strong enough to do it. Giving was how I would be worthy of them. I never…I never thought of people needing me for me. I never even considered people taking care of me as much as I was them."

But they were.

My papers for the severance of my marriage were always expedited.

Now I can see Emily's hand in matters with the council. My mother was always giving me suggestions for sailing that ended up leading me to empty ports with eager merchants, easy to navigate and even easier to trade. My father always had a warm meal ready when I would return home. My crew, when the time came, risked their lives and gave up all their pay while doing it…for me.

"I don't—didn't deserve them. Deserve you."

"Victoria—"

"I was so lonely for so long, but I was never really alone, was I?" A dam breaks in me. Tears I thought I'd long since stopped crying come forth. My hands release his shoulders and fly to my face, covering it, trying to hide from the world. Trying to hide from my shame for not realizing it sooner.

Two arms wrap around me. Tight and firm. *Sturdy.*

One of his hands slides up my neck, to the back of my head. The other arm is circled around my mid back, clutching me tightly. I am drowning in a sea of pain and joy that I never knew I was filling all those nights that I wept alone.

"You are worthy of so much more than I, or anyone, could ever give. I could spend a lifetime giving to you, and it wouldn't be enough," he whispers. It almost sounds like he's whispering right in my ear, even though he speaks without the use of his mouth. Every thought is a caress within my mind, smoothing over the endless aches I've carried for far, far too long. "Every night I heard you cry, I wanted to tell you that it would all be all right."

I let out a noise somewhere between a laugh and a sob. "I wouldn't have believed you, even if you did."

"I know." He strokes my hair gently. "Because I know what it's like to feel as though you are adrift, alone in a vast sea."

"I could've done so much more with the time you gave me," I admit to myself and him.

Long after I left Charles, I gave so much time to him. He had a hold on me unlike any other. Paperwork completed or not, I was as free as the wind in my sails for years. Em was right; my heart had given up on that decaying marriage long before pen was put to paper by the council.

But I hadn't let go of the grip Charles had on my spirit. I lived every day thinking of him. Spiting him. Resenting him. Wondering, now and then, despite myself, how he was and what he was doing. Good or bad, it all boiled down to thoughts of *him*. Devoting energy he didn't deserve, that I didn't *want* to give, and yet did anyway time and again.

It took removing memories of him with godly magic, and the plight of a world, to finally break my focus from him. To realize that, more powerful than all my hatred and need for vengeance, is my indifference. The way to wound him was never to hurt him, it was not to care at all. *That* is what will finally free me of him.

"You did extraordinary things. You sailed through the end of the Gray Trench, avoiding Lord Krokan's emissaries and wraiths alike. I promise I didn't help as much as you might think with that. You went farther to the south than I have ever seen—past where the maps spill off the edge of parchment." Ilryth sounds genuinely impressed and his sincerity slows my tears. "You did more in nearly five years than most do in their entire lives."

"But it wasn't enough…I didn't do enough for them. To repay them for all the love they gave me."

His hand stills. Slowly, his arms unfurl from around me. I almost tell him not to let me go. I'm not ready, not yet. I have not been comforted like this in years and I am needy.

"Look at me, Victoria," he commands gently. And I do. I peek through my fingers, then lower my hands. Ilryth holds me now with his unwavering gaze. It's as reassuring as his embrace just was. "You don't have to repay someone for their love. It's given freely."

"But—"

"No buts. That's it. It's that simple. If someone loves you, truly loves you, it's because they want to—because they can't imagine a world in which they don't. Because you make their soul sing just with your mere existence." Even though his words are sweet and bright, his eyes are filled with pain I don't understand.

"But I am not someone who is easy to love," I whisper. "Perhaps as a sister or daughter. Maybe as a friend. But not—" I stop short.

"Not?" he probes gently.

I'm too raw, too bare to fight. "Not as a lover."

He caresses my cheeks with both hands, coaxing hair away from my face. "Whatever in this wide world made you think that?"

"It's something I was told," I admit. *"Who could ever love you?"*

It's incredible just how much my inflection matches Charles's even in my own mind. Even after months of finally being away from him. "I'm difficult, I'm—"

"Stop," he commands, though not roughly. I oblige. "I don't know who this person was. But they were clearly a sad, small, and cruel individual."

That much I can agree with. I've always been able to agree with. So why do Charles's words still stick with me so?

"You are worthy of being loved not just by friends and family, but by a lover as well."

"Well, it doesn't much matter…does it?" I try to shrug as though none of it matters. As if he's not still holding my face with both his hands as gently as I would hope for him to hold my heart. "It's not like I'll have any time to find another lover. It's not like I ever did. Some people just aren't made for it."

"I know what you mean." There's not a trace of hesitation, or doubt, or deceit on him, as if he really does.

"How?"

"I never wanted to fall in love. Vowed I never would."

It's a sensible enough vow. But odd to hear from a man who was just waxing poetic about the power of love. "Why?"

"I saw what it did to my parents. After…" I'm about to tell him he doesn't have to continue, I know how hard this topic is for him, when he persists. "After my mother died, my father began to wither away. His songmate was gone and the silence in his soul sapped his will to live. Nothing in all the seas was enough to replace her."

"I'm sorry," I whisper.

"We've both known loss, and pain." He releases my face and trails his fingertips down my arms.

"And we try to do the best we can because of it."

Ilryth blinks several times, startled. He dips his chin slightly and the intensity of his stare is too much. He's inviting me to peer into his soul, just as he's peered into mine. "Not because of it, in spite of it. Who we are is independent of the trauma that tries to mar our souls. It is a part of us, it might teach us, but it does not define us."

Those words have my eyes prickling again. I want to throw my arms around his waist and cling to him. To leech off his stability for a bit longer as my world settles back into place.

But I don't. I can't allow myself to get too close to him. Not just for the sake of my fragile heart but because doing so would be nothing but condemning him to heartbreak—if he truly is smothering the same budding affection I currently am. I'm headed for the Abyss, then the Great Beyond…and he has a long life ahead of him. It's best not to challenge the vow he's made for himself, nor my resolve. But that doesn't mean we can't find comfort with each other, and solace. That we can't care for each other as fellow leaders who share a unique experience. As two people who are worn and tired and so very hungry for the reprieve of a shoulder of someone who understands.

I rub my eyes, trying to press away any remaining sensations of stubborn tears. In doing so I notice the state of my body. I'm no longer solid. My outline is still a sharp silver, but my flesh is growing transparent.

"What the…"

Ilryth's fingers clasp around mine. "We've spent too much time away from Lady Lellia's magic."

"What's different this time from yesterday?"

"Perhaps you have more of the power of the old gods wrapped in you. Perhaps it is because you are not singing their words this time. Regardless of the reason, we must return you to the Eversea soon."

I nod and he goes to collect the chest he placed on a nearby plateau.

"Let's settle matters with your family."

"Yes." I situate myself on his back once more and we head for the surface. This is the last time I'll see the waters of Dennow. The last time I'll see my home.

After tonight…I am one with the Eversea and will commit myself to becoming nothing more than the offering to an old god.

twenty-four

THE SHIPS ARE ALL TUCKED IN FOR THE NIGHT. As we swim between them, avoiding their barnacles and sea moss, I can't help but wonder how my last six months might have been spent if my ship hadn't been attacked.

I would've had six more months with my sister and parents. Maybe I could've negotiated again with the council after Charles had left for his lighthouse. They called it a "final judgment," but Mother taught me there's always the possibility of squeezing in one more word before the negotiation ends. Perhaps I might have realized I wasn't on my own—that I didn't have to bear the sole responsibility for caring for everyone around me to make up for things I didn't actually lack—sooner. Maybe, once I realized that, Emily could've helped me win over the council.

What if...could've...what might have been... The words that bookend my entire existence. The wondering that will follow me to my grave.

"Will here—" Ilryth is interrupted by a sharp, deafening chime that ripples through the water. He winces, reeling, clutching his chest as though he were stabbed through the heart.

The sound is trying to tear me apart. The magical contours of my body vibrate and distort. I struggle to keep myself together, as though my sheer willpower is the only thing binding me together. Though it's hard to keep my thoughts clear amid the resonant noise of the bell.

The sound fades and Ilryth takes a moment to collect himself. I do the same.

"That was a lighthouse, wasn't it?" I manage to ask, even though I already know the answer.

"It was."

"Well, they work," I mutter. Not just against siren song, but the wraiths as well. If only there were a way I could tell the humans that. The sirens aren't our enemies, not in the way we thought. The notion almost makes me feel guilty for ringing the bell so often. But the emotion is fleeting when I think of a wraith-possessed siren coming to claim Emily as they tried to claim me.

Hopefully, when this is over, when I succeed, the bells and cotton-stuffed ears will become a thing of the past. Humans, not knowing why, will realize the seas aren't as dangerous as they once thought. It might take decades, but maybe there would even come a day where families would willingly sit along the beach and admire the horizons I took for granted every time I went out on a ship.

If Ilryth hears my muttering, he says nothing in response, instead continuing to swim along the wharf, underneath the shadows of the docks and pylons. The sensation of it is akin to falling into a mirror and landing in the world on the other side—somewhere that looks so similar to all you know, but different. Reversed. For the first time in weeks, I'm aware of every kick of my legs, each turn to glide nimbly through the water. This was once my home, I walked these docks countless times, and now I'm a shadow beneath them. A ghost of my former self returning to a place that I no longer belong.

The city above is quiet. It's late. But I can catch glimpses of familiar buildings through the wooden slats above me. I pause at one that threatens to bring tears anew.

The usually quiet tavern is pulsing with light and sound. I can almost feel rumblings in the water as dancing feet shake its foundations into the rock below. I'm unable to see into the thick porthole windows from this vantage. But the stream of people that leave, causing us to sink deeper beneath the surface of the water, is all I need to know.

"That's my family's tavern," I whisper. "And it's thriving." Perhaps it's pity. Perhaps I've become folklore. Or maybe my family was finally able to separate themselves from the black mark I brought upon them. Either way, seeing them doing well has me heaving a sigh of relief.

"Is it? I always wondered why you spent so much time there."

"It was my father's dream. My mother kept trading past when she would've otherwise stopped so they had the crons to do it. I pitched in, too. Em also…" I trail off, staring in awe. *You did it, Pa. Everyone knows how good your ale tastes now.*

"We shouldn't linger." Ilryth touches my elbow lightly.

"I know." Yet I don't move. I want to stay until it's late enough for Em, or Father, or Mother to come out and collect the sandwich board. *Just to see them one last time…*

"Victoria."

"Right. Over here." Jolted from the futile notions, I guide us to a collection of nets not far away. "We'll put the chest here."

"Are you sure it'll get to them like this?"

I nod. "These are my father's nets. He collects whatever fish lands in them for his broils and stews."

Ilryth moves when there's no one around, wedging the box into the heart of the net and wrapping the ropes around it several times. I can't stop myself from making some adjustments after he finishes.

"My knots weren't good enough?" Ilryth folds his arms.

"Not at all. But don't worry, you have a sailor for a friend now."

"Friend?" He arches a single, pale eyebrow.

"You've seen me cry. Only my closest friends have seen me cry." I shrug. In truth…only about three people have ever seen me cry, Ilryth included. But he doesn't need to know he's among such an exclusive party.

"You need to have some more positive thresholds for friendships." He continues scanning the docks above us. "We should leave before someone can see us."

"I know." On both accounts. I run my fingers over the chest one last time. I've etched my name into its top. It holds my compass. My family will know.

It'll be enough. It has to be. It's the last thing I can ever do for them.

"Victoria." He takes my other hand, but doesn't pull. He doesn't demand I leave. Ilryth just holds it. Though his touch feels distant. Even the carvings of my name underneath my fingers are barely perceptible.

I'm fading away. My body really has become more magic than physical. Now that this is done, I will use what's left of my existence to do right by the Eversea, Natural World, old gods, even my family... and Ilryth. I'm briefly left stunned by how much he is factored into my steeled resolve.

"All right, I'm ready."

He presents me his back and I grab on.

We swim away from the lights of Dennow, down into the shadow and gloom of the lower levels of the sea, racing away from the echoes of lighthouse bells that chase us. We swim past the graveyard of forgotten and discarded trinkets. Down, past the sludge and grime that clouds the waters above the deep currents.

"Thank you again," I say with all the sincerity I have in me.

"Think nothing of it."

"But I do." I squeeze his shoulders lightly. "When we get back, let's begin the next stage of the anointing. I want to make sure I'm ready for Lord Krokan. There will not be another sacrifice after me."

He glances over his shoulder, pace slowing. "You're truly committed, aren't you?"

I nod.

"Aren't you afraid?" The question is almost timid, uncertain. It's clear he has wondered about this more than once, no doubt many times following his mother's death.

"A little, perhaps." I shrug. My cavalier tone is not just a bold front. I've found some amount of peace with my lot. "I think I've finally realized—finally accepted—that it's the place I'm meant to be. I died in the water the night we met and have been dodging the reaper since. It's time to pay my dues. And whether I owe it to others or not, I can make my life truly mean something by my own measure, independent of anyone else."

Ilryth is silent. Then, softly, "For what it's worth, I think you will quell Lord Krokan's rage."

"Thank you for the vote of confidence." Something else has occurred to me. "Is that why Lord Krokan's emissaries finally attacked my ship? Was he drawn to me for cheating death for so long?"

"It's impossible to know. Nothing Lord Krokan has done for years has made any sense. Even demanding sacrifices is an aberration."

"I'm going to find out the cause," I declare. "I'll make him tell me the meaning behind his rage so that I can fix it."

He chuckles, but there's a slightly sad tone at the end that I can't fully decipher the meaning behind. "If you manage that, you would truly be the greatest sacrifice we could've hoped for." We've arrived at the traveler's pools. "Hold on."

I shift my grip and press my body closer against his as we near the pool. We've found a rhythm with our hips, his tail, and my legs. No longer are we bumping awkwardly against each other, but gliding, flowing, moving together. It's becoming easier to be around him. To be pressed against him…

But purely as a friend. I will admit to nothing more. Anything more would be ruinous for us both.

He plunges into the pool and I continue clinging to him. The same darkness and starlight envelop us before we reemerge on the other side. There's the usual slight spin in my skull as our orientation changes abruptly.

Ilryth halts, holding out his arms to slow us in an instant. The muscles in his shoulders bulge, expanding the markings down his arms. His whole body is rigid.

I follow his gaze to another man, seated at the top of one of the archways that encompass the traveler's pools. His aquamarine tail contrasts against his fair skin and is marbled with inked lines similar to the ones on my body. He wears necklaces of pearl, accented by shells of different shapes and sizes.

The man looks up at us through long lashes the same color as his brown hair. He has a youthful air about him, perhaps even younger than Ilryth. A slight smile curls the edges of his lips, but the expression only makes me clutch Ilryth tighter. I am glad for the sturdy man to be placed between me and this stranger.

Whoever this other siren is, he looks at me with a hungry gaze. He regards Ilryth with flashes of contempt in his emerald eyes that he doesn't even bother to hide. Even the water around him seems to collect the umbra of the sea at night, gathering power, and danger, and secrets.

"Duke Ilryth, isn't this just a tidy collection of crimes? You should know better," the man scolds lightly and pushes off from the archway. He glides toward us. Ilryth remains suspended in place, his muscles so tight I'm surprised he doesn't snap in two. "One: touching the offering and in so doing deepening her ties to this world. Two: taking her out of the Eversea. Three: using a traveler's pool without chorus approval. Which high crime should we address first?"

I look between the two men. *High crimes?* Ilryth spoke of the dangers of doing these things, but nothing about it actually being a *crime...* Even though I have the shell around my neck, I focus on keeping my thoughts to myself. I don't want anything escaping without it being my choice.

Ilryth says nothing but continues to simmer. I'm surprised the water around him isn't boiling.

"What would've happened if she faded? Do you want us to suffer a repeat of your mother?"

I fight a wince on Ilryth's behalf—it's a low blow.

"We left for but a moment, and it was an absolutely necessary venture," Ilryth says tersely.

The man seems to ignore the statement. "If you don't care about the rest of us, that's all well and good, but think of your poor sisters. I don't think they could handle another disappointment due to their older brother."

Ilryth lurches forward. I'm so startled by the sudden movement that he rips himself from my grasp. I'm left hovering in the sea as he grips the man by his necklaces, twisting his fists in them as if he intends to choke him.

"Keep my sisters out of your thoughts, Ventris," he growls.

"Assaulting the Duke of Faith? Three crimes wasn't enough? You want to add another?" Ventris remains calm, even though the chains are beginning to dig into his neck.

There's movement in the water in the distance. Like sea turtles emerging from the sand, seven other sirens pop up, shaking off the seabed. They wear serious and intense expressions.

"Ilryth—" I try to caution.

"I suspected you might be prone to rashness, so I brought support," Ventris continues, ignoring me entirely. "Guards, take him into custody."

"You would use the men my mother and I trained against me?" Ilryth balks, finally seeing the warriors coming our way.

"You might have trained them but they are not 'yours.' They serve the will of the old gods and the Lifetree above all else. A model I suggest you follow sooner rather than later."

Ilryth releases Ventris as the warriors approach. The men and women circle Ilryth, whose arms are now limp at his sides. He doesn't put up a fight. His chin dips toward his chest, but I can see his shoulders quivering with the barely contained anger still pulsing through his muscles.

"Wait, no, this isn't—" *I need to do something!* "—He went because of me. I *forced* him to. This isn't his fault."

"Your Holiness." Ventris approaches me, leaving Ilryth to his men. But Ilryth is all I can focus on. They're not manhandling him in any way. But seeing so many around him, armed with spears and intense stares, has my throat tightening with anxiety. "Do not fret for him. He is still a Duke of the Eversea; he will be treated with the respect that is deserving of his station…when he rejoins the chorus in song, assuring us that he still has a firm grasp of the laws of our people."

Laws I still hardly understand. So I know I'm playing with fire when I say, "If you and the chorus want to speak with someone, speak with me."

"That will also happen." He grabs my wrist.

"Unhand me!"

Ilryth spins in place, a flash of deadly rage in his eyes. "Let her go, Ventris."

"Suddenly you care about who touches the offering?" He tilts his head at Ilryth and smiles a thin, serpentine smile. "I am merely bringing her to the castle. It is well past time the Duchy of Faith took over her anointing—look at how much blank skin she still has." Ventris rakes his eyes over me, sending a chill down my spine. "Don't worry a moment more for your *little experiment*, Ilryth. I will personally take over her preparation from here."

"I said, *let her go*," Ilryth growls.

"I can speak for myself," I remind all of them sharply and rip my wrist from Ventris's grasp. That brings his attention back to me. I level my eyes with his, looking down my nose, squinting slightly with all the disapproval I can muster. "I am the sacrifice, already anointed, in part, for Lord Krokan. You *will* respect my severing connection to this world and will not manhandle me. I understand how the traveler's pools work now, and will go willingly."

It is odd to throw authority around, especially when that authority comes from the fact that I'm about to be sacrificed. But, in this moment, I don't care. *No*…not just now. I am Lord Krokan's sacrifice. I am the one who will end this terrible cycle the Eversea is trapped within. It is not wrong of me to command the respect of my station.

The waters are still. Silent. All the warriors are focused solely on the two of us. In my periphery I can see even Ilryth's lips part slightly in shock. I wonder if anyone has ever spoken to Ventris like this before. He clearly has a high opinion of himself, so I doubt it. But that makes me want to push the limits even more.

"Very well, Your Holiness." He brings the offending hand to his chest and bows slightly. "Then if you will, please follow me."

I look back to Ilryth, who gives me a slight nod. Ventris notices me deferring to the other duke and it draws a line between his brows as he obviously fights a scowl.

"I will indulge you." I muster all the airs I ever saw the lords and ladies put on at the Applegate parties as I speak to Ventris once more. "Lead on, Your Grace."

Ventris leans forward slightly to encroach on my space, Ilryth's expression grows more shadowed and intense as he draws near. The next words he says are just for me to hear.

"You are new to our world so you are ignorant, and you are marked for the old gods, highest of holies, deserving of reverence…but I will not tolerate disrespect, especially from a human. You *will* show me appropriate decorum."

I narrow my eyes slightly. "We'll see about that, Ventris." I intentionally avoid his proper titles, and it has the desired effect and then some.

He spins in place and swims down. I follow behind, glad Ilryth never delayed on my behalf when we moved about. My swimming has become stronger and more confident. I don't look like I'm scrambling to keep up with the siren any longer. Weeks in the Eversea have completely transformed my movements in the water.

Ilryth and the warriors are behind me. I glance over my shoulder, meeting the duke's brown eyes once more. They're filled with worry and...sorrow?

I dare to speak just to him, hoping that with the shell and enough practice, none of them will hear. "It'll be all right," I say.

"Don't speak to me again unless I address you," Ilryth says firmly. I would think he was being rude, if not for the worry that bleeds around his words. He's trying to protect me. I can feel it in the song that hums in my bones, stronger than ever.

I nod slightly and look forward once more, bracing myself for whatever waits on the other side of the traveler's pool.

twenty-five

SWIMMING DOWN. Night and starlight. Swimming up in a new location. I think I'm beginning to get the hang of moving by way of traveler's pool as I'm less disoriented with every time I pass through.

The traveler's pool I emerge from is nestled in the center of an underwater garden, teeming with life, framed in by stone walls and a birdcage trellis over top. Anamneses, larger than the ones Ilryth magically grew in the trench, cast a pale light over the space, protecting it from the red rot floating through the currents just beyond the birdcage. The ghostly trees stretch up from beds of mosslike vines of seaweed, dotted with rocks and coral that have been sculpted into swirls and geometric shapes, framed by gently swaying fans.

Ventris hovers in the glow of one of the anamneses, hands behind his back, as he waits for everyone else to emerge.

"Take the duke to the judgment chambers while he awaits the next singing of the chorus," Ventris orders his guards.

Ilryth still wears a scowl but doesn't object. He has far more self-control than I, as I can't stop myself.

"You are not going to throw him in jail," I say firmly.

Ventris blinks at me. "Jail?"

"It's the place where humans lock each other in cages," Ilryth explains.

"Ah, thank you. Your endless knowledge on humans never ceases to astound." The way Ventris says "astound" leads me to believe he doesn't truly mean it. Ventris looks back to me.

"Your Holiness, there are no 'jails' in the Eversea. We do not cage people like beasts."

"You...don't?" The concept is foreign to me.

"No. Duke Ilryth will be kept comfortable, as any would, but especially befitting of his station, until the chorus can gather and discuss the best path to any reconciliation for his crimes."

"There were no crimes. I was the one who demanded to go. I *forced* him." It's not fair for him to bear the burden of my mistakes. I made my family suffer in that way; I won't allow it to happen again with him.

"That is for the chorus to decide. I do not question the ways of your people. It is not for you to question the ways of ours," Ventris says to me, tone as cool as the nighttime sea.

"Don't worry, Victoria." Ilryth summons my attention, locking eyes with me and giving a small smile. It does little to reassure me when he's still being escorted by an entire pack of guards. Would they need that many to subdue him? He's not even armed. "I'll be all right. We'll see each other again soon."

His ease is the opposite of the warning he gave me moments ago. Ilryth appears relaxed and calm. But I know appearances can be deceiving. As a duke, he is as skilled as I am in concealing true feelings.

"Very well." I nod. "I look forward to seeing you again, Ilryth," I add for Ventris's benefit. I want there to be no doubt that I will not be calm and quiet if any ill were to befall my duke.

Ilryth is escorted away. I'm relieved that the warriors don't lay a hand on him. He seems at ease, at least on the outside.

"Now, if you will follow me, Victoria," Ventris says.

"I prefer 'Your Holiness,'" I say coldly. I want distance between us, not familiarity. This man gives me an uneasy feeling and I have long since learned to trust my gut.

Ventris's face betrays no emotion. "Of course, Your Holiness. I wish to see you to your chambers so that we may continue your blessings and preparations. Goodness knows there are many still that we will need to place upon you to make a human even partly worthy of standing before an old god."

"You seem to hold an odd amount of disdain for the human who's going to be your people's sacrifice."

Ventris leans forward, his mouth visibly fighting a frown. "If I had been there the night Duke Ilryth claimed you, you would never have born the markings of Lord Krokan as the sacrifice. If it had been solely up to me, I would've swum to your sad, magicless world and expunged the markings myself before it was too late. But I was outvoted when it came to this little experiment."

"You'd rather see one of your own be sacrificed instead?" That's a better alternative in his mind?

"It is an *honor* to give one's life to Lord Krokan for the sake of the old gods—a blessing I doubt you comprehend." He's right. I definitely see this as more of a curse than a boon. "But what is done is done. I just hope this risk Ilryth has chosen for all of us doesn't result in Lord Krokan's rage increasing."

"It won't," I vow. If I hadn't been determined before, I am now. Ventris reminds me of all the men who told me I couldn't make a good ship captain because I was too young, or too emotional, not cutthroat enough, or lacked the right morals as an oath breaker.

"Now, if you'll follow me." He might phrase it politely enough, but it's apparent that the sentiment is begrudging…and that I don't have much of a choice in the matter.

I glance back over my shoulder one final time, looking at the tunnel Ilryth was escorted into. He and the warriors are long gone. I'm left with no other option than to follow Ventris in the opposite direction. I never would have thought the man who took me as a sacrifice could feel like my safety.

"Where are we?" I want to begin collecting as much knowledge as I can on my new circumstances, even if I'm going to verify all the information he feeds me with Ilryth later.

"We're in the heart of the Eversea, the oldest foundations of our forefathers, near the base of the Lifetree and the edge of Lord Krokan's Abyss—the halls of song."

When I first arrived here, I remember seeing a castle in the distance. I assume that's where I am now. "And where are you taking me?"

"The room of the offering."

"I have a whole room?" I arch my brows.

"Don't get ahead of yourself, human."

"For revering Krokan so much, you seem to take a disrespectful tone with his sacrifices often." Constantly pointing out my impending demise is not a particularly joyful experience, but I'm growing used to it. More importantly, it seems to be driving Ventris to new heights of frustration and I am having far too much fun with *that* to leave it be.

"That is *Lord* Krokan to you." Ventris whirls on me. His youthful brow is marred with deep lines, as if he's spent his entire life to date scowling. "Do not think that, just because you know some words of the old ones and have Lord Krokan's blessings on your body, you are suddenly in control here."

"Aren't I though?" I lean forward, hands on my hips. "You all need me."

"And we will get what we need from you, one way or another."

"You want me to fear you." My words are soft as silk, but as strong as steel, and I am not backing down as he continues to try to loom over me. "But I don't."

"Then you forget your betters."

"No, I know that you need me to engage in the anointing. You can't force it upon me. I must learn the words. And I also know it's too late to find someone else. There are only a few months left until the summer solstice." I ease away with a smug smile. "So let's cut the posturing, shall we?"

Ventris looks as though bubbles might come from his finlike ears from all the pent-up rage he's keeping behind his flushed face. But, without another word, he starts down the tunnel. I follow and leave the matter be, for now.

Ventris leads me to a lavish room of encrusted marble and silver-edged mirrors. There's a nested bed of kelp and sea foam. Two dressers flank an opening to a balcony beyond, and small pots above them glow with anamnesis saplings. The whole castle has been dotted with them, and I suspect they're all behind the barrier that surrounds this place, keeping out the red rot.

"Please make yourself comfortable," Ventris says, but I doubt he cares much for my comfort. "But don't think for a moment of leaving. I am the Duke of Faith and it is my sole responsibility, and honor, to be the most in tune with Lord Krokan's songs. I will know if traveler's pools are used, or if you leave the protection of my duchy."

*No wonder he knew I was gone to begin with…*I wonder if the more anointing I've had, the easier it has become for him to sense me. I rub the markings on my arms subconsciously, stopping the moment I'm aware of the movement. *Don't show your discomfort, Victoria.*

"I wouldn't dream of leaving," I force myself to say, ignoring the unease that only grows the longer his eyes are on me. A slimy film coats me at the thought of this man watching my movements. I hope his insights into what I'm doing are not that granular, but more of a general "if I leave the Eversea," as he said. But given Ilryth's warning…I don't trust anything to be that simple. I must be careful and get to Ilryth as soon as possible to learn what more I can about Ventris and his magics.

"Good. We will begin finishing your anointing as soon as matters with Ilryth are settled."

"I would like to go see him," I say before the duke can leave.

"He will be sequestered until he stands before the chorus tomorrow."

"In the morning, then, before he goes."

"You should not care so much to see a person of this realm," he says with a cautionary tone. "You need to be severing your bonds with life to meet death."

"I also need to deepen my bonds with the old ones, which is what I am focusing on," I insist. "Duke Ilryth is the one who marked me for Lord Krokan. He is the one who started my anointing and taught me the songs of the old ones. We already have an established rapport to my teachings. The anointing will go faster if he can continue to teach me."

Ventris regards me warily. I can almost feel him probing between my words, trying to pick them apart. I know men like him—he's looking for some kind of weakness to exploit, or leverage to use against me. I won't give it to him.

"Of course that is all it is. I will see it arranged." With that, Ventris leaves.

I believe that he will arrange it. But I don't believe that he buys that I purely want to see Ilryth out of a sense of duty as the offering. Not that I blame him. He's right to be suspicious, after all.

Tethers to this world or not…*I care for Ilryth.* He is my friend. He is…becoming more. But I refuse to allow those emotions room to bud and grow. For my sake, for his, and for all our peoples. I am accustomed to walls around my heart, and swallowing my emotions.

Rather than heading for the bed, I swim to the archway that leads to the large, half-moon-shaped balcony. I'm finding I grow less weary than

I used to. First, I needed less—no food at all. Now sleep is becoming optional. Will there be a point where I need any at all? Will my heart someday stop beating while I keep moving, and I will be sustained by magic alone?

The balcony is the only one positioned on this side of the castle. Little wonder, since it stretches over the vast Abyss below. Surrounding the whole castle is a faint, silvery aura—it must be the bubble I saw around it when I first arrived in the Eversea. It's identical to the hazy barrier that surrounded the Duchy of Spears. I suspect that, in addition to the anamnesis, there is another spear, like Dawnpoint, lending its protection.

I'm even closer to the surface here than in Ilryth's estate down by the trench. Perhaps only a one-story building's worth of depth, would be my guess. The moonlight reaches me in brighter beams, but that's not the only source of light. Swaying high, high above the surface of the water, like silvery clouds are the boughs of a massive tree that I can only assume is the Lifetree.

Its roots plunge through the water and emit the familiar red haze the farther they sink into the depths, running unfathomably deep. The underwater shelf arcs around, back and away from the castle, half the tree perched on its sheer ledge. The other half stretches into oblivion.

Down, into that deep, deep darkness of an ocean so vast that it has never known light, there's the faintest outline of movement. Massive tentacles glide through the rust-tinted water like the tattered cloak of Death itself. I move to the railing of the balcony—utterly unnecessary underwater and entirely for aesthetic. But it gives me something to hold onto. It helps me feel as if there is some barrier between me and that yawning abyss that threatens to swallow me whole.

A flash of green briefly breaks through the gloom and, for a moment, I know the eyes of an old god are upon me. It can sense me. It knows I'm here and that soon I will be ready to meet it.

I cannot suppress the chill that runs up my spine. Clots my throat with the taste of bile. Soon…I will be given to the darkness. Soon it will have me in its clutches.

Come to me, I can almost feel it say. *Come to me, and know Death.*

twenty-six

Dᴀᴡɴ ʙʀᴇᴀᴋs, sʜɪɴɪɴɢ ᴛʜʀᴏᴜɢʜ ᴛʜᴇ ᴀʀᴄʜᴡᴀʏs ᴛʜᴀᴛ ʟᴇᴀᴅ ᴛᴏ ᴍʏ ʙᴀʟᴄᴏɴʏ, ᴛᴜʀɴᴇᴅ ᴀ ʀᴇᴅᴅɪsʜ ᴀϙᴜᴀᴍᴀʀɪɴᴇ ᴀs ɪᴛ ꜰɪʟᴛᴇʀs ᴛʜʀᴏᴜɢʜ ʀᴏᴛ ᴀɴᴅ ᴏᴄᴇᴀɴ. I spent the night in my bed trying not to worry too much for Ilryth, or to think of the beast lurking beyond the barrier. Yet, with the sun, I'm drawn to the railing again. If only to confirm my suspicion from last night.

Light truly doesn't reach into the Abyss. The sun's rays illuminate the trunk of the Lifetree, but the glow quickly fades as the wood splits into roots. The water changes from a pale blue-green color at the very top, to a deeper, richer blue that's tinted with red, then, ultimately, to the color of the sky between the stars as the rot transforms the ocean into a deep, swirling purple.

Oddly, Krokan is somehow less visible in the daylight. Perhaps he slumbers. Or maybe I didn't see him at all last night. Perhaps it was just fear and anxiousness at finally being presented with the Abyss I will be cast into. I grip the railing of the balcony tightly. What stops the god from coming to claim me now? Surely not the flimsy, silvery barrier. That might keep out the rot, but I suspect it'd do little against a primordial god.

What else lurks in those depths? More emissaries of Lord Krokan? Probably. Lost souls…waiting to cross to the Beyond but unable to because Lord Krokan bars them in his rage. Souls that will become wraiths as they steep in that sea of death.

The thought makes my mind wander to my crew. Did they all become those haunted spirits? Or are some of their souls down in that realm of eternal night? Trapped and waiting to be led to the Great Beyond? Guilt courses through me yet again for them. No matter how many times I try to rationalize their loss—rightly or not— the feeling of fault won't completely abate. I doubt it ever will.

I swallow thickly and wrap my arms around myself, fighting a sudden chill in the water. If they are down there…I will have to face them yet again.

Closing my eyes, I let out a sigh. There's only ever been one challenge in my life I abandoned—Charles. He was the one mistake that it was better to step away from, rather than throwing good time and effort after bad. But, after him, every other challenge has felt surmountable. If I could thrive after him, I can do anything.

I open my eyes once more and stare into the darkness, hoping that Krokan feels me as keenly as I felt his presence last night. Let the old god know I'm ready for him. That I have faced death before and I am not afraid. He is nothing more than one more storm to charge into.

"Your Holiness." Ventris breaks into my thoughts. I turn to find him and two warriors on either side at the entrance to my room. "I trust you have found your accommodations comfortable this past evening?"

"They're fine." I swim back through the archway and into my bedroom. "What of Ilryth?"

A slight smile works its way onto Ventris's lips. It doesn't seem sincere. "I would expect you to be more focused on communing with Lord Krokan, now that you are before the Abyss, than thinking of the Duke of Spears."

"It is hard to commune when my duet partner is far and the future of my anointing is uncertain." I speak as though that should have been obvious to him, a small, unperturbed smile playing on my lips.

"You doubt I would see to your anointing?" Offense is heavy in his tone.

"Calm yourself, Duke of Faith, no need to be so emotional." Expectedly, that sets him off more and I gain no small amount of pleasure from it. "I simply do not know you."

"Well that is actually why I am here," he says hastily. As though he wants to prove me wrong. Ventris is young and obsessed with his power—challenge him and he's going to overcorrect. "The chorus is gathering now to discuss his crimes—"

"He committed no crimes," I remind him.

"That is for the other dukes and duchess to decide when the chorus meets for song." Ventris clasps his hands before him, trying to be the vision of poise. I see right through it. "In the meantime, we should continue readying you for your offering. There is little time and many markings still to be made."

"We can make these markings after I see Ilryth," I insist. The greatest leverage I have here is my compliance—or lack thereof—with their rituals and preparations.

In truth, I don't think I'd have it in me to postpone this duty that's been thrust upon me for too long. Now that I have seen the Abyss, all I can think of is the possibility that some of my crew might be in those depths, wandering and lost. More will drift back through the Gray Trench, trying to return to the world they came from. In my mind's eye, they're lost and confused and Ilryth's warriors are hunting them. No wonder ghosts lose all emotions beyond hatred and anger. They likely don't understand what's happened to them, all they want is to go home, and now people are trying to kill them for a second time.

They need me. All the souls down there need me to quell Krokan's rage and restore the natural order. I can't abandon them. But I can feign nonchalance if it helps me get to Ilryth. He's the only one I think I can trust here, and without his guidance I shudder to think what trouble I might get into in this strange world.

"There is little time before the chorus gathers."

"But there *is* time."

Frustration that he tries to veil as amusement lights up Ventris's eyes. "Your tenacity will serve you well in guiding all the unruly, waiting souls to the beyond."

"I look forward to it...after I ensure Ilryth has been well taken care of." I swim over to Ventris, hovering right before him. "Now, take me to him." Ilryth did me countless favors since I arrived, even before then. I owe him the life I knew for the past five years and my family's futures. Sticking up for him now is the least I can do.

"As Her Holiness desires." He bows his head and turns, heading out from the room. I follow behind him. The warriors take up the rear.

We swim through the tunnels, rooms, and halls of the castle. There are small, intimate areas contrasted with larger, sprawling salons.

Ornate gardens overlook the sea, protected from the rot that festers in the open water by the silvery barrier, as well as cramped coral tubes that have been carved with markings similar to what's inked on my flesh—what I saw in Sheel's home. I wonder just how much of the designs are placed there for protection, added over the last fifty years of Krokan's rage.

We arrive at an opening covered by a curtain of kelp, on what feels like the opposite side of the structure to where I'm staying. Two more warriors hover on either side. They straighten, holding their spears at attention as we approach.

"Duke Ilryth, Her Holiness has come to pay you a visit," Ventris says, hovering right before the kelp curtain.

"Enter, Victoria."

I swim forward, around Ventris's side. When he moves as well, I stop him by holding up a hand.

"I wish to see Ilryth alone." I don't bother with speaking directly to Ventris. Let them all hear, Ilryth included. Before Ventris can get a word in, I continue. "Thank you for your understanding. I won't be long so your chorus won't be delayed."

"I appreciate your consideration." The words are as tense as his pursed lips.

I swim ahead, leaving them behind. The kelp is thick, blotting out all light for a moment as I cross through. I emerge into a room that is much smaller than mine, but no less well-appointed. Large windows—void of glass—open to the city beyond. It certainly feels more like a guest room than any kind of prison, and that unravels a knot of tension that had been tugging against my ribs.

But Ilryth is nowhere to be seen. I turn, looking for him, only to have two hands reach forward and grab my cheeks. He must've been waiting on the side of the door for me, ready to pounce.

His large palms cradle my face between them. His shining eyes hold all the intensity in the world as he stares down at me. Ilryth is still moving. He pulls me toward him slightly, coming down to meet me.

Without warning, his face is close enough to mine that were we above the water I could feel his breath. I can see every fleck of honey, every hickory depth, as rich as forests mottled with late afternoon sun, in his eyes. He has freckles, I realize. Incredibly faint ones, dotted across his nose and onto his cheeks like the constellations that guided me for years.

My whole body is tense, but now for completely different reasons than with Ventris. The knot has left my chest and dropped into my lower stomach. I ache from top to bottom, yearning for something I haven't had in years—for something I never thought I might have again.

Is he about to kiss me? His eyelids are growing heavy. His lips are relaxed. I find myself tilting my head forward despite myself. My own eyes are fluttering closed.

I can't... *I shouldn't.* This is dangerous territory. I am marked for death. He is forbidden to touch me and we are no longer in his domain, where he can bend the rules. I can't risk his well-being like this...

Entangling myself with this dangerously handsome man, even if only for physical indulgence, is a risk neither of us can take.

Because you can't keep things purely physical, Victoria, my mind cautions. *Kiss him and you will fall for him.*

I can't honestly be growing affections for the first man with bright eyes and a warm smile that I let get close to me since Charles, can I? I'm stronger than that. I'm more levelheaded than the girl I was. I've learned from my mistakes of falling too fast and wanting too much.

Panic now competes with lust and desire. I must stop him for both our sakes. I raise my hands, placing them on his chest, ready to push him away. But all I feel is warm, sturdy muscle under my fingers and my will is sapped. I forget I need to project my thoughts for him to hear. I move my mouth on instinct in a weak attempt at an objection.

His nose brushes against mine. *Oh, old gods*, he's going to kiss me and I don't want it to stop. I want his hands to slide from my face down my shoulders. I want his fingertips to brush over my chest, teasing me in all the ways that have been forbidden.

Once more, before I die, perhaps I will feel again. Perhaps we will throw caution to the wind and indulge in passion and lust. I have hidden the shattering of my heart before; I can do it again. And maybe the pieces that are left of that infernal organ won't be enough to fall in love. Maybe I can forget that it ever happened once I'm satisfied. One song of the old ones would be enough for me to forget Ilryth and I ever existed, if it came to that. Maybe—

His forehead touches against mine. But he does not move. I open my eyes and find his still closed, his brow furrowed slightly in intense focus.

"We'll only have a moment before he begins to wonder why we're not speaking," he says. "It's risky to speak here without touching. Ventris no doubt uses the wards and blessings to listen in on this room. Touch will help make the connection stronger and more private."

I suddenly realize how cold the ocean water is as it douses the budding flame that'd been growing in the pit of my stomach. I hang limply in the water, held in place by his hands.

You fool, Victoria, he wasn't trying to kiss you...he was trying to talk to you. Why would a man like him, with so many prospects and so much life ahead, want to kiss a woman marked for death? I'm grateful for the necklace Fenny gave me for keeping those bitter thoughts and the internal, harsh laughter that follows to myself.

But is it necessary for him to be so close if all that's required is touch? I don't dare ask. I hardly think so. But I don't want him to stop... Is it so wrong for a woman to want a little bit of warmth before her life is over?

Ilryth's eyes open slightly, meeting mine. The stare is intense, this close. "They're going to take me before the chorus. It shouldn't take long, and then I'll come and find you again."

"Is everything all right in there?" Ventris calls in.

I hear Ilryth curse in the back of his mind. I push him away gently and call back to Ventris, "Of course, why would it not be?"

"It seemed very quiet."

"Can two people not talk amongst themselves?" I glance over my shoulder at the kelp to make sure he's not swimming through.

There's a brief pause. "Certainly, they can. I simply desired to make sure all was well."

If he wasn't trying to listen in then he wouldn't sound so confused and alarmed. I smile, taking no small amount of pleasure at the idea of thwarting Ventris. I hope he's racking his brain, frustrated as to the reason why he can't listen in. No doubt the carved symbols I've seen all over this place are also the markers of his grubby little magic trying to get into every corner.

Leaning back in, I press my forehead against Ilryth's once more.

I savor the sensation of initiating the closeness, even if it's only for practicality's sake. "What can I do to help you today?"

Ilryth shakes his head, his nose almost brushing against mine. "You can't come."

"I will."

"But—"

"I'm going to and that's that," I say definitively. "I will help. I'm the offering, I know words of the old ones, surely all that means *something*? Tell me how I can be of use."

Ilryth narrows his eyes slightly. He wants to object, but he doesn't have the speed or eloquence to continue doing so. And I remain resolute. Instead, his expression relaxes slightly and the focus shifts to something more internal. He props his right elbow on his left fist, bringing the latter across his body, and strokes his chin with his right hand.

For a moment I am very, *very* distracted by the way his fingers glide over his cheeks and lips. He grabs me again, this time pressing his cheek against mine as though he is going to whisper in my ear. I barely resist holding his cheek with my free hand to feel his closeness.

"While there are general guidelines for anointing the offering, there's a lot of room for interpretation depending on what the offering needs. The whole process is relatively new in our history and is still being experimented with," Ilryth says, resting his hands on my shoulders to keep us together. "Because of this, it could be difficult for them to question the nuances. If you said we had to go back to the Natural World to anoint you in the waters of your home—that you heard in the hymns of the old ones that you needed clean sea, free of rot, and that it was Krokan's will…they couldn't object."

I nod. "I can do that. When is best for me to—"

"The other singers in the chorus are here. We should make way to the meeting hall. *Now*," Ventris interrupts. His tone is curt. I hope it is because he's annoyed by not being able to hear our thoughts. "The hour is growing late and there's much to be done."

I can't get in a word faster than Ilryth.

"We're coming."

"But—"

Without warning, his right hand glides against my cheek, fingers pressing lightly behind my ear, gently hooking my jaw. The movement draws my entire being against him. The momentum is stopped only by my body meeting his. The barbs of desire have hooked me once more, instantly upon his touch. Our lips nearly meet.

So close. Agonizingly...close.

Just once more before I die, I'd like to kiss a man. Kiss him... maybe?

Ilryth presses his forehead to mine. "All will be well, don't worry," he says, the words deep with purpose. "I will look after you no matter what. I swear it."

The sentiment is innocuous enough that he could have said it aloud. It would've hardly been a problem if Ventris had heard him reassuring me.

But he didn't. Ilryth kept that comfort for me, and me alone. He releases me, but the words cling. I hold them in my thoughts as delicately as I would an egg. They are warm, fragile, and carry something unknown, but possibly wonderful, within them.

twenty-seven

I KEEP ILRYTH'S REASSURANCE CLOSE AS VENTRIS LEADS US INTO A LARGE CAVERN. It appears naturally made, embellished with relief carvings of stone pillars against the walls that don't appear to support the rough-hewn ceiling. Silvery vines trellis down from a trough carved around the top of the room, casting everything in the truest shade of blue I've ever seen.

Five shells are positioned in a semi-circle. The one in the center is placed upon a pillar of stone. Two each are positioned to the right and left of it.

With the way he's been acting, I would've expected Ventris to take the top seat—the one that looks most like a throne for a king—but he occupies the one at the far left. The center seat is occupied by a pale, older woman with short-cut, dark brown hair that's lined with salt.

Ilryth positions himself before them and I hover just behind at his right. The other two dukes regard us thoughtfully. One of them has long, thick black braids and brown skin. The other is tawny skinned and brown haired. I'm not sure where to go, or what to do. So I linger and wait. The dukes and duchess glance at each other and I know things are being said that I can't hear.

Ventris takes a conch shell and places it on a flat, round stone in the center of the semi-circle, right in front of where Ilryth is standing. Much like the shell around my neck, it has been adorned with carvings and silver inlay of swirling lines and symbols that are reminiscent of the markings on us all.

The four dukes and one duchess begin to sway slowly,

humming. Song vibrates from them, rippling through the water. The notes are in perfect harmony and the markings of the shell light up in gold.

"This chorus of the five duchies of the Eversea is now in session. It is year 8,242 of the divine twining," Ventris says as the singing dies down. "Those in attendance are myself, Ventris Chilvate of the Duchy of Faith."

"Sevin Rowt of the Duchy of Scholarship," the man to Ventris's left with the black braids says.

"Crowl Dreech of the Duchy of Harvest," the man with the brown hair to the right of the center throne says.

"Remni Quantor of the Duchy of Craftsmen, and conductor of this chorus." The eldest woman places both hands on her tail, leaning forward and staring intently at me. I try to avoid her piercing, hazel eyes.

"Ilryth Granspell, Duchy of Spears," Ilryth says last, adding, "Standing before the chorus for review of conduct regarding this five-year offering to Lord Krokan."

"Indeed." Remni wastes no time getting the first word in, as seems befitting of her station. "Ventris, seeing as you were the one to call this meeting and catch these supposed offenses, I think it is only right for you to explain why we are spending a morning on it when there are anointments to be given to the offering and matters to be attended to before the waters are high."

Perhaps I misjudged the grizzled woman. Her tone suggests she views these affairs as tedious at best. I spare a glance to Ilryth. I should have trusted him more to know if this chorus merited worry or not. All I could feel in my gut was my own fear going before the council back home, Charles standing opposite me. There's a trembling in my muscles, telling me to run from the mere thought of that strange man—a fear I don't quite understand.

Charles… The name is synonymous with fear in my mind. But what did he do to me? *We were married.* That much I know because I remember standing before the council to nullify that contract. But almost everything before that is blank. A huge void of my life.

Whatever it was must have been horrible enough that I needed to wipe him from my personal records. The next memories I will choose to be expunged will be of those appearances before the Council of Tenvrath. Merely thinking of him is a reminder of everything that's gone—everything I don't know. It's not worth the emotional strain to keep any memories of him.

"I was made aware of the oddity late last night through a dissonance in the humming of the water—a shift in the songs of the old ones," Ventris says. "As is my responsibility, I have been preparing here for the offering's arrival. Naturally, the anamnesis alerted me to her presence when she first arrived in the Eversea and subsequent blessings only strengthened that awareness."

"You've been spying on me?" I blurt. Not even the shell can hold back that thought.

"Not *spying*," Ventris says, mildly offended. "I have been watching over you to ensure that you are well taken care of."

"Did you doubt Ilryth's ability to take care of me?" I ask pointedly, offended on my duke's behalf.

Ventris's eyes dart between Ilryth and me. From the corners of my eyes, I see Ilryth smirk slightly. It's a very minor movement, enough so that the rest of them don't seem to notice. But he's been the only foundation I've had in this strange, new world. I've paid very close attention to the man.

"Ilryth has acted in dissonance with the council before, especially when it comes to matters of the offering," Ventris says curtly. His hands are folded in his lap, shoulders away from the salmon-colored fins on either side of his face to give the appearance of ease. But every muscle in his expression has been trained into place. He clutches his hands so tightly that his knuckles are nearly white. What really gives his distress away is the incessant flicking of his tail.

"The matter of Ilryth selecting a human for the offering is long settled, Ventris. It is done. Stop echoing the final note." Crowl leans back in his sponge-filled shell, his brown hair swaying about his face. He has the air of seniority and the ease that comes with it. I suspect that he must be the second in command. As far as I can tell, the hierarchy seems to be structured by age.

"It might seem little to you, Crowl, because the obligation to find and anoint the offerings does not fall to you. But Ilryth and I will be finding offerings long after you are gone. We have a standard to uphold." Ventris narrows his eyes at Ilryth. I can feel the barely contained rage radiating off of him. "A standard that is meant to be followed, or else there are unfortunate mistakes and the offerings lack the proper potency."

Ilryth stiffens slightly. Was that intended to be a sly attack on his mother not being able to quell Lord Krokan's rage? I ball my hands into fists, digging my nails into my palms to keep myself from verbally launching myself at him in Ilryth's defense and my own. How dare he imply I'm not up to standard, too. Only I am allowed to question my own adequacy.

"Watch your tongue," Crowl says lightly, but with a dangerous look to Ventris.

"Enough, all of you," the eldest, Remni, says tiredly. In that moment she looks twice her age. "Let us stay focused on the matters at hand—taking the offering from the Eversea via traveler's pool without permission, and engaging in physical touch with the offering."

So it really is forbidden…

Sevin, Duke of Scholarship, picks up where Ventris left off, speaking to Ilryth. "So Ventris found that you had taken the offering out of the Eversea by sensing her departure via the use of the traveler's pool." *That explains why they don't seem to know of our departure through the Fade to the Gray Passage.* And the Duchy of Spears—at least Fenny, Lucia, and Sheel—are keeping it a secret. "Surely your mother or father taught you that once the anointing begins, the offering is tethered to the Eversea and removal risks her disappearance?"

"I was informed." Ilryth's tone is completely different—harder, more closed off—when talking about his parents.

"And Ilryth explained as much to me," I interject. With a small kick I swim forward, hovering next to Ilryth rather than off to the side. I am careful not to touch him. "He told me of the risks but *I* was the one who insisted. As I listened to the songs of the old ones, I realized I needed clean sea, free of rot, to be blessed in. I needed to be close to other humans—those crafted by Lellia's hands." I try to levy all the information I've collected on the Eversea until now. It rings true when spoken with confidence. "Leaving was an act to sever my ties to the Natural World. It was absolutely necessary or I would have remained tethered to this plane. Now that I have returned and severed those ties, I am better prepared to meet the Abyss."

All eyes are on me. Ventris wears a scowl. But the rest of them seem fascinated—as if they're amazed I can speak at all. I feel a bit like a toddler performing a parlor trick to cooing parents, but I carry on anyway.

"His Grace was very cautious, of course. He taught me how to review the songs to make sure I hadn't misunderstood Lord Krokan's will. We went at night," I continue. "And we kept a close eye on my status to make sure I didn't fade away and that no harm came to the elements of the anointing that had already been completed. Ilryth ensured that we returned before any real risk was posed to me."

"And were you able to sever these human tethers that would've prevented your descent into the Abyss as the offering?" Remni asks.

"Yes." I nod and place a hand on my chest. "Where there was once turmoil, there is now peace. I know in my heart and my song that I am wholly ready to be the offering that will bring Lord Krokan peace."

The four of them stare at me, occasionally sharing a glance with each other. I'm surprised when Ilryth leans forward to speak, holding out his arms, beseeching all of them.

"Victoria might be our tenth offering, but she will be our last. We have presented the best the Eversea has to offer to Lord Krokan, but it was not enough. Victoria will be." Ilryth looks back to me with a warm smile, his eyes alight with nothing but compassion. "She is smart, astute, and capable. She has a zeal for life, and I swear on my mother's life that I can see the spark of Lady Lellia within her. Never, in all my years, have I known a woman finer than Victoria."

My heart swells at his words, pressing with a sweet ache against my ribs. Has anyone risen to my defense so eagerly before? Has anyone ever said such sweet things about me?

It contrasts with all the times before the council with Charles. How he screamed of my failings until he was red in the face. The names he called me. The lies he spun…

"More than anything else though…" Ilryth turns back to the council. "Victoria has proved to me, time and again, that she is a woman of her word. She will keep all promises and oaths above all else. Her every action is the picture of honesty."

My heart deflates, leaving a hollow in my chest. *Stop, please*, I want to say. All the names the rumors of Dennow called me are back, reverberating around all the blank spaces of my mind. *Contract ender, oath breaker, deserter...*

But he continues, ignorant to the truth about me. "She would never, under any circumstances, go back on her word or break an oath. So if you refuse to believe me, then believe her."

I float in pained silence. It's hard to keep my face passive and relaxed. *Never broken an oath...* If only he knew. My earlier thoughts return: *What would happen if he knew what the money we retrieved was really for? If he found out it's because I nullified my marriage? That I am not the woman he thinks I am?*

My mind begins to spiral like a whirlpool.

"Then it seems there is no cause for concern." Crowl shrugs.

Ventris sulks. "This is a dangerous precedent."

"He took appropriate precautions. The offering is fine and has given us her word that it was necessary—a word Ilryth would have us believe is as virtuous as Lady Lellia herself. Moreover, there are no more risks of them leaving. Are there?" Crowl glances to me.

"None," I assure them. Ilryth is right about one thing: I'm ready to accept my fate.

"Then let us put this matter to rest. We—"

"What of the matter of him touching her?" Ventris interrupts Remni. "I have multiple witnesses of it."

"Yes, what of that touch?" I interject just as quickly, pinning Ventris to his shell with my stare. "In fact, I was touching him. It was necessary for transportation through the pool and nothing that could anchor me to this world. But"—I continue speaking even as he tries to get a word in—"what of *you* grabbing me? Was *that* necessary? A touch those same knights of yours could corroborate?"

Ventris leans back in his shell, face draining of what little color was there. I think I hear the faintest reverberation of a chuckle from Ilryth. My duke is fighting a smirk with all his might. The other dukes seem equally amused. Remni has the expression of one dealing with a gaggle of young children.

"Ventris, would you care to put this matter to rest?" Remni rephrases her earlier statement as a very pointed question.

Ventris glowers at me then looks to the duchess. His expression drops before returning to me. I tilt my head in a gesture to suggest, *your move*.

"Very well," he begrudgingly says, sinking farther into his shell.

"I think that's wise," Remni says curtly. "As I was saying, we have more important concerns, like the remaining preparations and the organization of court for the final blessing and send-off."

"If you would care to take your seat, Ilryth." Sevin motions to the shell at the far right.

Ilryth swims effortlessly over to it, settling in one fluid motion. Even though he's the one settling into his place, something in me softly *clicks*. My muscles unlock and thoughts slow. As though I needed to see all was right with him to truly feel at ease.

"Shall the offering be escorted out while we discuss these matters?" Remni asks.

"I wish to stay," I say. All eyes are on me. I want to make sure they don't go after Ilryth when I'm gone and...I'm curious. I've grown fascinated with the sirens and their ways.

"That is quite irregular," Sevin observes. He doesn't sound disapproving, nor pleased. Merely factual.

"You have additional anointments to be made," Ventris says as if I am an unruly child.

"Anoint me later."

"There is little time," he counters.

"I think there are a few months left till the solstice, aren't there? It's time enough." I smile slightly.

Ventris scowls and goes to speak.

But Ilryth interrupts him. "I doubt we will meet for long. Most of the details were discussed before I even collected the offering."

"This offering you have brought us is truly fascinating...a human, with such zeal!" Sevin appraises me. The feeling that I am more of a thing than a person to these people returns. It is a sensation I haven't felt since I first arrived and it is deeply uncomfortable yet, oddly familiar... *I've known this feeling before, I think?* "Perhaps there is something to be said for your unorthodox methods, Ilryth, after all."

"I told you all, I was compelled in the water that night by an urge that hearkened to the old ones. Victoria will be the last offering ever to Lord Krokan. We will soon know peace in the Eversea once more. Now, regarding the remaining anointments…"

I'm not really a part of the conversation any longer, merely an observer. None of them address me, even though it's clear they're speaking about me. Ilryth's eyes are the only ones that dart over to me, from time to time, offering a reassuring and somewhat worried look. I keep my face passive. The last thing I want is to be dismissed for acting out of turn and miss an opportunity to gather more information on what awaits me.

Ventris details the remaining anointments in quickly glossed-over terms. The rest of them nod and hum along, agreeing with seemingly everything the Duke of Faith has to say. Then they discuss the court—the lower nobility gathering for a great presentation, a final anointment, and then the final send-off. A grand affair that—so far as I can tell—is going to make up my last day on this plane of existence.

After somewhere between thirty minutes and an hour, they conclude their meeting with one final song. It is in perfect harmony. Ventris collects the shell at the center. It flashes brightly for a second as he picks it up.

"As always, lady and gentlemen, a pleasure." Sevin straightens off his clam shell and starts for the exit, wasting no time.

"I'll see you all in soon enough for the final court, blessing, and send-off." Crowl smiles, gives each of them a nod—myself included—and leaves.

As Ilryth and Remni straighten, the elder swims over and clasps Ilryth's shoulder.

"You did well with this one." She motions to me. Yet again, I'm spoken about as if I'm not actually here. But I bite my tongue. "I know you have risked much for her. But sometimes the greatest risks are the greatest rewards."

"That is my hope as well," Ilryth says solemnly. His tone stills me. The anger and frustration I felt at how they've been talking to me abates some.

I've never seen Ilryth with such an earnest, delicate hope in his eyes. It's something that he has kept hidden the entire, albeit brief, time I've known him. For a moment, he looks like the boy I saw in the vision—fragile and frightened.

"There is no way a human will be Krokan's peace," Ventris seethes quietly. "Especially not one found and cultivated outside the rules of the Duchy of Faith."

"Ventris—" Remni tries to caution.

But the Duke of Faith leaves with little more than a glare over his shoulder. Those angry eyes are still aflame on his face as he swims past me. In his mind, I clearly share some blame for whatever wrong, or wound, he carries.

"I expect you to be in your anointing chambers shortly," Ventris says curtly, right before he vanishes into the tunnel that connects this room to the greater castle. I can't tell if it's only to me or not.

"An honor to meet you, Your Holiness," Remni says before departing as well.

Ilryth and I are alone.

"Well, what did you think of your first siren chorus?" he asks. His body language is casual, but his tone betrays a bit of nervousness.

"It was enlightening," I say. "Was Remni elected as the leader?"

He nods. "No, the head of the chorus is the eldest among us. Before Remni, it was my mother."

Mention of his mother reminds me…

"There's something else I want to know but I feel it might be a bit personal," I say delicately.

"There is nothing I won't share with you, Victoria." The sentiment stills me, warms me. It's not a fiery passion trying to rile me to the point of agony if I don't find release. Instead, this is a calmer heat. One that envelops me like sunshine on a cloudless day.

I work to keep focused. "It's about Ventris."

"Ah, I think I know what it is you want to ask." Ilryth folds his hands behind his back.

I glance over my shoulder. The warriors are speaking with Remni, all looking in the other direction. I dare to reach out, touching his firm bicep. "Should we speak like this?"

He shakes his head, and I withdraw my hand before any can see and get us in trouble all over again. "It's safe in the meeting hall; just focusing on each other will be enough. Even though this is in Ventris's domain, parts of the castle belong to all the duchies. For him to have ways to listen in, or track, what happens in this room would be a grave error on his part, resulting in deep offense."

"Would the offering's quarters be a deep offense as well?"

Ilryth sees right through to the heart of my worries. "I believe so."

"Good." I keep my thoughts and words focused on Ilryth.

"Now, to answer what I believe you wanted to ask... Ventris blames me for the rocky start to his leadership as the Duke of Faith, and for the circumstances of his father's death." Ilryth wastes no time and doesn't mince words.

"What do you mean? How so?"

"His father gave up much to learn of the offering fifty years ago. My mother worked closely with him on helping to decipher the words of Lord Krokan and their meanings," Ilryth says. No wonder he had his own theories about the words Duke Renfal heard from Krokan. "After the first eight offerings had failed, my mother offered herself as the ninth. Duke Renfal could try communing one more time as they were working together, trying to learn all they could about the anointing. Connecting with the old god again was too much and he perished."

"So Ventris blames your family for his father's death?" I reason.

"In part. But Duke Renfal was already deteriorating from his earlier communing with the god. That might have been the moment of his undoing, but he was well along the path," Ilryth says with genuine sympathy.

"Grief is rarely logical," I say softly, thinking of a young Ventris, not quite understanding why his father's body and mind were so weak.

"Then I didn't ascend to the mantle of Duke, as I was supposed to, which caused my mother's anointing to be delayed." Ilryth's tone turns solemn and sad. "So Ventris not only sees my family as the cause of his father's death, but me the reason behind that death lacking purpose. I held my mother back, and for that reason both she and Duke Renfal died for nothing."

"That's not true," I say softly.

Ilryth just shrugs and moves on with his tale. "That night, I made my vow no other siren would die. I chose you—marked you as the next offering without consulting the chorus or the Duchy of Faith. It was a slight to Ventris right at the start of his rule. He looked like he no longer had the control his father wielded with such grace. Now, he resents me and my duchy."

"That will change when I quell Lord Krokan's rage," I say firmly.

"I hope so." The words are faint, almost sad.

"Let's carry on then." I swim toward the entrance of the room with even more purpose fueling me. I cannot let Ilryth down. I will not.

twenty-eight

Ventris is already in my chambers, and barely looks our way as we arrive.

"Thank you for bringing the offering, Ilryth. You may go."

I glance between Ilryth and Ventris. Ventris's tone is casual enough, but he's already taken Ilryth from me once. He's stricter about the amorphous rules surrounding the offering. I've little doubt that, if Ventris wanted, he could find a way to keep me from Ilryth entirely for the next eight weeks. That shouldn't matter to me, but it does, and I'm too tired to fight it.

I don't want to be alone.

My attention lands on Ilryth. I bite back words and force myself to look away. I can't speak now or I'd ask Ilryth to do something I know he shouldn't.

Somehow, Ilryth seems to read my mind. Even more incredibly…he acts on it.

"Actually, Ventris, *you* may go."

"I beg your pardon?" Ventris turns from the Abyss, wearing a shocked expression.

"I will continue overseeing the anointing for the offering," Ilryth declares. His boldness in the face of Ventris's authority has a depth of meaning I wouldn't have picked up on had I not just learned of their shared history.

"The Duke of Faith has always overseen the anointing after the halfway point," Ventris says coolly.

"You're right," he agrees with almost dangerous ease.

"But this is Victoria's and my duet. We are the ones to determine how it is best sung."

"The chorus—"

"Made it clear that they trust my judgment when it comes to the offering, however unorthodox it might be." Ilryth drifts forward. His powerful aura makes him feel taller. He seems to loom over the younger man, making Ventris look like little more than an insecure child. "I was the one to first teach her the hymns of the old gods. I will oversee her anointing until the very end. It will take Lord Krokan himself to take me from her side, so there is little you can do."

A flush rises up my chest and hits my cheeks. I try to fight it but my body has a mind of its own. I know Ilryth shouldn't be doing this...but seeing him stand up for me in this way has my insides knotting with a sensation that borders on the unbearable.

Ventris's eyes dart between us. They narrow slightly before returning to Ilryth. "It is incredibly inappropriate, Your Grace, for the offering to have only one person anointing her. The process is about removing the bonds with this mortal plane, not tying her to it."

"I would never do anything that would tie her to this plane," Ilryth says defensively, perhaps a bit too much so.

"Good, then you will not object to me—" Ventris reaches for me but Ilryth spins, positioning himself between me and the other man.

"Have I not made myself clear, Your Grace?" Ilryth bites out. There is no tone of formality in the words. He speaks with all the air of authority of a king. One look from me—one moment of hesitation on my part—and he's putting his neck on the line for me.

Though, he has been this entire time. From daring to touch me so I could get out of my head and learn the words, even when he knew it'd be forbidden, to taking me to Sheel's house and having me practice my magic to gain my confidence before the trench. Helping my family... Ilryth has risked so much for me.

I don't deserve him. Especially not when he thinks I am the epitome of trustworthiness and honor. I can't remember all of what I've done anymore, but that thought is as bright and sharp in my mind as the north star.

"Do not allow a human to turn you foolish, Ilryth. Even if that human is the offering." Ventris folds his arms, scowling openly.

"Do not allow history to blind you to progress, Ventris," Ilryth fires back.

Ventris purses his lips. The mental war he wages is visible on his face. I wonder what pros and cons he's weighing. But I'm shocked when it seems that something Ilryth said might have made it through to him, actually working in our favor.

"Very well. We shall *share* in this responsibility." A compromise is clearly the closest Ventris will give us to what we want. "I shall return later to anoint her, and leave her in your care for now. Do ensure she meditates on the Abyss. We wouldn't want another failure because of you." With that biting remark, he swims off, leaving us alone in my chambers.

"He's a real piece of work," I say when he's gone.

"You're not wrong." Ilryth drifts over to the table.

"Are you sure this is all right?"

"It's what you wanted, isn't it?" The question sounds like a genuine inquiry. One of concern and gentle probing. It's also a deflection.

"Yes, but how did you know?" I look back to him.

He doesn't answer for a long minute. "I could hear it in your song."

"In my song?"

Ilryth swims over to me. I stand perfectly still as he presses his fingers gently along my jaw. His fingers linger. The side of his thumb grazes the shell of my ear.

"I told you once that we all have a song in our soul."

"Yes...and you can hear mine?"

He nods. Why does it make him look so sad? Do I bring him such sorrow? I couldn't bear the answer, so I don't ask.

"Would you like company for while you 'commune with the Abyss'?" Ilryth's expression is guarded, utterly unreadable. Does he want to stay? Or have I already put him out too much?

"Only if you would like to." I try to strike an indifferent tone.

There's a long enough pause that my heart sinks. But then it soars once more with fluttering beats when he says, "I would like to."

The distance between our bodies feels an ocean wide. And yet he is so close that I could cross the gap in a heartbeat. My hands could be on him with a thought. I could run my fingers over those markings across one side of his chest like I would pore over a map…finding my way around him. Learning his most uncharted territories.

"What do we do now?" My words are a little breathless, even to my ears.

"We can do whatever you think you would enjoy." He folds his arms and lifts a hand, stroking his chin in thought. The familiar motion almost brings a smile to my face. I barely resist quipping that I could think of quite a few things at present that I would enjoy doing alone with him. "I could request some games that might be of interest. Or a scroll that details the old language of the siren. Perhaps one written in common tongue that tells more of Krokan." He drops his hand and flashes me a dazzling smile. "Truly, whatever would please you. Say the word and it shall be yours."

"None of that sounds like 'communing with the Abyss.'" I grin slightly.

Ilryth shrugs, unbothered. "I could make any of it happen."

"Why are you being so kind to me?" I can't stop myself from asking.

"Have I not been kind to you until now?"

The question is justified. He has been. But it… "It feels different," I admit.

For a moment, he doesn't know how to respond. He stares at me with those deep eyes. Eyes that seem to hold more colors than I ever noticed previously.

"Does this have to do with what we spoke of in the Natural World? Of you being 'undeserving' of love?"

"I said nothing of love." I avoid his eyes, otherwise he'll see right through me. I can't think that way about us. Neither can he. It's a risk that's too grave for either of us to take.

"You didn't have to. That fear of yours is much more than just love…" Ilryth drifts a little closer, the small fins on his tail propelling him without help of his arms. Does he realize what he's saying? What the intensity of his stare implies? "Let me be the one to tell you, Victoria, without doubt or hesitation, that you are worthy of kindness, compassion, and love. And I will tell you it a thousand times over if that is what it will take for you to believe it." He dips his chin, trying to meet my eyes.

Every instinct tells me to push him away as hard as I can. The lessons that have been etched onto my very soul were to trust no one deeply, to count on no one.

But…perhaps I could've trusted a bit more, long ago. There were all those around me that I kept at arm's length because I was the one who had to take care of them, not the other way around. But they stayed, ready to fight and sacrifice for my benefit. I can't change the past, but I can correct the future—what little I have left.

Now there's an oddly freeing notion that hadn't occurred to me before.

Rather than looking at my impending demise as reason to hold myself back, perhaps I should consider it freedom, of a sort. There is no "after." No payment that will come due for whatever choices I make. I am about to march to the Great Beyond. What do I have to lose by living a bit for myself?

Without a word I swim toward the balcony. Ilryth follows when I motion to the space next to me, settling alongside me as I perch myself on the railing. There's no sign of Krokan below this afternoon.

"Go ahead, ask me anything."

"Pardon?"

"You must have questions about me… about why I am the way I am." There are two conversations happening between us in tandem. What we are saying, and everything we aren't—everything we can't. Perhaps, if I'm brave enough, I can tear down the barriers a bit on the latter. "I'll tell you anything you want to hear. Even things I haven't told my family, or friends back in the Natural World. If you ask, I will answer you wholly honestly."

Ilryth considers this for long enough that I'm bracing myself. "*Anything* I want?"

"Yes, anything." It's too late to back down now. And, just once…I want to be vulnerable to someone worthy of that vulnerability.

"And you'll answer truthfully?"

"I swear it." He's going to ask me about who made me feel unworthy. I'm already trying to string together what I remember around the voids of my mind the words of the old gods ate through. Who would've thought that whatever it was that I so desperately wanted to forget, is now something I'm trying to remember.

"What is the purpose of the cloth that adorns your ships?"

"Excuse me?" I blink several times, as if my misunderstanding somehow comes from not being able to see him clearly. I run a hand through my hair. "I don't think I—"

"The ships. They have large flags tied to their center poles." He pantomimes a ship and its mast. "Yours had three. I've seen them countless times but I've never been certain as to the reason."

I'm fighting a smile with all my might. He's so enthusiastic. So enthralled.

"It's difficult to get plans or dioramas of ships. So I've worked to rebuild them as best I'm able in small model. My suspicion is to catch the wind. But how can wind move a vessel so large? Perhaps I could bring one of my reconstructions back from my treasure room to the surface and you could show…" He trails off. I've lost the battle with my face. A grin splits from ear to ear. Ilryth straightens and looks away. He has the pout of a boy who hasn't been taken seriously enough for his liking. "Forget I asked. It's a foolish question, I know. So obvious, so silly of me not to know. But it's nothing a siren duke should be concerning himself with."

The final statement has the echo of other people's words to it. I shift on the railing and my fingertips brush his lightly. It wasn't intentional… but I don't move my hand either.

"Ilryth, it's all right. The question isn't offensive and isn't anything you should be ashamed of, either. Besides, I find it endearing that you want to know." His fascination for ships came from me, after all. It's only right that I'm the one to teach him about them. "You're right. The sails catch the wind and help give the ship forward movement."

"I knew it," he whispers triumphantly.

I nod with a smile. Ilryth looks rather proud and that only makes me smile bigger.

"The ship, while heavy, is much lighter in water. It's called buoyancy." I elaborate a bit more on the mechanics of ships and how the sails and rigging works. Even though I'm using technical terms that I'm sure would bore most people, he hangs on my every word. When I finish, I say, "I imagine there are many things about our worlds that we think are obvious until we're presented with the gaze of someone unfamiliar."

"Is there something you'd like to ask of me?" he offers.

I think about it. There's so much unknown about the world of the sirens. About Ilryth himself. But he asked an easy enough question of me to start, so I'll keep my inquiry simple, for now.

"Do sirens hate humans?"

"Why would you ask that?" He seems startled. "Have I ever—"

"Not you, or most of your duchy, really..." I give his people the benefit of the doubt. "But here, I feel like a caged animal. Brought out for the fancy of others."

"Humans are never seen in Midscape, save for the Human Queen... and some sirens do blame them for the demise of Lady Lellia."

"Why?

Ilryth stares out into the Abyss, thinking. His eyes are drawn to the roots of the Lifetree when he speaks. "It was shortly after the humans were crafted that Lady Lellia stopped walking among us. Some say it was shame for their lack of magic. When the Fade was made and humans were separated, her song was no longer heard."

"But wasn't the Fade made to protect humans?"

"It was."

"Then why blame the humans?"

Ilryth shakes his head sadly. "When people are wounded, they look for an easy person, or people, to blame. The humans weren't there to defend themselves, so they made for simple targets for the ire of many." He brings his eyes to me. "But I think most sirens today have little feelings one way or another toward humans beyond mild fascination."

I nod. "All right, then, your turn."

We go back and forth for hours. I learn of his favorite memory growing up with Lucia and Fenny—of kelp-fishing with play spears. I learn of the siren performances around yule to sing in the new year. I tell him of my own childhood. Of the vast and mysterious places I've seen while sailing for Kevhan Applegate, choosing to speak fondly of how I remember him in life, not as I last saw him in death. How I was the best of the best among the sailors—thanks to Ilryth's magic.

I sigh wistfully, thinking of my early days among the waves. A rogue thought from those times resonates through my mind: *Those early days, I felt like I was truly free of Charles. Even though he still held my soul and on paper my name. I felt like I could sail far enough and escape him.*

"Who was he?" Ilryth asks softly, gently.

"Who?" I look to him, my heart seizing. My musing got away from me, my thoughts wandering beyond my tight grasp. *Don't say it. Please don't say it.* I can't stop myself from clutching the shell necklace, hoping that somehow, I'm wrong. That it protected me even from my deepest thoughts. It's futile.

"Charles."

twenty-nine

"It's going to be hard to tell you about him," I say softly, when I've recovered from my shock of him outright asking about Charles. I've worked so hard to erase him from my history but he continues to haunt me…even if I don't fully understand why.

How can I tell Ilryth who Charles was to me in a comprehensible way? All I know, now, are the broad strokes. But how could I communicate those without Ilryth losing faith in me? It has taken us months to build this foundation of trust. The mere thought of losing it turns my insides to lead. I grapple with my next words.

"You don't have to tell me, if you don't want to," Ilryth reminds me gently.

I shrug, pulling my eyes from his. Somehow, compared to his affectionate and yet piercing stare, the Abyss is a welcome alternative. "It's…it's all right. We're being honest with each other, aren't we?"

"Yes. But that doesn't mean you must share something you might otherwise not want to."

"Stop telling me not to, or I won't." I laugh, though it is a joyless sound. "I really haven't talked with enough people about him." If there's one thing I learned from going back to Dennow, it's that I should have been talking more, to everyone, for a long time. I can both be relied on, and rely on others, at the same time. "Besides, what does it matter if you know? I'll be gone soon anyway."

"You shouldn't say that." Ilryth's tail twitches slightly. It's the only movement on his body, but it betrays agitation and alarm. The tiny fins on the sides of it ripple several times. There are all these small things about the sirens and their mannerisms—about him—that I'm still learning. I'll likely never have the chance to study every movement and indicator the way I would want to know him. My shoulders feel even heavier.

"It's true, isn't it?" I try to shrug, making light of it. Facing it head-on rather than by cowering in fear is the only way I know how to keep moving on when the world gets tough. Hide my pain not just from everyone else, but from myself as well.

"It's hard to be reminded of it…" He trails off, then hastily adds, "And that's speaking for me personally. I can't imagine how it might feel for you."

"I'll be fine."

Ilryth looks at me skeptically, but doesn't object.

"Anyway, when I said it'll be difficult to tell you of him, I didn't mean just emotionally. It'll be difficult because I seem to have eradicated memories of him first."

His skepticism shifts to surprise. Ilryth's brow furrows, and there's a flash of rage in his eyes. His words take on a protective edge. "What did he do that would make you target him for complete removal from your memories?"

"I don't think I could tell you anymore," I reiterate. The Abyss is as dark as the voids in my mind. "But I'll tell you what I know, what I can still piece together…

"I grew up on the outskirts of a small town. My father and mother both worked—as hard as they could. But it was difficult for either of them to hold down any kind of steady job. My father because he sustained an injury that made it hard for him to work the manual labor that was abundant in our area, and he didn't have the book skills to work as a secretary for a local merchant noble…and my mother because it just wasn't really in her blood to stay in one place for long. But they made do…" I wax poetic about my childhood. About the long days down by the creek that ran by town catching bugs with Emily. About the cold nights that I didn't hate as much as I thought I did in retrospect because it meant we were all snuggled close.

Ilryth holds no judgment. He listens with quiet, earnest fascination. I admit to the bad times as freely as I describe the good. Hiding nothing is freeing.

"Then…" I pause, squinting slightly, as if I could cut through the murk of my mind to find memories that have long since been consumed by magic not meant for mortal understanding. "I was eighteen, barely… I still have a memory of my birthday celebrations for that year… I went into the market. Something about lighthouses… It becomes fuzzy." I shake my head. "After that there's a large swath of my life that's just gone. The next point I can remember is tumbling in the water that night. Then, standing on the beach, alone, staring at the lighthouse. Twenty and—" *Married.* I glance at Ilryth to see if he heard the rogue thought.

"And?" His face betrays nothing. I can't tell if he heard or not.

"And I had markings on my arm. I've kept most of the memory of meeting you," I say brightly.

"Surprised you chose to keep that traumatic night." The faintest blush highlights the barely-there freckles of his cheeks. "Do you remember anything else of him?"

"I remember going to court… It took me years to let him go," I say softly. "I only just managed to right before you took me…that was why my family was in such debt."

"You owed money because of a relationship?"

"That's right…" *How can I keep myself from admitting the full truth, while still not outright lying?* All I want is to preserve some of the esteem Ilryth has for me. "I helped him at the lighthouse. The council said I had to repay what Tenvrath invested in me for my time as an attendant. Almost everything in Tenvrath can be bought and sold. It's why the highest crime is owing money you can't pay. At the lighthouse, I was supported by the taxes of the people. They demanded I pay back that debt and if I didn't they'd—"

"Send you, or your family in your place, to that horrible debtors' prison you mentioned." He frowns. "I remember."

All my muscles are tense. I grip the railing under me with white knuckles. I can't remember what happened during those two years with Charles. They're as empty as the Abyss beneath me. And yet, my throat is tight. My breaths catch. I feel as if I want to fight, or run…weep or scream. My body remembers what my mind has readily forgotten.

"Victoria…" Ilryth touches my hand, leaning toward me. "What is it?"

I don't notice my eyes are burning until I look at him. I imagine they're red and puffy. Tears cannot fall in the ocean, but eyes can burn, mouths can twist.

"I don't know," I whisper. "I can't remember anything. I don't know why I feel like I want to burn the world down around me."

Ilryth's lips part slightly. He seems to lean closer. "It's all right."

"I know. I—Even if it's not, it doesn't matter, right?" I shake my head. "All this will be over soon, anyway. It doesn't matter."

"Of course it matters."

"Why?"

"Because everything, good and bad, is a part of who you are. It might not define you, but it informs you. Teaches you. We fought, and struggled, and bled to get this far in life. And while I wish you never had to suffer as I fear you might have…if you did, that, too, is part of the Victoria I admire."

"Perhaps I don't want it to be a part of me," I murmur, lowering my eyes. "I might not remember the memories, but I can remember choosing to remove them first. Perhaps I am better for it. There's a strange comfort to this unknowing. Wiping out what I can only assume are the worst parts of myself."

"It's not just what you think are 'worst parts.' It will all go," he says gravely, looking out over the Abyss. The thought is spoken so quickly that I don't know if he intended for it to come out or not. But he doesn't backtrack.

"What… What do you mean?" The sentiment mirrors a terrified wondering I had weeks ago.

"You must sever *all* tethers to the mortal world. One day, soon, you will forget it all. Not just the bad, but the good. You can't choose forever what you want to keep." He doesn't look at me as he speaks. It's somehow worse. This truth is so horrible, he can't even face me.

"I'll forget…everything?" Emily's embrace. The smell of the wind on my first sailing. The taste of my father's ale. How the stars shone the first night I taught Jivre how to navigate by them. The feeling of the fine silks my mother would bring home, gliding between my fingers.

"It's the only way."

"How fast will it happen now?" Panic is rising in me. There's only two months left before the solstice. I realize that I'd allowed myself to believe I could keep the parts of me I wanted. Maybe not *all*, but at least a few... I replay every bright spot in my life, imprinting it on my heart, as though I could physically hold onto memories that have no shape or form.

"Much faster, now. When my mother arrived at the Duchy of Faith... she couldn't recognize my sisters and I within the month."

I lean back, reeling. They'd told me what I was doing—what had to be done. But I never took it to the logical conclusion.

I will be a shell. A husk. I—

My panic is interrupted as Ventris swims into the quarters with two warriors in tow. His presence reminds me that he could've been listening to our conversation this entire time. Even though Ilryth said this space should be safe, the mere idea of him knowing about my family, about Charles, my fears and all those ugly and hidden parts of me that I only wanted to show Ilryth, would be a violation I'd never forgive Ventris for.

Though, Ilryth's and my hands were touching the entire time. Perhaps it wasn't an accident or a sweet sentiment on Ilryth's behalf— he was trying to ensure our discussions were private. He's shifted before Ventris can notice the contact.

"I hope your meditation has gone well. It's time for your next round of markings before the Abyss," Ventris announces. The warriors move forward.

I eye them warily. Every time one of these sirens comes to anoint me...I'll have to give up more and more of myself. Soon, there will be nothing left of me. I want to swim away. To take Ilryth's hand and tell him to flee with me.

For the first time in a long time, I feel like running.

But this is the duty I accepted. This is the oath I took. I can't run, not now. I might not remember my family when the time comes. But I will still be giving my life to protect them. I will give everything to keep them all safe.

I push away from the balcony railing. From the corner of my eye I can see Ilryth's resigned, sad expression. "I'm ready."

Ventris approaches reverently. For the first time it feels as if he actually sees me as a sacred individual. His eyes are downcast. He moves with purpose, bowing before approaching.

Just like at the manor, I am marked across visible sections of my flesh. I imagine by the time I am offered to Krokan, I will be more drawings than bare skin. A beautiful husk. Even though Ventris is the one marking me, and the warriors remain present, heads bowed in reverence, it's Ilryth that I'm aware of.

He's moved to hover over Ventris's shoulder, watching intently. His broad chest rises and falls as though his breaths are labored. His expression is closed off, muscles tense.

Ilryth seems almost…alarmed? Scared? Put off? I'm not quite sure which, or why, but I tilt my head slightly to catch his eyes and offer a slight smile. Trying to tell him with the expression alone that I'm fine, not to worry.

No matter what my reaction just was, I can do this.

He returns the expression, briefly, but then reverts to his worried look with a furrowed brow as he stares a hole between Ventris's shoulder blades. It stays on him until Ventris is done. The Duke of Faith excuses himself, leaving with his warriors, and, like clouds burning away with the afternoon's sun, Ilryth's expression recovers.

"Are you all right?" I can't help but ask, boldly resting a hand on Ilryth's shoulder.

"I should be comforting you, not the other way around," he murmurs.

"It's all right. Talk to me," I encourage gently.

"I don't like seeing him near you. The idea of him marking your soul is nearly unbearable," Ilryth admits. I'm too startled to say anything in response before he says, "But, no matter, where were we?" His smile is so jarring from his previous tone that I almost have whiplash. "I believe it was your turn to ask me something."

I almost ask him to elaborate more on what was going through his mind when I was being marked, but ultimately decide against it. If he wanted me to know the details of what those thoughts were, he would've shared them. Maybe I'd rather not know. Safer this way.

But there's another question I want to know the answer to. My time has suddenly felt so short. The risks of taking chances less than they've ever been.

I'm losing everything anyway. What does it matter if I am bold? Brash?

"Have you ever been in love?" I ask.

His eyes widen slightly. Ilryth drifts back to where we sat previously, staring out. "I'm twenty-seven years of age. Like you, I'm not a stranger to matters of the heart. Though, it sounds like, unlike you, I have not found anyone serious." He sighs. I resist the urge to tell him Charles was nothing but damage. "Though that will have to happen soon. As you know, I need to wed in short order. I've postponed while managing your upcoming sacrifice, but that excuse will run out soon."

The idea of him marrying fills me with an odd sense of sorrow. The sea is stiller, the swirling rot denser. A wondering of what might have been…but never really could have been—not in this world, at least—overcomes me.

"That's not what I asked though," I remind him gently, drifting over to his side. The urge to take his hand is overwhelming. I've held it so many times. And yet now, I'm held back. Now is different, somehow.

"I…I have no current prospects for a wife." The words seem difficult for him to say initially. He shifts and our fingers brush again, sending jolts up my spine.

"That's *still* not what I asked." A little firmer. I'm not backing down. "Have you been in love? Are you?"

"There might be someone I'm interested in," he admits, attention dropping to our knuckles brushing together slightly in the currents. My chest tightens. "But it's complicated."

"I see," I say softly. I want to ask more. But he doesn't let me.

"Tell me about how the lighthouses work?" Ilryth sits, as if the tension was never there to begin with. As though my question meant nothing.

Biting back a sigh, I sit next to him. My thigh brushes against his tail. He doesn't move away. I read into it deeply as I indulge his question.

"There's a water wheel that turns a mechanism within the lighthouse. The attendants must…" I tell him all I can remember of lighthouses. Most of my knowledge comes from basic, educational memories that I think everyone in Tenvrath knows—not from my personal experience. Which is odd, knowing that I was a lighthouse attendant, for a time.

Our conversation ebbs and flows like the tides, each topic giving way to the next effortlessly. We are two ships on a calm sea, moving in unison, carried by the same wind. Never in my life has it been so easy to talk with someone about everything. I imagine, had we been using our mouths to speak, our throats would've been sore by now.

Hours fly by, and the ocean has grown dark. Flecks of gold dance across the surface, casting weak beams of light that no longer quite reach the castle through the gloom and the rot. Night is already settling.

Ilryth is working his way through the food they brought not long ago. It was all for him, really. I still have no hunger and clearly no need to eat. But, despite that, he still offers me some. I politely refuse and my lack of interest elicits a brief, strange look from him that I can't decipher.

"I can't believe we've spent the entire day doing nothing but talking." I grip the railing and lean back, pushing up my hips and suspending myself in the water in an odd balance of tension and relaxation. "I can't think of the last time I spent so much time doing so little."

"Little? Speak for yourself." Ilryth snorts softly. "I've spent the entire day learning about the Natural World and its peoples. That is a day well spent under any circumstances. But the company has made it exceptional—learning about you has made it exceptional."

I settle back on the railing with a smile. "You're being polite."

Ilryth shakes his head. "I've decided I enjoy your company, Victoria. Is that really so hard to believe?"

"I admit I wasn't sure at first."

"You are a complicated individual for me."

"Complicated?"

"There have been times when you frustrated me and there have been times when…" He sighs quietly and I think he's not going to continue. When he does, it's so soft I can barely hear. "When you make my soul sing with notes I never thought possible."

I smile faintly. "I'm going to do my best to keep all of the Eversea singing." That wasn't what he meant, and I know it. He knows it; I can almost feel as much. But neither of us say anything more. We are both trying, with all our might, not to cross the line that is right before us.

"I believe in you. If anyone could, it's you. You've already overcome so much."

I shrug. "I merely carry on, as anyone does."

"And you make it look easy." He flashes me a brilliant smile, as dazzling as the sunset.

"Today was an early morning; you should get some rest." I don't know why I say that so suddenly. I don't want him to leave.

"I should, especially since I have plans for us tomorrow."

"Another day of sitting with me on the balcony?" I can imagine worse fates.

"No, we are venturing out." Ilryth smirks slightly.

"I thought I had to commune with the Abyss?"

"This is an excursion as important as that."

"Where to?" I tilt my head. He's piqued my interest.

"Where's the fun in my telling you?"

I roll my eyes. Ilryth is getting too much enjoyment out of teasing me. "Fine, keep your secrets."

He leaves the balcony, taking the remaining food and containers with him. I remain at the edge of the Abyss, alone. I'm immediately aware of his absence after having his company for almost the entire day. It's a solemn reminder that I'm going to have to face this vast unknown without him.

There's a shift in the currents. A rush of cool water sweeps up from the depths. It carries on it the whisper of death. I push away from the railing, kicking off it and pressing back against the castle wall right as Ilryth returns.

"What is it?" He looks at me, halfway up the wall, as flat and white as parchment.

"Krokan has returned."

Ilryth swims up, looking down, squinting in the same direction I'm looking. There's a flash of green in the abyss deep below. I rush over to him, grabbing his hand with both of mine, and pull him back over the balcony.

"What the—"

"You were swimming too far into the open water. You were almost out of the anamnesis's protection." I look up at him. My heart is hammering in my chest. "Krokan had turned his sights on you."

"Lord Krokan would never harm a duke of the Eversea. Especially not the one that wields Dawnpoint."

If only that were true, instinct whispers within me. I've no reason to believe it. No reason to think I'm right and he isn't when he's the one who's lived in this world his entire life.

"Still, I... Please, for me. I saw my entire crew die before my eyes to the old god." The mention of them stills him. "I'm sure you're right, but...please never venture too far over the Abyss. For me."

"For you, anything." Ilryth squeezes my hand and follows me farther down, back onto the balcony. I've no idea why this little ledge feels as though it could protect him and me from Krokan. It's like thinking when you're a child that the monster in the dark can't get you if you keep underneath the blanket and all your limbs are on the bed. Foolish. But the illusion of safety is better than nothing. "But it's good that he's here. It should make your next round of markings even more potent."

"Ventris isn't insisting on doing it himself again?" I ask.

"No, marking your bare skin is my honor tonight." He brings his fingers to my neck. They hover, a moment, before pressing against me, just beneath my ear. Even though he doesn't have to touch me to mark me, he does so anyway. Ilryth sings a breathy, sweet melody that fills my mind with memories of home. Of lazy summer afternoons and autumn apples.

He drags his fingers down my neck and across my collarbones. They dance and dot, pulling and swirling. My flesh presses into him as I inhale breathlessly. He presses back as I exhale. It feels...so good to have someone touch me when they do this. To bring warmth into the process.

It is as though he is drawing desire into existence. As though these markings are a map by which I can find passion I'd long since given up on. I want him to kiss every dot his thumbprint makes. I want him to lick up the long, swirling line he draws from my knee all the way up underneath the hem of my shorts, pushing the fabric slowly up. A flick of his eyes locks his gaze with mine.

The intensity of his stare is maddening as he uses those dexterous, skilled fingers. I'm left imagining all the other uses I could have for those hands. What would it feel like to have him bring me to the heights of passion? Could I still feel everything in this form as I know it? Or would it be different? Better? Worse?

How would it even work logistically for him? Though, I did see him with human legs in his memories. Perhaps he could summon them if it were for the sake of tangling them with mine?

A thousand questions beg me for answers. I shouldn't wonder them but I can't stop. I know there are many creative ways for two people to fit together. Even if I have not indulged, I've heard stories. But does he even have a...

My cheeks are burning and the slow stroking on the backs of my thighs isn't helping either.

Finally, there's relief as he pulls away. But I'm not sure if relief *from* his touch is what I wanted. I think I would've much preferred relief *because of* his touch. Either way, I have time to collect myself as he eases away.

"That's all for tonight."

"What is it?" I can tell by his tone there's something concerning him. It's a miracle my words aren't a squeak.

Ilryth doesn't seem to be able to look in my direction. His body is a lean line against the fading light. Biceps bulging as he fidgets. Even clearly anxious, he's one of the most handsome creatures I've ever laid eyes on.

"Over the next few weeks, we'll finish the markings on you..."

"All right?" I urge when he trails off.

"When this happens, we'll need—" He shakes his head, straightens a bit, and looks back to me with forced, almost clinical detachment. "The remaining anointments will be on the *rest* of your body."

"Oh? *Oh.*" It takes a moment, but what he's really saying dawns on me. "You mean I'll have to take off more of my clothes?"

"Yes. Though I've already sent for Lucia and she should arrive soon. I felt she'd be preferrable to Ventris making such markings." He glances my way, as if to be sure in that assumption.

"Much preferred," I say hastily.

"Good. I wanted to warn you it would happen."

"Right, of course." Disappointment courses through me unbidden. I wouldn't mind that delicate touch of his on my most sensitive parts. Was that not the source of my fantasies just now?

But he doesn't give me a chance to object. "I bid you goodnight then."

Ilryth begins to swim away by paddling backward. Our eyes are locked. It's as if he's waiting.

The way he touched me...

It was just for the anointing.

There've been all the other times.

Accidental touches.

"Ilryth, wait," I say, despite my better judgment. Not knowing what I'm going to say next.

He halts at the corner of my bed. "Yes?"

Those eyes of his...I could get lost in them forever. I could subsist on their intensity alone. Perhaps—

The words "*used woman*" echo through my mind in Charles's voice.

No. I'm not going to allow Charles to dictate my own inner voice any longer. I've given him too much power over that across the years. So much so that it's hard to even tell what is in my own voice, and what he planted within me.

There are only a few weeks left for me to live. How do I want to spend it? Not cowering in fear. Not wishing I had done something differently.

I put to rest my internal struggle—let that be the only thing getting sleep tonight. I cross the gap between me and Ilryth and grab his face with both hands, kissing him with a fierceness I didn't know I still possessed.

thirty

ILRYTH DOESN'T PULL AWAY. The opposite. He grabs me by the hips and draws me to him with force. A dozen bodiless voices sing through my mind at once as our mouths meet in glorious harmony.

I break away, forcing myself to stop. My lips quiver, yearning for him still. Trembling with passion that I'm barely containing. *Touch me*, my whole being screams. I wonder if he can somehow hear it, because his palms dig into the meat of my hips.

"Tell me we shouldn't do this." My fingers trail down the muscle of his neck. They finally, *finally* trace over the markings inked into his skin. At long last, I permit myself to touch them and I fear I might never want to stop.

"We shouldn't do this," he obliges, but doesn't sound convincing in the slightest.

"Tell me this will end in disaster," I demand, knowing full well it's true. That's a fact I came to terms with long, long ago.

"It *most certainly* will end in disaster," he affirms with all the confidence of someone who's thought about this as much as I have. Yet, his arms tighten around me. The pads of his fingers dig wells into my flesh. "I do not expect my heart to survive meeting you unscathed. Though, I've known that for years."

"Years?" I whisper.

"Years. Ever since I first laid eyes on you. Even if I refused to admit it. You ensnared me. Inexplicably and effortlessly became the object of my every desire."

"But, you... I wasn't... How? Why me?"

One hand releases me to caress my cheek. He pushes a wayward strand of hair away from my face as gently as someone would shoo a butterfly. One hand touches me with tenderness. The other is still wrapped around me, gripping me so tightly his muscles tremble, as if forcibly restraining himself from taking me here and now.

I crave him with a ferocity I've never known before. I want him to move slowly, to cherish my mind and heart. To be gentle with all my tender wounds. Yet, at the same time, I want him to unleash himself upon me, to ravage me and leave me breathless.

"Why does the sun rise, Victoria? Why do the tides swell or the fish swim in groups? Some things simply *are*. They are forces of nature and it would be an affront to the divine beauty of this world to question them. I do not want to question."

"You care for me even though you know I was somehow involved with another?" I dare to ask. I wish I didn't have to. But I do. *I should tell him I was married...* He has a right to know, doesn't he? But maybe it doesn't matter. Maybe knowing I was serious with another is enough. Maybe it won't matter soon when I forget everything related to Charles...

"I am not threatened by a man you tried to expunge from your memories." He has an almost arrogant smirk. That confidence, the ease by which he remains so unthreatened, couldn't be more attractive. "History is just that, Victoria, history. The only bearing it has on the present is what it taught you and what you choose to carry forward. I wouldn't change the woman you are now for the whole of the seas."

I close my eyes, pressing my cheek into his hand. His thumb strokes gently, as light and tender as the markings he draws across my flesh. "Ilryth, tell me we can't do this."

"I already told you we shouldn't." His fingers curl slightly against me, as if beckoning once more. With one taste, I heard a song of passion, of pleasure, of all the goodness in the world that had previously been forbidden to me. And I want more.

"Tell me we *can't*."

"You know it is forbidden for me to even be touching you." It's not my imagination, he is drawing me closer. Both of his hands are pulling me down.

"Then we can't."

"I never said that." He leans in ever so slightly, eyes consuming mine. "It might be forbidden, but we certainly still can."

"I don't want to hurt you like that…" I press my eyes closed. My heart will also be left in tatters if we do this. But I have only a little bit of time to endure it. He has years.

Yet, despite knowing all this, I'm not pulling away. For all the reasons we shouldn't…I can come up with one, singular reason why we should that trumps all others: *I don't want to stop.* I am selfish, and cruel, and needy.

"What if I give you permission to?" His words thrum against my thoughts loudly, as though they originated from my own mind. "What if I want you to?"

"You want heartache?"

"I want you—and every risk and delight that comes with you."

"What will happen to you, if they find out?" My hand traces down his collarbone and splays across his chest. Every thought says no but my body—my obstinate heart—says, *yes!*

"They might try me again."

"You have so much you have to live for, so many you are responsible for. I can't ask you to risk all that."

"You're not asking, I'm offering." Ilryth leans away, as if gaining the clarity of distance. Allowing me to see the resolve that's not just in his gaze, but his shoulders and stance. "I have only ever done the 'right' thing. I've stayed in line and sacrificed for my people. Even with my mother, I quickly fell into place. I have silently stood by and given up all else as I'm told. Just this once, I want to be shameful. I want to pursue something solely for myself."

How do I argue with that? How could I when my motivations are just as self-serving?

He closes the gap between us again and my lips nearly burn from proximity to his. It takes every last scrap of sense and self-control not to kiss him until I'm dizzy. He whispers with his mouth so close to mine that even our hair struggles to drift in the space between.

"Lay yourself bare to me. Tell me, what do you want?"

"Everything I haven't had in years. Everything I thought I'd never have again." I shake my head, rubbing my nose lightly on his. "I want passion and pleasure. I want reckless abandon even when I know it's the wrong choice to make."

"Let's be horribly wrong together, then." His hand slips around the back of my neck and into my hair. My legs wrap around his middle and our bodies are flush and I am drowning in new, different, and unimaginable sensations.

His firm muscle provides a steady base underneath warm flesh and scale. Tiny currents tease my body like a thousand tiny fingers caressing me. I am weightless. There is no pressure or tension, no awkward sorting of limbs. Everything ebbs and flows as if we are the sea itself. Effortless. As he said…a force of nature.

I hold on for stability as my head spins, bringing my lips to his. Ilryth moves slowly, as if giving me enough time to pull away. *As if I would ever want to.* I grip his shoulder with my left hand, the right still on his chest.

His lips brush against mine and he stops. They quiver slightly, barely touching. My whole body shudders at the sensation. Ilryth holds me even tighter. His hand slips from my hip to my rear, kneading the muscle as his lips crash against mine again.

We are soundless underneath the waves. There is no noise of bodies or mouths or breaths as we shift against each other. There is only blissful silence and the makings of a new melody that takes shape with our every movement. With each pressing of the words inked into our flesh, notes fill the back of my mind. They trill and swell as he drags his hand across me.

New inkings form. Up my arms, around my neck, down my back and thighs. Wherever his hands are on me, music follows.

His touch is both tender and needy. With hands as possessive as his mouth, both demanding what only I can give—all I can give. I am left breathless by his hunger, by feeling that it will be an impossible task to satiate but left wanting to try even more at the prospect.

As for Ilryth's kisses…his is a mouth worth living and dying for. I surrender to its force. My stomach flips as if I am riding the crest of a tall wave every time we twist, shifting our angles while hovering weightless, suspended. His tongue slips into my mouth and my mind goes blank.

It has been years since I was last touched like this. Years of slowly reclaiming my body and soul. Years of accepting who I was and who I was becoming.

The actions of kissing and touching aren't new to me, but the sensations are. I thought I knew all there was about the indulgences of the flesh. But I was wrong. Terribly wrong.

His hand moves around my neck, hooking my jaw with his thumb and fingers. Ilryth breaks away and tilts my face away from his, kissing down my throat. His tongue runs along the lines that are a part of me now. I shudder and my lips part with a soundless gasp that somehow manifests as a single thought: *More.*

Ilryth is ready to heed the command. He spins and my back meets the bed, the water easing our fall to the sponge. His hands caress my hips, pushing waves into the thin fabric that floats around my lower regions. His teeth press into the flesh of my shoulder. I keep my legs locked around his hips, holding him to me. Ilryth explores every bit of my exposed body from my bust up, eventually kissing his way back to my mouth. I map out the lines in the muscles of his back, tracing every edge of his own markings, and cementing it all to my memory.

If I am to die, these are the feelings I want to take with me of a man. Of passion and pleasure. Of a love that is as foolish as it is liberating. As Ilryth's kisses slow to mere pecks, my knees unlock from him, settling to either side, and a smile crosses my mouth.

"You seem pleased, Victoria," he murmurs.

"You have given me more tonight than you realize."

"I wish to give you even more than this." The intensity of the sentiment has me staring up at him, confused but eager.

"Ilryth…"

"Not here, for…reasons." His tail thumps lightly against the bed.

I can't help but laugh. "Is it shameful to admit I was wondering?"

He hums in thought as he eases off me, lying on his back and staring up at the ceiling. "Only if it's shameful to admit I am all the more excited by your wondering."

To want and be wanted…it's a good feeling. Even if it can be nothing more than carnal urges. Even if the love that's stubbornly grown underneath it has no future.

Before I know it, I'm rolling on my side, curling against him. Ilryth shifts and I expect him to push me away, but instead his arm wraps around my shoulders and he pulls me close. I rest my head on his chest on instinct, our bodies fit together as if they were made for each other. The sound of his heartbeat is a symphony.

"I'm going to have to leave," he says somewhat apologetically.

"I know." I close my eyes. "I know you have to leave to keep this a secret—for their rules regarding the offering…but I need you to know something else."

"Yes?"

"I know that doing this with you is selfish of me."

"As it is of me," he gets in quickly. "I'm the one who's demanded everything of you. You have no room to apologize or feel selfish."

I shake my head, nuzzling his neck. "You are incorrigible, Ilryth."

"So are you, Victoria." He kisses my forehead.

I continue on my earlier thought, "But I want you to know, I don't need this to be love. Let's keep things simple for us both. Physical desires only."

Even as I say the words, I already know I am helpless to the force that's trying to sweep me away despite myself.

That's not something he needs to know, however. I can't lie to myself, but I can lie to him. I can pretend none of this matters beyond crawling into his arms. Beyond the raw physical desire. I've seen enough women and men who can treat such as a casual affair that I can use their example.

If I fall in love, that will be my burden, my secret that I will carry to my grave. I can't hurt him like that. Nor can my heart handle another failure in the arena of romance. I might not remember everything that surrounded my past relationship, but I do remember it failed… and, based on what scraps I can recall, and the feelings I have, I've a sneaking suspicion that failure was because of me.

He searches my expression as I speak, as if he somehow can see through my farce—my claims to the contrary. Ilryth's brow furrows slightly. I almost expect him to object.

But he seems to accept my words at face value, nodding slightly. I imagine he's taken many lovers. That's what I choose to believe. This is easier if I think it's nothing serious to him. If a casual fling is easy for him to have.

And, if it is more than that for him, as well…it is better for us both to pretend otherwise. If we don't speak about any further affections, then they can die in doubt. In the unknown and unsaid.

"As you wish, my lady."

I give him a slight smile. I expected this… He knows I am a dead woman walking. It'll be easier for us both like this. If I tell myself that enough times, maybe I will believe it.

"You should rest," he says softly. "There is more work to be done in the coming days and weeks in anointing you."

"You should leave." I choose to ignore the mention of work.

"I should, but I think I'll stay until you fall asleep…assuming that won't disturb you?" Ilryth's deep voice is filled with concern at the idea.

"Not in the slightest." I yawn. "In fact, you make me feel relaxed— safe." I close my eyes and enjoy the feeling. Even though there are gaps in my memories, I am confident that no one has ever made me feel so wanted and protected in my life. For the first time I feel like I can rest my head somewhere and not have to keep one eye open, or worry about anyone or anything else.

Sighing softly, I bid a silent, final goodbye to my family and the few friends I had back across the Fade and above the sea. They will be fine without me; they have to be. I cannot return now and there's nothing more I can do for them than be a worthy sacrifice to an old god. So I let them go.

For the next few days, and weeks, or however much time remains, for the first time in my life I will live solely for myself.

thirty-one

WHEN I ROUSE, I'M ALONE, JUST AS HE TOLD ME I WOULD BE. I prop myself up and push away from the bed, my hands sinking into the soft sponge. Sure enough, there's no sign of him, making the whole affair feel like a sumptuous dream rather than a reality.

Likely for the best, I think as I collapse back onto the bed with an internal sigh. It'll be easier to pretend all of this means nothing if we don't spend the morning lounging in the embrace of each other like the lovers we aren't. Yet, I close my eyes. I imagine what it might feel like to rouse with the dawn, his warmth still enveloping me.

I snap open my eyes, banishing the dangerous daydream. These were *exactly* the emotions I couldn't allow to happen. But ignoring them isn't made any easier when mere hours ago I fell asleep in his arms.

It was the best sleep I've had in a long time, yet instead of waking well rested, I am tired.

I don't really know exhaustion in the corporeal sense anymore. But every single one of my joints seems to ache from the muscles being wound up so tightly by his kisses and caresses last night. I roll over with a groan. Despite myself, my hand slides down my side, smoothing over the swell of my stomach; it slips under the top of my shorts, and lands between my legs to touch myself in the one place I so desperately wanted Ilryth's hand to be last night.

Rubbing slowly, gently, my middle finger rolls over the

most sensitive spot on my body. My lips part and a soundless sigh of delight escapes them. In my mind, Ilryth is still next to me. He's waking me with these delicate caresses. His lower half is no longer scaled, but possesses all the desired parts of a human man.

I imagine him leaning over to me and biting my earlobe. He'll whisper the details of everything he wishes to do to me straight into my mind, penetrating my thoughts. My left hand slides down my front, groping my breast over my corset as the images playing before my mind's eyes grow more and more vivid.

Last night was merely the appetizer. The temptation. The proof that our bodies will respond to each other. All I want now is to explore just how far we can go. Just how deeply we can know each other.

My lower abdomen is knotting. My toes are curling. Release isn't far. I've had enough practice getting myself there over the years and this fantasy is sweeter than any I've ever come up with before because it's tangible. It's almost possible and that—

"Your Holiness, are you awake?" Ventris's voice is a bucket of cold water being dumped on me.

I rip my hand from my shorts, the other releasing my chest and pushing off the bed. I try to smooth my hair away from my face, attempting to tame it on instinct, even though in my current form that's absolutely unnecessary. I've managed to catch my breath and banish the fantasies by the time he arrives up the tunnel with his guards.

"Ah, good morning. You seem to have slept well last night."

"Excuse me?" I panic, wondering if there's any sign of Ilryth in the room. Perhaps there's some siren sense where Ventris just knows the lines we've crossed. What will that mean for Ilryth?

"You are in your bed this morning, rather than on the balcony," he says casually. "It's good to see that you are getting the rest you need to ensure that you remain focused on learning the hymns of the old ones."

I relax some. "Yes, of course. Meditating before the Abyss has been quite taxing on the mind and body."

"Speaking of anointments." He motions and another set of guards emerges with a familiar face.

"Lucia." I push away from the bed with a smile, gliding through the room.

"It's good to see you again, Your Holiness." The end of her tail curves back and she dips her head. Even though the two of us weren't exactly the best of friends, she made a kind enough impression on me. And in Ventris's realm, I'll take any friendly faces I can get.

"Lucia was one of the best students during her time in the Duchy of Faith. She'll be taking care of your anointments these next few days as it becomes improper for myself or Ilryth to do so."

I remember what Ilryth told me last night, that there would be some markings he wouldn't be the one to do. I hide my lingering disappointment that it's not him administering these markings to my more sensitive areas. Another fantasy attempts to creep up and I refuse to let it here and now. Those are best savored privately. And, if someone other than Ilryth is going to make those markings, I'd much rather Lucia than a stranger or, worse, Ventris.

"Thank you for being mindful of my modesty," I say as if modesty has ever been something that's meant all that much to me.

"Do you need anything else of us?" Ventris asks Lucia.

She shakes her head. "No, Your Grace, I have all I need."

"I will leave you to it, then." Ventris leads the four guards from the room.

Lucia folds her hands in front of her, waiting until they're gone. Her fingers lace and unlace, betraying discomfort. "Please forgive me, Your Holiness, but I'm finally going to have to ask you to remove everything."

"Just Victoria is fine," I remind her. "We're not strangers."

"It is only right that I show you the utmost respect as the shepherd. Anything less would be an affront to Lord Ventris's good training of all the acolytes of Lord Krokan."

She's afraid he's listening. "I don't think he can hear in here. Ilryth said this room has protections."

Lucia's eyes widen slightly. She glances over her shoulder in the direction Ventris left.

"If you're nervous, we can speak like this." I close the gap between us and rest my hand on her shoulder.

She nods. "That's good to know, Victoria." I smile at her use of my name. "But you should refrain from touching me. We are getting close to your offering, so it is even more important now."

"Right." My smile falls and I release her. "Should I undress?"

"If you don't mind." Lucia averts her eyes, despite her being about to see me in the very state of undress that she's offering me modesty about.

I reach around to the back of my corset, hooking the knot and untying it. Tugging at the Xs that line my back, I get enough slack that I can slot out the small knobs from their hooks in the front. I pull it off me and hang onto it for an extra second. The last of my clothes, carefully tailored to fit my needs. Quality over quantity.

And the last ties I have to the world I came from.

Unfurling my fingers, I release the garment, watching as it begins to unravel like magical threads into the water. In a blink, it's as though it never existed in the first place. The shorts are easier to let go of. Though, once they're gone, I'm standing as naked as the day I was born.

"All right, I'm ready."

Lucia swims over. She still seems a bit uncomfortable, but not too awkward with the nudity. For which I'm glad. I give her credit that most of her curious glances are concealed. I can only imagine I look as strange to her as a siren does to most humans.

"My crew was mostly women. Not all, but most," I say, in an effort to make her feel a bit more at ease about the circumstances. "One of them could hardly keep her clothes on. Every time I turned around it seemed like she had stripped down for one reason or another." I laugh softly, thinking of Geniveve. "Once in a while, when we sailed far to the south where the waters are as blue as your Eversea, I'd drop anchor and we'd all go swimming. Geniveve never had more than her small clothes on, if that."

"It sounds like you were all fairly open with each other," Lucia remarks as she sings swirling marks into existence between my shoulder blades.

"You have to be when you're putting your life in someone else's hands."

"Perhaps that's why I have always felt so comfortable with you—all of the Eversea is relying on you to quell Lord Krokan's rage."

"You feel comfortable with me?" I ask. Lucia hasn't been unkind, but there has always been the barrier of etiquette and propriety between us.

"You wound me with how surprised you sound." There's a slight quirk to her lips, as if she's fighting a grin.

"I always saw this as more of a professional relationship." Though, it doesn't feel professional to be hovering stark naked before her.

"It is...should be." Lucia sighs softly as she swims behind me to begin the anointing. Her finger hovers low on my hip, by my rear. "I know what you are destined for. I saw in my father the toll the sacrifice will take on any who are too close. So I did not want to tempt the situation."

"I understand that." She's protecting her heart, even from friendly compassion—something Ilryth should be doing.

Her finger draws up my side and pauses on my shoulder, hovering where I remember Ilryth biting and sucking last night. A tingle runs underneath my skin. Her silence is telling. Somehow, she knows. She can feel him on me.

"Did you hurt yourself?"

"Oh, I'm not sure," I murmur. "I must have bumped into something. I'm still growing accustomed to swimming all the time."

"Right." Lucia leaves it at that. But warning bells are tolling in my mind.

She knows.

thirty-two

SEEING ILRYTH LATER IMMEDIATELY QUELLS THE RELENTLESS CHURNING OF MY STOMACH FOLLOWING LUCIA'S DEPARTURE. I'd been on pins thinking she might have told Ventris of her discovery—or merely her suspicion, of Ilryth and me. The logical parts of my mind want to argue that there's no way she could know for sure the bruise was from Ilryth, not really. But magic defies all logic I've ever known.

If she did know, and could prove it, would she turn her own brother in? Another thing I'd like to think not…but I can't be sure. Lucia is loyal to the old ways and, if she were smart, she'd see telling Ventris as a way to protect her brother. To pull us apart before we could get too close.

Ilryth emerges from the shadow of the tunnel, flanked by two warriors. But they aren't manhandling him. All seems well.

The moment I lay eyes on him my core turns molten. The mere sight of his hands makes me think of him tracing his fingers across every contour of my body, smoothing away years of aches and pains. Vivid fantasies return in full, but they are tainted by my interaction with Lucia—they seem more than dangerous now. Deadly.

"Good morning, Victoria," he says politely.

"Good morning, Ilryth." Awkwardness overcomes me and I smooth my hands over the wrapped fabrics Lucia brought to replace the clothes I lost. I've never been more aware of other people's presence, namely the two warriors. If they weren't here, how would he greet me?

"I trust you slept well?"

"I did," I say. When what I mean is, *I would've slept better if you'd stayed with me the entire night.* "And you?"

"Of course. The comforts of the Duchy of Faith are unparalleled." Does he mean it? Or is that a subtle reference to last night?

"Good, I'm glad." I've never been very scholarly, but all I want to do right now is read too much into everything.

"Siren attire suits you." Ilryth's eyes drag over my body with obvious intent. I glance toward the warriors; they don't seem to notice. "You look lovely."

I suspect finding a siren tailor who could make something for a human must have been difficult, seeing as the wrap that hugs my hips barely covers my sex. Judging by the currents I feel on my rear, the back leaves just as little to the imagination. However, it does show off the colorful markings of my legs and I believe that was the goal.

In place of my corset is a short vest that ends at my lower ribs and is fastened with a ribbon at my bosom. It offers very little in the way of support and just one swimming error could result in my going topless... an idea I've been wondering if I can use to my advantage around Ilryth the next time we are alone.

"Thank you." I cease my inspection of my clothing. "As do you."

He's wearing fabric wrapped around his lower half as well. It's odd to see, as he usually wears nothing, but the garment frames his tail nicely. Ilryth merely grins.

"We're going to go on an excursion today so I needed to dress appropriately for the occasion," he announces. I remember him mentioning as much last night, but I wasn't sure if it'd happen.

"Where to?"

"Where we are going will serve to further strengthen your anointments and prepare you," he says, giving me no more information than last night.

"Well then, lead the way."

Rather than going through the tunnel, Ilryth leads us to the balcony. I follow him, the warriors behind me. I assume their presence is because of this excursion—an escort. Did Ilryth ask for them? Or did

Ventris send them? I suppose it's possible that this is just their general obligation—where I go, they go…but I feel like Ventris trying to keep an eye on us is far more likely, given how adamant he was about my not leaving the Eversea again. Or, really, stepping out of line at all.

The depths of the Abyss are calm this morning. There's no sign of Krokan. Still, I'm glad we swim close to the castle as we ascend. Though I suspect they do so to stay in the protective haze of the castle's anamnesis and out of the rot swirling up from the Abyss rather than because of any fear related to Krokan. The red murk seems thicker today, as if it's worsening with every passing hour. I can't help but wonder if the old god of death can sense my presence and is growing restless with each day that passes without his sacrifice.

We swim up past the highest tower of the castle, near the large roots of the Lifetree that knot and spill down the cliff it and the castle are perched on. The roots are jagged and scarred with deep gouges. Some have been cleaved entirely in two. The red haze thins as we ascend, as though burned away by the light of the sun. The higher we swim, the brighter it becomes and the clearer I can see all the carvings that have been made into the roots.

That's when it dawns on me, as bright as the afternoon sun, that we're going to break the surface of the water. The beams of light that are filtered to ambient haze on the sea floor now strike my cheeks. I blink upward and smile. It's felt like an eternity since I saw the sun unfiltered, and I didn't realize just how much I was missing it until this second.

Breaking the surface, I take a deep breath on instinct. The action is still there, but unsatisfying. I no longer need to breathe in this mostly magical form. Still, the motion brings me some comfort.

We bob with the waves. For a large body of water, the Eversea is surprisingly calm. The swells are small enough that I have no problem seeing where Ilryth and the warriors have crested.

They glide toward the massive tree, which looks as though it's supporting the sky itself in its mighty branches that sway in winds unfelt under the water. Silvery leaves spiral and loop through the air like falling snow. I saw the Lifetree in Ilryth's memory, but seeing it in person is an entirely different experience. All thoughts still as I stare up at the sentry, which truly looks befitting to hold a god.

"Victoria, this way," Ilryth calls me over.

I fall back into line beside Ilryth, the warriors right behind us. The underwater shelf the tree sits on slopes up, the gemstone water becoming shallow enough to see the sandy bottom with crystal-clear ease. Ilryth guides us through a maze of gnarled roots. These, too, are scarred with the markings of axes and other cutting implements that sheared away their bark. Applied to each cut and scar are ropes made of kelp and adorned with shells and coral, like haphazard bandages that do little to stop the crusted, red sap that still oozes from the savagery.

The water soon becomes shallow enough that I can stand. Ilryth continues swimming, wriggling until it seems too difficult to carry on. I'm about to ask him just how far we're going when he lets out a note and the water around him begins to hiss and bubble.

"Ilryth?" I say worriedly.

As he sings, his scales slough off his body and turn into sea foam, revealing two very human legs underneath that bear markings which give the illusion of scales. He stands, the water pooling around his knees. I now understand why he wore clothing on his lower half today. Though my cheeks warm at how the soaked fabric clings to every line of his body.

"Yes?" The water is only up to his knees when it is nearly halfway up my thigh. Even in a human form, he's very tall.

"You...you're..."

"You saw me with legs in my memory." He still speaks without moving his lips. Telepathy remains the only way sirens communicate. "This shouldn't be a surprise."

"I knew it was possible, yes, but seeing it is..." I drag my eyes from his toes, still underneath the waves, up his powerful thighs, to the skirt he wears. *Is it* all *human?* I want to ask, but don't.

"The transformation could be a bit jarring for someone who's never seen it before," he admits, and looks back to the warriors still in the water. "You two may go and pay homage to the sacrifices of the Lifetree for your weapons. We'll be a few hours."

"His Grace instructed us to follow you," one of the warriors says uncertainly. So Ventris did send them to keep an eye on Ilryth and me. Predictable.

"The air is deep with chill," Ilryth says. I don't feel it. I wonder if it's because I can't anymore with my body as it is, because he's more sensitive, or if it's just an outright lie. "The next Human Queen has yet to reinvigorate the seasons. It would be uncomfortable for you."

The warriors exchange an uncertain glance.

"I will be working on the hymns of the old ones," I say with an air of authority. "You shouldn't risk the impact hearing the words might have on your well-being as you have not practiced singing underneath the hymns to protect your minds, as Ilryth has."

"That is true..." one warrior admits. Self-interest is a powerful motivator. "We will await you here and offer our songs to strengthen Lady Lellia and the offering."

The two duck back under the water. It's shallow and clear enough that I can see them as they descend, heading toward one of the scarred and ornamented stretches of root. They place both hands on the wood, closing their eyes. I can hear a soft song coming from beneath the waves and the water around them shimmers slightly.

"It's a prayer, an homage to Lellia," Ilryth explains. "The Lifetree roots life itself into this world; it has also given us the weapons and armor we use to protect ourselves from Lord Krokan's rage."

"It's...stunning." I look back up to the tree in awe.

"The tree is one anchor of my society. It was important for me to share it with you. I wanted you to know that there is more than death and turmoil in the Eversea. There is brightness, and life."

"I'm honored you have trusted me with this pilgrimage," I say sincerely. I want to take his hand, but I don't dare do so when the warriors could see.

I'm still speaking with my thoughts, rather than my mouth. Even above the surface I find it's now more natural to think what I need to say. Perhaps I'll have enough control of the ability soon that I'll no longer need the shell Fenny gifted me to protect me.

"Come, I'll take you to the door." Ilryth attempts to take a step and stumbles. I move to help him but he holds up a hand, stopping me, glancing back at the warriors. "I'll be fine; my land legs always take some getting used to. I don't come up here that often. Land is a bit awkward and uncomfortable for us sea folk."

I smile and think of his obsession with ships. "You know, for humans, it's the opposite. We call them our 'sea legs' to refer to getting accustomed to being out on the ocean."

"Really?" He seems genuinely fascinated, as he always has when a ship is brought up.

"Truly." I glance back toward the warriors. "Are you sure I couldn't help you until you get a little more confident?" Neither of the warriors is paying much attention to us…but all it would take is one look. I know it as much as he does. So I expect his refusal before it comes.

"While I would appreciate the assistance, it's probably safer if we don't."

"I understand." My tone is as dejected as his.

It's uncomfortable to the point of enraging to walk slowly at his side as he struggles. Every time Ilryth slips, catching himself on his knees, I must fight with myself not to reach for him. I resent the systems in place that prevent me from just helping him.

"Would this not be a practical touch?" I ask. We're nearly to the mass of roots ahead of us.

"Ventris is looking for any small step we might make out of line. We must be careful. We'll be out of their eyeshot soon."

The moment we pass between two large roots, I wrap my arm around his strong middle, allowing his arm to drape over my shoulders. The man is an entire statue's worth of carved muscle. All that strength means little when he can hardly balance himself.

"I'll be all right."

"I know, but you were still a bit unsteady." I give him a small, sheepish smile. "Forgive me for wanting to touch you?"

"It's embarrassing having you see me like this," he admits with a faint blush on his cheeks.

"Why? It's only natural to need help, now and then," I say. He snorts. "What?"

"I find that sentiment amusing coming from you."

"Do as I say and not as I do." I know exactly what in my personality he's referring to. "Besides, you have no reason to be embarrassed around me, ever."

"Pardon?" He seems genuinely confused.

"I'm not as good of a person as you think I am. It's not as if I have any room to judge."

"You're too harsh on yourself. You're one of the best women I've ever met," Ilryth says softly. Oblivious to the knife he's twisting. *I should just tell him the whole truth about Charles and end my agony over it.* "You're perfect, Victoria. I wouldn't change a thing about you."

"I'm really not perfect," I murmur.

"Yes you are," he insists.

"Liar."

"Watch your tongue," he cautions. "You are speaking to a duke of the Eversea." There's a playful overtone, but a depth to the bass of his voice that makes my insides squirm.

"Or what?" I ask coyly.

"I will be forced to watch it for you." His eyes dip to my lips with sensual intent. I grip him a little tighter, fighting the urge to kiss him. Could I? Now that we've crossed that threshold, am I free to walk it whenever I please?

"Don't tempt me, Your Grace."

"Perhaps tempting you is exactly why I brought you to this secluded place."

My throat is thick and the sun is suddenly too hot and my skin a size too small. I clutch onto him tighter, feeling his body move alongside mine. Ilryth chuckles as though he knows—*he must know*—what he's doing to me.

"First, we shall go pay our respects to Lady Lellia. Then, perhaps, I shall worship at the altar of your hips, should you be willing to have me."

thirty-three

THE AIR IS SUDDENLY VERY, *VERY* HOT.

"I'm going to drop you if you keep talking like that." Despite what I say, I clutch him even tighter.

"Have I offended?" He looks genuinely concerned.

"Hardly. You've made my own knees weak."

Ilryth gently strokes my shoulder. The swirling of his thumb is so distracting I almost forget how to walk. "Good. I prefer my women primed and eager." *Oh yes*, the man knows *exactly* what he's doing to me and I daresay I like it.

"And just how many women have you had?" I think of our conversation last night. He hadn't exactly denied that he'd been with women, just that it had never been serious. But what "serious" means to each person can vary wildly.

"A gentleman doesn't tell." He gives a small wink and even that is somehow sensual. "However, I'll assure you I've had enough experience that I won't leave you disappointed. Yet, not enough experience that you'll have to worry about any jilted lovers coming after you."

I hum. If this is the game he's playing then I shall be coy right back. "Last night begs to differ."

"Excuse me?"

"Well, I can't speak to jilted lovers, but you were going to leave me unsatisfied after spending an entire day with me."

"*Ah*, but, as I said, I am a gentleman, after all... I would not presume to know your desires if not told. We spent the day *talking*. A gentleman doesn't assume a woman desires him in the carnal sense just because she spent some friendly time alone with him." He sweeps wet hair away from where it clings, running his fingers lightly over the mark he left on my shoulder with his kisses. Ilryth seems to be finding his land legs just fine now that he has something else to focus on. Even though he'd probably have no trouble if I let him go, I'm not quite ready to. "So let's remove all doubt. Why don't you tell me: what do you desire, Victoria?"

A weak smile crosses my lips as I stare up at the Lifetree and its mighty branches. "It's hard to have desires as I am now…with only two months left to live."

His embrace tightens as stillness overtakes him. His body becomes heavy with the truth we both willingly ignore. I almost want to ask what has him so melancholy, but I resist. I know what has overcome him—the truth is like an anchor, pulling us both down. Ignoring it is impossible, no matter how much we might want to. It's a reminder of the obvious—we would be so much better off resisting these forbidden indulgences.

Yet I can't bring myself to move away. I don't want to. With every step the crunching sand whispers, *damn my heart and damn his*.

I am selfish and impulsive. Clearly, in all my years, I never learned how not to be. Too much of the life I can still remember can be summarized with: *Everyone warned her that what she was doing was a bad idea, but she did it anyway.*

Ilryth slows his pace. "Perhaps because you have such precious little time, it is ever more important to make the most of it." He looks me in the eyes. "You were reckless last night. Be reckless again."

If he's giving me permission… My hand glides across the contours of his back, down his strong forearm, to where my fingers interlace with his. Neither of us is ready to move away from the other. "I yearn for the freedom to desire whomever I please. To live with reckless abandon. I've allowed my entire life to be wrapped up in this fear that if I didn't fulfill others' expectations of me that I would be unworthy of their affection and loyalty. Even in death, I'll be offered as a sacrifice for the greater good.

"So for however much time is left between now, and then…" We slow to a stop. I look him in the eyes and take his other hand in mine, turning them both over, feeling the many calluses left behind by years of carrying his spear into battle. Tracing my thumbs over the lines that trail up his arms. Savoring how the barest caress sends shivers. "I want you, Ilryth. I want to feel you. Be with you. I want your hands and lips to ease away my worries and pains left by others."

"I would be lying if I said the desire wasn't mutual."

Are there any better combination of words than hearing that you're wanted? Than knowing a person you desire, desires you in return? My heart swells against my ribs. Breath catches. But I hold it. There's a but here.

"But"—*there it is*—"like you, I must also look after the people I care for. Those whom I would give everything to. I must be mindful of your tethers to this world."

"I can indulge in the flesh without love or meaning tied to it." If it's not true now, I will make it true before I am offered up. The last thing I want is for whatever is blooming between us to wither on the vine. For him to pull away and me not be able to catch him ever again.

His face is a guarded mix of emotions. He glances between our hands, still interlocked, and my face. His chin dips slightly. "Are you sure?"

"I won't risk your people or the vows you made to them, or my family's lives, for a tryst in the sheets." I can promise that much. Even if it costs me my heart, I can walk away. I've done it before.

His fingers tighten around mine and he brings my knuckles to his lips. "Then you shall have me."

"Are you sure?"

"I am." He seems so resolute it squashes all doubt in me. My heart pounds and my core heats with anticipation, with what this means.

How long has it been since I last knew the touch of a man? Years, I believe, even with the holes in my memory. Judging from the readiness of my body...*years*.

"But there's something I should tell you, before we continue to progress things between us," I continue. "I saw Lucia this morning. She came to continue my anointing."

"I had hoped her presence might make you a bit more comfortable than a stranger's."

"It did, thank you. But she noticed this." I touch the faint bruise on my shoulder. It's hardly visible between all the markings.

"I see. Did she say anything about it?" Ilryth's tone is hard to read.

"She asked how I got it. I told her that it was an accident from swimming. But I don't think she believed me." I rub the marking before lowering my hand. "She didn't press the matter, however."

"Lucia has good sense, and is more loyal to me than to Ventris— much to his annoyance. She won't tell anyone of her suspicions."

I now suspect there was more to Ilryth having Lucia come to me than purely for my own comfort.

"Can she prove those suspicions if she wanted?"

"She wouldn't. Lucia might have been raised and trained as an acolyte in the Duchy of Faith. But she's my sister, foremost, not one of Ventris's zealots," he continues to insist.

"If she was forced, then?" I refuse to let the matter drop. I need to know how much danger I am allowing him to be in.

"She could extrapolate on her theories…" Ilryth strokes his chin. "But Lucia wouldn't."

"Ventris is ready to believe the worst."

"And his belief would mean little without solid proof."

Pressing my eyes closed, I try and push my cowardice away. "Are you sure being with me is a risk you want to take?"

"Are you worried for me?" Ilryth pauses, leaning against one of the oversized roots that dwarfs us. The pathway we've been strolling along leads under a natural archway, away from the beach we first walked up on. He has a slightly smug grin.

"I am," I answer honestly. "I'm worried that others will find out about us and it'll make problems for you that you shouldn't have to face."

"Is that all?"

"I'm worried you're being careless with your heart," I admit.

He turns it right back on me. "If I can trust you to handle this, can you trust me?"

I have no retort. We both know, don't, under any circumstances, ever call it love. Because that will be the moment that it all comes tumbling down around us. *Let's just pretend*, that's what I think we're both saying. *Even if we know there's more to this, lie, say there's not.* This is all going to end soon, and nothing between us will matter when it does…so we can pretend and enjoy ourselves for just a little bit longer.

We emerge from underneath the archway the root creates and onto a swath of beach that's familiar from Ilryth's memories. A nest of roots completely encircles the area. If not for the sound of the waves breaking in the distance and small glimpses between the roots, it'd be impossible to know we were right at the sea's edge. The sand is sugar-white, finer than any I've seen in the Natural World. The waters and beaches of the Eversea would put to shame even the finest southern shores.

Directly across from us, at the highest point of the island, is the base of the Lifetree. All the roots part like a lady's hair down the middle, revealing a doorway barred by woody vines. The beach is spiked with spears bleaching in the sun, basking underneath the boughs above. Axes, of all shapes and sizes, with worn handles and chips in their blades, are lined up against the roots, perfectly spaced.

The air is filled with invisible effervescence. It makes my skin tingle with a thousand unseen bubbles. It is tangible enough that I feel as though I can breathe again—that I am briefly more flesh and blood than magic. Much like the strange waters of the Eversea itself, this land is anything but normal. Even Ilryth seems to walk easier as he steps ahead, leading me by intertwined fingers toward the base of the tree.

"Every spear has been cut from the tree," he explains. "The Duchy of Faith oversees it. Ventris's father, Duke Renfal, was the first to do so and none have made finer weapons since him. He made a great many spears from the Lifetree. But five were stronger than the rest, each containing a scrap of wood from Lellia's door. Each given to a duke."

"Dawnpoint was one," I surmise.

Ilryth nods and motions to the spears skewering the beach before us. "These are not nearly as good as those early cuttings, back when Renfal was aggressive in taking from the tree what we needed—though Ventris would vehemently object to my saying so."

"Don't worry, I won't tell him," I say. He chuckles.

"But they will serve the warriors. The best among the fighters is awarded one when they pass their training with their first venture into the Gray Trench. Then, they will pilgrimage here and use their spear to mark out where their armor will be cut from, should their merits to the Eversea ever warrant receiving such a boon."

"No wonder the Faith and Spear duchies have such a close relationship," I observe.

"We did, before me and Ventris." Ilryth pauses, staring at the spears. "I sometimes wonder if I'm even worth the Granspell name."

"You are a good man, Ilryth," I insist, knowing how he feels all too well. "You have done nothing but help your people."

He looks away. "Except indulging in you."

I swallow thickly and step in front of him to catch his eyes. I hold them firmly. "I will be an incredible offering. I swear it to you." I rest my hand on his chest and he grabs it.

Bringing my fingers to his lips, Ilryth kisses them lightly. Though this time he doesn't stop at my knuckles. He gives three kisses up my forearm toward my elbow, pulling me a step closer that I take gladly. "You're biased in how you see me."

"Maybe so." I grin slightly. "But do you care if I am?"

He chuckles softly, the sound rumbling in me. "I suppose not. Now, come. Let's pay our respects to the goddess of life."

We finish trekking across the beach, right up to where the wood of the tree trunk meets the sand.

I am certain that there are mountains smaller than this tree. I am humbled by something that only an old god could create. Much like I saw in Ilryth's vision, it seems to be multiple trees woven together as one. I imagine Lellia in the center of a circle of trees arching above her, reminiscent of the altars I saw in the Gray Trench. The trees continued to grow around her, keeping her in, like bars of a cage to hold the old goddess in her place, rooting her to this land against her will.

It's an odd thought, I realize, but the suspicion is compounded by how the vines over the door have turned gray and hard with age and time. Woody ropes that are no doubt stronger than any metal chain from my world. Still, there are five notches in them, one for each vine.

"You said that Krokan and Lellia chose to stay in this world after the Veil was made, right?"

"That is what our stories tell us," Ilryth says. "Long ago, there were many gods and goddesses that walked this earth, side by side with the living, the dead, and the immortal spirits. When the first Elf King sought to bring order and hierarchy to the young world and its first crop of mortals, the old gods agreed to his plan. They assisted him and then they were the first to traverse the Veil. The path their passing made was the way for our immortal souls to join them in the Beyond. Lady Lellia remained to look after her creations and make more. Lord Krokan stayed as well, to guard his lady love and the passage to the Beyond."

"I see…" I tilt my head and continue to stare up at the tree. The way the leaves rustle sounds almost like a song—faint and whispering, as though it is trying to tell me a long-forgotten secret.

"You seem skeptical," Ilryth says. I don't know if skeptical is the right word for it…but I do have a nagging sense of *something* more.

"I have no reason to doubt your stories," I say. The last thing I want to do is offend him. "Perhaps the history is just so wondrous, so seemingly impossible, that it is merely hard for me to fathom." Just laying eyes on the Lifetree begs a reverence to a greater force, one that can be felt but never fully understood.

He smiles faintly. "This is the first time I have come here in a long time."

I say nothing. As he speaks, he stares up at the leaves above as well. Tiny slivers of silver foliage fall to us with each sway of the tree, like rainfall on a moonlit night.

"I've only been here twice before," he continues. "The first time you saw. It was with my mother, when I was supposed to pledge myself to the Eversea as the Duke of Spears before Lady Lellia. The second time was when I returned alone to actually accomplish that task." His voice grows soft, eyes sad. "I wish my mother could've seen it."

"I'm sure, in a way, she knew. She could feel when your oath was made."

"I hope so." Ilryth grows still. He's a statue in a breezy world of swirling sand and gently falling leaves. "I thought that if I could put off becoming a duke, I could change her mind. That she would hold on for longer. My selfishness only made more problems. If I hadn't clung to her as I had, perhaps she would've been a successful sacrifice."

My hand returns to his and he doesn't pull away. I shift closer. "If you're right, and it's a human Lord Krokan desires, then there's nothing that could have been done for it."

"Perhaps…"

"Because of your grief, you went into the trench that night. You found me." I hate to shift the focus onto me, but I feel as if he needs something more to hold onto—to find meaning in.

"A silver lining worthy of Lady Lellia's light." He brings his face to mine with a small smile. "If all my misfortune has led me to this moment, if every pain and hardship I endured was to meet you, then it would've all been worth it."

I stare up at him in no small amount of awe. Has anyone ever spoken so kindly of me? I am a balm to his troubles. An explanation that is an ease and comfort. I…I wish I could give him the world and more.

"Come. There's much more of the holy island of the Lifetree to show you." He goes to move away but I end up lingering for another moment at the door. I can't seem to tear myself away. "Victoria." He tugs lightly on my hand.

"Yes, sorry." I step backward away from the door. I should leave matters of the gods be, but I can't help but ask, "Behind that door—"

I don't get to finish, as he knows exactly what I'm about to say.

"Yes."

Behind there is where a goddess slumbers… "Have you ever seen her?"

Lord Krokan swims freely through the Abyss. But Lellia is trapped within the tree. Confined.

Pain for her floods me. There is now a new verse of the hymn of the old ones that lives in the back of my mind—a different way to interpret the words. Same sounds, different meanings. This song is one of sorrow and agony. Of injustice.

Did she choose to be here? Or has she been trapped for millennia? I rub the markings on my flesh, as if they will tell me. As if this understanding I feel as though I'm on the edge of will take shape.

It does not. And Ilryth confirms my suspicions and my fears. "When the magic wars happened, Lady Lellia's heart broke for her children and her pain was said to be felt in the peoples across the land. The Fade being erected and quenching the bloodshed calmed her. The first Human Queen, even, was said to have come and planted a tree to shade the old goddess of life. Lady Lellia sheltered under it, and then became one with it.

"As the tree grew, her song seemed to waver. She rooted into the world, but her people faded. The dryads vanished. Her song hasn't been heard in thousands of years."

"I see."

He tugs on my hand and this time I follow behind as he leads me back, away from the tree. But instead he crosses the beach opposite of where we entered and into another tunnel made of roots.

I can't help but look over my shoulder, back at the tree and its mysterious door. Ilryth called it Lellia's home...but what if it is her prison? If it is, what does that mean for the Eversea, for the sirens, and for the relationship of the god of death with the goddess of life?

Is Krokan husband, or captor?

thirty-four

THE ROOTS CREATE A TUNNEL ONCE MORE. They are so dense that the only light that reaches us is from the beach behind and what I assume to be another beach farther ahead. The scars of cuttings are here, too. The sap that oozes from them is a bright red, still glistening in the dim light. Still wet.

"Are these carvings recent?" I ask.

"They shouldn't be; Ventris has banned more carvings. And I believe I remember them from the last time I was here."

More than five years old, and they still bleed. I reach up to touch them and Ilryth doesn't stop me. As my fingertips meet the wet sap, a jolt courses through me, like when my skin met Ilryth's immediately following his return from the trench. But this sensation is different, stronger. A trill of sharp words screeches through the recesses of my mind. They're unlike any language I've ever heard before. Unlike the words of the sirens, or even the old ones.

I yank my hand away before the incoherent noises fill my mind with unbearable chaos. Pain rips through my temples, begging for a place currently occupied by a piece of me. A memory vanishes before I could pick which one.

Rubbing my temples, I try to recall what it is I lost. But a life is long and filled with thousands of small moments that seem inconsequential until they're gone. It's impossible to run through them all…to know what it was.

"What is it?" Concern is on his face. Ilryth moves for me.

I stop him with a hand, but do not touch him. The last thing

I want is for whatever just happened to me to somehow jump to him. "I...I felt something strange."

"Strange how?"

"It was a song, but unlike any I've ever heard before. Any I've ever learned." I straighten, the pain subsiding. Though the twisting, uncomfortable sensation of having a memory ripped from me without my choosing still exists in the back of my throat. It felt like I had so many to give at the start, but now that they're leaving unbidden, now that pieces I *want* are being taken from me, I feel the need to hold on to what I have left with all my might. "I think it was Lady Lellia."

Ilryth takes a small step forward. I lower my fingers from the root, still not daring to touch him. He must pick up on my concern because his hands hover just off my flesh, as if he can barely hold himself back from enveloping me in the safety of his embrace.

"You...heard Lady Lellia's song?"

"It wasn't like Krokan's. It wasn't like your siren songs. And the language was unlike any human tongue I've ever heard." I stare at the oozing sap, then down at my fingertips. It's already gone. But a faint reddish tint has dyed my three center fingers from tip to second knuckle. I rub my thumb over my fingers. Like all the other markings and colors, it doesn't leave. "It required a memory, just like all the other hymns of the old gods. I can only imagine it was her."

Ilryth can no longer hold himself back. He seizes me with his powerful embrace, and spins us with wild laughter. Grip slackening, I slide down his strong form, my body instantly awash with sensation. He takes my face in both hands, pulls me close, and kisses me breathless. My mind is still with thoughts of Lady Lellia and my lost memories, but my body rushes with dizzying desire that roots me to the here and now.

"You are truly magnificent."

"I—"

"I was right. It must be the desire of Lord Krokan to receive a human. One blessed by his lady's hands. Even *she* sings for you."

I try to get a word in but Ilryth is speaking too quickly in his excitement.

"She must be delighted that one of her own has returned. She is singing hymns of your joy and—"

"The song didn't sound joyful, Ilryth. It sounded *painful*," I force in. "It was more like a cry for help than delight." I brace myself for him dismissing me outright.

But Ilryth hums, considering this. "It's nearly impossible for mortals to understand words of the gods," he says finally. "It was centuries in the making to hear the hymns of the old ones in a way that could be recorded for mortal minds. It took half of Duke Renfal's life to merely commune with Lord Krokan for a few, brief moments. Decades to even begin understanding the anointment. And even now, we are constantly adjusting because of how little we can comprehend."

"I understand that, but, Ilryth, you must take my word on this. I know what I heard." I try to think of another angle. A different approach. As much as I want him to believe me, I can also understand why he might not. He is, after all, a product of his world. He can't see it as objectively as I can. "You said that carving from the Lifetree didn't happen until recently?"

"Yes, when Lord Krokan began to rage in the past fifty years."

"Perhaps *that* could be the cause of her pain?" Another thought occurs to me. Something else he mentioned surrounding our trip to the Gray Trench—something I saw coming here, today. "The roots, in the trench, you said they were severed."

"To try and stop the rot."

"And who dictated all of this?"

"Duke Renfal."

It is not lost on me that the man who was in charge when Krokan began raging was the same man who led the carving of spears from tree cuttings. I stare at my hand as the tingling fades away, trying to choose my next words as delicately as possible. I know I'm treading on dangerous ground, but I must ask all the same.

"Was it ever postulated that perhaps Krokan's rage and the aggressive cutting of the Lifetree could be related?"

Ilryth shakes his head. "The Lifetree was cut *in response* to Lord Krokan's increasing irregularity. Not the other way around."

I can't seem to shake this nagging feeling. I do not wish to test the limits of Ilryth's patience but something continues to stand out to me. "The tree was never cut before Duke Renfal?"

"Yes, and all cutting has been limited since." Ilryth shifts his weight. "What are you getting at?"

"Does the Duchy of Faith make any money from the creation of the spears?"

He lifts his brows at the question, initially startled, but then they ease back down as a smile slips across his lips. Ilryth slides his arm around me and shakes his head.

"The Eversea is not quite like your world in that way," he says thoughtfully.

It is good of him to have the sense to know that this matter requires a delicate approach, as it could easily come off as an attack on my home. Though I suppose if he was able to tolerate my inquiries about Krokan and Lellia without growing upset, then I can do the same with my human world and customs.

"Here, not everything revolves around buying and selling and trading. The chorus ensures our world remains in perfect harmony. Sometimes that requires the sacrifice of a few. But in return, we are all looked after by each other. This balance in song has ensured that we all have enough to sustain ourselves in body, mind, and spirit. Moreover, there are some things that we view as too special, too sacred to buy or sell."

I admit *that* notion is strange to me.

"All this is not to say your world is bad," he says quickly. "Only that our worlds are different."

"You don't need to worry, Ilryth. I understood your intention, and what you said isn't wrong." I hope he understands the same of me. That my inquiries aren't implying anything. Though, I suppose I am…

What did Duke Renfal have to gain from weakening the Lifetree? The question nags me. If the Lifetree was keeping the Eversea safe by holding back the rot and Krokan's rage…why cut it? He wasn't profiting off it. Another possible explanation strikes me.

"Did Duke Renfal begin this cutting after his communing?"

"No, though it increased after."

Perhaps then it *was* an order of Lord Krokan. Perhaps the god of death and goddess of life are not lovers at all, but enemies…trapped in an immortal struggle. Commanding the Duke of Faith could be a ploy to kill her on Lord Krokan's part. Make a blight and then make the solution killing the Lifetree.

Duke Renfal could've communed with the god well before he let anyone know, too. Krokan could've commanded the start of the cutting; it's impossible to be sure. His mind became twisted from communing over time, but perhaps it happened faster than anyone imagined. What if he was Lord Krokan's puppet?

"Victoria, what has your expression so serious?" Ilryth frowns slightly.

"I'm afraid there's more at play here, Ilryth," I admit.

"Of course there is." He's frustratingly blasé about the matter. "The old gods aren't meant for our minds to understand. I'm sure there is much we cannot comprehend at work."

"It's not just that…I can't shake the feeling that Lady Lellia…that she's in trouble." *That someone might be trying to kill her*, is what I can't bring myself to say.

Ilryth's expression turns serious. He tightens his arm around my shoulder. "She probably is." His voice is deep with concern. "The rot is no doubt affecting her and I shudder to think what Lord Krokan's rage might do to her if it's not quelled."

"*Why* would he hurt her? If he is supposed to love her above all others, if she is without peer, his chosen songmate…why hurt her?" The question stings my eyes. It causes something forgotten in me to ache. A wound I bear that is reminiscent of the roots around us—still oozing. Though I no longer know its cause.

"Because, sometimes, despite our best efforts…we hurt those we love." He's thinking of his mother. I can see it in his eyes and hear it in his voice. "We ask too much of them, or put them in harm's way. We are a danger to all that we care for."

I open my mouth and close it. It's not good enough. The explanation doesn't satisfy me.

"Love shouldn't hurt," I murmur.

"Victoria—"

"He does not love her."

Ilryth begins ushering me away, as if he can physically move us from this topic. "Lord Krokan is not well… I believe he doesn't know what he's doing. But when he comes to his senses—thanks to you—he will. He will be mended, and maybe you can help mend his relationship with his lady wife, too. Maybe he is her bane, but, if he is, he can also be her cure."

I wrap an arm around Ilryth as well as we begin walking with more speed. I stop resisting. I want to move on from these torturous notions, even if they cling to me.

"Will you indulge me one more question?" I ask.

"I will indulge you anything you desire."

Heat tries to rise to my cheeks at the unintended implication of those words. "Do you believe me?"

Ilryth halts all movement to lock eyes with mine. "Yes. I believe you have a deeper and greater sense of the old gods than any who have come before. And I believe *that* will help save us all."

I take a small step forward. "Will you help me find these truths, if I seek them?"

"I will be at your side every second you are on this plane." There's more unsaid there. He stops himself short.

Placing my hands on his hips, I shift us even closer together. It's odd not to feel scales. Yet, also, somehow inviting. "I need you to support me until the very end."

"I swear it."

What I'm about to ask is cruel. I know what he endured with his mother. He was going to try to avoid that pain again. But perhaps he was right...*we do hurt those we love*. "Then don't leave."

His eyes widen with recognition and a subtle crease furrows his brow. Ilryth knows what I'm asking and, he doesn't appear cross with me for it. If anything, he seems determined. "Victoria, I've long resigned myself that I'm helpless to you. For better or worse, ill or good, I will be at your side until the very end. Mine will be the last song you hear."

"Thank you." Two words don't encompass my gratitude, but they're all I can offer him.

Worries about old gods abate as the sound of soft moans fills my ears. Of sighs and squeals of delight that make it impossible to focus on anything else. Ilryth stops and shifts. He glances behind and then back ahead.

"What is it?" I'm unable to see what awaits us at the other end of the tunnel we've been walking through, but now it wholly consumes my thoughts. The sunlight is so blinding reflected off the pure sands ahead that all I see is brightness. The only clue I have of what awaits me beyond are the noises that my mind is objecting to identifying.

"I was hoping there wouldn't be others here," he murmurs.

"Others?"

He purses his lips a second and then looks back to me with a somewhat sheepish smile as he rubs the back of his neck. "Perhaps it would be best if we go back. You don't really need to see the rest of the island of the Lifetree." His words say one thing, but his feet refuse to move.

And now I'm even more curious.

"What's wrong?" I ask—no, demand firmly. He swallows uneasily. I try a gentler approach. "You can tell me."

But still he says nothing and shakes his head. I have never seen him look so uneasy or embarrassed and I cannot fathom what could possibly have him in such a knot.

"I have bared my soul to you, Ilryth. I have said more than I should. Expressed skepticism toward your home, and you took it in stride. Allow me a chance to return that kindness."

His chest swells slowly as he gathers his courage. "The beach out there is much like the rest of this island—a sacred place for my people. This is one of the few places in all of Midscape that we can walk on land without experiencing any discomfort or having to expend a great deal of magic to maintain our two-legged forms." He shifts, his voice deepening no doubt despite himself. "So, it is here that we— my people—" He clears his throat and seems to gather the courage to continue. "It is here that we ensure future generations."

My gaze darts back and forth between him and the exit of the tunnel. There's been no change, no movement. But the noises persist, growing louder, reaching a crescendo that makes my own lower abdomen clench and grow hot with anticipation. But I refuse to let it get the better of me. I am not a blushing maiden, unknowing of the ways of pleasure. I gather myself. "You mean this is where the siren come to engage in the act of lovemaking?"

He nods. I am about to agree with him that we should go when he says, "Would you like to see it? The shores of our passions?"

I am still stuck in place. I stare up at him, feeling like I should say no. We have no business being there, do we? And it's not something I *need* to see. I know how children are made. I have all the reasons in the world to refuse.

But instead, with a great amount of curiosity, and the slightest bit of eagerness for what he might truly intend by taking me here, I say, "Yes I would."

thirty-five

FINGERS STILL INTERLACED, ILRYTH LEADS ME OUT OF THE TUNNEL AND INTO THE SUNSHINE. Here is another beach, another part of the island that the Lifetree anchors to the surface of the Eversea. Unlike the area directly before Lellia's door, this beach resembles the first that we walked up from. Roots are tangled on two sides. The trunk of the tree is at the back. Open water laps against the shore…and in the sea foam there are men and women, bare and exposed.

They are writhing, thrusting, gyrating, and sliding against each other in the heights of passion. While there are three couples in different areas of the beach, they do not seem to engage with others beyond their singular partner, focusing solely on the individual I would assume they came here with. I have never seen anything so brazen or bold when it comes to matters of the flesh.

The general immodesty of my crew is a very different thing compared to this. When I have seen my crew in various states of undress, it is either at necessary times or in entirely platonic ways. But this, this…

My heartbeat quickens. *This* is something altogether different. Ilryth squeezes my hand, drawing my attention away from the fornicating couples and back to him. He regards me thoughtfully, I suspect trying to parse out what I make of this strange place.

He can no doubt see the flush on my cheeks. I wonder if he sees the slight heaving of my chest as I try to breathe on instinct, combating the immediate sense of embarrassment. All my previous notions of having little concern for modesty are gone.

"We can go if you would desire," he reminds me gently. "I don't want you to be uncomfortable."

I shake my head. Uncomfortable isn't the right word. Shocked? A little. Deliciously tempted in a forbidden sort of way? Also, yes. "I admit…this is *very* different than anything I am accustomed to. Or anything I have seen before. But these are your people and your ways. It is beautiful and not a cause for shame, nor something that should be hidden or shied away from."

He beams as though I could have paid him no higher compliment. His shoulders seem to relax a bit, and I wonder if he thought this element of his people would've scared me away somehow. The thought only makes me want to hold him even tighter, even as our fingers unravel to avoid being seen touching. I wish I had the courage to say that there is nothing in his culture that could turn me away from him. He could be from the ugliest, most brutal, horrible corner of the world, and I would still want to know all there was about it…because it's part of *him*. The words burn my tongue, but I can't bring myself to say them. To expose the depths of my tenderness for Ilryth and everything that surrounds him.

"It was my hope that you would feel this way. This place is one of great magic, of life itself." He nods toward the beach. "Siren come here with their songmates to consummate their love, to sing for Lady Lellia in the hopes of a child. This is one of the few pieces of land all sirens can come onto in our two-legged forms, necessary for conceiving a child, without any kind of discomfort." He wears a slight smile. "Arriving at this shore is a dream come true for any siren who would one day want children."

"You seem to have given it some thought," I observe. "Odd for a man who hasn't even taken a wife yet."

He laughs. "Yes, well, despite my delays in seeing it through, I have always known that my duty would extend to having an heir. That I would come here is simply something I long since accepted." The joy I initially heard in his tone when speaking about this place fades some.

"Does the prospect not excite you?" Had I misread him?

Ilryth doesn't immediately answer, giving my question some

thought. "I cannot say it 'does not' excite me because the act certainly does." He smirks and I fight laughter with a snort. "But I have spent all my life knowing that I will be *expected* to have children. I have never much given thought to if I *want* them. Frankly, it is not something I think I should consider."

"Why not?"

"What if I discover that I do not desire a child, knowing that I'm expected to have one or more, anyway?" He redirects the question to me, even though I know he cannot expect me to have an answer for him. Ilryth shakes his head. "But those are worries for my future self. Let's not dampen this day with my concerns for a year from now."

We are both determined to ignore the troubles that plague the backs of our minds for the sake of this moment. Each passing day feels as though it could be our last, as if every passing hour is all we'll have to truly know each other. The seconds slip away too quickly, time that seems impossible to fully appreciate until it's gone.

"Would you like to see more?"

"More?" I'm not sure what "more" there is to see. But I am achingly curious. "Are you sure it's all right? I wouldn't want to make anyone uncomfortable." We've been intentionally focused on each other, rather than the couples at the water's edge.

"There are shallows and tide pools for those who wish for privacy in their intimate acts. If a couple is out in the open, it is because they do not mind the presence of others. Or even invite it, so that their songs of love might harmonize with others as a lovely offering for the goddess of life."

I am certainly blushing now. Ilryth smirks slightly, but doesn't comment on my slight scandalization. Instead he leads me down the beach.

Despite not wanting to stare, I find my gaze drawn to the distant couples in the surf. Their hair is slick with saltwater and clings to their bodies that glisten with sweat, highlighting the markings drawn across them and faint outlines of where scales would be. Their fanned ears stick out from the sides of their faces, even more noticeable when in their human forms. They are undoubtedly siren, even on land. And, were their physical features not enough of a giveaway, the songs of pleasure would be. It is a chorus in its own right, every couple lending to the melody—a beautiful song made in happenstance harmony. I smile faintly. My initial surprise aside, Ilryth is right. This place, and the act it is designed for, is beautiful.

We cross the beach and enter another area of woven roots splitting off the Lifetree. The entire time, the backs of our hands brush against each other like an illicit secret. Unlike the first two passages, the roots do not form any kind of specific tunnel here. Instead, they loosely weave together like the thick knots of nets, making a maze that is also filled with the sounds of more couples. I assume this is the place that Ilryth mentioned earlier—for those who wish for privacy.

My suspicions are confirmed when I catch glimpses of movement on the other side of roots in the corners of my eyes. But I do not outright look. If they are here then they do not want to be seen.

Though all this does make me wonder where he's taking me...

I don't ask. My thoughts have gone wild with nerves and excitement from all the moving bodies, the hot desire that fills the sun-bleached air and calls to my own arousal. The need that Ilryth has been building within me is reaching its peak.

Is he taking me to one of those sheltered alcoves? Is he going to kiss me again? Here? Alone? Will I find out exactly what is underneath that skirt of his? I glance at it from the corner of my eye.

"We can go any time you would like," he says, pulling me from my thoughts.

My eyes drag up from his skirt, across the divots of his abdomen. There's a knowing gleam to his stare when my gaze finally lands on his face. I've been caught. I give him a somewhat sheepish grin.

"I never said anything about wanting to leave."

His eyes seem to darken with intensity as he stares at me. Ilryth licks his lips and the movement nearly drives me mad.

"You do know why I brought you all this way, don't you?" His voice is low, husky.

My focus wanders from him long enough to become vaguely aware of where "here" is. We have found our own sheltered alcove. The walls of roots that surround this secluded place extend into the sea, embracing us and offering much-desired privacy. I'm unable to form words for a moment, but then collect myself.

"I think I do," I whisper in reply.

"We don't have to," he says.

"We *shouldn't*," I correct. But I'm resting my hands on his hips and leaning into him. "But I want to. Do you?"

"More than anything."

The words are a spark—lightning in the dark—arcing across the waters we've made between us. Jolting us into movement. His hands are in my hair. My back crashes against a root. He has me pinned and never have I been so delighted to be immobile.

I open my mouth for him and his tongue is there. Ready. Eager. It slides against mine and explores. I tilt my head back to give him better access. Ilryth knows what I want—what I *need*. His hand is at my chest, pulling at the ribbon of the vest Lucia found for me. I feel it ease around me and yet it is still too constricting. Just the knowledge that soon it will be off and soon I will be exposed to his fingers makes any fabric feel as though it's constricting me to the point of breathlessness.

Ilryth does not allow me to suffer long. He leans forward, tipping up my chin as he takes the ribbons in his fist. With one confident movement he pulls. My back arches, arms back, to accommodate the removal. I am left gasping.

He pauses, but his expression doesn't seem hesitant or unsure. If anything, it looks as if he is savoring this moment. He looks at me as though I am a work of art that he has been waiting to bear witness to for his whole life.

It is possible that we have been waiting for this very moment, each in our own space and time. For five years, our souls have been bound together in an unconscious duet. Our movements were in tandem, even worlds apart. Every action, every decision and deed has led us to this very point—the moment where we will come together. We are aware of each other on a level that is innate, that transcends logic.

Even though our better senses are screaming that our actions are wrong, our souls remain assured. We exist only in this glorious here and now, casting off shame and doubt. This moment might well be— probably will be—the only one we ever have.

Ilryth moves for me again. As his fingers slip into my hair, his lips part slightly and his jaw relaxes, but his brow furrows almost as if he's in pain.

"What is it?" I am afraid of what he might say. If there is some flaw that he finally sees upon me. Something I always knew was there but tried to hide from him because I so desperately wanted him to see me as enough.

Ilryth shakes his head and it is as though he read my mind. "You are *perfection*. You are as radiant as Lady Lellia herself."

It is possible that our duet is clouding his judgment, but I don't question him. I don't want to argue. So I take his praise with a warm and ready heart.

"You are equally so," I reply. "From the moment I first laid eyes on you, I thought you were magnificent."

The compliment seems to catch him off guard. The first time he averts his eyes from my body is not out of disapproval, as I might have once expected, but, it would seem, embarrassment. I press my hand against his chest, leaning away from the root and looking up at him through my lashes.

"You are *stunning*," I emphasize again. How a man as fine as Ilryth might think himself otherwise is lost on me, but I will say it as often as he needs to hear it. "And I want you to touch me and hold me until I lose all sense of self. Until the world drifts away and all my worries and pains with it."

I want to feel while I'm still alive. If only just one more time...

"I think I will be able to accommodate your request," he says, pressing his hands against my hips and sliding them upward, gliding over my breasts. I let out a gasp. My eyes close and I bite my lower lip, savoring the feeling. He continues moving up, tracing the markings on my chest, shoulders, and arms, down to my hands.

I am your canvas, I want to say. *Make me.*

Wordlessly, he leads me toward the water's edge, guiding me down as he sits. My knees frame his hips as I straddle him, grabbing his shoulders as he kneads my thighs and ass. We kiss well past the point that I would think I would have grown tired of kissing. And yet I cannot bear the thought of stopping. I am consumed by a need for more, more sensation, more of this feeling that pulses through me like a fever—like salvation.

"I want more." The thought escapes me and he smirks against my mouth. "Give me it all."

Holding me tightly, Ilryth leans forward and lays me down in the sand and surf.

"I have every intention of accommodating your request," he says. "But all in due time."

"You are an unbearable tease," I say with a gasp as he bites my collarbone and kisses down my chest.

"I must admit no one has called me that before." He lavishes special attention on my breasts.

"I am certain someone has." My words are breathless.

He makes a show of thinking about it and I groan as his movements stop. He laughs once more and continues showering his affection upon me. "No, I do not think anyone has."

I am sure I'll be the first of many. The errant thought is unwelcome and unwanted, though it stays in my mind alone. I do not want to consider just how many countless others will be sure to follow, drawn by his allure and undeniable charisma. I won't theorize about which of the beautiful women I saw in the Duchy of Spears will become his bride. I can change the future as much as I can change my past—all I can do, want to do, is be helpless to the here and now.

Ilryth continues down my body with eager hands and kisses, pushing up the tightly wrapped skirt, hands gliding over my thighs as they undo the fabric. I groan, back arching off the sand. Just when I think he is about to reach for the apex of my desire, he stops and leans back onto his knees. The only thing that keeps a whine of objection from escaping is when he reaches for the tie of his skirt. He undoes the knot and the skimpy piece of fabric falls away, exposing *all* of him.

We both get our first real look at each other at the same time. We stay in a moment of mutual silence. Of awe.

Somehow, this does not feel like the beginning of the end for us. Only the former. It is as though, together, we can somehow escape the harsh fate that is inked into our very flesh.

Ilryth shifts and settles atop me. Our bodies flush, I can feel every inch of him between my thighs, pressing against me. Seeking entry without word. A sense of guilt overtakes me; it's sudden and unwelcome—its root I can't place. Ilryth freezes. He must see the momentary panic in my eyes.

He caresses my cheek lovingly and says, "We can stop."

"I know," I reply. "I don't want to."

"You're sure?"

"I am," I insist. The first time with anyone is at least a bit awkward. The first time with a man who is not the one you married seems to be even more so. But *I am doing nothing wrong*. I remind myself that I am free in mind, in law, and in spirit. I can hardly even remember the bindings that were on me to begin with.

It is as if Ilryth knows the turmoil—every doubt and insecurity—that haunts the seas of my mind. He waits patiently as I work through them all. As I spend my time worrying away my insecurities until, finally, I can give him a nod. The smile he returns is not one of lust, or unbridled passion. Rather, it is earnest, filled with genuine joy and affection.

Ilryth leans forward and kisses me one more time—gently, almost chastely. But there is nothing chaste about the way he rolls his hips, pressing forward and into me for the first time.

I let out a gasp at the momentary pain of expanding to accommodate his substantial size. While I haven't had much experience in the ways of the flesh, that I can recall, I suspect Ilryth is particularly blessed. He seems to know it, too, as he eases slowly into me, searching my face for any sign of pain or hesitation.

Finding none, he presses forward all the way until our hips are flush and our bodies are one. The sun shines brighter. The chorus in my mind is louder, clearer, as if the universe itself is opening to reveal a long hidden, great secret. I am as light as a song, as intense as a prayer. I relax as the sweet feeling of fullness overtakes me. And then, just as I have grounded myself in this new reality of our own making, he begins to move. Every thrust destroying and remaking my entire world.

His hips pound against mine, slow at first and then picking up speed. I wrap my legs around his waist as I did last night, hanging on to him as though my very existence depends on his. Ilryth kisses me fiercely, lips pressing hard against mine—as though he wants to capture every moan that passes between my lips, exhaling it back to me as a song in my mind. His pace reaches its steady point, stamina unyielding, sending waves of pleasure across my body.

My moans echo so loudly I cannot tell if they are only in my mind or if I am now leading the songs of pleasure sung on this beach. A part of me almost hopes it is the latter. I want him with a desire that is all-consuming. I want them all to hear—for the old goddess herself to look out from her tree and smile that somehow we have uncovered the great secret. That *this* was what it was going to take all along to make an offering that could quell Krokan's rage.

It had to be a duet that would honor—harmonize with—the promise Krokan made with Lellia. Two lovers. Not cold and unfeeling sacrifices. But an offering made of passion.

Ilryth slows and leans away. I look at him, confused and fighting a whimper. He smiles, a wicked glint in his eyes, and leans back. My legs stay locked around his hips and without him leaving me for an instant, he is now on his back. I am astride him. He grabs my hips, goading and guiding me. It is my turn to set the pace. My turn to be in control, and I revel in it. I move fast, enjoying the moans and cries it elicits from him as I do. And then at once, without warning, I stop.

His fingertips dig wells into my flesh as he tries to yank me into him, but I do not budge. My hands splay against his broad, strong chest and I smirk as I rock my hips slowly, purposefully. His head tips back and Ilryth lets out a groan that devolves into a growl. He knows I'm teasing him and he's relishing it as much as I am.

I repeat—fast then slow, fast then slow. We continue creeping toward the edge of that wonderful sweet release, but never quite get there.

With a frustrated grunt, he pushes me off. I think for a moment that I've gone and teased him too far. But his eyes are still filled with lust and intensity. He twists me, guiding me onto my knees and hands. Hands still gripping my hips, he thrusts into me in one fluid motion, taking me from behind as an animal would. Even with holes in my memories, I know I have never felt a man from this angle. I have never known that there were so many ways to feel pleasure—different spots within me that could be struck again and again *and again*.

And as it is already becoming too much, he leans forward. With one hand he grabs my breast; the other reaches around my hips, stroking at the apex of my thighs as he continues to thrust in and out of me relentlessly, begging surrender. It is too much to resist.

I let out a cry. I shudder and I find my sweet release. Ilryth grips me, supporting me through my passions. His chest against my back.

He stays within me as he kisses down my shoulders, moving his fingers over my body as though he is drawing new lines upon me.

When I finally collect myself enough to speak, I say, "That was incredible."

Ilryth bites my shoulder. I can hear the smirk in his words without having to see it. "That was only the beginning."

thirty-six

WE DRESS IN SILENCE, THE AIR BETWEEN US THICK WITH THE LINGERING INTENSITY OF OUR PASSION. It's not uncomfortable or awkward in the slightest. If anything, it's a pleasant intimacy. We share small glances and knowing smiles underneath flushed cheeks. Every look underscores that we now share a dangerous secret.

We share a lot more than that.

I can feel him on me—deeper than the markings inked upon my skin. He doesn't need to touch me. A mere look is all I need to feel the phantom outlines of his hands smoothing across my breasts, grabbing at my hips, or his mouth on my neck. The memories make me shiver; phantom sensations of him are almost too much. And yet I want more. If we could do it all over again I would in an instant. I would give myself over to those heady passions without remorse.

Even though what we shared was intense, I can't help wishing we had more time...not just today, but months, or years, to get to know each other. A lifetime to explore everything we could, and couldn't be—to see if these budding affections could blossom into something truly profound.

And yet I also want everything all at once. Damn moving slowly, I want it all, now. The idea of us doesn't have the hard-earned instincts in my gut twisting. There are no warnings or concerns rising in my mind when it comes to Ilryth. Maybe, if the seas weren't rotting and an old god wasn't raging, and everything didn't hinge on my life being sacrificed…we might have a genuine chance at something *real*.

It's a bittersweet thought. But not bitter enough for me to push it away. I think, if I had the chance to do it all over again, I'd try harder at love. Even though there's this odd sense in me telling me to avoid it at all costs.

You're not worthy of love.

I pause at the errant thought. It was said in a voice that didn't entirely feel like my own.

"What's wrong?" Ilryth rests his palm on my shoulder.

I shake my head. "I had an odd notion."

"About us?"

"No." I smile up at him. Reassuring.

"Anything you want to talk about?"

"I don't think so." I take his hand and lace my fingers with his, kissing his knuckles. "Do you ever just have a rogue or intrusive notion cross your mind without warning?"

"Sometimes," he admits. "Though they're usually tied to something. Are you sure you don't want to discuss anything?"

"I feel incredible, Ilryth. It was a passing thought that deserves no credence."

"Right, then." He lets the matter drop with a smile.

Hand in mine, he guides me back through the basket-weave of roots to the beach of passion, releasing me when we're out in the open once more. It's mostly empty now. There's only one couple at the ocean's edge, leaning up against a root where it meets the water. I don't know if they were there when we arrived or not. But I don't pay them any mind. I'm still too caught up in what we just shared. Focused on his magic, which is still sizzling across my skin.

I glance at him and I wonder if we will speak of this ever again. Once more, the idea of love crosses through my mind. It would've been nice to be able to fall in love with him. To feel that anxious flutter of excitement. To be able to look at him, at the ridge of his nose, the strong line of his jaw, the slight pout to his lips—to admire him as shamelessly as I am now, but have the opportunity for it to become something more.

But what we shared can't grow into love. At least…not a love we will ever acknowledge. We must let whatever is budding die on the vine. All today can be is an afternoon of forbidden pleasure. Of finally satiating ourselves and alleviating growing tension. *It will be alright if I must pretend this didn't happen,* I tell myself. I don't need to speak about it, or tell anyone, for me to know that it was real. I can find peace in that. At least I *think* I can.

Yet a different part of my mind is already wondering when, or if, we might find an excuse to return here. If he might sneak into my room in the night and whisk me away by moonlight. I can't help but hope he will and that it will be soon, but I do not have the courage to ask.

We come to a stop in the tunnel just before the beach where we first arrived. The guards that escorted us here are no doubt still waiting beneath the water's surface. While out of eye shot, Ilryth takes a moment to give me an apologetic look.

"I'm sorry," Ilryth says. I blink, trying to think just what he could be apologizing for. He picks up on my confusion and continues, "When we arrive back, I will have to pretend that—"

"Nothing happened," I finish for him with a small, and hopefully reassuring smile. "I know. I didn't expect it to be any different. We made our choices knowing our circumstances." When he still seems hesitant, I emphasize, "Really, it's all right."

"It doesn't feel 'all right.'" He sighs. "It feels as though I am betraying you—as though I have used you."

"If anything, I used you." I shake my head before he has a chance to get in another word. "I am a woman grown, in control of my own wants, and have done what I desire. You've done the same. There's no slight. We both knew our circumstances. Truly, Ilryth, think nothing of it."

"I suspect I will spend many, many delicious hours thinking of this afternoon." He leans just a bit closer to me as he says it. I bite my lip and his eyes fall to the motion. In my periphery, I can almost see him reaching up to touch my face.

But he is stronger than the temptation. Which is good, because if he crossed the line again, I doubt I could be the better of the two of us. Risks be damned. I would take another chance. Ilryth starts to move again and I do as well. But he stops once more without warning and looks at me with renewed purpose.

"If I were to come to you in the night…would I be welcome?"

I can feel my jaw drop open. I didn't honestly expect there might be an opportunity for more indulgences between the two of us, though it is very, *very* welcome.

I nod, not caring how eager I seem. Playing coy or denying is pointless now. "It would be my literal pleasure."

He seems to breathe a sigh of relief, as if he wasn't sure if I would say yes to him. How could he think anything else? Especially after the day we shared?

As I suspected, the warriors are waiting for us just beneath the waves. They don't seem suspicious in the slightest about what kept us for half the day. Perhaps they don't want to know, or think it's better if they don't ask questions.

I hold my head high and act casual as we return to the castle. With a nonchalant farewell, Ilryth and I part, going our separate ways. It takes every bit of my control not to look back at him when we do. Not to hope that he might already be swimming back to me.

It is too soon for it, I know, yet I can't help myself. I can't stop my hoping for his arrival as the remnants of the day slip into night. I wait on the balcony, ignoring Krokan churning up the currents of rot below and instead scanning the waters above, searching for any sign of Ilryth instead.

But there is none. The night comes and goes, dawn breaks, and Ilryth is still not here. I remind myself that he said he wouldn't be able to come soon without arousing suspicion. Moreover, I am sure he has many responsibilities to attend to beyond me. I insist to myself that I will not think too much or obsess over his absence.

I spend my time dedicating myself to what I'm supposed to be doing—working on the hymns of the old ones. I sit on the balcony railing, where Ilryth and I sat the other night.

Alone, I sing.

The words come from low in my stomach, are drawn up through my chest, and pull up to the top of my mind. As they drag through my thoughts, they pull parts of me with them. Stripping me away from the inside out. It's harder each time to pick memories than the last. Briefly, I consider sacrificing the memory of Ilryth's and my passions…but I don't. I want to carry that with me for as long as I can.

Instead, I pick memories of council meetings. The last vestiges of the man named Charles. Those can burn away. Whatever happened with him is of no consequence to me any longer. It feels so vastly unimportant to where I am now.

The notes rise, lighter and lighter with every thought I let go. It feels as if my soul is soaring with them, unhindered for the first time in my life. I try to sing with all my chest—to reach the tallest boughs of the Lifetree that sways above me. But the words are weighted by the still, heavy water, pulled down into the clotting rot.

My song sinks into the Abyss. I can almost hear a faint echo resonating back up to me. The sound is lonely and far colder than I feel. I still, tilting my head slightly. I sing another note. The reply is filled with longing and pain.

I pause my song, trying to make sense of what I heard. Was it merely an echo? Or was Krokan singing back to me? Closing my eyes, I try to repeat the sound in my mind—to understand it—but I'm interrupted.

"Your Holiness?" Lucia calls up.

"I'm here." I push away from the railing, drifting into my room as she arrives.

She knows instantly what we've done. I don't know how she knows, but she does. The moment she swims up through the tunnel she halts, staring at me. There's a sudden shift to her expression from wide to narrowed eyes.

I stand a little taller and I give her a slight smile as though I am acknowledging that she knows without needing to say a word. Lucia shakes her head and crosses, giving me a pointed look of disapproval. I hadn't expected her to say anything about her brother and me. But, apparently, I was wrong.

thirty-seven

SHE GRABS MY HAND. Her words are hasty, whispered even though she's speaking directly to my mind. "I worry for you both."

If not for my years of training, I wouldn't be able to keep a straight face. "What are you talking about?"

"You…and my brother…" It takes her a second to formulate the words, as if she can't believe she's saying them at all. Or perhaps she's inwardly cringing at the notion of her brother being intimate. Either is possible.

"I don't know what you mean." I continue to play dumb, wanting her to elaborate and tell me exactly what she knows—what she sees or hears—so that I might hide it better to protect Ilryth.

"Your markings have shifted a bit."

"They have?" I hold up my arm. The tattoos appear mostly the same as always.

Lucia inspects the markings as well. "Yes. Somewhat on your skin. Definitely in the song your soul resonates with—it no longer quite matches what we've inked. I can only assume it was quite the monumental shift to adjust your duet so significantly."

"I heard Lady Lellia's voice." I offer the explanation to see if it's a viable substitution to her suspicions in case someone else notices.

She stills, eyes darting up to me. "You did?" Her voice is

still a whisper, but no longer one of fear and worry. But, rather, awe… and a fleeting hope as delicate as the words.

I nod. "I'm certain of it. Perhaps that was the cause of the change in the markings?"

Lucia eases away, gaze darting between my arm and my face. "Such a monumental thing would impact them… But I know my brother's song." She sighs. "I can hear it in you, now."

What does that mean? My heart skips a beat and stops, as if it can't decide between joy and breaking. Ilryth's song is a part of me now, written on my soul. What does that mean for him when I depart this mortal realm? What will it mean for me?

"Will other people be able to tell?" I focus on keeping him as safe as I'm able, despite the risks we've chosen to take.

"Likely not," she reluctantly admits. "I suspect I can because I've seen almost your entire anointing and know the song of your soul well, and my brother's better."

That gives me hope. "And has the anointing been damaged?"

"Not that I can see." A relief. "But it *could* be if you were to persist. You both are doing a dangerous thing. Connecting in this way could jeopardize you being able to properly descend into the Abyss and stand before Lord Krokan. You are forming more ties to this world." She looks up at me, brow furrowed with worry.

"We know the risks," I say, trying to infuse some of my calmness into her with my tone. The monster of guilt for our decisions tries to rear its head again. But I refuse to allow it to get a hold of me. There's no going back now. "I understand your worry, we both do, but we have it under control."

She sighs and drifts away, leaning against a column and staring out at the Abyss.

"Lucia—"

"Our mother…she gave *everything* to try and quell Lord Krokan's rage. It wasn't enough and Ilryth has always blamed himself for rendering her sacrifice 'meaningless.' He saw it as his fault that she was still too tied to this land to properly descend." Lucia's stare is a thousand leagues long, as though she is trying to pierce the Veil that separates this world from the next and see her mother one more time. "Fenny and I had to sit by and watch as the weight of his duty slowly dawned on him. As he lost the opportunity to mourn our mother's passing by holding onto her.

"Now, he's taking the same risk all over again." She twists slightly to look at me. Her wounded stare is sharper than any dagger and it finds a soft spot between my ribs. "You will kill him."

"No, I won't," I say fiercely. "I would not let any harm befall him."

"You will be *gone*," she says curtly. "And if the guilt of you failing as an offering doesn't put him over the edge, the weight of loss will. Just like it did my father."

I swim over with a shake of my head. "Ilryth doesn't love me like your father loved your mother." She stares at me blankly. "*He doesn't,*" I insist again. "I've ensured it."

"If you've 'ensured it' then why can I hear the harmony of his soul's song mixed with yours?" Lucia's eyes are filled with steely determination. It's the look I'd give anyone who would even dare think of bringing harm to Emily. Before I can answer, she continues, "Tell me why I shouldn't report you both to the chorus."

The words are as cold as ice and freeze me in place. "Because I give you my word that—"

"Your word?" There's judgment in those two words that runs a shiver down my spine. In them, I hear all of those in Dennow calling me an insult I no longer understand: *Oath breaker.*

Why did they call me that? I can't remember and the jab is unfair and cruel.

"You gave us your word—gave *him* your word you would be dedicated to the anointing if he helped your family," she says.

"And I am dedicated, with all my being."

"Not if you do things that compromise your very goal!" she snaps. I rear back.

"Lucia...please," I say softly. "It was a moment of passion, nothing more." It is odd to lie while trying to defend my integrity. But the most important thing, out of any of it, is ensuring Ilryth doesn't suffer for what we did. "I don't love him. He knows it." The words are uneasy as a lie. I just hope they don't sound like it, too.

"Does he?" Lucia asks skeptically.

"He does. I told him outright before...anything happened." This discussion is made deeply uncomfortable by having it with his sister.

But I press on. "Please. I wanted to indulge in a bodily pleasure before I died—scratch an itch, as it were. If anything, it helped sever a bond more than build one. I have no lingering wants."

Lucia continues to regard me warily. With a sigh and a flap of her tail, she sits on the edge of my bed and stares out once more at the Abyss. Her elbows rest on the curve of her tail. Chin in her hands.

"I hate this." The words are honest and raw. "I hate that the first time I've seen my brother genuinely happy in six long years is with a human who's marked for death."

"I'm sorry." I swim over and settle into place next to her. "Ilryth's a good man...he deserves all the happiness in the world. And I'm sorry I can't be the one to give it to him."

"He'll survive. Fenny and I will make sure he does. Just, please don't make it harder on us than it already will be." The plea is desperate and broken.

"I won't." I'm torn in two. Between what I want, and what I must do. Between my oaths and obligations and a man that I never asked for, or even thought I wanted. "He'll be all right, though. I'm sure of it. He has both of you." Fenny and Lucia have held the Duchy of Spears together for a long time, I think.

"When he actually listens to us." She sighs and pushes off the bed, halting mid-drift. With her back to me, she says, "I'm not going to tell Ventris."

"No?" I can't help but question. For a moment, I was certain she would.

"There's no point... It's not as if we could anoint anyone else in time. And you've already been marked as the offering; we'd have to kill you first if we wanted to try." Grim, but works in my favor. "So even if you're a subpar offering, you're better than scrambling or, worse, nothing. I'd shudder to think of what might happen if we present no one to Lord Krokan. Moreover, I don't want to see my brother get into any more trouble than he usually does."

I push off the bed as well, drifting over to her. "Thank you, Lucia. I know it's not for me, but it means a lot to me that you've done this."

"Yes, well, prove that your word is all that Ilryth makes it out to be."

"I will," I resolve. In all I can remember of my life, I have never broken an oath. "I swear it to you. I will quell Lord Krokan's rage and bring back calm and prosperity to the Eversea."

"Good. Oh, and make sure Ilryth and I are the only ones to mark you from now on…let's not risk anyone else finding out."

"You're a good woman and a good sister, Lucia. Thank you." I wish there might have been more time to get to know her. Perhaps befriend her properly. Much like my feelings for Ilryth, there's the start of a connection with Lucia—a friendship, but it's not going to have time to mature into anything.

She gives a small nod. "Just don't make me regret it," she says, and gets to work.

Her movements are relaxed and purposeful. Confident. She's just about finished when Ventris swims up.

"How is she?" he asks Lucia without so much as a greeting to me.

"I am just finishing." Lucia does another check of her lines— the ones that were new, and adjustments to the old. I hope she was right when she said that she could cover the shifts Ilryth made in my markings.

Ventris swims over and I remain perfectly still, working to keep my expression relaxed. *I have nothing to fear. You have no reason to be suspicious.* I repeat the thoughts, keeping them for myself.

"She looks good," he says, leaning away. I fight not to let my shoulders sag with relief. "Excellent work, as always."

"Thank you, Your Grace." Lucia bows her head. "If I may, when do the markings need to be completed by?"

"Our astrologers and tidal readers say that it shall be less than fifty nights until the summer equinox."

Less than two months, I think to myself. It's so close. Twenty-five years was all my life had. It's too short. I might have accepted my fate, but for the first time it hurts. Today highlighted everything I'm letting go with painful color.

How did I allow myself to get to this place?

I try to remember the circumstances, but they're hazy. I knew Ilryth when he came to collect me aboard my ship. I knew he would come and take me. *So why…*

"Now," Ventris continues. "If you would please come along."

"To where?"

"We are going to begin the preparations for the final verse of your anointing."

I do as I'm told. But not for him and not because he tells me to. I do it peacefully because I think there's a chance that I might see Ilryth again. It is dawning on me how little time I have left with him. This will all be over before I know it; I must savor every moment. I have things I need to ask him...things about myself.

We glide gracefully through the twisting corridors and oddly shaped rooms of the castle. I pay little attention to the direction we take. It doesn't seem like something I need to know; it's not as if I will be here for much longer. Instead, I focus on the multicolor beauty of it all. The intricate and organic skill by which the sirens build their homes that begets a seamless fusion of form and function—a stunning merger that I feel as if I'm seeing for the first time.

We end at another large cavern, not unlike where the chorus met. This one is filled with sculptures similar to those in Ilryth's armory. On one side is a carved rendition of Krokan. On the opposite is one of Lellia and her Lifetree. However, unlike in Ilryth's armory, the roots that wrap through this space are not carved from stone.

These are the real roots of the Lifetree, shimmering with a ghostly haze, much like the anamnesis spectral trees hanging from the ceiling. They illuminate the space with their glow. As if a forest has grown upside down, cradled and supported by the roots of the Lifetree itself. I briefly wonder why these roots shimmer with the same glow as the anamnesis when other roots—outside the castle, the ones that descend into the Abyss—are rotting. Perhaps Ilryth was right, and it is the waters of death poisoning life.

My thoughts are stilled by the two large emeralds that are inlaid as eyes for the carving of Krokan. My gaze locks with it, as if the real Krokan can see me through his stony counterpart. I can almost hear the whispering of words that I cannot understand because they were not made for mortal ears. They pool in the back of my mind, calling me, beckoning me closer and closer.

He is waiting for me in that endless pit of water and rot. The old god of death calls relentlessly, demanding my very soul as payment for a crime. A chill panic sweeps across my skin. I want to leave this room—to go anywhere other than where he can see me. I swim backward.

Ventris notices the reaction and he can no doubt see the panic on my face.

He stops and asks tiredly, "What is it now?"

"I..." Words are stuck, unable to be freed from the corners of my mind.

"What is wrong with you?" Ventris demands.

I shake my head again. I try to open my mouth, as if by physically doing so I could coerce the words into coming out in the same way I would when I still could speak with my physical voice. But none come.

"Tell me." Agitation has crept into Ventris's voice. "Or I shall begin to think that you might be defective."

The words echo something lost within me. Something someone said to me once, *I think?* But I can't recall. Still, they elicit a response in my body that my mind can't explain.

Before I can muster a response, a warm and protective presence envelops me. I glance over my shoulder to find Ilryth there, as if my fear summoned him and he responded with my defense. He gives me a small but gentle smile. But he's careful not to touch me, even if he positions his body partly before me.

Then he turns to Ventris with ferocity. "Is that any tone to take with the holy sacrifice?"

"It is merely one of concern," Ventris says calmly. "I need assurance that our offering will not falter when the time comes. If she's wavering now, then the anointing is not working and her ties to the world are yet too strong."

My thoughts settle. Thanks to Ilryth's presence, I can focus on the here and now.

"I will not falter," I say with even more confidence than I showed Lucia. "I was merely taken aback at how stunning this room is...and how perfect that sculptor's rendering of Lord Krokan is."

Ventris looks behind him, clearly skeptical of my claims. Even though he's right to be, he doesn't have any room to argue or protest. It is not as though he could prove that what I have said is untrue. And I'm paying his lord a compliment.

"It *is* a magnificent depiction of Lord Krokan," he admits with a note of reluctance. "And it is good to know that it appears a faithful rendering, even to the offering, for if any were to have an innate sense of what our old god looks like, it would be you."

I cannot refute him, and not just because I don't want to. But because I am overcome with this innate sense that I *do* actually know what Krokan looks like.

The urge to take Ilryth's hand is nearly overwhelming. All I want is to feel his fingers against mine. To remind myself that I am still among the living, and safe. That I am not yet cast into that Abyss, surrendered to a god whose intentions I cannot fathom. I wish he could offer me some kind of reassurance. I wish I could leech off of his stability, but I know I cannot.

We have our roles to play...and that will be the hardest part of all of this.

So I stay poised and calm as Ventris begins to outline the gathering of the siren court and the final anointing that will happen before my soul is sent off to that old god once and for all.

thirty-eight

W<small>HEN</small> V<small>ENTRIS HAS FINALLY FINISHED DRONING ON ABOUT THIS</small> <small>AND THAT,</small> I<small>LRYTH PROMPTLY SAYS,</small> "I <small>SHALL ESCORT HER BACK.</small>"

Those words bring me back to the present. The entire time, my thoughts were wandering to the roots above us—to the Lifetree. As if, by staring at them long enough, I could connect with Lady Lellia, rather than Lord Krokan, and perhaps catch a glimmer of understanding from her.

What is Lellia's role in all of this? Maybe I have it wrong. Perhaps I'm thinking of her as the captive when she is actually the cause of the rot. Perhaps the goddess of life ended up resenting the chaos her children caused, resentment led to the decay of hate and that is what's causing Lord Krokan's rage.

There's the edge of understanding in my mind that has been consuming my attentions all afternoon. I've been replaying the hymns of the old ones, trying to find some scrap of understanding that I hadn't been afforded yet. As if hidden in their unintelligible, barely comprehensible words is the key to all of this.

"I do not mind escorting her," Ventris says with a note of skepticism.

"Of course not, but as the Duke of Faith you no doubt have other important obligations." Ilryth smiles. "Allow me to relieve some of your schedule. Besides, I can proceed with her next set of markings."

"Very well." Ventris swims away with an air of washing his hands of us. I suppose it's better than suspicion.

Ilryth and I leave. He says nothing the entire way back to my room. The warriors on either side of the entrance to the tunnel that leads to my chambers do not follow behind us. They barely acknowledge us beyond a respectful nod.

The moment we're alone in my room, Ilryth shifts, swimming in front of me, a hand dragging around my waist. His other hand moves to tangle his fingers with my hair. He claims my mouth—gentle but demanding.

A soft whimper escapes me. It reverberates between us. He responds with a low, resonant note that seems to rumble deep in my core. A sound that feels as if it originates within me, rather than from him.

Ilryth's tongue slips into my mouth, finding mine eager and waiting. I do not breathe, and yet my chest burns as though he has stolen the heartbeat from between my ribs. When he finally breaks away I am dizzy and yearning.

He presses his forehead against mine. "I am sorry for not coming sooner."

"It wasn't *that* long," I say, as if I hadn't waited the night for him.

"It felt long to me."

I laugh softly. "Me as well."

A dazzling smile splits his lips. I stare at it, barely resisting the urge to kiss it off. He must see, or sense, my want, because he leans in once more, lips brushing against mine, replacing cool water with the warm taste of him.

"I spent the night awake…" His words reverberate across my mind as he kisses me. I am surprised he's able to form a coherent sentence. I certainly could not when his lips are on mine. "Thinking of all the reasons I could not go to you—*should* not…shouldn't even want you. And yet." He shifts, deepening the kiss once more. "For every reason I thought of, I wanted you all the more. When it comes to you, every no becomes a yes."

"As if this is the one thing you know is right in the world." My words are a whisper as he pulls away with a slight nod, his nose brushing against mine.

"I wish I could redesign the stars to give us more time."

"Let's not waste the time we have by focusing only on how quickly it will be over." I meet his brilliant eyes and bring both my hands to his face, running them along his strong jaw. "Let's focus on nothing but each other, for the brief moments we can be together."

"What if there were a way that we could stay together?"

"What?" I blink up at him. The idea seems almost comical. A way to stop the wheel of fate from grinding us into the dirt, after all this? "What are you talking about?"

"I could consult the old scrolls—everything here in the Duchy of Faith. Perhaps there's something in Duke Renfal's records. Perhaps—"

"Ilryth." I stop him firmly but gently by his name alone. "We cannot."

"But—"

"I gave my word. To you, to Lucia, to all of the Eversea, and to my family," I remind him. Something creeps up from the recesses of my memories. A vague notion that is formless. A feeling, more than tangible thought. "I can't go back on this. You told me how much an oath means to the people of the Eversea."

"More than anything." He sighs, cupping my hands with his. "And yet you mean—"

"I don't mean anything to you beyond the offering," I cut him off. "And maybe an indulgence." I add the last bit with a coy smile.

He shares the expression, briefly. But it doesn't quite reach his eyes. Lucia's warnings earlier return in force.

He's falling in love with me.

I can see it, plain as day. Feel it. If I don't stop this then he is doomed for a world of heartache.

But…how can I stop something that part of me secretly, desperately wants? I want to be loved. Needed. I want to be touched and known.

"I'm not ready to lose you yet."

"We have almost two months," I remind him.

"Less than."

"When the time comes, you will be sick of me." I release him despite every fiber of my body yearning for him. Wanting him. The less I hold on to him, the better.

"I doubt that could ever happen." He regards me warily as I swim out to the balcony.

"Don't try me. I can be a lot."

He huffs and comes to sit next to me in what have become our usual spots. "I'm not sure, if it came to a war of wills between us, who would win."

Me. But I don't say so. I'll prove it by staying our course. I've charted against the stars, sworn to the crew that is the Eversea. There's nowhere to go but forward.

"I actually had a question for you." I shift on the railing of the balcony. Something about this question—despite my needing to ask it—chafes because it's something I should know. But can't…for the life of me…recall…

"Yes?"

"How did this arrangement come to pass?" I finally ask.

He shifts to face me. "What do you mean?"

"I know that I was going to be claimed by you. I remember… waiting for you." I run my fingers over my forearm. "But tell me, how did I know that? How did I come to be chosen as the sacrifice?"

His lips part slightly and then close as his chest swells. He looks like he's bracing himself. The affection that was in his eyes runs away from the sorrow that's filling them. Pain…at the idea of me not remembering. At what I've lost.

That will be it, the key to destroying everything when the time comes. It will be to let him go in a way that only I can—in a way that he has no control over. A way that there is no going back from. I won't falter. When it is right, I'll kill this budding love memory by memory, stripping it from me, and him.

"You…made a deal with me…" He starts slowly, finding his stride as he speaks. Some of what he says I remember from things he's told me in the past. Others are gone completely.

Why was I in the ocean that night? He doesn't know, and neither do I anymore. When he is done speaking, I rest my temple on his shoulder and allow my eyelids to grow heavy. They close slowly.

"I'm glad we met," I admit, even though there are still blanks in my memories. There are things he's not saying.

"Me too." He kisses my forehead, lips lingering, quivering slightly. "A human and a siren. What an unlikely pair."

"No more unlikely than the human breathing underwater…or being sacrificed to an old god."

My singing is better than ever. I practice with Ilryth as I have before. But I also sing by myself—for myself. There's peace in the words. In letting go. In the sweet blankness that follows every song.

Vast swaths of nothingness overtake my mind. The lacking makes room for me to focus on my work in learning the words of the old ones. But Ilryth has other intentions.

It is as if he wants to fill those voids solely with thoughts of him. His life. His body.

He takes me back to the shores of the Lifetree and we tangle in the surf. His body is ecstasy. Our moans a song. Every time feels as though it is the first.

The next time I sing, every time becomes the last.

If I run my fingers lazily over the marks Ilryth drew on me earlier today, I can still feel him touching me, holding me. His hands magically summon paints and pigments underneath my flesh, smearing and shaping them as he kisses my every worry away. I do not hear music when I study my skin tonight. Instead, I hear the song of our lovemaking ringing in my ears, a rhythm of sound and percussion of hips.

It churns a deep and fierce need within me. A beast has been awoken within, more fearsome than any old god, and I welcome the opportunity to become the monster.

Night has fallen across the sea, and I wait on the balcony, wondering and hoping he will come to me again. Will he steal me away to the shores of passion? Will he lie with me in my bed?

If his body and mind are too weary from the day's preparations for such forbidden delights, then I still hope he comes to me as I would like to delight in his mind. There's so much I wish I knew about him. So much I know I'll never have the chance to learn.

Every day he tells me more. He fills my head with stories. This man with the handsome face, and his loving tongue…and sad eyes. He tells me tales of a deep, dark trench, filled with monsters. Of a great escapade to brave it for rare silver. He tells me of a woman who saved him once when he was on the brink of death.

The stories stir something in me. Warmth, at first. But then restlessness. Nagging. Something…not quite there.

I look over the Abyss once more.

The water is murkier than normal tonight. The rot is churned by currents unseen. I wonder if Krokan is restless. I imagine the monstrosity writhing and slamming his tentacles across the sea floor, kicking up silt. He knows I'm *so* close to being his. He must feel it, because I can.

The pigment that has soaked into my flesh is beginning to constrict around me. It won't be much longer now until the stars are aligned for my offering. I'm nearly ready.

Yet, one thing pulls me back. One thing keeps me here, for now. I look toward the edge of the castle Ilryth swam around previously. Hoping he will come to me… We don't have many nights left.

But I still know better than to expect it. He still has other obligations and we must be careful. Biting back a sigh, I turn back into my room and settle back into bed as the evening verses have begun. The sea is filled with siren song that begs for peace, and protection. It enhances the throbbing glow of the anamnesis.

I tune it out, lie back, and sink into the sponge. Expelling my worries. I relish in the delightful ache that has seeped into my bones thanks to Ilryth. While I do not have any need of sleep any longer, I don't think that will stop me tonight from dreaming. My eyes flutter closed. I drag a hand down my breast to smooth my palm along my stomach. Even without him here, my core within is already on fire.

My fingers slide farther down, nestling between my thighs. I make lazy circles with my middle finger, sighing a second time, easing into myself and the motion. I think of how he felt within me, under me. His hips colliding with mine. Our breaths and moans a song of our own design. My other hand grabs my breast, pulling, twisting, teasing like his tongue did. I increase my speed and my hips arch slightly with need.

Through heavy lids I notice movement and I pull my hands from my body instantly. A cold sweat overcomes me, trying to douse the heat that had been building. Luckily, it's not extinguished as my gaze quickly focuses on the man floating in the entry to my balcony.

There he is. In all his glory. I relax.

Ilryth looks at me as though he wishes to devour me whole. Consume me one delicious bite at a time. Wordlessly, he glides over and perches himself next to me.

"Don't let me interrupt." His voice is silk and his hand rests on top of mine between my legs. His other hand slips behind my neck, holding my head as he kisses me slowly. Each gliding of our lips takes me to the edge of all reason.

Something as simple as a kiss has never felt so delightful. So forbidden yet desperately needed. He breaks away just as I try to enter his mouth with my tongue. Shifting, he presses his temple to mine; the words he utters feel as if they are whispered in my ear. "I told you once that I would like to worship at the altar of your hips. Do you remember?"

"I do," I say. He hesitates, searching my expression. "It was on the beach, the first time we went," I add, to prove it to him that I do, indeed, remember. He's trying to see if the woman he made these memories with is still here. Despite all else that I have become, and so much that I am not, by now.

"Yes. So, tonight I have come to show my dutifulness to you."

A flush rises up my body, though not from embarrassment. He continues to kiss my face and neck as our hands begin to move again. Ilryth pulls away slightly and I lock eyes with him. I want him to watch as I reach the pinnacles of pleasure. Every gentle caress and twist of my fingers feels all the better with the pressure of his hand over mine.

His lips reach my chest. He pulls aside the meager scrap of fabric with his teeth and encircles the peak of my breast. My back arches off the bed, leaning toward him, yearning for him. For more.

My thoughts are a hazy blur, but pleasant. I focus on nothing but him and this feeling of his body next to mine.

I release my breast to touch his face when he pulls away, shifting to the other. He pauses and looks at me with all the admiration in the world. He looks at me as though he loves me even though I know he could not because we both know our fate. We both know what destiny is waiting for us.

But in that moment, I don't care, and I don't think he does, either. He is here with me. Not because he wants to take something, because I have already given everything that I have left to give. I have given him my body. I have given him my thoughts. I have traded away my life with him. There is nothing more that he has to gain from indulging me. There is no other promise he could be seeking to solicit.

No, I must believe that he is here because he *wants* to be. Nothing more or less. Perfect in its own way. Having always measured myself in the context of what I can give to others—defined my value in terms of what I can offer—the idea of him wanting me with no other ulterior motive is the most attractive thing I have ever known.

And I want him in equal measure. That thought, combined with the sustained movement of his fingers, is enough to push me over the edge, to have my nails dig into his shoulder and my chest press against him as I float off the bed and drift away from my body for several blissful moments.

"I can hear them now," I say as I stare out into the Abyss. The Abyss stares back at me tonight. Waiting. Growing ever more impatient by the week.

"Hear what?" he asks from beside me. He gently caresses my arm, as if he seeks to remind himself that I'm still there.

I wouldn't be anywhere else. There are still two weeks until the summer solstice. I cannot be sent into the Abyss yet. But soon.

"The songs of the dead," I answer.

He's silent for a long moment. I wonder if this information has displeased him. Finally, "What do they sound like?"

"Screams."

The warmth of his arms feels like a long ago, forgotten home. His touch is bliss and comfort. It is not unlike the hymns I sing by day. Ilryth and I sing a different song by night. One that is wholly ours but in harmony with Krokan and Lellia's.

He drags a finger up my collarbone. The touch grows more distant by the night. It reaches the tip of my chin, bringing my face to his. He leans down and kisses me sweetly. Longingly.

I shift, responding to his need with my own. This is the only thing I know in the world—this need of him. This want.

Ilryth pulls away from the kiss, rubbing his nose against mine. We float through the room, weightless, carried on the currents of bliss. "I know, you are resolved...but I cannot help wishing that there was still another way. If I could take your place as the sacrifice, I would."

"You cannot." I smile, somewhat sad...because I can feel the sorrow within him, even if I struggle now to fully comprehend it.

"I know. And—"

"Your Holiness?" another voice interrupts. It's the young woman who has been coming to attend me regularly.

Ilryth releases me and we drift apart as she enters. Her eyes dart between us, disapproving. She says nothing as she paints upon my flesh with song. Then she gives a slight nod of her head and leaves promptly.

"I do not think she likes me any longer." At first, she seemed a bit fond of me. But that's faded.

"Lucia is worried for me, is all." He sighs and runs a hand through his halo of golden hair. "You know how sisters are."

"I do not."

Stillness overtakes him. His wide eyes stare at nothing. The man looks as though he has been stabbed in the gut.

I swim over to him and place my palms on his chest. The contact of his skin fills my mind with notes that burst like bubbles on a summer's day. A symphony of sound and delight.

"Do not look so disappointed...we only have a few days left. Let's enjoy them, together, as we have been," I say, leaning up to kiss him.

Ilryth takes my hands on his chest, holding them, but he pulls his face away. He doesn't allow me to kiss him. His eyes redden slightly. The fins of his tail go limp.

"Why...are you going through with this sacrifice?" The question has a slight tremble to it.

"Because it is my honor to be the offering for Lord Krokan," I say. "The hymn commands it."

"Is there any other reason?" He releases my hands to grab my shoulders. Ilryth's stare is intense. He's desperate for something that I don't know if I can give.

"Why would there need to be another reason?"

His grip slackens some. "Nothing else compels you other than the hymn of the old gods?"

I slowly shake my head. He releases me and his warmth retreats with him. I dash over, trying to catch him. Trying to pull him back to me. I don't want this to end. I don't want to lose him. He's the last thing I have that I know is mine, and the thought dredges up panic that feels like it belongs to a wholly different person.

"Wait, are you leaving?"

"Yes."

"But you…but we…"

"Not tonight." The sad smile has returned. He sees my confusion and leans forward, placing a soft kiss on my forehead. With a sigh, he hunches over me. His thoughts are fraying at the edges. "I cannot lie with a woman who has lost her sense of self."

"I know who I am," I insist. "I am Victoria."

"Where did you live before the Eversea, Victoria?" he asks. I don't have an answer. "Where did you grow up?" Still, no answer. "Who were your parents? Your siblings?"

I pull away slightly to look up at him. Why is he doing this? These questions are filling me with panic. I can feel shadows clawing at the walls of my mind, begging release. Begging for clarity to dawn upon them and bring them back into focus.

"You might know your name, but you've lost all of who you are, and I…"

I hang on the word. I lean closer, as if maybe I can steal one more kiss. I need it desperately.

"I love you," he whispers softly. "I love you too much to kiss you, to have you, if your mind isn't with me."

"I know what I'm doing."

"Yes, but I can't help but wonder if your choices would be different, should you still possess every facet of yourself. I…I don't want this version of you," he admits, and I can hear how painful it is to do so. "I want the woman I fell in love with."

"Ilryth—"

"It's time to let this go. Forget me, Victoria." He leans in and kisses me one last time. It's goodbye.

thirty-nine

I sit on the balcony, singing my song. My body thrums with the words of old gods. Markings upon my flesh shine in the sunlight filtered through rot.

A young woman comes to me with fair hair and sad eyes. She checks my anointing in silence. But, before she leaves, she asks, "Have you seen Ilryth lately? He hasn't been showing up to his meetings as expected."

My brow furrows. "Who?"

forty

THE DAY HAS FINALLY ARRIVED.

The woman with golden hair comes to dress me. Her eyes are sad, but her hands are attentive. She adorns me in finery.

From head to toe, I am painted in the bright splashes and swirls of the old ones. I can hear their music in the lines. Raw power, plucked from the unseen weavings of the world. Remnants from a bygone era that I belong more to now than the present. Even though my physical form hovers in the sea, my soul is already with the old god deep beneath the waves that calls to me endlessly...

Endlessly...

I am given a fresh wrap around my hips. The young woman applies shells over my breasts with a gooey substance that sticks them in place. It's used for other shells and small crystalline rocks that are stuck all over me.

A choker of many stranded necklaces and pearls arcs over my shoulders and around my sides—underneath my arms. My hair is pinned back with needle and spiny shell. She has slathered oil all over me. This substance is not pigmented but it creates an opalescent sheen to my skin. When she is finished, I am complete—a ready and willing sacrifice.

They lead me through the castle, low hymns already humming through the water. The sirens' songs are more muted than the ones I know, than the masterpieces I've been listening to as I've stared out over the Abyss.

We arrive at a cavernous room with sculptures of Lellia

and Krokan. A large dais has been positioned in the center. More of a pedestal, really, as it is a single wide column stretching up halfway through the hall. At its top is the lower half of a large clamshell, filled to the brim with pearls and gemstones.

We swim up and she positions me atop. I settle delicately onto the finery, grateful for the waters of the Eversea and their unique properties that allow me to hover just above the rocks, rather than putting my full weight upon them. It'd be rather sensitive, given how little I wear on my lower half.

"It will begin soon, Your Holiness," the young woman says, and then leaves with the warriors that escorted us in.

I sit quietly, shifting to face the statue of Krokan at one end of the room. Meeting its emerald eyes, I fall into a trancelike state. The room around me fades into nothing.

My attention is called back to the present by movement. A brown-haired man approaches me, warriors encircling him. The latter begins to chant, and sway, as the former begins to draw music across the pedestal in a thick greasepaint. The swirling lines carry music. The song that has been written on my flesh, on my soul, is reaching its crescendo.

More voices fill the cavern. Dozens of singers, all harmonizing together, and I can't help but sway to the rhythm their pulsing words set. My eyelids become heavy. The song seems to envelop me all at once and without warning.

A group of men and women swim in. They each hold a wooden staff with a silver ball of tentacles at one end. For every beat of their song, they wave it through the air, rocking in time with the music. Their clothes are strips of multicolored fabric of all colors and patterns that drift around them like pennons fluttering in the currents. They lead a procession of people that press in to the point of being flush, shoulder to shoulder.

I am overwhelmed by them all. It only takes a moment for the room to feel cramped with bodies and sound. Though perhaps the sensation comes mostly from seeing and feeling all their eyes on me and me alone. They lift their hands in unison as the song reaches its crescendo. It is as if they are reaching out to me. Begging me.

End it, they sing. *Calm our restless god. Quell his rage. Be a worthy exchange for peace.*

With the climax, the song is over and silence floods the room.

The man who drew music around me now swims over me. Layers of silver fabric around his shoulders swirl and coalesce. He addresses the room, turning as he speaks. "Today is the day of the five-year summer solstice. The day that we shall present Lord Krokan his offering as he has demanded. Who has brought us this offering?"

"I have." A man with pale blond hair swims above the rest. The moment I lay eyes on him everything else falls away.

A slow, delicate melody trills in the back of my mind. It's sung by a lone singer, somewhere deep in my soul. A song that's just for me…

And for him.

Who is he?

"Duke of Spears, tell us of your offering."

"Victoria is a woman of esteemed character. A woman who has sacrificed much to be here. Who has sworn to me with her life, with all she is, that she will bring peace to Lord Krokan's rage." As he speaks, every pulse of my heart tries to pull me closer to him. It begs me to leave where I sit and swim to him. Hold him…

Strange.

"As my father foretold," the first man with the brown hair begins again, "when he communed with the old god: *Krokan wants a woman, rich with life, and the hands of Lellia, to descend into the Abyss, only every five years.*"

Thumping fills the room as wooden spears are struck against the roots that line the walls in response to the man's proclamation.

"Today is the day of send-off, the day we will impart our songs and our wishes upon the offering for her to carry to the ears of our Lord Krokan. We invite you to bestow your blessings upon her. To finish her anointing. And to reaffirm your faith in the old gods to whom we owe our lives, and our deaths."

The men swim away, leaving me alone in the center of the room. I am a slab of meat, offered up for carving. Everyone stares at me with hungry eyes and desperate gazes.

Singing starts again, a low humming in the background. As though everyone is murmuring softly all at once. There are no words, no intrinsic meaning this time, so far as I can discern. I am so focused on trying to decipher the song that I do not realize someone is approaching me until they are at the pedestal.

It is a young man, no older than seventeen. He bows his head and clasps his hands above his chest in prayer. The siren lets out a long and lonely song. In this hymn, I can hear words:

"Guide my mother to her rest. Care for my brother who followed her, succumbed to the rot. May the seas be calmed and purified. May the Eversea become an ocean that can be home to joy and peace." When he has finished, he holds his hand before me. A single dot appears on my shoulder that encompasses his whole song, then he eases away.

The next one to approach is a young woman. Just like the young man that came before her, she clasps her fingers in front of herself and bows her head before she begins to sing.

"May our fields be blessed with warm, clean tides. May the wraiths not haunt our shores. May the rage in your heart, Lord Krokan, finally calm."

Her markings appear on me as a different color—on the backs of my hands. When she meets my eyes a final time, I hold her gaze. There's something almost familiar about her...

She releases me and the next person approaches.

The sirens and their private songs, sung only for me, are seemingly endless. One after another, they come before me. They sing their desperate verses tinged with sorrow and longing. Their touch hovers above me, and with a single finger they bestow the weight of all their hopes on my shoulders.

It is crushing.

They all are desperately awaiting—begging for—the day when they hear those sweet words, *It's all right, you don't have to worry any longer. You are safe.*

I want to tell them as much. What little hope I can wring from these tired bones of mine, I want to give. I begin to quietly hum in response to them as they sing. Then I begin to sing louder, with them. I don't say any words, nor do I try and imbue any intent. This is their moment. I do not wish to take it away from them. Rather, I want to harmonize in solidarity. The only thing I would wish to say, if I said anything at all, would be, *I hear you. I see you.*

The hours drag on. One after another they come to me. I am painted over, and over, and over again by their voices. My body feels as though it has truly vanished into every blur of color and sound. Any discomfort I could have felt at all the strangers touching me leaves with my physical awareness.

There is just our solemn song. This prayer we share.

My send-off.

And then all at once, the room is quiet. My body returns to me slowly. I blink up at the ceiling, at the ghostly trees that stretch down toward me like the hands of Lellia herself, reaching out to embrace her living children. My chin follows the movement of my eyes, dropping. I don't remember tilting my head back in song. Nor do I remember this man with the strange melody that thrums in time with his heart as he approaches.

But now he hovers before me. One steady look from him and the world comes crashing back to me.

I want again. I feel again. The memory of *him* lingers on me, grounding me here in this place. Just as they all warned it would. He is my tether to this world and will always be. I know that immutable truth in my soul.

But instead of causing strife, it cements my conviction. He has become the single representation of everything I still have to fight for. I might not remember every man or woman who came before me and sang. But I will remember *him*. Even in the farthest reaches of the Abyss, where the sunlight has never touched, when all else fades away...there will be the light he has placed in my heart. The happiness and joy I had long since written off ever feeling again.

But what is his name? The question burns my mind as he sings for me, for what I know will be the final time. He reaches out and drags a finger through the water, drawing on my body without touching. He does the same with his left hand. And then his right again. And again. And again.

The song starts out soft and lonely, just as it always has been. But I can finally hear words in it.

I hear the story of a boy trying to be worthy of the title that has befallen him. Of a people he fears for. The grief of seeing his home... and his mother...fading away.

His story shifts into the present, and his voice shifts with it. There are trills of happiness, of sustained notes. He has met someone in this tale that he weaves with sound and there has never been a happier voice. A more joyous refrain. I don't know if he sings only for my ears, but I am too enthralled to worry about the rest of them.

Sing for me, my heart says. *One last time, sing for me.*

Sing for me, he seems to echo, just as he had all those months ago. And so I do.

I raise my voice in tandem with his. He extends his hands to me and I take them, trembling slightly. We swim above the gathered sirens, up through an opening in the ceiling that was obscured by the anamnesis trees. The rest of them follow behind; I sense as much as hear them as they join our song. But the only voice that matters to me is this man's.

He holds our hands between us, propelling us upward by the might of his tail. His eyes are locked with mine, as steady as he has always been. As if to say to me, *do not be afraid,* with a look alone.

I am afraid, I wish I could tell him. But I am not afraid for myself. I am afraid for him. For what will follow my departure from this realm.

We emerge into the open sea, out through the top of a large chimney of coral, growing organically from the castle beneath us. A large, unfinished archway, like a bridge cut in two, extends out from this chimney; it is a construction that would be impossible to support above water. I can see it for what it is: a long plank stretching to the Abyss.

My final swim.

The man with the sad eyes takes me to the very end of it, our hands still interwoven. The rest of the sirens pour out into the open sea, like bats from a cave at dusk, to bear witness. But they do not scatter or approach; instead, they all hover and watch from a distance. A chorus of four assumes their place halfway down the broken arch, at the midpoint between us and the rest of the sirens.

The song slows, all the voices fade away. His is the last to remain. Though even it fades as he releases my hands.

Don't go, I wish I could say. *Don't leave me.*

He gave me so much, and in the end all I could want is more. Memories return, as brief and hazy as the flickering of lanternlight on a ship wall. One more day to look into his eyes. One more night of kisses, of falling asleep in his arms. One more moment of passion that would make me feel more alive as a construct of ancient power than I ever did as a woman of true flesh and blood.

There is no sound now. The sea is unnaturally still, as if it is holding its breath, waiting.

"Ilryth," I whisper.

His eyes widen. He sees me seeing him. My knowing. My hands grab for his again, trembling like the dam that's been constructed in my mind, trying futilely to block me out.

"Ilryth," I say with more confidence. "I—"

"The moon rises!" Ventris sings with a shout. A roar that threatens to split the sea in two is his response.

The sea floor rumbles, waves churn, spiraling down in a vortex of red rot and death. Every drawing on my skin condenses. The ink vibrates as if trying to tear me into pieces. Thousands of songs, overlaid on top of each other, in dissonance with thousands of screams coming from deep below. I can hear all of them, every broken and terrified word—the sirens depending on me and the souls waiting for me.

I cling to Ilryth. To this man whom I can hardly remember anything about and yet know with all I am. But it's too late. It's all crumbling.

"Victoria." My name is a whisper from his mind to mine—said like a promise that all we had, every glimpse I can remember and all I cannot, was real.

"I love you," I say as I am ripped from the world of the living and pulled down, down, and farther down into the Abyss of death from which there is no return.

forty-one

I AM PULLED DOWN AT AN IMPOSSIBLE SPEED. Skin and muscle are ripped from bone. Color and light mixes with sound, with flesh and magic. The weight of the sea crushes me to dust.

And yet, I persist.

Fear is ripped from me. My worries and pain go with it. Even errant thoughts drift away. It is as if every last scrap of what I was is being torn from my soul. Scattered among the nighttime sea and swirling rot.

I'm not sure what's left. Who I am now. *What* I am now.

All I know is I am not dead. Yet again, I have been forcefully pulled from one realm to the next and my eyes do not shut for a final time. My lingering consciousness is as persistent as the song that still envelops me. Some part of me still lives.

This is Death's secret, the great mystery of the old god hidden in the hymns: There is no end. Not really. We continue past the point of oblivion. Where one world stops, another begins. At the end of every exhale is a new breath.

Death is not a finality, but an irrevocable change. It is a continuation, but past the point of no return. A truth that cannot be seen until you are undergoing the metamorphosis.

The distant singing of the sirens becomes a pulsing in the back of my mind. Their grief and pain brews a storm, howling beneath the waves. The waters turn violent and I am thrown about carelessly. It is as though they resent me for the misfortune that has befallen them. They want to tear me apart so there is more of me to offer. Pull me in different directions. Their lines become sharp—bladelike—and I am undone.

But I do not fight it. I keep my consciousness rooted in the single, dissonant song that continues to thrum in my heart. Ilryth's voice continues to reach me. Persistent. Reminding me that all of them are depending on me—that *he* is. I cannot forget that one mission and goal.

I won't fight this fate. I know I am helpless to it. Every forgotten choice that brought me here. Every step I took that I can no longer recall.

My descent slows the moment I give myself to it. I relax back into the swirling sea with a sigh. There is song around me, but none louder than the song in me.

I love you.

He—Ilryth—told me that. And I loved him back. I do not know why but I do not have to because it rings as truth within me.

I continue to drift like one of the silvery leaves of the Lifetree, falling on the sea breezes to the frothy waves. My momentum slows. And I tilt. No longer am I falling on my back, but my feet are beneath me.

The swirling waves and rot condense into shapes. Mountains and valleys—a whole other world—lined with steaming vents and glowing lava extend as far as the eye can see in the very pit of the world. The underwater landscape fades away as I descend farther, submerged into a cloak of eternal night.

My feet lightly touch down onto an icy, rocky earth. As my eyes adjust to the odd light, details come into focus. It feels like what was day has become night. What was dark is now light. Everything has been reversed and it takes my mind time to adjust.

In the distance, there is the faintest glimmer of silver. It feels like an invitation, though I don't expect I can count on anything to be as it seems. The Eversea was magical, unique, and different from the Natural World. But it was also familiar, in its own way. There were laws of mortal and nature that persisted. This place truly feels…otherworldly.

I push off with my toes, expecting to be propelled through the water as I have been until now, but I do not glide upward. Instead, I stumble and fall. My jaw smarts with pain from where it cracked against the rocky earth and I rub it, pushing myself onto my knees. My hair still drifts around me, unruly, defying gravity as it would in the Eversea. But it seems that whatever substance surrounds me is not water. At least not any water I can recall ever knowing.

And I can still feel pain. I pull my hand away from my chin. There is no blood. I appear to still be stuck between life and death, human and something...more.

I walk.

The silvery light I saw cutting through the gloom is an anamnesis. Small and frail, flickering, as though it is a candle flame about to go out.

I come to a stop before the small tree and find myself compelled to touch it. I reach out a hand, running my fingertips along the silvery leaves.

The moment I come into contact with it, I find myself overcome with a song that dulls my other senses. This is a new song—one I do not understand the words of, but can clearly comprehend. Light blooms within; no longer is there a perpetual night pressing down upon me.

Just like the markings upon my body, the anamnesis is a physical manifestation of music. The song trapped within its ghostly form tells a story. Or tries to. The events of the tale do not follow a logical order. The beginning occurs in conjunction with the end. The middle is strewn throughout, making it challenging to get a sense of what is real, what is emotion, and what are fragmented memories of something far beyond me—memories that are trapped within the Lifetree itself. *This must be Lellia's song.*

I see a young world, occupied with spirits of light and darkness, nature and destruction, life and death. A garden so large that it could be the whole of the known world. Peoples, held in the warm embrace of the eternal.

There were no lines here. No barriers. No living or dead. Oneness.

An elf. The first of his kind. A king.

He parlays for a world with more order. A tidier world. They comply.

The song shifts, pitching into the highest registers of notes. It's filled with longing as the shapes of gods vanish. They're leaving...

The song fades and, with it, the visions. I ease my hand away. The tree shines brightly, branches trembling, new leaves budding, as though it is surging one last time with power. Like a brilliant star, it extinguishes after that final act of beauty. It unravels into silvery strands that dissipate into the water and are carried by a current through the darkness, before they condense again and ignite on a different rocky pedestal in the distance.

The song grows once more as I near the second anamnesis, and so, too, do the visions.

The dryads, carved in her image. The sirens, made for Krokan. The elves. The fae. Vampir and lykin. More in the skies and more on the land. The world is full and so too are the notes. Sung with full-bellied joy.

Once more, the anamnesis fades and the silver dust from it speeds away, guiding me along. I follow the motes like breadcrumbs through the Abyss. Each has a song that gives me another piece of Lellia. Another morsel of insight into the trapped goddess.

I hear her sorrow and feel her pain during the magic wars. Her song wavers with visions of seclusion. Of winters that seemed unending. Of a pain that could not be lessened by a mere Elf King and Human Queen.

My path through the darkness is unhindered. There is no longer the screaming of souls or relentless song the sirens imparted upon me before my departure. There is no movement at the edge of my vision. The water—or perhaps *ether* is a better word for the substance I am suspended within—is calm and quiet. I feel…*safe* here, oddly enough.

The anamneses continue to sing me their songs and guide me out of the fog of night to an underwater river of molten rock. A stone boat is moored, tethered, as though someone knew I would be coming. My hands close around its bow. My toes dig into the rocky sand as I push.

I've done this before.

When…?

The vessel is free and I leap into it with confidence. My feet were never at risk of touching the lava. It's like I've done this a thousand times.

Drifting away from the shoreline, I begin to paddle with an oar made of what feels like bone. I don't have to apply much effort as the river has a strong current and for the most part I can just sit back and watch this strange, slowly illuminating world drift by me. I can't see much, but what I can see are the withered carcasses of the massive roots of the Lifetree. They are wrinkled and shriveled. Spindly things compared to the massive structures up among the sirens or even in the Gray Trench.

Dotted among them are the bony remains of Lord Krokan's emissaries, nestled in forgotten graves.

Soon, roots and bones turn to nothing but dust. Consumed by the same rot that is eating away at the goddess.

A faint haze grows in the distance, a pale fog that is reminiscent of a distant light. As the haze coalesces, I finally begin to see movement on the banks of the river. Silhouettes stumble forward. At first, I think I cannot make out their details because they are too far, or the fog is too thick, but then, some come up to the water's edge.

They are living shadows, voids condensed into the outlines of what were once human. No, not just human—there are others among them. Some hover with the tails of sirens. Others have points, jutting out from the sides of their heads. Some have wings and others horns. There are men, women, beasts, and creatures I do not recognize. While I cannot see their eyes, I know they are all looking upon me.

We have been waiting for you, their silence seems to say.

I know, my heart sings with a sigh in reply.

The boat comes to a stop, grinding up on a rocky shore. It's hard to tell how long I rode upon it; time is as ephemeral as the images that pass before me. There a moment, gone the next. Even though the river turns and carries on through the barren, mysterious landscape, this is where the current took me—where the boat stopped. The message seems clear. So this is where I disembark.

I hesitate a moment. The spirits still linger, barely visible to the fog. But well within the realm of my perception, because I feel them more than I see them. I wait to see if any will approach but when none do, I begin to walk.

They part for me. None of them get in my way. A few begin to walk with me. I find their presence oddly comforting, rather than uneasy. We begin to descend into a deep valley. I know who I will find waiting for me at the deepest point of the Abyss. I can already begin to see snakelike tentacles writhing in the distance.

I scramble down over rock, and leap across chasms. I am nearly to the bottom when an oddity catches my eye. Granted, this whole world is quite strange…but this is something—*someone*—out of place and wholly unlike the rest.

A soul in the distance still has a silvery outline that encompasses the faint remembrance of color and shape. He climbs up the rock, slowly determined to get away from death's Abyss. Every movement seems to hurt him. His edges fray, as if invisible hands are trying to drag him back.

Farther up, I see the makings of the start of a deep trench. He's scrambling to get up there. Though I can't comprehend why. I glance between the man fighting to escape and the swirling shadows deep below, deciding he is not my concern.

I continue to descend through the gloom and shadow and rot. Deep underneath the waves, a current picks up and pulls on me. It tugs me in one direction and then another. When I heed its wishes, there is a soft whispering in the recesses of my mind that grows stronger as I no doubt get closer to Krokan. If I move in the wrong direction, the whisper-singing becomes fainter. It is like a child's game with life and death and the fate of an entire world in the balance.

In the distance, there is a silvery outline of an anamnesis that I recognize instantly. Once more, I am directed by Lellia. Life carries me to death.

I continue, past the anamnesis and the last scrap of light it offers. There is truly nothing now. The sea has become a cold, *cold* void. Nothing but smooth rock and sand beneath me. Nothing above or around me.

Fear tries its hand at me, but I refuse to let it take hold of my resolution. Instead, I hum to pass the time as I continue walking. It turns to singing, as if I can fill the emptiness around me with my voice.

Rather than singing the words inked on my flesh, I sing something else. It's that same song that's tied up with the name "Ilryth" and "love." I have the sense that I've heard this song countless times. That it has somehow been my life's great work. The thing I know deep within me, despite all odds, was right. A great "yes" in a life full of "no" and false starts.

Minutes seem like hours that extend into days. Time is condensed under the weight of all this water. Yet, in what also somehow seems like a blink, I've arrived.

forty-two

I KNOW I'VE MADE IT THE MOMENT A NEW SONG COURSES THROUGH MY MIND. There are no words to the lyrics and yet, I can understand them as clearly as if someone had sat me down and asked me a question outright.

"Who are you?" the mighty voice demands through its dissonant and yet also harmonious song. A brief pause and then, "You are not my love."

"I am not Lellia." Though now I wonder if the markings made on me—the ones that seem to be able to summon and gain protection—are to mark me as her. That way I can be guided by the anamneses that surround him. Cross through Krokan's guard to reach his audience. "But I am here to serve you. To be sacrificed to you so that you might find peace."

"Then they have failed once more." I cannot see Krokan in the perpetual night and shadow that is alive here.

"Tell me, how have they failed?" I dare to ask. *You* have failed, a quiet voice tries to taunt me. Despite all else, and all my efforts. I am somehow not enough.

There's a flash of green. Movement all at once. I am surrounded by a thousand writhing tentacles that condense from the currents and shadows. They cage me in place with his anger and rage, blocking all exits. A mirror to the roots of the Lifetree. "There is not much time left before the Blood Moon rises and the barriers between worlds will be at their thinnest."

The old god finally emerges from the darkness. He is of

incomprehensible size—a mountain of a creature—with eyes of green, the same shade as the rare flash that happens when the crest of the sun dips beneath the horizon of the sea at sunset.

"But perhaps you will be a worthy vessel." The tentacles close around me, agitated and angry. "Give her to me. Take her into you, human, her dear and yet so fragile child."

The old god writhes. Tentacles thump against the sea floor with such force that it creates cracks in the rocks under me. The world itself seems to quiver. To the beat of his own making, Lord Krokan begins to sing. My mind, empty of myself, yet full with the hymns of the old gods, comprehends the meaning, if not the literal words.

He sings to the distant sky he has not seen since those early, primordial days of gods, mortals, and beasts. He speaks of loneliness and longing. Of waiting for thousands of years for someone that was promised.

The words are low and slow, sung by a thousand unified voices. When Krokan sings, every spirit and creature of the depths pauses to join him. They are calling…calling…

I was called once.

I blink, staring up at the silvery light that is beginning to collect in the water, spinning down. Krokan continues to hold me in place, slowly hoisting me. As though I am a thing to be presented—a sacrifice for a second time.

Take this vessel, his song says. *Take her as your own.*

Lellia. My eyes flutter closed. My heart sings with him. So much pain and hurt. For what? Why? The Abyss was made not from turmoil or from trauma that scarred the earth long ago. But from the ocean of tears Krokan wept for his lady wife.

For his goddess. Gone.

At the edges of my consciousness, I can hear her trembling words. Unlike the essence trapped in the memories of the anamnesis, which was mostly clear—strong enough—these words are frail. Like a warbling dove with a broken wing.

It's all right, I try to sing in reply. *I don't understand, but it's all right. Take me. Make me.*

No is the response.

My eyes snap open at the reply. The moment they do, the silvery light and power that had been gathering around my form explodes into starlight on the dark sea. Krokan's tentacles unravel and I am sent, once more, plummeting down. Though I do not land violently, but with a sigh.

The last of Lellia's song leaves me.

"You...were not enough to free her." Krokan begins to retreat.

"Wait—wait!" I scramble to my feet. To run after him, even though I feel like the distance might be unfathomably large. "You cannot run from me." There is no response, just the sense of the old god retreating farther and farther away. "I have given you everything—my life, my bones, my memories!"

"And we gave this world our essence!" Krokan roars, returning in force. The thrumming in my skull has returned. He speaks with a thousand voices in song. A thousand languages, spoken and unspoken, condensed together in a cacophony of sound. "We gave all so that you and your kind might not just survive, but thrive. Do not speak to me, human, of sacrifice."

"And that is why you demand sacrifices of your own? As payment for all you gave? Retribution?" I plant my feet, staring up at the old god without a trace of fear. What more can he take from me? There is nothing more that I haven't already lost or given.

"*I* do not demand sacrifices. I do not know by which perversion the people who once so loved and revered me have demanded such."

I...I don't know either. I try to sift through the recesses of my mind for an explanation. But it is lost. I cannot recall who I am, what I know and what I've seen, while also comprehending an old god.

"The only use I had of you was to see if you could host the spirit of my lady and thus free her. But a mortal form could never be a substitute, even anointed as you are."

The moment that Krokan goes to pull away, there is a shift in the old god's demeanor. His attention diverts. A voice so beautiful it pricks tears into my eyes cuts through the still waters. My lids flutter and my body relaxes.

I know this voice... It beckons and calls. Begging for...me.

At first, I cannot tell if this sound is merely some memory pulled from the recesses of my mind during the final moments of existence. But as the voice grows louder I know my senses don't deceive me. The tentacles shift and part for a beacon of shining, radiant, silver light in the shape of a siren man with platinum blond hair, and brown eyes that hold amber within them.

forty-three

ILRYTH.

I know this man. With all my heart and soul and body. I have wondered about him, resented him, resisted him, and revered him. I have tried to keep all I am from falling into his hands only to delight in giving him everything.

His eyes lock with mine. He sings for me. With every word, my memory returns. Every verse is one I can sing along to and its familiarity begs more of what I know in my bones. This is the song he sang that night in the sea when I first gave myself to him. It is the melody he braved leaving the Eversea to use as my lullaby—soothing me, giving power to me, protecting me. This is the song he sang to me, *for me*...the song that became ours.

My voice joins his. We rise, higher and higher in notes. Every sound is a symphony of two. Our whole selves are poured into the music. For once, for always, we don't hold ourselves back. We give each other everything and it is more than the union of flesh on a beach, or minds on a balcony.

When the last note fades and we are breathless, and the world is still, there is nothing but each other.

I blink, trying to make sense of what is before me. The haze of our song is fading and, with it, my mind is almost painfully full. Names, places, people, and events all return in force.

The sounds of my ship creaking and my crew buzzing about it with words and heavy steps. I can feel Emily's hair—

my sister's hair—as I clutch her tightly before sailing off again, every time treated like the last. The scent of my father's cologne, applied a little too thick, yet still pleasant, makes me almost want to sneeze. The smooth caress of the silks Mother traded in...

Memories, all of them, return to me. Even the ones I chose to rid myself of—the ones I was so ready to part with. Charles...I can imagine every line of his face, carved by the relentless sea and the cruelty of his own heart. Every freckle and birthmark that once formed constellations of desire, then pain and fear. But now, looking back at him, he is not the monster I remember, but a tired, bitter man. He elicits no fondness or pity...or fear.

I do not look back upon him and feel as if I need to expunge him from my memory. He might always be a part of my story that I do not wish to linger on. But he is little more than a chapter. Started, ended, and no longer relevant. So brief in the grand scheme of things that, from where I stand now, it seems almost comical to make him out to be more. There is no more hatred, fear, resentment, or regret surrounding him. Toward Charles there is...nothing. A cool indifference.

But the man who hovers in the ether of the Abyss, at the upper edge of this forgotten, godly place? He is everything. My heart. A future that I can hardly imagine.

Oh, Ilryth... How, *how* is he here?

Silver light has been woven around him with lines and dots inked upon his flesh, coating it in its entirety. He looks in every measure my mirror. I wonder, if we were to stand opposite each other, if our markings would line up as a perfect match.

Even now, here, throughout it all, he remains. The song we never meant to sing won't die. I can't believe my eyes—don't want to, more like. What does this mean for his well-being?

My stomach knots. I move toward him and away from Krokan. Drawn despite all odds and everything that I know better.

"Why are you here? You can't be...*shouldn't* be." Those two words continue to define us. The sight of him is ripping me apart. It is trying to pull me back to the upper sea, where life still thrives. Though, not for much longer, since I have failed so magnificently in my oath to quell Lord Krokan's rage.

"You know why I'm here," Ilryth says calmly, eyes locked with mine. I hear his song almost purring in the back of my mind.

"No," I say instantly. I know what those markings mean. Even if he shouldn't be able to wear them. It should be impossible. *I am the sacrifice.* Unless...the moment I was thrown into the Abyss was the moment a new offering could be marked. "I won't allow you to sacrifice yourself."

His brows shoot up. He tilts his head slightly then gives it a small shake with a gentle smile. I finally reach him. I feel as though I've crossed the world to get to him, but I'm finally here. I can touch him. Our hands clasp around each other's and I nearly choke from emotion.

"Victoria, I'm not here to sacrifice myself," he says gently. "I'm here to bring you back."

"But..."

He twists to face Krokan. The old god seems amused by this turn of events. At least so far as I can tell from the wriggling of his tentacles and the gleam in his emerald eyes. His rage has dissipated...at least for now.

"I have come before you, Your Greatness, to ask for you to return this woman to me. If she cannot quell your rage, then permit her to stay with me in the Eversea until the end of our natural days when we will come to you again, as willing offerings."

"She has been marked for me. A promise has been made by your people—an oath. Such things are not so easily broken."

Don't I know it? I've paid and paid for broken oaths. And...I'm so tired of the cost.

"Weren't you going to cast me aside?" I take a half step toward Krokan. The old god bristles, tentacles tensing briefly. "You said I was not worthy. That I was a failure of an offering. If I was so terrible, then let me go."

Ilryth weaves his fingers with mine. "I am here to change what we must, to change fate itself. Lord Krokan, I would like to propose we come to a different arrangement. As I am sure you can see, we will stop at nothing to be together. Your storms have grown worse, the rot thicker. It is clear she is worth more to me than to you. Give her back, I beg of you."

"Tell me what she is worth to you," Krokan demands.

Ilryth nods. He stretches out his arms as if he's trying to hold the whole world in his reach. Instead, he fills the entirety of the Abyss with sound. The notes, shapeless and as flowing as the sea, radiate off him as strands of pure light that break free of his glow. They drift through the ether that surrounds us, curling, splitting, changing shape. I recognize them as a variance of the marks on my skin and his. This is how the language of the gods was born. From this ether where all life crawled from, and where all will return.

The song is a variant of what Ilryth sang at my send-off but I can truly hear it now in all its meaning and glory. It tells the same story of our love, but holds nothing back. It isn't curated or curbed for any reason. It is raw and powerful. He beats his chest with his fist. He pleads and begs through music.

It makes my soul feel so light that my feet barely touch the ground. He wants me, truly and completely. *He wants me.* I never thought it could feel so good to be wanted again. That it could ever happen. Even if Ilryth's plea doesn't work, this moment is more than enough to give me peace for the rest of eternity.

But I wonder if it will be enough for Krokan to agree to Ilryth's proposal. The old god has gone still, listening. He sways slightly with the rhythm of Ilryth's words.

Ilryth falls to his knees before the divine being, holding one last, sustained note, and then is silent.

If I had breath to breathe, I would be holding it. Ilryth doesn't move. We are both trapped in the stasis of awaiting judgment. I do not expect my lover's plea to work, but then Krokan turns to me.

"And what of you? What is your song?"

"My song?"

"Yes, he has so eloquently laid himself bare. But we wish to know, are his affections one-sided? Do you feel as he does?"

As he does… The words repeat in my head. I heard his song now, and when I left the mortal world. I know what every sound meant, and yet I still doubt. I still question what I felt—what he feels.

This is all so fast, so sudden, so soon. I feel as though I have known Ilryth for my entire life, and yet not at all. We only existed as we were because we *couldn't* exist. We shouldn't be together and so, when we were, there was no fear, or doubt, because there were no expectations.

There didn't have to be a future. Or the questions of whether we could work. Everything could be a dream, rather than the concerns of a practical reality.

And yet...I want to find out. I want to know what our possibilities could be.

That is where my song begins: With the end. With the here and now. With wondering what we could be if we were given the chance, if the world was designed a little differently.

My song is as slow as I wish Ilryth and I could've taken our relationship. It is as delicate as the mending pieces of my heart. I never allowed myself to wonder what could be next. I never thought there might be love for me again someday. I wasn't supposed to feel these emotions in the aftermath of heartbreak.

All of this was supposed to be simple. I was supposed to selfishly live to my fullest during the five years I was granted and then die without much thought. But none of it happened the way I thought. I lived for my family and for my crew as much as—if not more than—myself. My death wasn't quick and thoughtless. It has become a bundle of complexities that I wasn't supposed to hold and don't want to let go of.

I find the notes as I go and pour myself into every single one. When I'm finished, I am on my knees next to Ilryth. Krokan is still.

"You have moved me, mortals. But perhaps, more importantly, you have moved my bride." Lord Krokan's eyes go dim, as though he's closing them, communing with his entrapped partner high above the waves. I think back to when Ilryth took me to the beach, to when I imagined Lellia looking down on us from her wooden prison and thinking to herself that finally an offering had honored her and Krokan correctly.

Not with sacrifice and estrangement...but with love.

"I shall give you one final chance," the old god decrees. "You shall return to the surface and have your opportunity together. But how long that opportunity lasts will ultimately be up to you."

Ilryth flashes me a look of disbelief, a relieved smile that stretches across his cheeks. He thinks we have won. But I am far too experienced in negotiations such as this to think that it will be so simple.

"What must we do to ensure the opportunity lasts as long as possible?" I ask outright.

"To understand what we will demand of you, you must first understand the ancient truths of how this world came to be..."

forty-four

LORD KROKAN SPINS A TALE. Much like the anamnesis that guided me here, the story is not words but an ancient song that paints a picture in my mind that's so vivid it's like I'm living every moment—like the memories are my own. However, unlike the wavering anamnesis, Krokan's hymns are strong and even. Where Lellia's memories are splintered and faded, Krokan's are a portrayal that's as clear as daylight.

The world is young.

All the old gods are present in their might. Even through the eyes of Krokan, the beings are beyond the realm of my comprehension. They are both large and small. Infinite and finite. But, through his words, I feel as if I know them. We are kin.

Among these eternal beings are offshoots, spirits that structure the world—from water to fire and air. They walk with mortals, the latest exploration in divine carving.

The Veil is erected.

Lellia refuses to leave. Her people are here—her mortal children. They need Krokan as well. For Death is much a partner to Life. He will not leave her, cannot. He will not leave them.

So the two gods stay, right on the edge of the Veil from which their kind depart. Krokan ushering the souls of those lost to the Beyond. Lellia seeing to safeguarding the budding new life of the realm she helped make. And, for a time, it is peaceful.

Warmth floods me with the making of the early sirens. Creatures strong enough to touch the depths of her beloved. Their cousins, creatures of the land, the dryads. More. So much more.

Time passes. Both impossibly fast and slow. I see the centuries as a mortal that are mere blinks as a divine, otherworldly creature.

The first peoples die and Krokan ushers them away. Their children die. And their children. The cycle is unbroken and effortless. But it also begins to put distance between those alive and their divine caretakers. Their stories fade, lost. Every generation is less and less able to stand before the old ones—to comprehend them.

The magic wars begin.

Humans are hunted. Lellia bleeds for them—kin fighting kin. She can no longer find the right words to communicate with her children. They cannot—or will not—listen to her begging for peace.

The Fade is erected.

A heartbreak with all the ferocity of an earthquake that can rattle the foundations of the world. A song that is more akin to screaming. Pain that is only lessened some by a Human Queen returning to the world where Lellia resides. With her hands, a tree is planted at the base of Lellia's altar. A home for her heartbreak. For a weary goddess whose children no longer sing to her as they once did. For a goddess whose voice has become frail and tired. She retreats into the tree, if only for a moment, to nurse her wounded heart.

The roots grow ever deeper.

She sinks into the earth. Into the rock of a mortal world. It anchors life and nature and magic. But her own strength begins to wither.

Come with me, my love, Krokan begs. *This is no longer a place for us.*

They still need me. A little bit longer, she replies. Fainter, and fainter, each time more than the last.

Their duet continues. He sings for her up from the darkness. Yearning for light. Yearning for her. Krokan sings with all the voices who have come before and Lellia responds with all the voices of those yet to come.

But it grows weaker and weaker. Fainter.

Soon, the duet is a solo.

Come with me, my love, Krokan begs. *There is little time left.*

There is no reply.

The song fades. My chest is tight and throat is raw. My eyes prickle. Three millennia of longing. Of service to people who can't remember, or comprehend their words any longer.

Next to me, Ilryth doubles over, one hand covering his mouth, the other clutching at his breast as if he could rip out his heart. I throw my arms around him, alleviating the spine-breaking burden of loneliness with our touch. He lets out a long, sorrowful note. One I can't help but echo.

The song we sing has shifted. It is still our own, but forever changed with the burden of what we have seen. With what we now know.

"I was wrong," I rasp. "I was wrong, about you. About it all. I had thought you were perhaps enemies. I thought that you kept her captive. But she was the one who *chose* to stay, even knowing what it might mean for her to continue pouring her power into this world... All you wanted was to free her and return to your kin—to save her." I straighten to look at Krokan. His emerald eyes shine in response.

There is good love out there. True love. Love that will go to the highest mountain or to the depths of the deepest sea. I know it before me and know it beside me.

"How do we fix it?" I ask as Ilryth collects his composure.

"No one knows of this on the surface," Ilryth says weakly. "We had no idea."

"Because you no longer listened," Krokan says with an almost thunderous growl. "When she screamed, you did not listen. When she whispered, you turned your backs."

"It was not our intent!" Ilryth pleads for the old god to understand.

"Your kind continued to demand more, more and *more*, magic and life your world sapped until there was nothing left of her!"

"How do we fix it?" I cut through the two men with my own ferocity. "It doesn't matter any longer how we got here. Fighting over the past won't help her. What do we do now?"

Krokan stills, his emerald gaze swinging back to me and turning more thoughtful, though still intense.

"Within three years, the Blood Moon will rise, and with it the last chance to bring Lellia back to the realms of the eternal. You must free her before this happens. For after, the Veil will thicken once more; it will be impossible for ones such as us to cross, then. We must leave during this time of thinning, no later than the night of the Blood Moon, for after we shall be trapped in this realm for another five hundred years. A length of time my beloved will not survive again."

And with the sirens sending an offering only once every five years... there will not be any other to come to the Abyss after me, and Ilryth. We are her last chance.

"She will not survive..." I echo, paying close attention to his choice of words. "Why? What is hurting her?"

Krokan shifts, giving life to the waters around us. "She, like myself, was not made to be in this world when the time of mortals came—when the Veil closed us off to the primordial essence of the cosmos. Our brethren left long, long ago but she wished to remain, to look after the fledgling life that was here.

"I stayed with her, caring for her, watching after her and her creations as much as I have been able. I crossed the Veil and brought back power from our kind on the other side... But this could only sustain her for so long.

"The first Elf King promised that once our powers were anchored into this world, a new keeper would be appointed from among his worthy mortals to oversee the anchor of life in this world that her tree has become, so that we might leave. But there are none. There never have been. Now she is withering and dying; my lady will not survive many more decades." His pain and anguish split through my skull, rippling. I try to hide my wince.

"Is there a way to fortify her?" Ilryth asks. He's also struggling to speak. Our minds weren't built for this. It is no doubt due to the protection of the anointing—and perhaps Krokan's will—that our consciousness has not shattered.

The tentacles close further around us, agitated and angry. "Do you presume to think that you might find a solution for a divine problem that I could not, mortals? That you hold the might of the first Elf King, a young mortal, he who treated with gods?"

The pressure is suddenly overwhelming. I swallow physically, trying to catch my breath, to expand my chest so that I can generate enough space to think logically once more without moving. It's as though the old god has me in a chokehold without touching me. Krokan must sense it, because he eases away.

"I know," he says softly, almost apologetically for his temperament. Ilryth breathes a sigh of relief as well. "There is no other way, no other path to saving her. She must be freed from the Lifetree or she will die and take this world with her. Life needs her power to exist. But if she stays here any longer, with the life she made, it will be the end of her."

No matter what, the world will lose the goddess of life.

"Let us return. Grant us safe passage, and we will see her freed." Taking a step forward, I reach out my hands, pleading with him to understand the ways of mortals. How can I make a god comprehend how short our lives are? How brief it all is and how little we know as a result? Truth among mortals falls as effortlessly as grains of sand through the hourglass of time, lost among the ages. "As my love said, they don't know any of this above the Abyss. But we can be the messengers if you will bless our minds and bodies with your protections and grant us safe leave."

Krokan stills, as if considering it. "I have tried to reason with every one of their ilk," Krokan says with disdain. "The holy men, as they call themselves. To them I have tried to convey what must be done."

I was right. Duke Renfal was communing with the old god for longer than he let on. But there was more to it…

"Duke Renfal was trying to kill the tree," I whisper.

Krokan lets out a hum that sounds like a *yes*.

"What?" Ilryth gasps.

I face him, briefly, to explain. "He knew there was no way the sirens would abide cutting down the tree to outright free Lellia. So he began weakening it as he was able while Lord Krokan tried to free her as well with the rot. Because of what we knew as 'Lord Krokan's rage,' Renfal had an excuse to weaken the tree enough that maybe she could break free."

Ilryth considers this and turns back to Krokan. "If we free Lady Lellia, what will happen then?"

"I will take her into my embrace—as is the natural order of life and death—and then, together, we will depart this world," Krokan says with little emotion. As if he is not somehow damning us.

"You said life needs her to exist. If she's removed, what happens to life here?"

"Life is a cycle. Death is an inevitability. We do not concern ourselves with such things."

"But we mortals do," I blurt out. "We want to live, to thrive. To have an opportunity to build the best life we can afford ourselves. You know she wants that, too. It was why she didn't free herself from her cage. Even when weakened and rotting, even when she knew what path she was setting herself upon...she wants to see us tended to."

"Eventually, in its time, life would return to these lands. Or find a way to persist."

I resent the old god's calmness, his peaceful detachment from the world. But I suppose I could not expect much else from the god of death—living is not his role, responsibility, or concern.

"Like my love, it is audacious," Krokan finishes.

I rack my brain trying to think of what else could be done. What has not been pursued... "You mentioned a keeper?"

"It was something discussed by the first Elf King," Krokan admits.

"To do what?"

"That was between my love and him. I only concerned myself with seeing her wishes done."

I bite my lip, thinking. My mind is so full it nearly hurts. There must be a path forward. One that has been uncharted. But one I *will* find. All I know is that we must liberate her. If Lady Lellia dies in the tree, the world is lost anyway. Perhaps, in freeing her, we'll find another solution.

Krokan shifts, emerging from the gloom once more. It's just his massive head and shining green eyes. But he stares me down—straight to my marrow, testing my make. I stand as tall as I would to face off against the Gray Passage. As tall as I stood against Charles in the council chambers.

"I will teach you her song and allow you to depart." He's made up his mind.

Tentacles wrap around me once more. But this time they hold me with all the delicacy of a child cradling a treasured doll. I am weightless as he lifts me up.

"Victoria—" Ilryth drifts forward, still hovering as if swimming.

"Don't." I hold out a hand and look over my shoulder to him so he can see I'm calm. "I made an oath to save the Eversea, and the world. One I will see through."

Pain flashes through his eyes. He is afraid for me. Perhaps he should be... I don't know what will come next. But I do know that this is the right choice. And no matter what awaits me, I will live without regrets. My life feels full. I have sailed every sea, and ventured to the deepest depths. I have known and lost love and found it again. I have chosen a purpose when I could've avoided the responsibility.

My song is complete.

I shift to face Krokan once more and soft words fill my mind. I have spent months learning and repeating the words of the old ones. I am ready to accept these just like I accepted Krokan's hymns. Part of me already knows them. I heard them in the anamnesis. In banishing the rot of Sheel's daughter Yenni. In the bleeding roots of the tree. In the shifting of the branches overhead when Ilryth and I made love.

The song fills me with meaning and purpose. Light floods the water, turning every last marking on my skin—even the newest—silver. When Krokan releases me, my mind sings in harmony.

Mortal minds cannot comprehend fully the songs of one god. But both? A duet... I cross to Ilryth without word and press my forehead against his, singing a few words to stabilize his mind and bathe him in Lellia's blessings enough for us to leave without harm.

"We will go now," I say.

"Go, and be successful. For the Blood Moon rises in three years. One way or another, my wife will be one with me once more. Even if I must tear down this world to achieve it." The tentacles around us begin to writhe, kicking up silt and spinning the current into a vortex. "So return to your world. And do not fail us."

forty-five

THE CURRENTS SLOW, AND THE BUZZING IN MY EARS COMES TO A HALT. The waters grow still, and there is no longer the feeling of writhing movement around us. We stand on a large, rocky outcropping, overlooking Krokan's deepest den, transported. Both of us are too stunned to say anything for several long seconds.

I recover before he does. "What are you… How?" *Okay…I didn't recover as much as I thought.*

Ilryth still glows with radiant light. I notice that small pieces of wood have been fastened with ribbon around his arms, legs, neck, and torso. No doubt wood from the Lifetree to keep him safe. Another theft that unknowingly wounded the tree…but to good end.

Rather than answering me, Ilryth takes my face in both of his hands. He draws me to him with deliberate purpose, and he kisses me. It is firm, yet sweet. Tender but needy.

Thoughts vanish. I grab behind his arms, above his elbows, and pull myself to him. Our bodies crash together, all distance collapsing into a breathless moment of relief, joy, and passion.

"I realized I couldn't do it." He breaks away and presses his forehead against mine. His voice quivers, as though he is close to weeping. "These past three months have been unbearable. I've had nothing but time to think about what I had with you, and what I lost. About everything we could've been. About what I knew in my very soul to be the one brightest spot in my life—us."

"Three months?" I repeat. Out of everything he said, that's what I'm focusing on. The rest is too overwhelming and threatens to break me with emotions. "No… It's only been a few hours, a day at most."

He frowns slightly and slowly shakes his head. But he does not dismiss my experience. "Perhaps for you, it has been; I don't know. In this realm—this between of life and death—time doesn't flow the same as it does above."

"Then we must move quickly. Every minute here might well be an hour, or a day." I lead our ascent, scrambling over boulders and marching up narrow, sandy paths between the rocks. Ilryth assists me. In this weird ether that surrounds us, he hovers—like swimming—though not entirely, as every now and then he seems to sag to the ground. "Your markings?"

"They are a form of anointment, yes. Once the sacrifice was gone, a new one could be marked."

"Which gave you passage to the Abyss." My earlier suspicions are confirmed. "I can't believe you sacrificed yourself."

"I can't believe I sacrificed you." His fingers slide against mine. "My songmate."

That stills me. I meet his eyes. I can almost feel our hearts beat in tandem through the pulses in our fingers.

"The duet we sang down there…" I start softly, abandoning the thought.

He finishes it for me. "It was the song of our souls, harmonizing as one."

"You, me, we were destined to be together?" I realize I've spent so much time learning about the old gods that I've learned very little of what "songmate" means. Though, falling in love hadn't been my concern.

"It is not destiny." Ilryth begins moving again, reminding us we have little time. I help find the way as he continues to speak. "True, there are stories that say the songs of some souls might be more naturally compatible than others—destiny, if it pleases you. But our songs evolve as we do. They are learned and taught, shifted and changed with our choices and experiences. We make our own song—the song doesn't make us."

I smile faintly. All my memories have returned and I can see the full scope of everything that has brought me here like a dazzling canvas unfurled. "I never thought I'd love again."

"Do you resent me for it?" He seems genuinely concerned.

"Not in the slightest." I squeeze his fingers. "Though it is terrifying. Terror is a matter of perspective and right now I have other, far greater matters to fear." I nearly tell him about Charles. But this is not the time or place. That is a conversation I want to have when it can be focused upon and settled once and for all.

We emerge out of the deep gloom, continuing to ascend from the depths. In my soul, I can feel Lady Lellia's song. The small warbles that are guiding me from the Abyss just as Krokan's song led me to him. As we head for the boat on the lava river, a silvery outline catches my eye.

Even though I wasn't myself, I remember this man from my descent. Something had made him stick out to me beyond simply being a spirit trying to ascend out of the Abyss and into what is no doubt the Gray Trench. The memories of the angry wraiths that filled the trench rush back to me. I cannot escape the feeling of guilt that followed as I ended their entire existence. Even if it is just one man, one soul, I will not let him become one of those creatures of hate and rage. I am Victoria, and I leave no man behind.

"A moment."

"Victoria—"

"I'll be quick about it. But one less wraith is better for us all." I start for the man, Ilryth following.

My movement is faster than the escaping soul. I'm not as encumbered as he is; I'm free to move around this Abyss. I make it across the distance and up to him in the same amount of time that it takes him to clear one boulder. Thanks to the fog, and the meager ambient light, it isn't until I am completely upon him that I recognize the coat he wears. It is plainer than his usual finery, but still betrays his wealth and material and craftsmanship. Perhaps that's why he stuck out to me so clearly in the first place…

He mumbles to himself, not aware of my presence. It's odd to see someone using their mouth to speak. It seems in this place either form of communication is possible.

"I have to get back. They need me. Katria needs me. I never told her the truth. She should know the truth. Damn ship, damn monster, damn them all."

The words are harsh and cold. I've never heard him speak with such hatred. He is already losing the warmth and compassion he once held in the struggle just to make it to the Gray Trench. He won't make it all the way back to the Natural World. And even if he did, he would burn away with the sunlight, little more than a memory. He will never see his daughters again.

"Do you know this man?" Ilryth asks softly, bringing me back to the present. It's then I realize that I've released his hand, covering my mouth with my fingertips in shock.

"I do," I reply with my mind only to Ilryth. "Lord Kevhan Applegate. He was my employer. No, he was my friend and like a second father to me. He was on the ship when it went down. Ilryth, I can't let him become a wraith."

Part of me expects Ilryth to say no. But, time and again, the way he cares for me astounds me. "If he is important to you then he is important to me. Let's guide him away from the trench."

"Thank you."

"Victoria, anything for you," Ilryth says it so plainly, leaving no room for hesitation or doubt.

I kneel next to Kevhan and place my hand on his shoulder. He flinches, head turning, and his eyes go wide with recollection. I try to give an encouraging smile despite my immeasurable guilt. It is my fault he is here. Helping prevent him from becoming a wraith is the least I can do for now—until I settle the matter with Krokan and he can cross the Veil when he is ready.

I speak as gently as possible, making it a point to shape the words with my mouth so it's more familiar for him. "Lord Applegate, let go of your struggles. It is all going to be okay."

"V—Victoria?" he stammers. Kevhan's face crumples. He leans back, sits on his heels, and begins to howl with an unbridled outpouring of grief. My own eyes sting, seeing the man as I have always known him, rather than the corpse in the depths. "The siren have sent their monsters upon us. They have taken us. We are trapped here in this wretched domain of nightmares."

"No... It's not..." I don't know how to explain to him what's happened. How can I tell him he's died when he doesn't seem to realize that himself?

His gaze shifts, landing on Ilryth. "That—that *monster*! I won't let you keep me," he continues with fervor. "I *will* escape this place and get back to my daughters."

"Of course you will," I say softly, knowing that this will require a delicate hand. "But first, let us sit a moment and talk."

"*Talk?* You expect me to sit when there is one of our enemies among us?"

"He's a friend," I emphasize.

"A…friend?" Kevhan looks between us. He grabs my shoulders. "They have taken you. Stolen your mind with their songs."

"No. Let me explain—"

His eyes widen, as though he's seeing the truth for the first time. "Those early rumors…they were right all along. You made a deal with the siren for your skills as a captain."

"I did." It's painful to admit. Not because I'm ashamed, but because I hate the feeling of how long I lied to him. "But it's not that simple—"

"It seems simple enough to me." He stands, looming over me, radiating rage. So much for trying to calm him down and bringing peace. "You led us to them, *fed us to them*."

I don't rise to his level, staying seated, my voice an easy tone. "If my goal was to lead people to the siren to meet their demise, why did I go for years without losing a single crew member? Why would I wait and lose only one ship rather than feeding them souls all along, little by little?" I hope he can still be calm enough to see the logic.

"You waited until *I* was on the vessel."

"Kevhan," I say flatly, somewhat exasperated. "I know as a lord you think yourself rather important, and I know you are to Tenvrath. But the siren do not care about our nobility."

"No," he agrees easily, catching me off guard. "But they do care about their own nobility." I don't follow, so I sit in silence and wait for an explanation that he doesn't waste time delivering. "You made a deal to return me to the fae." He thrusts a finger in Ilryth's direction, who remains silent, allowing me to lead this interaction.

I am now certain that these are the ramblings of a dead man slowly losing his mind and better sense to grief. "We are dealing with the *siren*," I remind him gently. "Not the fae."

Kevhan turns, as if forgetting about me entirely. "I must get back to my daughter. She needs to know the truth of why she can't go to the forest, or they will hunt her."

"Wait..." I stand as well. "Are you saying that one of your daughters is involved with the fae?"

"Don't pretend like you didn't know." He glares at both Ilryth and me.

"I didn't! How could anyone have known that?" I look to Ilryth and he shakes his head as well. "Neither of us have any idea what you're talking about, Kevhan. I promise, I've only ever lied to you about one thing and that was where my abilities came from—which you now know the truth of. There's nothing more."

He studies my face, looking for deception, no doubt. I meet his eyes and hold out my hands in a gesture that I have nothing to hide. Kevhan relaxes. "You really didn't know about it... Then why?"

"Our ship wasn't supposed to go down." I allow my pain and guilt to bleed into my voice. "It was my fault, yes. But not because I fed the crew to the siren. You're right, I made a deal with the siren—this one, in particular, no one else—and that deal gave me my abilities as a captain. But the bargain was only for *me*, and me alone. No other humans were supposed to be involved. The ship went down because I was there, but I was going to try to sacrifice myself to avoid it. How everything happened was an unfortunate twist of fate."

Kevhan stops trying to get away. He doesn't sit again, but he does linger. I take it as a good sign.

"What do you last remember?" I start there.

He shakes his head, bringing the heel of his palm to his temple. "We were in the Gray Passage. The ship was rocking so violently. And then an...explosion? Everything went dark. When I next came to, I was here.

"Some of the crew were here, too...some weren't. But I'm the only one left now. The rest of them heard the song. They said that it sounded like peace. Though all I have heard is screaming." He shakes his head. "I warned them not to give in. I told them to be wary. But they said that they would go willingly. That they were ready and I should be too— that there was nothing to fear. The fools." He scoffs.

An odd bodily pain fills me. It is one of contracting and relaxing at the same time. It hurts, but it is also a weight leaving me. There were those among my crew who accepted their fate. They hadn't lied when they told me that they knew the risks of the passage and were ready to take them. Whatever matters they still had on land, they could let go of, they could find peace. All of them were far better than I, in life and in death.

I did not deserve my crew, not a single one of them. Each of them was the best version of myself. Because where I struggled and fought against my ultimate demise for so long, they met theirs with grace. If I were not already committed to bringing peace to the world so that their souls could pass effortlessly to the Beyond, I would be now. I owe it to my crew, to every other waiting soul, and to every future crew who deserves peaceful seas to sail through.

"I'm sorry, Victoria. The crew I saw became the siren's dark shadows and wandered deeper, saying that they had to heed the call. As I tried to chase them to drag them back, they were stopped."

"Stopped?"

"I couldn't understand it, but I took it as a blessing. Whatever halted them from getting to where they needed to go also gave me the chance to escape." He shakes his head. "I'm sorry. I left them. But I had to leave to find my girls."

I rest my hand on his shoulder once more, grateful he doesn't pull away. I point up the passage he was trying to scramble up. "If you go up that way, it will lead to the Gray Passage. You will become a wraith—a ghost of nothing but hatred—and lose your mind. You will *never* see your daughters again if you pursue this."

"Then what am I to do?" he asks dejectedly. "I cannot go as the other sailors did. I must see my girls once more...my Katria..."

A thought crosses my mind. "Come with me."

"Victoria, I'm sure I'm misunderstanding...are you bringing a soul with us out of the Abyss?" Ilryth's voice resonates between my temples.

"I'm not leaving him here," I say plainly, speaking to Ilryth alone, hoping it's clear that there's no room for argument.

Objection seems to pain Ilryth. "We can't take him back."

"Why not?" I look him in the eyes, keeping my focus only on him in the hopes that Kevhan won't hear our debate. "Souls wander back all the time."

There's a shift in how Ilryth's voice sounds, almost like he's whispering through a short tunnel to me. He's speaking for me alone as well. "He will turn into a wraith."

"I was told that wraiths were created out of resentment, and hatred. Yes, he was on the way to becoming one when I first saw him. But with a little explanation, and time, he now understands what his circumstances are. He's not going to resent the living so he will not become a wraith," I reason. "When he is ready, he will cross over to the other side—he'll become one of the shadow spirits we see here, waiting for his chance to cross the Veil. But until then, he stays with me. If anything bad happens, I'll take responsibility. I'll do what must be done. I have the power to, thanks to Krokan and Lellia." I just hope it doesn't come to that.

Ilryth grabs my hand. "You're sure about this?"

I nod. "I don't leave my people behind. He's all that's left of my crew; I can't abandon him down here. Besides, it'd be more irresponsible to leave him. He might go back to wandering up the Gray Trench on his own; he was already close to doing so. At least this way, if he turns into a wraith, we're there and can banish him instantly. Plus, you never know, he might be of help convincing the chorus of what we have to say. Or perhaps can help me understand Lady Lellia in some way we don't yet know." I'm reaching, but I'll make any excuse not to leave Kevhan behind.

The pad of Ilryth's thumb lightly strokes over mine. The movement is oddly intimate. As much as any of the other carnal pleasures we've indulged in. It is a motion of easy confidence and tenderness. Of compassion and understanding.

"I can see why Krokan chose you," he says thoughtfully. "You truly are a magnificent creature."

"Shall we?" I turn back to Kevhan, stealing his wandering attention from the opening of the trench. He seemed to have been utterly obsessed with it, missing our debate entirely.

"All right, I'll come with you."

"You're sure you can trust me? Even though I lied about working with a siren?" Despite getting what I want, I still question. The edge of feeling unworthy of his trust snakes up within me like a bad habit.

"Did I not tell you that you are like a fourth daughter I never had?" He clasps my shoulder. "What kind of second father would I be if I didn't trust you now? Beside, we both had our secrets, didn't we?"

I smile weakly through the pain that his words fill me with. Raising a hand, I pat the back of his. "I never told you enough how appreciative I was of you. I never realized how much you looked after me. All the times that I could have—*should* have—been more grateful to you. I'm sorry for not recognizing it all sooner. For not giving enough credit."

"Victoria, I'm going to say something and I want you to listen well: if there's anyone you don't give enough credit to, that you've never given enough credit to…it is yourself. You've done all you could. The level best that could be expected of anyone. Find peace with that and leave the rest behind."

"I'm working on it." I nod and then start forward, back up to the Eversea as an unlikely trio.

forty-six

LEAVING THE ABYSS IS MUCH HARDER THAN ENTERING. Every step over rock and up steep hill is more challenging than the last, and both men fight to follow closely behind me. I continually look over my shoulder at them, ensuring they're still with me, afraid that if I were to let them out of my sight for a little too long they'd vanish completely.

"Sorry for slowing you both…it's…" Kevhan is out of breath. "Surprisingly difficult to crawl out of here."

Ilryth gives me a worried look on his behalf. I release the siren's hand to outstretch mine to Kevhan. My former employer seems to take note of our previously interlaced fingers.

"Here," I say with forced calm, treating Kevhan like I would a leery stray cat. The idea of him snapping and running back to the Gray Trench is prominent in my thoughts. Somehow, I've convinced myself that neither of them is truly safe until we're out of the Abyss. "Take my hand. I won't let you fall back to that place, unless you want to."

"I assure you, I won't 'want to' until I have a chance to see my daughters again," he vows. I believe him wholeheartedly, and that's what helps me keep a steady hand, his fingers closing around mine as I help him scramble over a rock.

It occurs to me that his wife isn't counted among his reasons to return. In fact, Kevhan never speaks of his wife beyond passing, businesslike mentions. I can't help but wonder what the design of their relationship is. Is it love? Or more of an arrangement?

When I was young and my head was blissfully full of storybooks, I thought every couple who fell in love desired to be wed. And, therefore, every marriage was one of love—that love was passion and fire and so every union that ended with a ring was one of bliss. That was how I mistook lust for love when Charles first came to town. One look, and I thought I knew. He hardly had to do anything but flash me a dazzling smile.

It's because of him that I learned, all too well, that love is not made of fairytales. I took it as a bitter lesson. I saw every love that worked, like my parents', as a fluke. Every one that failed, like my own, as an inevitability.

Now…I see that lesson in a new light. There are many different forms love can take between partners. A love based on passion is no less than a love based on shared experience, or business, or whatever other connection brings two individuals together. Every couple has their own opportunity to define what love is to them. Whether that is an arrangement like Kevhan's, or a love that is so world-changing the days stop when your partner is gone, like Ilryth's parents'.

My attention drifts to him. Shamelessly, I study the sharpness of his jaw. His youthful features that glow with their own light, his pale hair cutting harsh lines against this realm of eternal night.

I'd never thought of marrying again. I didn't feel it suited me. For so long, I believed Charles wholly when he told me I was hard to love and difficult to be around. But now I know he was wrong. He was a sad and bitter man who desperately needed control after his life upended with the deaths of his family, and I am no longer beholden to his cruel catharsis.

Ilryth has loved me, deeply enough to stand before an old god for me. He has come to the literal edge of the earth to plead for me. It is a love I had only ever dreamed of and long since written off. But here he is beside me, fighting with and for me. He is a man of flesh, and blood, and virtue, who wants *me*, out of everyone in the world, and I want him in equal measure.

But if we were to steal time enough for a future together, could I give him what he needs? Even if Lord Krokan's rage is quelled, he still needs a wife and an heir. He needs to lead his duchy and Ilryth deserves a duchess who will relish those duties alongside him.

None of that is me. Not anymore. Maybe not ever. So where does that leave us? Is our love perfect, yet doomed, no matter what happens with old gods?

I don't have the answers…but perhaps part of what we're fighting for is the ability to find out. The right to ask the questions for ourselves and find our own path. Whatever that might be.

We finally reach the boat on the molten river. The current now flows away from the Abyss, which I take as a good sign. I help Kevhan into the vessel and then motion for Ilryth.

"I'll go in last," Ilryth says.

"Captain's orders," I insist.

"But—"

"A word to the wise, good sir, I wouldn't challenge Victoria when it comes to a vessel," Kevhan interjects.

I grin up at Ilryth and tilt my head toward the boat. "He's right, you know. Plus, I'm the only one among us that's really equipped to navigate the Abyss."

Ilryth chuckles and gets in by drifting over the side. He sits on the edge, his tail bent and curled along the hull. He still moves in a strange hovering-almost-swimming way. He flashes me a smile. "Very well, lead on, then."

"With pleasure." There's an innate pull in me. One that I put into my back as I push the small rowboat off the shore and into the lava, chasing after it and leaping in.

"Are you both…speaking?" Kevhan seems equal parts unsure and genuinely excited by the notion.

"We are," I affirm.

"How? I hear nothing."

"We're speaking with our minds…" I briefly explain telepathic communication to him, trying to offer a better primer than the one I was initially given.

He hums, brow furrowing with focus. "Like this?" he asks both with his mouth and his mind.

The words are practically shouting. *Goodness, did I sound like that when I first arrived?* No wonder Ilryth and his family were so tense speaking with me at first. My head is splitting from the sudden noise. He'd alert half the Eversea to our presence had we already ascended from the Abyss.

"More or less." I try to turn my grimace at the sharp sound into an encouraging smile. "Keep working on it while we leave here. But, here, this will help." I pull the necklace from my throat and place the shell around his neck instead.

"A good thought to shield him before we return," Ilryth praises. I'm pleased he doesn't seem upset with me passing his shell along.

"I thought so," I reply, focusing only on him. Kevhan doesn't react to the thought. I truly have learned how to keep my thoughts to myself and my communications focused—shell no longer required.

"Thank you," Kevhan says, pursing his lips to keep them from moving. I fight a smile of my own. His eyes dart to Ilryth. "Can he hear me?" There's no reaction from Ilryth. "Ha!" Kevhan seems rather pleased with his discovery. And his volume is already at a much more tolerable level.

I begin rowing, allowing him to test this newfound ability with Ilryth and me. We talk about the Eversea and the siren, about the Lifetree, quickly filling in the broad strokes of our circumstances. Kevhan picks up telepathy quickly. Though, I can only assume that a man who is somehow involved with the fae would adapt quickly to the world of Midscape.

When there's a lull in the conversation, I ask Ilryth for an update on present circumstances, rather than the events that led us here. "What's waiting for us when we return?"

"Nothing good," he says grimly. "The seas are worse. The other duchies were beginning to turn against me, blaming me for subjecting the Eversea to this fate by choosing a human as the offering."

I snort. Little do they know that somehow that human is still their best shot for lasting peace. Ilryth seems to pick up on my thoughts without my saying, because he gives me a small smirk. We share a look.

"That wasn't telepathy just now, was it?" Kevhan has attentive eyes. Or a lucky guess. "I take it you two have known each other for some time?"

"Years, technically," Ilryth answers. "Though I have only had the privilege of getting to know Victoria on a more personal level these past few months."

I focus on rowing to fight a blush at the words "personal level."

Kevhan considers this. Even having some preexisting familiarity with Midscape, I can't imagine the burdens he's having to deal with coming to terms with everything that has been presented to him. So I'm even more shocked when he stretches out a hand to Ilryth.

"I suppose a thank you is in order, good sir," Kevhan says. "Her skills made me very rich."

Ilryth considers the offering a moment, but ultimately accepts it. However, he doesn't let Kevhan's hand go, his expression turning stony. "Then it is you who failed to pay her properly so her family was at risk?"

"Ilryth," I interject curtly. "He paid more than enough. There were other circumstances that had set back my finances independent of him."

Ilryth slowly unfurls his fingers and murmurs, "Apologies."

"It's all right. I appreciate someone looking after our dear Victoria." Kevhan smiles, massages his palm, and then gives me a knowing glance.

"Kevhan, can you tell me more of what you know about Midscape?" I ask hastily. There's not much distance left for us to cover and I row a bit faster. The last thing I want is for the two of them to have uninterrupted time to talk between themselves. Kevhan knows too many of my secrets and too much of my past.

A past I still need to tell Ilryth. I *will* tell Ilryth, once we are safely back in the Eversea. Hopefully once everything is sorted, but sooner than that, if need be. He deserves to know. I just...want to tell him when we don't have an audience and aren't trying to escape the god of death's Abyss.

The shore where I found the boat appears around the bend. Conversation dies as I guide them up the maze of anamneses and finally to the circle of stones I first arrived at. Holding each of their hands, I close my eyes and search within myself for the right words to sing. This close to the Lifetree, I can hear the whispers of her song.

My intention clear, I open my mouth and let out a high note.

We're coming, Lellia, I say without words. *You'll be free soon.* The first time, we sang to Krokan and solicited his guidance for the descent. This time, we sing to the Lifetree high above. Kevhan is utterly entranced by Ilryth and me. His jaw slackens slightly and his eyes glaze. He sways, succumbing to the trance of the siren songs.

Tiny bubbles surround us. My body feels light, detached. My feet leave the ground, and the two of them come with me. We begin to soar, far beneath the waves. Higher and higher and higher. Everything is a blur until we blink and, all at once, our heads crest the surface of the Eversea.

forty-seven

KEVHAN GASPS LOUDLY ON INSTINCT. As if he still needs to breathe. I still feel a draw to do the same, but refrain. I've grown much more accustomed to my magical form.

Ilryth blinks up at the gray sky above us, calm and collected. He doesn't gasp for air. He doesn't immediately dive underneath the waves. There's a tired smile curling his lips. The light of the Lifetree glistens on his wet skin, highlighting all his paintings in silver and gold. He truly is stunning, beyond all compare.

But a harsh wind sweeps across the ocean, churning it until it's as gray as my eyes. I fight a shiver and watch as more silvery leaves than ever fall from the Lifetree.

"That is the Lifetree?" Kevhan whispers.

"It is."

"She would speak of crowns of glass, people that lived in the seas, spirits of the deep woods, and kings that could cleave worlds," he muses softly to himself. The words seem personal enough that I don't want to interject. "I never expected I would see such magical things with my own eyes."

"You'll get a much closer look," I say, beginning to swim. "The Lifetree is where we're headed."

"Victoria, we need to act with caution," Ilryth warns, but still follows. "The moment the chorus knows we've returned, they will sequester us. And I can only assume Ventris has sensed a disturbance from the Abyss."

"I've no doubt." This is thoroughly without precedent. I

expected as much, as the way of the Eversea seems to be: lock someone in a room until you know what to do with them. "That's precisely why we're going to the Lifetree first. We need a safe place for Kevhan to stay."

"You're leaving me?" Kevhan asks, hastily swimming to catch up with me. I hadn't realized how much faster I'm able to swim until I wasn't comparing myself to sirens.

"You will be safe here," I assure him. "The Lifetree anchors life itself to this world. It will protect you from falling back into the Abyss." I hope. It's a bit of a guess but it's the best I have. Briefly, I wonder if I made the right decision bringing him back...but I can't hesitate now. I couldn't leave him, and Ilryth seems to accept my decision as well.

We swim around to the back of the Lifetree—the roots that hang over the Abyss. I've never seen sirens swimming here thanks to the rot and I hope that means that it is marginally protected from their prying eyes. The water becomes clotted and the air is heavy with a putrid stink. To save our noses, we dive underneath the surface once more.

Kevhan goes to swim up for air after a few moments, but I catch his hand.

"You're a spirit," I remind him. "You don't need to breathe."

"Right..." He stares at the wrist I'm holding. "How is it that I can feel? Or smell?"

"I suspect it is the magic of the old gods," Ilryth postulates on my behalf. "To ascend to this world from the Abyss, you have heard their songs through Victoria and myself. I suspect it stabilized your spirit."

Which gives me hope he won't return as a wraith. "You're a bit like I am, I think." I offer Kevhan an encouraging smile and release his wrist, returning to the task at hand by gesturing to a small alcove in the roots. "Stay here. Keep yourself hidden from *anyone* but us. We'll return soon." *I hope.*

"What will you do?"

"We're going to try and free a goddess," I say with forced calm. As if it's not an impossible thing to even think. "But you need to hide, for now. If a siren finds you, they're likely to think you're a wraith and could attack. Once things are settled, we'll figure out how to get you back to your daughters. I promise. But it might take a day or two."

"All right. You've never let me down." Kevhan swims into the nest of roots. He pauses, then adds with a grin, "Except for that one time you got me killed."

"You're looking good for a dead man," I retort with a chuckle.

Kevhan's attention shifts to Ilryth. "Keep her safe."

"I will. Though I'm sure it'll be much the other way around." Ilryth takes my hand. "We should go."

I nod and lead the way. Rather than back to the castle where the chorus no doubt waits, I swim toward the Lifetree.

"Wait, Victoria, where—"

I glance over my shoulder. "Frankly, Ilryth, I don't care what your chorus thinks or says. Krokan has tasked me with one job: to free Lady Lellia. I see no point in delaying."

We round the roots and arrive at the beach. It isn't until I'm halfway out of the water that I hear the song resonating over the island.

"Lucia was leading a prayer to the old goddess, begging for peace," Ilryth explains. He hasn't shed his tail. "There are worshipers there. We *must* go through the chorus."

"How many sirens?" I ask.

"What?"

"Could we handle them?"

"Victoria." He swims back with a pump of his arms, gazing up at me in shock. "I won't fight my kin."

"The longer we delay, the closer we are to the whole world dying." I gesture to the tunnel that leads to Lellia's door. "We're *right here*. We go. I grab one of the axes leaning against the roots, then I hack open the door while you hold the rest of them off. You're the Duke of Spears, I've seen you fight."

"You can't just charge in like that." He shakes his head slowly.

"Why not?"

"They will kill you."

I gesture to myself. "I have already walked the deepest part of the Abyss and returned of my own volition. I am not afraid of any mortal."

"Please, I do not wish to see you as the villain of this tale," Ilryth says softly.

I wade into the water, kneeling before him. The waves lap against my chest. Ilryth's arms frame me on either side. Our faces almost touch as I cup his cheeks.

"Ilryth…I spent *years* where people saw me as the villain. Years where I believed their words—that I was a wretched, unlovable creature," I say softly. His eyes widen with shock. I continue before he can object. "But I know now…I'm not. I never was. I kept telling myself that I knew, but my heart never believed.

"But now I know it in my soul. I hear my own song so clear and true that there is no doubt. Let them try to sing over me. They will not. I will scream, if I must, to make myself heard. My truth and you are all I need. So long as you know the design of my heart—you don't see me as evil—then I don't care about the rest of the world. They do not matter."

"Victoria," he murmurs softly, leaning up to kiss my lips gently, tasting of him and saltwater, but also sorrow. So much pain lives in him on my behalf. I caress his cheeks and try to smile—to reassure him that it's all right. For the first time in my life, it will all be all right. I have not only the power to lead my destiny, but peace with the past.

"Let me go, if not to break down the door then to sing with Lellia. To ask her for the first time in thousands of years what *she* wants. We will do as she directs before all others."

"Very well." Ilryth only gets out the first note of the song to shed his scales when a familiar voice interrupts us.

"Old gods above and below, the shift in song was true. The conspirators have returned to damn us all." Ventris fumes at the opening of the tunnel.

I turn quickly, my hands dropping from Ilryth's face. Fenny stands next to Ventris, at the lead of a host of warriors and sirens that must have been among the worshipers. On Fenny's right arm and shoulder are markings identical to what I had always seen on Ilryth's skin. She carries a familiar spear in her hand—Dawnpoint.

"Fenny?" Ilryth blinks, confusion seeped into the name.

"That is Duchess of Spears to you, traitor."

forty-eight

WE ARE TAKEN BACK TO THE CASTLE BY FORCE. While neither Ilryth nor I are manhandled, the message is clear enough from the brandished spears and harsh gazes: step out of line and it will not end well. No time is wasted on holding rooms or discussions. We are immediately escorted to the hall of the chorus, awash in the deep blue.

The other sirens have departed, no doubt forced away with words I'm not privy to. I think, had they been given the option, they would've much preferred to stay and watch our trial. The warriors and worshipers leave the hall with sharp notes cast in our direction. Hateful sneers.

I take it easily. I'm all too accustomed to such things. But it's new to Ilryth. These callous gazes from the people he loved—sacrificed much for—wound him. I can feel it in my very soul as his eyes flash with pain even though he works to keep himself composed. I debate taking his hand, but resist. I don't know what they know of our relationship, *if* they know of our love and all the lines we crossed. I can only suspect they have some idea, given that Ilryth defied all law to get to me. But, for now, it's best not to give anything away until we must. Even if it pains me not to reach for him.

A few warriors hold their positions at the entry, forming a line to bar our escape. Even though we've done nothing to suggest we would try. Sevin, Remni, and Crowl are as still as statues upon their shells. Ventris and Fenny make a full chorus.

It is strange and painful, even for me, to see Fenny take Ilryth's shell. She rests Dawnpoint across her lap. Each of the other dukes and duchess do the same with their own legendary spears. I wonder if their magic will be what it'll take to open Lellia's door. Or perhaps it doesn't need such power and the door is shut only because no one has ever tried to open it and Lellia has grown too weak to do so herself even if she wants to.

Remni, head of the chorus, extends her spear into the center. All the others do the same. A faint glow ignites from their tips, lighting an anamnesis where the carved shell formerly was the last time I stood before a chorus.

"The chorus is in session," Remni announces.

I waste no time. "I can explain—"

"Explain how you have ruined our seas? How you have betrayed us?" Ventris seethes. "Now you have come to mock us and swim in the waters of our doom."

"Enough, Ventris," I say curtly, loud enough for them all to hear. I hope the whole Eversea hears. I assess him with a cruel stare; he has never looked so small. "You're nothing more than a sad little boy, hoping and trying *desperately* to live up to your father's legacy. But you never will. You're so wrapped up in trying to be him that you aren't focusing on what made him great."

"How dare you." He tries to continue, but I won't let him.

"You spend so much time putting on airs that you've never taken the time to do the work. You can't even hear the words of Lord Krokan, can you?" It's part guess, part truth that I gleaned from what Krokan said.

Ventris rears back, hands twisting around his spear. Shocked expressions have been carved into the chorus's faces. Ilryth wears a slight smirk.

"Your father could, genuinely, but you cannot," I continue. "You've spent so much time and effort on your displays of power and the prominence of your castle with its wards and carvings that *he* made to compensate for what you're lacking in substance. Your insecurities and hubris risk costing your people everything. It is because of you that the headway your father made went to waste."

Ventris glowers at me. I'm surprised the water around him doesn't bubble with the heat of his rage. "That is quite enough from you."

"Is it true?" Remni, Duchess of Craftsmen, interjects coolly. She has her strong arms folded over her chest. It is not necessary for her to hold the spear to be imposing. "Have you been deceiving us? Can you not hear the song of Lord Krokan as your father could?"

Ventris's head whips around. The movement is so sudden and violent that his whole body drifts in the water, nearly propelling him off his shell. "You can't honestly—these lies—she's—"

"A traitor," Fenny finishes.

"Yes, a traitor," Ventris says quickly. He looks at Fenny as though the woman is the key to his victories. "Her mind is twisted by depravity and, were it not for that, then the rot, which has only grown worse since—"

"Let me speak!" I say, louder than him. All their eyes return to me. "When I first met the chorus, I was shown how you all use measure and good sense to lead. How you treat all with respect and civility and do not jump to conclusions on important matters. I ask you to grant me the same, now. Let me speak." My tone has calmed by the time I repeat myself. I motion to Ilryth. "Let him speak, too. We have the answers you're seeking because the old gods have chosen us as their messengers."

Crowl taps his spear against his thigh. "The human has a point."

"You cannot honestly—" Fenny starts.

"You are fresh to this council, Duchess," Remni interrupts coolly, "and your place among us is up for debate now that your brother has returned." Before Fenny can even think of another word to say, Remni gestures to me. "Speak, then."

"I stood before Lord Krokan. We both did." I gesture between Ilryth and me. "But it did not lead us to madness. It led us to *clarity*. Lord Krokan sent us back—both of us—because there is something that must be done." I take a moment to think of my next words. I must choose them with care. It's up to me to convince these sirens that we must go against years of tradition and risk what has been the balance of the world until now in the process.

"And that 'something' is?" Remni asks, arching her eyebrows.

When I don't respond immediately, Ventris can't help himself. "See? Her mind is already fraying."

"Lady Lellia is dying and Lord Krokan is revolting as a result—he wants to take her away so he can save them both," I blurt. They all stare at me as though I've suddenly grown a tail like one of them and begun swimming. So much for trying to be tactful...

"Freeing Lellia from the Lifetree? Fellow chorus members, we aren't going to entertain this drivel, are we?" Ventris's voice has a note of relieved smugness. He thinks I've proved his point. I fear he might be right, given the expressions of the chorus. "I propose the best thing to do is return them to the Abyss, not through the anointing, but by force, and allow Krokan to do with them as he pleases. They no doubt subverted him, treacherous little wretches."

Is Ventris honestly suggesting what I think he is? By *force*? Does he mean to try to kill me again? I dismiss the idea of arguing over the possibility. It's not even worth entertaining when there are more important matters. And if I spend more than a second thinking about how Ventris is suggesting that they kill Ilryth, then I really will lose every last scrap of my self-control.

"I'm telling you the truth," I insist. "Lord Krokan and Lady Lellia must be allowed to pass the Veil and join their godly kin in the world beyond..." I tell them of all we've seen. Of the ancient histories forgotten by mortal minds for thousands upon thousands of years. I tell them of Krokan and Lellia's love. Of her sacrifice.

I try and lay everything out as openly and honestly as I can manage. It might all seem impossible. The truth might be the last thing they want to hear. But they deserve to know everything.

"... the late Duke Renfal spoke with the old god and knew some of these motivations. He wasn't able to understand every word from Lord Krokan since he wasn't anointed, but he captured the general idea. That led him to harvest from the tree under the guise of protection. But in truth, it was to weaken the tree to try and free Lellia. Lord Krokan attempted to help the process, from the rot to refusing souls and causing the buildup in the Abyss that led to more wraiths, which, in turn, led to more trimming of the tree. That is, until you stopped it." I glance at Ventris, but continue before he can react to the slight. "Free Lady Lellia, return her to Lord Krokan, let them return to the Beyond and reunite with their other godly kin."

"I will not sit idly while she disparages my father's name with her lies." Ventris rises. Ilryth moves slightly in front of me.

"Sit, Ventris," Remni commands. "You must keep your outbursts under control or we will never get to the truth, much less decide what to do next. Now tell me, could all this be *possible*?" Remni asks Ventris. The fact that she's asking him when I'm standing right here, telling her everything she needs to know, makes me want to scream.

"I would need time to consult the tomes. But in the meantime, we should send her back."

"There is no time." I practically speak over Ventris. "There is something called the Blood Moon. Leading up to this event, the lines between the worlds are thinning. If Lord Krokan and Lady Lellia are going to join their brethren on the other side of the Veil, they need to leave on or before this day. It will happen before you can send another sacrifice—there is no more time."

"Blood Moon?" Remni looks to Ventris.

"The holy astronomers have mentioned this," he begrudgingly admits. "But it is more the way of the vampir and has never been particularly important to our traditions."

"How could I have known of such a thing without Lord Krokan telling me?" I raise a hand to my chest. "It only happens once every five hundred years."

"But it is not for a couple years yet," Ventris objects. "Plenty of time to—"

"Do you really intend on gambling with Lady Lellia's life. She certainly will not survive until the next one; she might not even survive until this one. It's this or nothing, now or never, and that's why Krokan has resorted to drastic measures."

"Let's say we believe you," Sevin says. I wish he sounded more genuine and less hypothetical. "What are we supposed to do? Let you cut down the Lifetree?"

"How dare... Are we just... Are we going to let her talk us into destroying the anchor for life and one of our last old gods in this world with little more than convincing lies?" Ventris blubbers.

"That is a worthy question." Crowl rubs his chin. "What of the rest of mortal life if we free Lady Lellia from the Lifetree and she leaves this world?"

"Lord Krokan said that there is a possibility of another anchor... but I would ask her myself, if given the chance." I hold out both of my hands, wishing I could make them understand the emotions and machinations I barely can make sense of myself. "I'm sure that if we can speak with her, she would guide us. She loves this land more than anything—enough to sacrifice her very essence for it for centuries upon centuries."

"You presume to be able to speak to Lady Lellia?" Ventris scoffs.

"I do." I meet his gaze and am pleased when he looks away. "Maybe I can't promise what happens after, but I do know this…if you all fail to believe me now, then it will result in a great calamity."

"How can we trust you?" Fenny asks. She has an expression I can't quite read. It's almost…smug? While the rest of them are panicked or angry, she's worn a slight smile this entire time.

"Because I'm telling you the truth," I say. "I admit there was a time when I resented—hated, even—Ilryth and all sirens. But I have come to understand you. I have shed my human skin and have been anointed by your songs. Even now, having gone to the realm of death and back, your markings are still on me. So, I fully understand that what I've told you, what I'm asking you to accept and do, is no small measure."

"What you are asking for is the ending of those ways you say you understand." Sevin leans forward, resting his elbows on his knees. "We have thousands of years of history, passed down in our songs. But not one speaks of this danger you foretell—of our gods dying."

"Did anyone sing of the rot before it began seeping from the Lifetree? Or the rage of Krokan churning the seas? Or the increasing frequency of wraiths?" They're all silent. "I know, it is terrifying when the world you thought you knew, thought you had control of, is suddenly crumbling apart. When the things you've always counted on—the foundation you built your world on—crumbles."

Lonely nights. The illusion of safety, gone. Harsh words, heavy enough to break a young woman's back. A barren beach.

"I know what it's like when you've lost everything, and the terrifying realization that it was in no small part by your own hand, even if it wasn't what you ever intended. But you *must* keep going. Even if you don't know the headway…or even if you'll make it to that distant, hopeful point at all."

One muddy footprint at a time, pulled away from a cold, dark beach.

Down a road you've never traveled. To a city you've only ever heard talked about. To a life you haven't even dared dream of.

"We owe it—*you* owe it to everyone to take history in your stride and chart your own course. You can't let your future be chained to the past. Claim your own destiny," I finish.

My words reach them, I think. I hope. They all remain quiet. Expressions pensive.

"Listen to her." Ilryth swims forward slightly. "If you ever held any love or respect for me, listen to her. Victoria is the best among us. She is good and honorable. She has never lied or deceived any of us. If anything, she has always acted in our best interest."

Don't speak so highly of me, I want to say. *Don't say these things.*

But he doesn't stop. He continues his noble crusade that wars with my heart. "Men and women followed her in the Natural World because of her goodness and virtue. I have witnessed souls of the dead turned from rage just by her mere presence. She has swayed the heart of Lord Krokan himself to allow us to return. If she gives us her word, then it is so. And we—"

"Enough, Ilryth," Fenny interrupts, that smug smile widening slightly. "She is not the woman you think she is. And, now that I am the Duchess of Spears, it is my job to defend the Eversea from evil, wickedness, malice, and *lies*."

Fenny turns her eyes to me and the world grows still and cold. I watch, as if on a delay, as Fenny reaches into a pouch at her hip. A similar smile slinks across Ventris's face. I know what's coming before it does. It is like watching my ship sink all over again. Hopes pulled under the churning tides of fate.

She holds up a simple gold band. The same I lost in the water five years ago. The same that was in Ilryth's treasure room… The ring I trusted her to get rid of.

"Did you know that she was married?" Fenny asks Ilryth.

His head whips between her and me, landing back on Fenny. "What is this game, sister?"

"No game, just the truth, *finally*." Her attention shifts back to me. Fenny cocks her head to the side, golden hair swirling free of her spiky shell pin like angry serpents. "Will you tell him, or shall I?"

I am spinning, deeper and deeper, back into the Abyss. The sea is going to swallow me whole and this time not spit me back out as a conscious being. I will be nothing more than an amoeba. I will be one of those shadow creatures, waiting to be consumed whole by the monsters of the depths. I am small and pathetic and weak…

My body breaking down isn't happening fast enough. I'm desperate to have it all be over and yet it's *not*. I'm still in place. Very much in one solid piece. The conversation is still happening. *Why am I not putting a stop to it? Why am I not saying anything?*

"Very well, then," Fenny continues. "This fell from her, the night you marked her to be our offering."

"That could be any ring," he says cautiously.

"Her initials are within it." Fenny's words gut me. "It came off her finger when you performed the act. Isn't that true?"

Ilryth's head is still whipping between us. The moment he lays eyes on me, though, he knows. His body language shifts at my lack of denial of it being mine. He knows the truth without another word having to be said. "It did, but—"

"What finger was she wearing it on?"

"I…I don't recall," Ilryth stammers.

"Come now, of course you do," Fenny almost purrs.

"Left hand, second finger from the pinky side…"

"Sevin, as the Duke of Scholarship, I came to you inquiring about humans and rings months ago, did I not?" *Months ago?* If that's true, then the day I asked Fenny to get rid of the ring, she left…she was nowhere to be seen for a while after that.

"You did," Sevin admits.

"And what did you tell me?"

"There are records of early humans marking their unions with gilded bands of wood, carved from the trees of their forefathers. To signify their union with each other, and with the world, everlasting," Sevin says.

"I fail to see how any of these theatrics are relevant," Remni says curtly, tapping the tip of her spear against the floor. "Get to the point, child."

"The point is that she *lies*." Fenny looks to Ilryth. "Did she ever tell you of a husband?"

Ilryth is silent for a long moment. He looks back to me, searching.

What can I say, or do? *I was going to tell you*, I can't say fast enough, before Ilryth speaks. "No."

"She has lied to us, deceived us all. A human was never a fitting offering and we should have known it would be as such." Fenny rises, pointing in my direction. "She is a scheming villainess who conspired to bring low my brother and turn him against his kin."

"I did no such thing!" I finally find my voice. It's thick and clumsy and painful to speak, but I force myself.

"Were you not married? The truth." Fenny brandishes the spear at me.

"I was, but it ended—*I* ended it."

I am shocked when Ilryth, still, moves between us. Positioning himself protectively. I want to hold him. To weep my apologies for how this has unfolded.

"Then you confess to being an oath breaker." The chorus murmurs, exchanging glances. The word shakes me to my core yet again. It brings back every jape and jeer cast in my direction. Can I never escape my fate? Is this all I am? "Lucia, enter," Fenny commands.

"Lucia?" Crowl echoes as Lucia swims through the tunnel. "What does she have to do with this?"

"Further evidence of Victoria's deceit. How she corrupted Ilryth for her benefit." Fenny motions for Lucia to come and stand before the council as well. "Tell them what you told me."

Fenny knows of Ilryth's and my love. Of what we did. I have damned him, and myself, the Eversea, and the whole of Midscape. Maybe the world.

Lucia drifts to a stop, looking between us and the chorus. After what feels like an impossibly long time, she says, "I don't know of what you speak, sister."

"Lucia," Fenny growls.

"I will not speak against my brother."

"The chorus commands it!"

"You are not the chorus," Lucia fires back. "You are merely a stand-in for our brother and a sad one at that. I thought better of you, sister."

"How dare you! I am trying to *save* our family."

"Enough," Remni says.

As the sisters begin to squabble, Ilryth shifts to look back at me. His expression is unreadable. He's not betraying any of what he thinks, even for a moment.

"It's true? You're married?" he whispers, only for me.

"I can explain…"

Ilryth shakes his head and looks away.

"Let's kill her and be done with it," Ventris demands.

"It is possible for human traditions to change," Sevin points out. "Perhaps we are staking too much on ancient records to determine her character."

"None of this helps alleviate our problems with Lord Krokan, or this claim of Lady Lellia's ailments," Crowl points out.

Everyone speaks over each other. Louder and louder. But my ears hear none of it—nothing but quiet ringing as I stare at Ilryth, who still won't meet my gaze.

What have I done?

"Enough!" Remni silences us all with a shout and a slam of her spear that causes a burst of light to strike against all corners of the room. "Enough. This dissonance will get us nowhere. Lucia, leave. Warriors, take Ilryth and Victoria to the chambers of the anointed and *do not* let them leave until the chorus has decided their fate."

forty-nine

WE ARE GUIDED BACK TO THE CHAMBERS I PREVIOUSLY OCCUPIED. There is a whole ocean between us, rather than just a room. My body is numb. Heavy. It's a wonder I can float or swim at all.

As we arrive, the chorus's song hums through the seas—if it can even be called a song. It's a cacophony of five voices singing at once, all off-key, not quite in the same time. Stopping. And then trying again to no success.

The warriors leave us in the room, positioning themselves at the start of the tunnel that leads up to it and on either side of the balcony outside. But, for the most part, we are alone. Especially since the spear-wielding men and women can't even bring themselves to look at us. I wonder if this was part of Fenny's plan. She knew we would be placed here, together. Alone. Perhaps she's hoping we can find a way to escape.

Or maybe she wants Ilryth to stew in hatred for me and that's how she plans on getting him back on her side so she can free him. *I am trying to save our family*, she'd said. If Fenny can convince the council that I deceived Ilryth enough to twist his morals…that I used some power I don't possess to steal his better sense…then maybe they'll spare him.

She was shrewd, a bit harsh, but never struck me as cruel for cruelty's sake. And what I do know is that she loves her home and family more than anything. Perhaps…it was all an act to save him. But not me. She never really cared much for me and I've crossed lines she wouldn't forgive. Fenny would absolutely let me die, again, to save her brother.

Ilryth…

He's said nothing. I turn, bracing myself. He's right there, yet half a world away, staring.

"All right, let's get this over with. I don't want to play your games," I say curtly. Maybe I'll rise to the role Fenny has arranged for me. Maybe I can hurt him enough—hurt *us* enough to break this. And then he can be spared from whatever fate awaits me.

But just the thought is a red-hot poker to the backs of my eyes. I'm not ready to let him go.

"Games?" His expression becomes shadowed as he drifts forward and out of the glow of the anamnesis planter on the wall. "I'm not playing any games."

"Aren't you though? Waiting for me to apologize? Withholding your words as punishment for me withholding mine? I know this dance all too well."

"I am not going to take childish swipes at you, Victoria. I was giving you space to work through whatever you needed to so that you could arrive at a place where you felt ready to speak. I am a grown man and you are a grown woman. I assumed we could handle this as adults."

I lean back, startled. *He wasn't trying to punish me?* Ugly instincts still left over from Charles try to tell me that this is a test. He's waiting to see how I handle myself and what I do. I hate that there is this streak within me that, no matter how hard I try, no matter how much my better sense might try to say otherwise, I can't seem to shake.

"I was married. But I'm not anymore. Believe me or don't." I go to swim to the balcony. "But we should focus on the task at hand. Perhaps I can commune with—"

"Don't run, Victoria." He stops me by catching my wrist, keeping me in the room and out of sight from the warriors. "You've been running your whole life. Going from one thing to the next. Always another duty. Another place to be. Another deal to make with someone—with yourself. You've kept yourself so busy, so wound up, that you could never unravel. The only time you ever gave yourself any room to feel were the last weeks before you were sacrificed. It took your own death to let go."

"What do you know about me?" I whisper.

"Clearly more than you give me credit for." The words are an echo of what he's told me before, a continued reminder. Gently, Ilryth spins me to face him. My chest tightens as I stare up at him. At those intense, thoughtful eyes that demand a person I don't know if I am—if I've ever been. "Stop running, *please*," he says softly. "I'm here now. I don't want to be anywhere else. So don't run from me."

How can the words be nearly the same as what Charles said when he tried to hold me back, but the feeling be so different? Perhaps it's because Ilryth releases me with ease. Perhaps it's because I know I could tell him to go and he *would*. I am free to ask him to leave me be. As is he to ask such of me.

And yet...we both stay. Even when it's hard, when it's ugly, when everything within us screams *run*, we stay because we can't imagine being anywhere else but each other's side.

"Do you hate me now?" I whisper. My thoughts are for him, and him alone.

"Hate you?" He blinks. "Victoria, I *love* you."

"Still? After I lied to you?"

"You were not entirely truthful...but you did not outright lie, not that I recall." Ilryth smiles slightly and shakes his head. "I only remember ever asking if you were married, presently. Not ever before."

We've shared so many words and moments over the past months that I can't remember completely if that's accurate or not...but I choose to believe him. He's offering me a bridge and I will not burn it.

"I *wanted* to tell you," I admit. "And I was going to. Soon. I swear it to you. I just hadn't found the right chance."

Ilryth frowns slightly. "There were plenty of chances."

"Once I had made the decision to, there weren't. Before...yes, at least while I had all the memories," I force myself to admit. "But I was afraid. I wasn't ready, then."

"And I respect that." He dips his chin to meet my eyes. There isn't a trace of doubt or hesitation. I am completely taken in by his steady gaze, as warm as an embrace. "I do. Though it doesn't stop me from wishing I had heard the truth from you. Or that you would've felt you could've been honest with me from the start—that I wouldn't have pried past what you were ready to share."

I lean forward, pressing my forehead into the center of his chest. Tiredly, he wraps his arms around my shoulders.

"I wish I were stronger," I admit.

"You are plenty strong. Strength isn't all-encompassing, nor without falter." He presses his lips into my temples, over and over again.

"I've never had someone like you," I confess. "Someone kind, trustworthy, *good*. I don't know what I'm doing in a relationship like this."

"Neither do I. And don't the old gods know how complicated they've made things by bringing us together in the way they have." He chuckles and his hands slide over my shoulders, up my neck, to cup my cheeks and turn my face up to his. "But I'm trying to navigate this uncharted territory with you. All I know is I am not ready to leave your side."

"I want to learn how to be better, too, constantly. I can't change the choices I've made…but…" I gather all my strength and look my worst fears and doubts in the eyes as I tilt my head back and meet his. I won't run from this any longer. "I would like to tell you now, if you'll listen?"

He nods.

"The debt my family was in was because I sought to nullify my marriage. That night you found me in the ocean…I was trying to get away from him—Charles. I was trying to reclaim my freedom."

"I see." Ilryth's expression becomes stony and more severe. His thumbs continue to stroke the swell of my cheeks in a motion that I can only describe as tender, juxtaposed with the pure murder in his eyes at the implication of Charles's actions against me. Ilryth manages to keep his voice level when he asks, "Would you be willing to tell me everything from the start?"

The last time we spoke of my history, my memories had been gutted. But now I can paint a full picture for him. I tell him things I've already said—of my childhood and my family—in more complete detail. I tell him of my girlish whims, how I thought Charles was mature, handsome. How we ran away and my family accepted but never warmed up to him. He listens with quiet, earnest interest. I admit to the bad times as freely as I describe the good. Hiding nothing is freeing.

When I'm done, Ilryth is quiet for a moment. Then, "Did you love him?"

Of all the questions I expected Ilryth to ask, that wasn't among them. I dare a look over to him. It's as if he was waiting for my eyes to meet his again. He holds my gaze steadily.

"If I'm honest..." I start slowly. "I wish I could say that I *didn't* love him. That I never really loved him, because I wish it were true. It'd feel like my heart betrayed me less. Like I could pretend I wasn't so fooled by who I thought he was." I grab my chest. "But...if I look back honestly on the woman I was, as much as it physically pains me to admit, I did love him—the man I thought he was. In the way I knew how for the person I was.

"But I grew. I learned truths about him that couldn't be reconciled. People change over time and the love needs to change with it." I smile softly, thinking of my parents. Of the married members of my crew and their spouses on land, or aboard that seemed to survive anything thrown their way. "Charles forever wanted the naive and perpetually optimistic young woman who made him her entire world. Someone who would never challenge him, who existed to make him feel good. She faded, with time, and the woman who replaced her needed so much more— needed a man he couldn't be. I wanted a partner; he wanted a servant.

"And every night, for years, I would wonder what I could've done better...how I could've fixed it. Where *I* went wrong." I shake my head. Looking back on it all, the sum of Charles's and my time together, there were times when he wasn't as horrible as I thought. And others when he was worse than I allowed myself to see. I wasn't as good as I remember. But I was also far too patient and forgiving. The burden is not solely mine to bear. "In some ways, we both succeeded. In other ways we both failed."

"Him vastly more than you, it sounds like. He had as many choices and opportunities as you did and it sounds as if he squandered them. He never had any idea of the treasure he had—" Ilryth stops himself before the rage can take over his words. I nearly tell him to go on; I'd love to hear him verbally eviscerate Charles on my behalf. But I refrain. It wouldn't be productive.

"Obviously, I got away. With the help of you and your magic...but what you couldn't do—what you *failed* to do—was truly free me." I'm drawing closer to him. Pulled by pain and questions I've harbored for years. Questions I don't know if I *want* the answers to but must ask anyway if I can ever truly bare my heart to the man who has claimed it from the protective prison I'd locked it within. "The markings you gave me—your song—said none would threaten or control me. Yet I spent the five years of borrowed time that you gave me running from him. Trying to escape his hold. Trying to expunge the marks he put on my soul. To think of anything but him.

"*Why?* Your magic could've ended everything for me…it could've given me a true fresh start. I could've made the most of my time rather than feeling Charles's grasp still around my throat. Why didn't you?"

Ilryth stares deep into my eyes. I've exposed more of myself to him in these moments than I ever intended. He sees a part of me that I wish, desperately, I could just let go of, or kill off. But it almost feels as if this wound will continue bleeding until everything that I've let fester has been cut out.

"I never wanted to see you tortured. I would *never* wish for that, or allow it to happen, if I could stop it." Ilryth's words are filled with all the pain in the world. I believe him without hesitation. This is the man who went to the edge of existence for me, after all.

"Then why—"

"When we forged our deal, I structured it that 'No plant nor man, bird nor beast, shall hold you back when *you* desire release.'" The words are said delicately. And for good reason. I hear his implication.

"You're saying that it is because I did not desire my release enough that Charles continued to have the power over me that he did?" I snarl, my mouth twisting with pain. "I would never—"

"I couldn't have known what bonds you did or did not want to keep. I wouldn't sever something you wanted to hold on to," he interjects firmly, continuing his explanation. "Oaths, bargains, our word means as much in the Eversea as it does in Tenvrath, you know that. I extend the same respect to you—to all humans—on instinct. If you had *chosen* to establish a bond, you would have to also choose to end it and take action to do so. What if I had broken a much-loved connection crafted by hardship and toil by wielding power indiscriminately?"

It makes so much sense. A wash of guilt rushes over me with sickening cold that I had ever suspected so little of him. "Then why didn't the magic break it the moment I wanted it broken?"

"The blessing I gave you wasn't designed that way. It didn't work retroactively," he explains. *And I didn't wish to nullify my marriage that night.* I just wanted to escape. "Moreover, even if I'd known, I couldn't. That oath was cemented and involved ties to others that I wouldn't have had the power to reach in that moment with my song. I was focusing ahead for you, not behind." He tries to catch my eyes. I look away. So he catches my hands instead. That brings my attention back. "But I am sorry, Victoria. I never meant to let you down."

My fingertips quiver under his calloused, warm grasp. My whole body begins to shudder and I swallow. I try to push all these overwhelming emotions down somewhere deep, deep inside of me where it can't be reached ever again.

"I resented you for years for not freeing me from him," I confess.

"Some things we must do ourselves. No amount of wishing or magic can free us or spare us the responsibility."

"It's unfortunate, isn't it?" I chuckle grimly.

"It is," he agrees with the ease of someone who's wished the opposite were true many times. "But we carry on. We have no other choice."

I nod in agreement. He gives me a small, almost gentle smile, one I return in kind. I can see his flaws as easily as his pain. The grim realities he's forced himself to accept and push through. I see something familiar in the mess of it all:

Myself.

"So, now you know everything."

"I don't think I know *everything.*" He smiles slightly, which softens the blow the words would otherwise be. "But, with any luck, I'll be blessed to learn in time. I could spend ages learning you and it would never be enough. You are worth every risk, and every chance."

He moves forward, wrapping his arms around me. Ilryth holds me without pretense. It's not needy, or passion filled. *Sturdy,* I'm reminded yet again. He is the immovable rock in the ocean. He's the safe haven where I can drop my anchor and rest.

"I thought…forgetting him might help me love you better, would make me more worthy of you. But I'm glad I remembered. I'm glad I could tell you all of it—all of me. If you are to want me, then I want you to want it all, the good and the bad." I want to be his—every tired, determined, bruised, and bold part of me. If he is to have me, then I want him to have it all. I want to know he *wants* it all.

"Good. You should never lessen yourself to spite another. The best revenge is to thrive."

My arms slip around his waist, reaching up his back, clinging to the hardened muscle of his shoulders. Ilryth presses his lips to mine, forceful, but not needy, erasing the last remnants of Charles from my body and thoughts. His fingers tense and relax, kneading up and down my back, unraveling the knots of so many years of pain.

When he pulls away I realize that the vast sea I felt when we first entered the room has condensed. Now there is only us. We steep in the moment and chart every detail of each other's eyes, like constellations that will guide us home.

Never have I done so little, been so covered, and yet felt so exposed.

This is an intimacy unlike any I've ever known and I want to give myself wholly to it. I crave it more with every passing second. It's like taking off my corset after a long day of work. Like a sip of iced lemon tea on a scorching summer's day—sharp to the tongue, sweet on the throat, refreshing to the core. It's the first breath I took after cresting the waves on the beach that night, long, long ago.

"Ilryth." His name is a caress on the back of my mind. "I love you."

The smile that spreads across his face is brighter than the midday sun. "And I love you." His attention drops to my mouth. He licks his lips and I squeeze him tighter still. "Victoria, I—"

We are interrupted by a sudden and ominous silence. Without warning, the singing of the chorus that has continued in the background has halted. I'd filtered out the constant noise. But its absence is noticeable.

"What—"

In response to my unfinished question, a single note hums across the Eversea—five voices in perfect harmony.

"They've decided," Ilryth says solemnly, his arms slackening. I barely resist pulling him back to me. *A little bit longer*. A little more time for him and me to simply exist.

But the tides of fate have been pulling us along since the beginning. It's impossible for us to find any kind of headwind that would be able to fight against them. Just as our arms relax completely and we drift apart, the chorus rounds the balcony.

All of them still carry their spears and their expressions are a mix of grim and serious. The only one who seems happy is Ventris, which further supports my theory over the game Fenny might have been playing. She'd been gambling for a different outcome. One that I now suspect she ultimately lost.

"We have reached a decision," Remni announces. "Your anointments shall be refreshed and then, come the dawn, you will be sacrificed on the shores of Lady Lellia so that your bodies might be offered to nurture the Lifetree—an apology for your affronts—and your souls can return to Lord Krokan. Hopefully, combined, it is enough to appease the old gods and end this once and for all."

fifty

THERE'S NO POINT IN ARGUING. Even though objections blaze across my thoughts, I keep them for myself alone, hidden behind a calm mask. Ilryth seems to have reached the same conclusion, as he remains perfectly still. Though the muscles in his jaw flex briefly. The only thing that betrays his agitation.

In trying to save their seas, the chorus has damned us all. But knowing where they stand—that they will be a hindrance and not a help—is progress in its own way. It cements that there's little point in seeking their assistance further. Ilryth and I are on our own.

My thoughts swirl like a tempest. Pressure propels me. It is the wind in my sails and the guide by which I chart my course.

"If this is what the chorus has chosen, then we shall abide by your decision," I say, bowing my head slightly.

"Good," Remni says. Ventris looks wildly skeptical at my compliance, but he keeps his mouth shut. Remni exudes an aura that now is not the time to try her patience. "We will take you to her sands now, so that you may be properly anointed before the Lifetree prior to your offering to our lady." Remni passes her spear from hand to hand, clearly looking uncomfortable with what she must say next. "However, given your talk of cutting down the Lifetree, we will need to bind and confine you."

The warriors round the balcony, wrapping thick ropes of kelp around our wrists that remind me of what Ilryth sealed his armory with. They lead us by bound hands up toward the Lifetree in complete silence. The chorus stays behind, but not without a final look from Fenny. She focuses mostly on her brother, but her attention drifts to me. There are volumes unspoken and she is too hard a woman to read for me to piece together what her true intentions are. She's out of sight before I can even try, a fading shadow.

Back on the surface, so many leaves have now fallen that the once white beaches have been turned silver. The foliage clumps in the surf that laps at our ankles as we emerge. I doubt it's my imagination that the boughs above seem to be more barren than even a few hours ago.

"She's dying." Ilryth's words are a ripple across the back of my mind as we enter the tunnel that leads to the main beach of the Lifetree.

"We'll save her." My determination is as clear as the daylight that awaits us on the opposite end.

The beach is empty now; there are no worshippers singing their prayers. Whatever contingent was here when we first arrived must've left, or was sent away by the chorus. Our only company are the handful of warriors, the spears that pierce the pristine sand, and the shining axes that are lined up neatly along the large roots that envelop this sheltered beach. I try not to stare at them with too much hunger in my eyes as we pass. But it's difficult when my fingers twitch, urging me to grab one and run to the door.

"In here," one of the warriors commands. He gestures to an opening between two of the massive roots. The other warriors make a semi-circle around us as their leader undoes the bindings on our wrists. "If we hear even so much as a note, we have orders from the chorus to end you then and there, anointing or no." He glares at me, as if he's barely holding himself back from making good on the threat right now. "The chorus will be sending someone to anoint you."

With that, he positions his back to the opening and Ilryth and I have no choice but to venture inside.

We squeeze through a narrow passage of roots. My eyes take a moment to adjust and, when they do, I'm reminded of a flipped-over bird's nest. It's as if someone has tried to capture us beneath a basket. Sunlight peeks through interwoven roots, casting beams of light that dapple the sand.

"I thought sirens didn't have jails," I mutter, massaging my wrists. Small wonder Remni looked so uncomfortable about this.

"We don't, especially not on the island of the Lifetree. This space is usually reserved for sacred prayers and silent meditation as it is nestled within Lady Lellia's embrace." Ilryth stares up through one of the holes in the woven ceiling of roots.

"The sirens' aversion to prisons will be our benefit. They could've kept us bound and tied. We have a head start on escaping since we don't have to worry about undoing those ropes." I start to walk along the circumference of the space. The walls are like a living tapestry, some of the roots thicker than three ship masts together, others thin enough that I could snap. I peer into gaps, looking for places that might open to form passages.

"There isn't another way out. I've been here before."

"Were you looking for one when you were last here?" I try and squeeze through one of the spaces between roots, even though I already know it's much too small.

"I can look around the entire space with a single turn." He does so for emphasis. "There isn't a way out."

Frowning, I place my hands on my hips. "So, what, then? Do you want to give up? Just, let them kill us? Let Lady Lellia die and take the whole world with her?"

"Of course I don't want that." Ilryth drags his feet toward the far end, away from the opening, and sits on one of the wide roots that slowly arcs down before plunging into the sand. "But I'm not sure what else we can do."

I cross the few steps it takes to get to him, still looking for any potential openings on my way, but finding none. "We could try and overpower the knights? If they untied us, they're clearly not thinking we'll try to escape. We'll have the element of surprise."

"I doubt it." Ilryth sighs and shakes his head. "There are too many of them."

I walk away, then back, then away again, beginning to pace. My feet dig a trench in the sand from the repetition. On one of my turns, I nearly slam face-first into Ilryth. He catches me with both hands on my shoulders. Our chests are pressed together and I'm instantly aware of how his heartbeat seems to match mine. The pulsing that underscores the song we share.

"Relax your mind, Victoria," he soothes.

"But—"

"Panic isn't going to help anyone. If there's a way out of this, it'll come to us when it's meant to. In the meantime, try to ease your worried thoughts." Ilryth's eyes flutter closed as his hands shift, grabbing mine on his chest, clutching them between us. His forehead gently presses into mine. Instantly, I relax into him. He murmurs, "I wish we had more time."

"No." I shake my head, pulling away. I see what he's doing. The resignation, the encouragement to let go. "Do *not* start with goodbyes."

Ilryth chuckles as he brushes a strand of hair from my face. "Goodbyes between us are pointless. I already stole you from death's Abyss once."

Yet, when he leans in to kiss me, there is an air of finality to it. The kiss burns with everything that's left unsaid. All the things we wish we had time to share in the slow unfolding of a relationship at its own pace—a luxury stolen from us. Our hands tremble. He pulls away, our breaths mingling in the damp haze of this place that has now become wholly our own. The walls are a little closer than the last time my eyes were open, the light a little dimmer. The sun is setting on what might be our last night alive.

"Don't," I whisper again, the word quivering upon my lips.

He smiles, and kisses me again as his response. This time he tastes of hope, but he moves with the hunger of desperation. Something within me breaks and I'm lost to it. If these are our final moments, then I submit to the need growing between us. The desperation. I submit to his tongue and fingers and hands pushing me against the back wall, slipping down my torso to grab my breasts.

Somewhere between my hands on his chest and them landing on his hips, he's pushed me onto the root where he'd sat. Ilryth looms over me. Eyes locked, shining with the tears we both refuse to shed.

"If these are our final moments, then let us make a song that will echo into eternity," he whispers across my face.

"No."

"No?" A frown tugs at his lips.

"No," I repeat with more conviction. "These will *not* be our final moments. But I will have you all the same."

His frown shifts into a smirk as he parts my lips with his tongue, deepening our kiss. I ache for him in a way that continues to both excite and terrify. Longing and despair swell within me, replacing any hesitation or sorrow with a burning that threatens to consume me. I cannot pull him close enough—grip him tightly enough.

Ilryth steals my breath as he grabs my waist and sends a jolt through my body. Our movements become frantic, kisses shifting with teeth and tongue. Hands urgent. There is too much of him, too much of me, and not enough of us. All I want is to condense the distance between us into nothing but burning skin and delighted sighs.

Grabbing behind my knees, he pulls me toward the edge of the root. My legs wrap around his hips on instinct and I arch upward, my arms gliding over his shoulders. Our eyes lock as he positions himself. I'm more than ready and he enters with ease. My eyes flutter closed and my whole body is alight—awash with waves of pleasure from a small, yet infinitely consuming act of being completely and utterly filled.

And then he moves, setting my every sense ablaze.

The rhythm is easy to find, tempo increasing with every second. I respond on instinct, helping as I'm able. When I press my forehead to his, Ilryth is all I see; his body is all I feel. There is nothing else but those deep, rumbling moans that thunder through his chest and resonate in mine. We are one entity, blended in an intricate harmony that is solely our own.

Shifting, he takes both my hands, eyes never leaving mine, and positions them over my head—wrapping my fingers around a root above.

"Brace yourself," he growls in my ear, hands moving to my hips.

I do as I'm told and I'm certain my soul leaves my body as he plunges into me with a ferocity that steals rational thought. His breath rasps against my throat as his teeth follow his tongue, as though he is trying to lick off the swirls painted on my skin. The way he ravages me is feral and I give in to the frenzy completely. I care not for bruises I might leave on him or the sounds I might make. There are only his hands—only the feeling of him sliding in and out as his thumb swirls attentively over every spot on my body that pleasure can be derived from.

My body quakes in anticipation. Back arching. Eyes fluttering shut. *Break me*, I want to say. All that escapes my lips are moans. Yet, I think he hears.

The climax comes hard and fast, leaving us breathless, gasping into each other's faces as Ilryth collapses over me, forehead pressing into mine once more. My fingers finally unravel and they glide across the glistening expanse of his chest. Cupping my face, he kisses me, over, and over. Sweet yet passionate. Hungry, and yet also satiated.

"I could have you a thousand times, and it would never be enough," he pants softly.

A tiny, wicked smile cuts my lips. "The night is yet young."

fifty-one

IT'S SO EARLY THE SUN HAS YET TO CREST THE WAVES. Not that we would necessarily be able to see it when it does from our nest of roots. Ilryth and I are side by side, lounging in each other's arms. Sure enough, we have yet to find a way to escape. We chose the guaranteed delight of each other's bodies, rather than the uncertain possibility of *maybe* finding a way out of our predicament.

"Are you afraid?" he whispers, fingertips gliding over my arm draped over half his body as we laze on the root that's been our support for the past few hours.

"Not really," I admit. "Are you?"

"A little, if I'm being honest." A soft chuckle. "I wish I had your will of steel."

"You do. You've already been to the Abyss," I remind him. "You've stood before an old god and lived to tell the tale. What more could mere mortals do to us? What should strike fear into us when we have the strength of the hymns of the old ones?"

"You have a good point. But there's still an instinct for fear in me."

"There are worse things than retaining your mortality." I wonder if, somehow, I've lost parts of mine along the way. Even though—thanks to the duet of Lellia and Krokan's songs, and their blessings—I have my memories returned to me. My flesh is still woven magic, shimmering like starlight along the gold and silver lines that have been etched into my body among swirls of color. My mind has been pushed beyond its limits and stretched to accommodate the shape.

Shifting sand distracts us. "It is time for your anointing," an unfamiliar and gruff voice resonates in our minds. We sit, pulling ourselves into order not a moment too soon, as none other than Lucia rounds the corner.

"Lucia!" Ilryth is on his feet instantly and I am immediately grateful that we had time to sort ourselves. He rushes over and yanks his sister into a tight embrace. All I can hope is that she can't smell me on his skin. But, thankfully, Lucia has other priorities.

"There's not much time," she says hastily. "Fenny and I have arranged a changing of the guard—our own men will be taking over right before the chorus and others will arrive for the sacrifice. It should give enough time for the two of you to slip away."

"Slip away?" Ilryth frowns. "Where would we go?"

"Go to a traveler's pool. Head to the southwest seas by the lykin. Go *anywhere else*," Lucia pleads with her brother. Ilryth presents reasonable objections.

Meanwhile, my mind is elsewhere. *A changing of the guard...a narrow window...* If we could create enough of a distraction—enough chaos. With the extra manpower... My thoughts speed a dozen a second. A wild idea forms, probably insanity, but it might work.

"That's it," I say, startling them both.

"What is?" Ilryth asks as he and Lucia shift to face me, confusion apparent in both of their expressions.

"How we're going to get the door open." I stand as well. Lucia moves to object, but I speak first. "There is nowhere to run. We free Lady Lellia, or it's all over. And this is how we're going to do it..."

Our window of opportunity is small. The warriors from the Duchy of Spears are arriving not long before the chorus. Originally, there was some debate over waiting for the changing of the guards to completely take place. But it was decided that wouldn't leave us enough time.

Ilryth and I stand side by side at the tunnel out of our small prison.

"Are you ready?" I whisper.

"As I'll ever be."

I wish he sounded more certain. But I can't blame him for his hesitation. Even if he knows what's at stake. Even if he heard the words of Lord Krokan. This goes against all his upbringing—his whole world, before me.

My hand slips into his and I hold his stare with confidence. "It'll be all right," I vow to him, to the whole world. "We'll see this through to the end."

"I believe you." He nods.

"Then here goes nothing." I close my eyes and my brow furrows with focus as I reach out with my mind. There's a single face in the forefront of my thoughts—one I know as well as my own flesh and blood father. From the salt in his hair to the stubble on his chin. "Kevhan?"

"Victoria?" Surprise is apparent in his voice.

I squeeze Ilryth's hand with anticipation and anxiousness. "Focus only on me, all right? And don't speak more than you need to." A stretch of silence. I take it as a good sign. "I'm going to need you to do something: be a distraction."

Another second of silence that, this time, I read as hesitation. Then, "What do you need me to do?"

I tell Kevhan about the island. How to swim around the far side, weaving between the roots and rot to stay out of sight of the upcoming warriors and any gathering chorus. I trust that, under the current circumstances, there aren't any sirens on their beaches of passion to scandalize him as he navigates through the maze formed by the Lifetree. Given his silence, I trust he finds his way onto the beach and into the root tunnel without issue.

"Now, Kevhan…" My thoughts sputter a moment, knowing the danger I will be putting him in. One jab from the spears of the warriors and, as a spirit, he will be ended. "You *must* run. The second the warriors come for you, run like your life depends on it. Return to the water and hide as you had. Go deeper into the rot where they won't follow. No matter what, don't let them catch you."

"I won't let you down," he reassures me. It's an echo of some of the first words I ever said to him. Begging him as a young woman on the streets of Dennow for a chance to make something better of herself.

For a chance to be the woman I am now.

"I know you won't. I trust you," I respond, a mirror of the words he said once to me. I turn to Ilryth and speak just for him. "Are you ready?" He nods. Then, closing my eyes once more, I return my focus to Kevhan. "All right... *Now*."

I hold my breath and listen. Even though sirens don't speak with their mouths on land, I can hear the grunts of surprise as Kevhan emerges from the distant tunnel and the sounds of the sand scraping as they give chase. With one look to Ilryth and a shared nod, we also launch into action.

Much like when I'd charged into the Gray Passage, I steel myself for whatever comes next. Whenever I tackled the passage, I had the protection of Ilryth. Now I walk with the protection of the gods themselves. A divine mission.

Ilryth springs from behind the remaining warrior that stayed back. The others are just a blur of sand sprinting down the tunnel. Ilryth wastes no time disarming the man and rendering him helpless.

I'm already halfway to the main trunk of the Lifetree, grabbing an axe on my way. Lady Lellia's door glows faintly in the gloom and gray of an early dawn, as though a fragment of the sun has been trapped inside. A subtle, warm pulsing—a rhythm I can now understand. I fight every compulsion to touch the wood and instead draw back my axe.

At the same time, friendly warriors burst through from the beach closest to the castle, led by Lucia and Sheel. They're those who patrolled the trench. Men and women loyal to Ilryth and the Duchy of Spears above even the chorus. There's enough of them to buy us time.

I swing the axe and it meets the wood. My eyes slam shut and I let out a song that has not been heard for thousands of years. *Let me be your voice*, I beg her.

I sing the words of the anamnesis down in the Abyss and the trench, not caring who might hear or if they can even understand. The stories that were placed upon my soul beg for release. I sing them for the silent goddess. For the fluttering heartbeat that I can feel reverberating through the handle of the axe. Each second weaker than the last.

Lellia, it's time to leave, I say gently between the words and notes, the scuffle behind me and howling wind.

My children...

I will protect them. Whatever you need, I am yours.

The silver axe comes crashing against the woody tendrils that have barred the door for millennia. The moment the blades sink deeper into the wood, they explode with silvery sap that glistens with iridescent rainbows in the sunlight. Axe still stuck, I pause, reaching out to touch the sap. It's as light as water and as lovely as mother of pearl.

It's not red. Even after all these years, the rot still hasn't reached Lellia's core. The tree still stood strong, holding Lellia in its grasp protecting her, but also trapping her in an embrace so strong that she couldn't escape even if she wanted to. It's small wonder Krokan was desperate. He could still feel how far she was.

Chaos begins to unfurl behind me. I see it with a glance over my shoulder as Ilryth moves to my side, an axe in his hand. Sheel and the warriors have formed a line. Lucia leads the other contingent toward the tunnel that connects with the beaches of passion. Blocking the warriors who had chased after Kevhan from returning.

Ilryth and I swing again in unison.

The wood is softer than I would've expected. The blades meet little resistance. Halfway through the woody vines, the tree begins to shudder. It's so slight that, at first, I think it's just the reverberation of the blows through the blade and into my arms. But more and more, the boughs above us sway. Silvery foliage rains down. Soon there will be nothing left on the branches above.

You'll be out soon, I sing softly, intending the words only for Lellia's ears. *You'll be with Krokan, soon.*

When I'm almost through the first vine, it begins to wither and sag away from the door. I grab it and pull with all my might. It strains. There's a horrible wrenching and tearing sound that rips through me. But at once, it's over. One of the bars of Lellia's cage is gone.

There's a burnt mark on the door, underneath where the vine once was—the wood has blackened as if singed. I imagine the vine was an invasive species, cutting off circulation for centuries.

Our attacks are stalled as the earth around us shakes and shudders. There is a groaning accompanied by a roar that comes from deep within the seas. At the same time, warriors burst from the tunnel closest to the castle, leading the chorus. Sheel engages.

"Krokan knows," I breathe, too focused on Lellia to worry about anything else.

Ilryth glances behind us and forward again. "Should we—"

"Keep going!" I say with confidence. "Krokan will be here to take her once she's free. He's coming to us and that means it's working." I know it in my bones. I can feel the old god's growing nearness as the song in my head grows louder by the second. But Ilryth has stopped cutting. "Ilryth?"

The chorus and their warriors are threatening Sheel's line.

Ilryth grabs my shoulder. "Keep going, Victoria. Free her."

"But you—"

"I'll hold them off as long as I'm able." He leaves his axe, starting down to Sheel.

"Ilryth!" I shout, turning from the door. He faces me as I run over, throwing my arms around his neck. The impact of my body crashing against his nearly knocks him over.

I kiss him with all my might.

His arms around my waist, he opens his mouth, deepening the kiss. His hard body presses into mine and for a moment the raging of the sea, the shaking of the earth, and all the uncertainty all fades away. When we break apart, all I see is him, framed by a shower of silver leaves, falling like a heavy rain.

"I love you, you know," I whisper.

"I know."

"I really, *really* didn't want to."

"I know." He smirks. Somehow the arrogance suits him.

"I don't know what the future holds. If we can even be together at all. And if we could, I doubt I will be good for you and—"

He kisses me firmly, silencing me. "Stop worrying so much, Victoria. If we can manage to undo thousands of years of history, free an old god, and *not* break the world in the process, I'm not too worried about anything else we might have to face in our future." Ilryth releases me. "Now, *go*. Free Lady Lellia."

We part and I race back toward the Lifetree, hoist the axe, and swing again. At the same time, Ilryth races toward the commotion of more sirens exploding from the tunnel. Fenny throws Dawnpoint to him, and he catches it. All the while, I keep swinging.

The sirens wage a war of song against each other. Krokan rumbles from the depths. Lellia screams. Altogether, it's a cacophony. Horrible, loud and wrenching.

Ignoring the voices, I keep swinging, keep pulling away viny bars. My axe strikes to the rhythm in the tree. Time and again. Relentless. The battle rages behind me. But I keep going until...

Until the last vine falls away.

For the first time in centuries, the door is exposed and, for a moment, the world is still as the axe slips from my fingers. The seas are calm and the wind no longer howls. The singing has silenced, and everyone and everything collectively holds their breath in a thrall as I pull open the door to what had become Lellia's unintended prison.

fifty-two

I AM BLINDED BY LIGHT. The slab of wood peeling away after ages upon ages hisses like the last exhale of a tired, wounded beast. Strings of membrane and goop cling between the door and the bark of the tree trunk as I continue to pry it open.

The blinding light fades and reveals the small, frail frame of an old god. Lellia is almost childlike in size, though she has the same air of timelessness about her as Lord Krokan. Her four arms are curled around her knees, three fingers on each hand clutching her sides, as she slumbers in the fetal position. She has two eyes, but they are large and circular, as a dragonfly's would be. Wings of gossamer gold feathers have broken away from her shoulders, fusing with the cocoon she has been encased in. Leaves coat her forearms and hands like gloves. Woody antlers extend from her temples, connecting her with the tree itself.

There is no movement. She doesn't rouse or open her eyes as the first breezes brush her cheeks. The world remains in an eerie state of calm. Even her song is silent and my heart pounds with fear that in my quest to save her, I created the shock that was the killing blow.

The sirens behind me murmur.

"Lady Lellia."

"… Lellia…"

"Our Lady is dead…"

"We have killed her."

"The rot came from her decay…"

I glance over my shoulder. Every warrior has dropped to their knees mid-fight. The chorus as well. All heads are bowed to the sand in reverence. A lonely, sad song of mourning rises from them. I can feel their worry and grief in my core, lamenting what they see as the death of all they knew and loved.

But they don't see what I see. They're too far. This close, I can see the twitching of the nubs on her back where her wings once connected. I can see eyes moving under the lids, as if she's trying to rouse. I breathe a soft sigh of relief that comes out as a hum.

She's not dead and gone. She's fighting with all the tenacity life fights with. Life is both a graceful and an audacious thing. Life does not relent. It can be broken, time and again, without relenting. Quivering and weak, her song persists. She holds on, waiting to be reunited with her husband. Waiting for peace.

I reach in.

In the heart of the tree, the wood is soft and has a slight give to it. She's suspended in the thick silver membrane that my hands plunge into. It's as solid and temperate as warm tallow. Like reaching into a beam of sunlight.

Lellia's body is solid silver, but surprisingly light. Her weight and size make it easy to cradle her in both arms. Leaning back, I free her from the godly plasma, holding her to my chest. She still does not stir, but I can feel her heart beat against mine. Her head is heavy on my shoulder, body stiff and cooling with the sea breezes.

I turn and, for the first time in thousands of years, mortals lay eyes on the goddess.

Life is pulled from the world itself. I walk and the last strings and strands of membrane peel off Lellia and me. Her tiny chest quivers as if she is attempting to take her first breaths in centuries.

The siren do not stop me as I progress through the remnants of their battlefield. They stare at me with tear-streaked eyes and hollow expressions of resignation. There's some rage and anger, but even those that hold contempt for me don't rise to try and stop me. It's too late for their resistance. For better or worse, my approach won out. My plan was victorious.

"Human," a soft voice says, only to me. It's as light as air. As bright and wondrous as moonlight.

"My lady?" I speak to her as I would to a siren, with my mind alone. I wonder if this was how early siren first learned to speak in that way. To sing with their souls rather than their tongues. Their primordial mother taught them.

"Thank you," Lellia whispers.

"You have nothing to thank me for."

"You will look after them, won't you?" she asks.

"I will." I smile faintly. "It would be my honor."

"Do not let them forget my songs," Lellia begs.

"I will not. I swear it."

The only one who follows us through the tunnels is Ilryth. He is at my side—just behind—as I carry Lellia to the ocean. However, from what I can tell, Lellia's words were meant for me alone. Or, perhaps, even if he could hear them…he wouldn't understand. I imparted enough of her song to him in the Abyss to stabilize his mind. But it would not be enough to give him comprehension.

I could yet teach him, though.

The carvings on the roots of the tunnel no longer bleed. The wood itself is beginning to turn as ashen as the spears usually left to bleach in the sunlight. The Lifetree is dying without its heart. But Lellia continues to grow stronger by the second. She is beginning to twitch, body slowly rousing to catch up with her mind.

We emerge on the other side of the tunnel to waves of tentacles writhing in the ocean, gripping against the roots. A massive face, as strange as Lellia's but one I no longer find monstrous, is halfway above the water. As the clouds above slowly part with a swirl, beams of sunlight strike the abyssal god. Seawater steams off him, as if he might burn from being exposed to the surface for too long. Krokan stares with emerald eyes that shine brighter the moment they rest on his bride.

"I have her," I say, with mind and mouth.

"So you do," he rumbles. Once more, it sounds like a song. But lighter, so far above the water. Or perhaps it's lighter with relief, because he sees his wife at long last. At the end of this long struggle they have endured on behalf of the world they helped make.

"Take her." I walk up to my knees in the water, laying Lellia in the surf before Krokan. She floats, as if she is nothing more than sea foam.

His tentacles surround her, drawing her under. Absorbing her into the core of his being. She will be safe, now. *Forevermore.*

"You have kept your bargain, mortal, so I will keep mine; I will no longer block the Veil. I will no longer plague the world. I will return with my lady love and it will allow souls to flow once more to the Beyond, henceforth and forevermore. There is no further reason for me to blight your seas," Krokan says. I expect that to be all, but he continues, "You have done us a great favor. Before we depart this realm, we shall bestow upon you a boon. Tell us, what do you desire?"

A godly boon. I could wish for anything. The might of two old gods is at my fingertips.

I look back to Ilryth. *A life with him.* A life to explore freely the world and my heart. I could make a similar wish to what I once asked Ilryth for all those years ago.

A chill wind batters me. The seasons of Midscape are returning to this sacred island—to all of the Eversea. The temperate climate the sirens have thrived in will be gone without the Lifetree to sustain it. Perhaps it is just the beginning of a new age of winter—of death, that could threaten to consume all of Midscape.

"She has already given me my boon," I say softly. Even though I'm speaking to Krokan, I allow Ilryth to hear. There's something in my words and on my face that prompts him to step forward. He crosses to me, gathering my hands.

"What's happening?" Ilryth asks.

"I made a promise to Lady Lellia as I freed her," I say. "I'm going to keep my promise. Her magic is still here, still in the tree. She poured so much of herself into it that it's there. But it needs an anchor to keep it in place, otherwise it'll fade from the world completely." Like it already is. Even as seconds tick by, there's less and less of her.

"No." Ilryth realizes what I'm saying. He shakes his head.

I catch his cheek, cupping it gently. "It's all right. I'm not afraid."

"You've spent so much of your life living it for others. Sacrificing, for others. Hunting for freedom." Ilryth's eyes redden on my behalf. "I can't let you do it again."

"But this is my choice, just like it was hers. I don't make it because I feel like I'm forced to. I'm not doing it to be worthy of love, because I already am. I'm doing it because I want to." I continue to offer him a slight smile, leaning in to kiss his lips gently. "And you, you need to go on and live. Reclaim your duchy. Look after the Eversea and make all the heirs that I will guard after."

"I don't want any of it. A life without you is a song without rhythm and notes. It is nothing. Less than nothing."

"Ilryth—"

"Your boon." He turns to Krokan. "Tell me how I can use it to stay with her. Grant us a life together where our world is safe and our future is secure."

The old god regards him thoughtfully. His tentacles are slowly unfurling from the roots, relaxing as he's slipping into the depths. For a moment, I think he will leave without a response. But then...

"Come with us, child," Krokan says, finally.

"What?" Ilryth whispers.

"Come," Krokan commands, the water nearly covering his eyes now. Ilryth starts toward the sea.

"No." I grab Ilryth's hand. "I won't let you."

"This is the only way." He squeezes my fingers and gives me a brave smile. "You do what you must, as will I. We both bear the words of the gods and a duet requires two voices."

"Ilryth..."

"Trust in me, as I trust in you." He kisses me, and I kiss him back, savoring the taste and feeling of him one last time.

He follows the old gods underneath the sea, disappearing with the tentacles and radiant light that was Lellia. I wish there was more time. It's all been so fast.

I march back for the tree. Alone but determined. Life is audacious. And even death isn't eternal. Our song will echo into the ages.

The siren are still there, kneeling in the sand, howling in their grief. I ignore them as I march up to the core of the Lifetree. The opening where Lellia once rested. I crawl into the ether suspended in the trunk and curl into a ball, positioning myself just as she was. Closing my eyes, I begin to sing the song I learned from the last remnants of the old gods.

The wood closes tightly around me.

fifty-three

IT IS BOTH LIGHT AND DARK, DAY AND NIGHT. Neither good, neither bad. Both simply…are. The world exists in a whorl that spins in time to my endless song.

But I don't sing alone. There are others who join me. They sing tales of the human who took the mantle of a goddess. Of her lover who descended into the sea and was never heard from again.

There are voices I know. Of old friends, long gone. And of new kin that were left behind. My heart sings for a family that thrives, safe and sound in a distant, coastal town. It aches for man who waits at my door alongside those that aren't his kind. Some of the songs are beautiful and skilled. Others are woefully out of pitch.

There are voices I don't know and have never met. Souls that stretch across space, and time. A woman ascends to a wooden throne, connected by root and magic to this distant tree. A man encased in crystal, the soul of his lover singing a dirge of longing and loss. The squeals of a young child of two worlds being taught by a new fae queen whose father has yet to know she is so near. A spirit that screams for freedom during a bloodred night. The curl of magic that whispers in the last bloodlines of a Natural World. Forgotten peoples and distant forces that ebb and flow with the shifting of days and years.

And then… at long last, there's another voice. One from deep below. One that somehow always knows the words before I sing them. Harmonies before I need them.

Even more time passes, I believe. *Time is such a mortal notion.* I understand that now, what those old gods meant when they tried to communicate as much to me.

But I am not one of those mighty beings from a time long before the age of mortals, not truly. Yet, I am also not what I was before, either. I have changed again. I am new. And yet also somehow ancient. Eternal but fleeting. The silvered and gold lines that coat my flesh tell the stories of the old ones that came before me. I am the keeper of the last vestiges of their magic, and their memories. The anchor for the final of the gifts they bestowed upon this world. I am also the overseer, the one who will help guide and protect the growth of all that might come after.

But I am not alone in this singular responsibility. That *other voice* continues singing. Louder and louder. He calls to me in a way that only he knows how. In a way that only I would heed.

I've come for you, just as you asked, he sings. *We have given to the world. We have sacrificed and stabilized. There is nothing more to fear. Now it is time again for us to live.*

At first, I am afraid to leave the confines of my new home. It is safe here and I am comfortable. His song is patient and reassuring, yet somehow also reminding me that being stationary does not suit me. Confinement, even one I choose, is not in my nature—it is what led to the downfall of the last woman who occupied this stasis, however alluring the comfort might be. For the sake of all those I care for, am responsible for, I must move.

At long last, I begin to wriggle against the confines of my tiny world. Stretching. Pushing. Trying to test the barriers that fight to keep me in place—keep me as I am. Already they have closed in around me, hardening into place.

No, that will not be the arrangement this time... I am not an ancient goddess, struggling to survive in a world no longer built for her. I was born of the mortal lands, molded by the people of them, I still bear their markings on my flesh. I am Victoria, sailor, explorer, lover, and fighter. There are too many different things within me to fade away quietly and allow these woody spears to pierce my heart and hold me in place.

It takes what feels like ages to push and pull, exploring my powers and exerting them over the cage I am within. All the while, my soul sings life into the world, and his distant voice calls to me. I finally find a way out. The tree finally heeds my commands and a tunnel forms before me. With a gasp, I wriggle and force myself through, pushing toward distant sunlight. I am bloomed back into the mortal world with the opening of soft petals and a whisper of promise.

The song is louder now. The duet that has filled the back of my mind for years. It's as forceful as a storm. As demanding as the tides that swell against the shores collected in the roots of my tree.

"Vic—Victoria?" Kevhan is there on the beach. He is appointed with siren clothing and medallions. Markings have been drawn all over him. Songs of protection ring in my ears. I can read the inkings with ease now—especially since I was the one to sing them for him. He is stabilized while underneath my boughs, but there is so much more I can yet do for him.

"Hello, Lord Applegate. It's been some time, I believe." I step from the woody flower that bloomed where the door once was, off a large petal that has unfurled like a carpet for me to descend. A haze of swirling silver surrounds me, trailing through the air following my movements, condensing into silver leaves that dot the sand below.

"It's been nearly four years." Lucia steps forward.

"Thank you for guarding Kevhan and ensuring his soul is as stable in this world as mine was," I say warmly.

"I'd hoped I'd heard your song correctly." She bows her head. Vaguely, I realize that one of the many voices I'd heard was hers. All this time, I had been communicating to her without thought. Humming new guidance to the sirens on how to thrive.

Kevhan's eyes are glossy. "How…how have you—"

"It's good to see you're still well." I clasp his shoulder and interrupt the question. He couldn't comprehend the answer even if I could explain it well. I am here thanks to a combination of time and harnessing the magic I inherited. Power that is now my honor and responsibility to wield on behalf of a goddess. In the end, I settle for a simple explanation that he might understand. "I am here in much the same way you are."

"Like a ghost?" That explanation is apparently the only way his mortal mind could comprehend his new circumstances.

"Of a sort." I turn to Lucia. "The rest of your kin?"

"The Eversea has never been better. Our seas are clear and our people are strong. Nearly so much so that there is talk of reaching out to the fae to our south once more. Perhaps restoring the land bridge that once connected this island to the rest of Midscape, at long last, so that others might come to worship at your altar."

"I am not one to worship." A slight smile crosses my lips. "Merely a messenger for the Lady that we should all still pay our respects to." Her sacrifices will not be forgotten as long as I walk this world.

"Understood." Lucia bows her head. I start for the tunnel that leads to the primary entry of the island—the one that it feels like I ascended mere days ago. "Fenny is still the Duchess of Spears. The chorus moved to position me as Duchess of Faith, given Ventris's decision to step down from his post." Lucia attempts to follow me. Kevhan is at her side. "But there's something you should know—"

I hold out a hand, halting them. "I already know. And this is a reunion I would like to make alone."

They wear smiles as I depart, nearly gliding through the tunnel in my haste. I emerge onto the other side and my gaze locks with another that is as familiar as the feeling of a song in my soul and the power in my veins.

My partner, the other singer of my eternal duet, emerges from the ocean. Sea foam and water swirl upwards, taking the shape of a man, solidifying into flesh that is just as I remember. Ilryth is as handsome as when I first laid eyes on him. As ethereal as I imagine myself to be now. His markings are the inverse to mine, but identical in all other ways. He is my match, my mirror and counterbalance.

"I was wondering when you would return to me." He opens his arms and, without need of any other invitation, I run to him. Ilryth crushes me in his embrace, kissing my face as though we have waited one thousand years for this reunion.

"It took me some time to acclimate to my new role," I say, somewhat guilty as we pull apart.

"Me as well."

"But now that I've become one with the remnants of her power, I can come and go as I please. Though, I must return to the tree eventually, at least for brief times, to keep the anchor." This truth is embedded in my soul.

"I know, and I will have to return to the Abyss on occasion for much the same reason." He leans in and brushes his nose against mine. "But these duties shall not keep us apart for long."

"Such is our duet, now." I run my fingertips down his chest. He feels as real as I do, as we always have. But I know we have become something more. Just as I was alive before, but not quite mortal, I have become something else again. Ilryth has as well.

"So, until then, my time is yours." His hands cup my cheeks. "Once more, should you have me, I would like to worship at your altar, my love."

With a coy smile, I take his hand. Rather than leading us through the tunnels and back toward the beaches of passion, he pulls me into the waves. We fall like two stars, spinning around each other into the depths of a clear Abyss, free of rot, monsters, and deadly currents. Into a world that is solely our own—made for our powers and our passions.

Duets are meant for two singers, and ours has always been the hymn of life and death and all that is woven between. A song of sorrow and joy, passion and longing. It was a song intended to be for Krokan and Lellia, but each time we sang those fateful words, they became more and more our own.

Now, our duet is of Ilryth and Victoria. The human and the siren. And it is a melody that will have no end.

How about a bonus scene?

Want a little bit more of Victoria and Ilryth? Kevhan's reunion, at long last with his daughter? Head over to my webiste to learn how you can get a special bonus scene from Ilryth's perspective that takes place after the end of the book. It also has some hints about what you can expect next in the Married to Magic universe.

Learn how you can get the bonus scene for FREE at:

https://elisekova.com/a-duet-with-the-siren-duke/

a DUEL
with the
VAMPIRE LORD

a MARRIED TO MAGIC *novel*

Learn more at

https://elisekova.com/a-duel-with-the-vampire-lord/

ON THE NIGHT OF THE BLOOD MOON, THE VAMPIRE LORD MUST DIE. But when it's up to a forge maiden to deal the killing blow, her strike misses the mark. Now, bloodsworn to the Vampire Lord, she must survive by helping end an ancient curse. Loyalties are tested and the line between truth and lie is blurred. When her dagger is at his chest, will she be able to take the heart of the man who has claimed hers?

a DANCE with the FAE PRINCE

a MARRIED TO MAGIC novel

Learn more at

https://elisekova.com/a-dance-with-the-fae-prince/

KATRIA SWORE SHE'D NEVER FALL IN LOVE. When her hand in marriage is sold, her new, mysterious husband makes that resolution very difficult. But what's even harder is surviving after she learns he's the heir to the fae throne in hiding. After accidently stealing his magic, she's taken to Midscape where she learns the truth of the fae and her heart.

a DEAL with the ELF KING

a MARRIED TO MAGIC novel

Learn more at

https://elisekova.com/a-deal-with-the-elf-king/

NINETEEN-YEAR-OLD LUELLA HAD PREPARED ALL HER LIFE TO
BE HER TOWN'S HEALER. Becoming the Elf King's bride wasn't
anywhere in her plans. Taken to a land filled with wild magic,
Luella learns how to control powers she never expected to
save a dying world. The magical land of Midscape pulls on
one corner of her heart, her home and people tug on another...
but what will truly break her is a passion she never wanted.

About the Author

ELISE KOVA is a USA Today and internationally bestselling author. She enjoys telling stories of fantasy worlds filled with magic and deep emotions. She lives in Florida and, when not writing, can be found playing video games, drawing, chatting with readers on social media, or daydreaming about her next story.

She invites readers to get first looks, giveaways, and more by subscribing to her newsletter at:
http://elisekova.com/subscribe

Visit her on the web at:
http://elisekova.com/
https://www.tiktok.com/@elisekova
https://www.facebook.com/AuthorEliseKova/
https://www.instagram.com/elise.kova/

See all of Elise's titles on her Amazon page:
http://author.to/EliseKova

More books by Elise...

THE
AIR AWAKENS
SERIES

A young adult, high-fantasy filled with romance and elemental magic

A library apprentice, a sorcerer prince, and an unbreakable magic bond. . .

The Solaris Empire is one conquest away from uniting the continent, and the rare elemental magic sleeping in seventeen-year-old library apprentice Vhalla Yarl could shift the tides of war.

Vhalla has always been taught to fear the Tower of Sorcerers, a mysterious magic society, and has been happy in her quiet

world of books. But after she unknowingly saves the life of one of the most powerful sorcerers of them all—the Crown Prince Aldrik--she finds herself enticed into his world. Now she must decide her future: Embrace her sorcery and leave the life she's known, or eradicate her magic and remain as she's always been. And with powerful forces lurking in the shadows, Vhalla's indecision could cost her more than she ever imagined.

Learn more at:

http://elisekova.com/air-awakens-book-one/

VORTEX CHRONICLES

THE COMPLETE SERIES

In a world on the brink of destruction, Crown Princess Vi Solaris must choose between her magic and her throne.

With her empire faltering from political infighting and a deadly plague, Vi's rare and deadly power may be the key to saving her people.

To master her powers, she trains in secret with a mysterious sorcerer from a distant land. Despite her initial fear, Vi finds herself increasingly drawn to him, and their forbidden love threatens to unravel everything she knows. With her heart torn between duty and desire, Vi embarks on an epic journey of adventure, romance, family, and destiny.

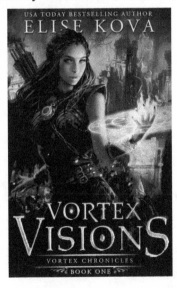

But the ultimate triumph will require the ultimate sacrifice, and Vi must make the hardest choice of her life: to play by the rules and claim her throne, or break them for magic and a love that could change the fate of her world forever.

For fans of young adult, epic fantasy world filled with elemental magic, friendships as deep as blood, shocking twists, thrilling adventures, and slow-burn romance.

Learn more at:

http://elisekova.com/vortex-visions-air-awak-ens-vortex-chronicles-1/

Acknowledgements

Robert – Thank you for helping me heal. Without it, I couldn't have even dreamed of attempting a story like this.

Melissa – This needed 7,000 rounds of edits (okay maybe just 4 or 5), but you stuck with me through it all. Thank you for giving me perspective beyond the line level and hanging in there until the very end of this monster of a manuscript.

Rebecca – I will always be grateful for every problem you catch in my narratives. This one was unwieldy, massive, and I tried to tackle so much, but you helped me get my hands around it and for that I'll always be grateful.

Kate – All of the last-second continuity errors, awkward sentences, repetitive words, and grammatical mistakes are gone because of you. Thank you again for turning this book so quickly, but being so attentive to all those details.

Amy – I know this looks nothing like the first pass you read, but I hope that you can see how all your feedback helped me get to this place.

Catarina – Thank you for coming in at the last-second to give me thoughts and perspectives as a reader. I really appreciate you lending me your views.

Leo – Not only have you helped bring Married to Magic to life for readers around the world in Spanish, but you've helped me so much personally. I will be forever grateful our paths crossed.

Danielle – You're the best. You know it. Or at least I hope you do… So I'll say it again: You're the best.

Michelle – I hope there are many more brainstorming and masterminding sessions in NYC ahead for us.

NOFFA – Endless love and respect to all of you insanely talented and kind-hearted ladies.

My D&D Crew – Thank you all for helping me escape into our fun co-made world whenever work became too much, and for always being some of my most steadfast cheerleaders.

Jaysea – Thank you so much for answering my message and agreeing to chat with me to give me perspective on ships, sailing, and being a captain. It helped immensely not only in this book, but for many books to come.

My Tower Guard – You all give so much to me, that it is my eternal goal to return that investment by bringing you the best books I can. Thank you for always being there and generally making our little group one of the best places on the internet.

Erion – Thank you again for working with me and bringing my characters to life. The cover illustration is stunning.

Merwild – I love how you continue to give faces to the names in my story. Thank you again for all the incredible character artwork.

My Royal Patrons – I love how I can put out a call for help, and you're all there. Thank you for giving me feedback on the first prologue I wrote. Your insights helped me get to this place.

All My Patrons – Charlee R., Amanda C., Kristen Ridge, Imzadi, Vixie, Caitlyn P., Kristin W., Rachael Leigh W., MasterR50, Rebecca R., Crystal F., Steffi aka. Lambert, Aniyue, Anne of Daze, Katherine, Laura R., Missy Anathema, Casey S., Sarah T., Nancy S., Laura B., Mandi S., Melinda H., Kayla D., Taylour D., Stephanie Harvey, Bridgett M., Sarah M., Gemma, Claire R., Liv W., Rachael, Kellie N., Rose G., Karolína N. B., discokittie, Teddie W., Kanaga Maddie S., Molly R., Kalyn S., Dani W., Liz D., Sharp, Emily E., M Knight, Kate R., Jamie B., Jennifer G., Marissa C., Monique R., Alexa Zoellner, Claribel V., Nicole M., Anna T., Ren, Lisa, Sorcha A., Tea Cup, Nat G., Caitlin P., Bec M., Paige F, Rebekah N., Tiffany G., Bridget W., Olivia S., Sarah [faeryreads], Macarena M., Kristen M., Kelly M., Audrey

C W., Jordan R., Amy M., Allison S., Donna W., Renee S., Ashton Morgan, MelGoethals, Mackenzie, Kaitlin B., Amanda T., Kayleigh K., Shelbe H., Alisha L., Esther R., Kaylie, Heather F., Shelly D., Tiera B., Andra P., Melisa K., Serenity87HUN, Liz A., Chelsea S., Matthea F., Catarina G., Stephanie T., jpilbug, Mani R., Elise G., Traci F., Samantha C., Lindsay B., Sara E., Karin B., Eri W., Ashley D., Michael P., Stengelberry, Dana A, Michael P., Alexis P., Jennifer B., Kay Z., Lauren V., Sarah Ruth H., Sheryl K B., Aemaeth, NaiculS, Justine B., Lindsay W., MotherofMagic, Charles B., Kira M., Charis Tiffany L., Kassie P., Angela G., Elly M., Michelle S., Sarah P., Asami, Amy B., Meagan R., Axel R., Ambermoon86, Bookish Connoisseur, Tarryn G., Cassidy T., Kathleen M., Alexa A., Rhianne, Cassondra A., Emmie S., Emily R., and Tamashi T. – Thank you for being such an important part of my worlds!

To all the readers, reviewers, book sellers, and everyone else who reads, shares, reviews, and talks about my books — Every day that I wake up and sit down to work, I thank you for all you've done for me, and continue to do for me. I see every effort, every recommendation, every post, and while I'm not always able to thank you individually, my gratitude knows no bounds. I hope that I am able to continue learning and growing as an author for all of you in the years to come.